Praise for Thomas Adcock's
Neil Hockaday Mysteries

DEVIL'S HEAVEN

"The action starts with a magnificent scene.... Thomas Adcock ... fires some sharp sociological salvos.... Fans of this fine series will be left wondering 'What next?' in the increasingly complex career of hero Hock."
—Ken Wisneski, *Minneapolis Star-Tribune*

"Adcock writes about New York like no other current crime writer. The author's streets are gritty and dark, and every shadow hides someone or something .... strong plot and fascinating characters...."
—Dan J. Szczesny, *Drood Review of Mystery*

Thomas Adcock is "master of a dark, dark world."
—Judith Kreiner, *Washington Times*

"Adcock is ... unsparing and acute in his descriptions...."
—Dick Adler, *Chicago Tribune*

"[Hockaday is] an effective investigator and what he finds is gory and gruesome."
—Mark Marymont, *Springfield News-Leader*

"Hockaday ... wades through blood and gore among the low-lifes of Hell's Kitchen and the high-lifes of Madison Avenue to find the answer behind the gruesome murders."
—Gary Svoboda, *Lincoln Journal-Star*

"*Devil's Heaven* continues a stellar series...."
—*Booklist*

DROWN ALL THE DOGS

"Smart, textured, immensely readable...."
—Richard Lipez, *Washington Post Book World*

"Drifting like a fine mist between legend and legacy, between dreams and waking, this dense and vibrant third work in a series is as charming as an Irish brogue...."
—*Publishers Weekly*

"A raucous, rollicking road show.... The plot's as big as Galway Bay.... Adcock's version of Ireland's mad, sad history makes as much sense as anyone's."
—Bob McCormick, New York *Daily News*

"A hauntingly articulate and action-crammed account of a man in search of a father...."
—Kiki Olson, *The St. Petersburg Times*

"The talk is lively and literate.... On the blarney meter, Mr. Adcock gives good value."
—Marilyn Stasio, *The New York Times Book Review*

DARK MAZE

Books by Thomas Adcock

Precinct 19
Sea of Green
Dark Maze*
Drown All the Dogs*
Devil's Heaven*

*Published by POCKET BOOKS

DEVIL'S HEAVEN

THOMAS ADCOCK

POCKET BOOKS
New York   London   Toronto   Sydney   Tokyo   Singapore

For Angelo, an absent friend

POCKET BOOKS, a division of Simon & Schuster Inc.
1230 Avenue of the Americas, New York, NY 10020

Copyright © 1995 by Thomas Adcock

ISBN: 0-671-77043-8

First Pocket Books paperback printing March 1996

10 9 8 7 6 5 4 3 2 1

POCKET and colophon are registered trademarks of Simon & Schuster Inc.

Cover design by Tom McKeveny

Printed in the U.S.A.

All of these you are
And each is partly you
And none of them is false
And none is wholly true.
　　　—*Stephen Vincent Benét*

Prologue

Me, a cop and a shamrock Catholic besides, in this unholy place.

Those songs! O Lord in heaven, if ever I needed a drink!

She started up again:

"Here's a little song entitled 'Let Me Go, Lover' ... or, 'Who Put the Glue in the Vaseline?' "

She was a three-hundred-pound face-lifted matron with skin the color of talcum powder and huge minstrel lips rouged up in candy apple red. She had inch-long fingernails lacquered in black, and teeth as big and shiny as the piano ivories in front of her. A rhinestone tiara nested in her tall bouffant of blonde hair, black at the roots. She wore a night-at-the-Grammys beaded white gown, matching mules, and a ransom in Chanel gold.

Big Irma smirked, glittering proudly in her blue spot. Heavy wisps of blue-gray cigarette smoke swirled in the light of her stage.

The audience adored her. With lips pulled back over polished teeth, hands fluttering at chests and drunk eyes dancing, she made them laugh. Too hard by my way of thinking, too long by Irma's. Maybe everybody thought it was the last time anybody would laugh.

"Hush now, boys and girls," she said. "You know your

Big Irma's only up here for just so long. Let's all pay attention, and I'll sing you some more nice dirty tunes."

The couple at the small table to my left, giddy from three rounds of drinks that had come with little paper parasols, shrieked joyfully. He wore chains and overalls with the bib lowered to his crotch to show off his washboard stomach. She wore a ponytail, and a pink string bikini the cocktail waitress had admired. *"Divine tuck, dear—and very excellent butt floss."*

At my right was a large table full of pumped-up body Nazis with stiff, young-Elvis pompadours, and their "dates"— would-be cover-girl idols with tan deltoids, fatless inner thighs, and feather-cut hairdos. The fluorocarbons from this room full of Aqua Netted belles and beaux were doing no good for the ozone layer.

Big Irma pointed at the shrieker in the bib overalls. The blue spot followed her lead, illuminating the subject of her exuberant ridicule. Nothing personal, all part of the act.

She said, "Looky looky, my pets. Don't our darlin' Billy-Bob-Joe-Jim shine tonight? Shall we throw a little shade on, darlin'?"

Her audience, like caged lions coaxed to a mass roaring by the sight of feeding-time beefsteak for the amusement of zoo customers, stamped feet and bellowed lusty encouragements.

Irma obliged. "Did you know he's been inside a woman? I ain't lyin'! Why, once upon a time he went all the way to the top of the Statue of Liberty."

More hard, terminal laughter.

A brawny Celia Cruz type in a miniskirt with her big feet jammed into a pair of sparkling yellow pumps tripped on something behind me. I turned at the commotion. Somebody in a purple Afro giggled and called her a "dumb cunt." Miss Cruz doubled a fist and slammed it deep into kinky purple. The contact sounded wet and sickening and painful. Celia then murmured to the dazed Afro, "Lose the attitude, sugar. Only a woman would want you."

Big Irma blew air kisses to the combatants, rolled her eyes, and pounded out a crowd-pleasing boogie-woogie medley. The floor soon vibrated with toe tapping.

Then she changed pace and sang "Somewhere over the

Rainbow," and this soothed many savage breasts, at least for a while. Long enough so Irma could take a beat. She sipped through a straw at the cloudy turquoise drink set up for her on the piano.

I put a slightly trembling hand to my dry lips and imagined Irma's colorful drink. Tinctured Bombay Sapphire gin with the picture of Queen Victoria on the label.

Merciful God, I wanted a drink. A real drink. Not what I had in front of me, seltzer over shaved ice with three kinds of fruit floating on top.

"You know," Irma said, smirking again, riffing the piano keys, "it's better to have loved and lost than to have married and gained."

A torrent of forced laughter.

"My boyfriend, I call him Ocean Liner because it takes a little tug to get him started . . . Me and Ocean Liner, we rushed out to the airport the other day. We wanted to fly united, but they wouldn't let us . . . Oh, don't you love those stewardesses? Not! They ask you what your pleasure is, then they strap you in and won't let you have it . . .

"Well anyway, here's a little song. It's called 'Open up, Richard'—or, 'Don't Close the Door on Me Dick.' "

The dark angel with the horns and pitchfork perched on my left shoulder was whispering in my ear now, and I wanted very much to heed him. In fact, I started rising from my seat with the bright idea of going up to the bar for a quick and blessed jolt of Johnnie Walker red. But before I could do the fallen angel's bidding, there was Ruby coming toward me, a bona fide female on her way back from the ladies' room. She attracted a few hostile glares, she being the only *she* in the room with the real goods.

I slinked back down in my chair.

Ruby sat, crossed her legs, and asked, "Miss me?"

I answered in something between a whisper and a snarl, "For the love of God, don't leave me here alone again."

Ruby could imagine what she might of that. What I truly meant was that I needed her right this minute to keep me from slugging down an honest-to-God *drink* drink. Here I was, after all, sniffing at the slightest scent of Scotch in the cigarette smog. Ruby being beside me would keep me on the wagon; Ruby and the angel on my other shoulder, too, the one with the halo. I had a very terrible battle going on inside, just as the assembled boys and girls laughing so hard had theirs.

Up onstage, Big Irma crooned a couple of misty Judy Garland signature tunes. When she was through, she leaned toward the slender redhead sitting alone at ringside, the one in the black body stocking with a cropped jacket of black ciré, the one with the sad, baggy eyes welled up in tears. In her throaty, plaintive voice, Irma cooed, "Honey, I know how it is. I might be too old to cut the mustard, but I can still lick the jar."

Maybe Big Irma was trying to coax a quiet moment with this remark. I have seen chanteuses play one mood against another this way, comic versus pathetic. Maybe some other time, and in quite another collective frame of mind, this crowd might have reflected on the bittersweet joke, as intended. But not tonight. The mood tonight, as much as the desperate laughter, was competitive. And the contest was deadly simple: Who would survive Halloween?

The popular girls in the room, the ones with their pick of gentlemen callers, flicked forelocks with deadly aim over cold shoulders in the direction of their less popular sisters. The wounded looked like the sweet dead face that burned in my brain.

Sweet Jesus, I needed a drink.

The needs of the wounded were deadly simple, too. They looked as if they wished nothing more of life than to leap up from their tables and dash from one mirror to the next, adjusting a wig here, smoothing a skirt there, in hopes that the ensuing reflection would reveal something worth suffering for.

1

Smooth and confident, he rose from the table as she approached, guided by the arm of the sleek captain. All six feet four of him in his charcoal gray Savile Row suit and his custom Turnbull & Asser bold-striped shirt and Hermès cravat and his carefully shaped hair, black with wings of silver at the temples. He took Ruby's extended hands, slender and caramel brown with pale white frosted nails, and kissed them.

"Back to the old salt mines, hey, kiddo?" he said with a smile, and with the lighter-than-air affability of the well bred. She thought, He always smiles that way when he wants something, like an elegant alligator.

"Table eighty-nine," Ruby said admiringly, her face uptilted to receive a kiss on the left cheek, then the right. He had introduced her to the continental buss years ago. She liked it. She liked nearly everything he had taught her, especially the things that took her far away from where she came. In her deepest privacy, she liked thinking of what might have been with this man had she taken the chance. She said, "Some salt mine."

"Well, one must eat, mustn't one? Welcome back to the beanery, Ruby dear."

Back? Was that where she was? Five minutes' worth of intriguing phone conversation that morning with the eminent Bradford Jason Schuyler III of Madison Avenue, followed by a frantic three-hour search through her theater wardrobe downtown for just the right thing to wear to lunch at the Four Seasons on a sunny October day, then a dollar-and-a-quarter ride on the uptown Lexington Avenue local since she was quite broke, after all—and already, she was *back*?

She wondered, A dubious welcome to a dubious return? And as usual when she found herself in Jay Schuyler's stylish company, Ruby Flagg could not prevent the fugitive thought, Can a Louisiana colored girl like me ever really look good enough to be with some Mayflower-to-Manhattan old-money white boy like this?

She smoothed the sleeves of her blue linen jacket and poked a finger in her nappy hair, and said, "Jay, I don't know about—"

He interrupted. "I do. You appreciate the perfect irony, right?"

"Sure . . ."

"Check. So hear me out on this project. It's ironic as hell."

"You're very sure of yourself, aren't you, Jay?"

"Check."

At the Four Seasons, one does not hear the coarse bustlings of waiter or wine steward. Instead, such men (for they are always men, never women) simply materialize. Thus did Henri appear at the table, with an iced bucket of Dom Pérignon and a pair of chilled champagne flutes. Without a word, Henri poured. And Jay Schuyler smiled his smile.

So it was to be one of those patented Schuyler luncheons, slow and boozy and politely crafty. In years past, she had been his comrade-in-arms when others were the subjects of these smoothy pitches; now she was to have the same treatment.

She knew all that was to follow: Jay would make her think everything he said was her idea, then he would send her home by limousine, a nice touch; then sometime that evening when she sobered up from all the drinks and alligator smiles, she would suddenly realize how much her wrists and elbows ached from all that Mayflower-to-Manhattan old-money white boy arm twisting.

Ruby should have figured as much, based on the tantalizing nature of the morning phone call. Schuyler had reached her at her theater, the Downtown Playhouse on South Street.

"*There's something very attractive in the wind, Ruby. I'd like to have you aboard.*"

"*So what's the sell?*"

"*It's big. It's more than big.*"

"*Please, that sounds like something from your jingle-writing days. 'Say there, folks—buy the new jumbo box of Suds-O detergent! It's big—it's more than big!*'"

"*Don't laugh. I'm talking immense.*"

"*I should laugh when a man talks immense?*"

"*There's money—*"

"*Big money.*"

"*Check. And lots more, Miss Smarty Mouth.*"

"*Such as?*"

"*The new world order, peace in our time . . . little things like that.*"

"*Jay, have you been talking to some plate-head who wants to run for president?*"

"*Hear me out over lunch today. You won't be sorry.*"

"Thank you, Henrí," Schuyler said.

The waiter clicked his Gallic heels, ever so softly. Then he vaporized.

Ruby began to feel sorry she had come. But damn, she was so broke! Then there was Hock.

. . . And who could say about Neil Hockaday, her husband of only five and a half months? Not Ruby. Certainly not during these past six weeks of Hock's being off where he had to go. Six weeks that had filled her with doubt and anger and regret and pity and fear such as she had never known. One minute she ached for Hock's big arms wrapped around her; the next minute, she was horrified by the short odds of his becoming the sorriest breed of spouse: a souvenir of love.

Should I fly home and ask Mama about it all? Oh, Mama, you know all about being strong for a man, don't you?

Ruby tried to keep such questions from her crowded mind, questions she considered girlish. Thus far during the luncheon at the Four Seasons, she had thought of home and

Mama merely a dozen times. Once for every thought of her absent husband.

The separation was for the good of poor Hock's body and soul, of course, not to mention for the salvation of his marriage. This was Father Sheehan's counsel when Ruby wept to him over the telephone, on those blackest of her lonesome nights; nights she believed she might go barking mad if she couldn't get a plane home right away and crawl into the big four-poster bed in Mama's room; moonless nights of no sleep as she paced the floor in the dark, worried about money, and her eyes all flooded from listening to the tape she put together of Billie Holiday's all-time saddest songs. "Moaning Low," and "The Man I Love," and "Foolin' Myself," and "Where Is the Sun?" and "It's Like Reaching for the Moon," . . . and, especially, "Gloomy Sunday." Ruby believed such wallowing in the lowest of low-down blues might expedite her mourning. But then again, who could say . . . ?

Of course, Jay Schuyler probably knew full well her sorry-ass situation: the money trouble, the theater trouble, the husband trouble; whatever, whichever, and however her damn troubles. All else might be uncertain, but of this Ruby was dead sure: Bradford Jason Schuyler III was bred to understand that one man's pain is another man's profit. Thus had he become a mogul of Madison Avenue.

"Some things never change," Ruby said, lifting a delicate crystal flute filled with roughly fifty dollars' worth of Dom Pérignon. With fifty bucks, she marveled, she could get her Visa bill back under the limit. "Do you think that's good or bad, Jay?"

"Yes."

"I see I'm right."

Ruby took a look around the room. From the corner vantage point of table eighty-nine, she had the whole sweep of the place: the big green-carpeted Pool Room, so-called because of the marbled square of potted palm trees and lily-padded water in the center; the copper link draperies that worked with the light from Park Avenue to cast the place in a faintly sepia tone; the Grill Room beyond, and the genteel hubbub of the bar; the widely spaced tables; the smattering of old-school celebrities—those able to use cutlery, chew with their lips closed, and speak in complete sentences.

Two tables over, for example, there sat Douglas Fairbanks, Jr. He was with a woman about Ruby's age, with fair skin and straight, upswept auburn hair. The fair one chattered while the still elegant matinee idol of long ago sipped his iced tomato juice. Douglas Fairbanks's spotted hand shook under the weight of a chunky goblet, but not a drop of red stained his silver mustache.

At that very incongruous moment, Ruby thought of her two homes. The one with Hock, now only half a home, and then the other one: the St. Bernard Projects on the northwest side of New Orleans.

Mama Violet stood in the dimness of early morning, already dressed for the day in her maid's uniform and heavy support hose, hanging up her own family's wet laundry on a line in the tiny garden patch behind the cinder block row house on Gibson Street. Upstairs in Mama's bed lay her husband, Willie, with nothing to do but complain about his long wait for death's deliverance. Ruby's beautician sister had come over the day before to press and straighten Mama's hair, and there was still the powerful whiff of processing fluids hanging around the kitchen.

Ruby thought of colors, too. Mama's hair was dyed auburn, the same shade as the white lady at the table with the movie star. At the Four Seasons restaurant that Violet Flagg would never know, here now sat her daughter Ruby, the one with the coal black nappy head.

"You notice Fairbanks?" Schuyler asked her, breaking the spell of Ruby's remembrance.

"Who's that with him?"

"A new beautiful woman. Some things do change."

"And others never do, like I said."

"Well then, here's to all of it."

Schuyler lifted his own flute, in a wordless toast. To the prodigal daughter who had found her way back to Madison Avenue? Why not? Ruby clinked her glass against his.

She looked beyond Schuyler to a large poolside table

framed by palm fronds. Five achingly young women in shimmery dresses chattered among themselves. The topic might have been business, but Ruby had her doubts as to whether it was corporate. There was also a sixtyish fat man at the table. He had a bald head and a puffy, olive-complexioned face half hidden by tinted aviator spectacles. He was very busy with somebody on his cellular telephone, his hands making a lot of looping motions as he talked.

"I see the Bullfrog is still holding out there by his pond," Ruby said. Schuyler laughed, remembering the tag Ruby had given him. She asked, "Did you ever manage to figure his story, Jay?"

"Not really. Everybody around here is sworn to secrecy. Nobody says much about him that means anything. Not even to me, and I give very brisk Christmas tips."

"Still the same routine?"

"It hasn't altered a bit in the four years he's been coming here. Every day, the Bullfrog arrives fifteen minutes before the place opens. Every day with his hands full. There's the fresh bottle of catsup, there's the greasy bag of bagels, there's the fresh batch of bimbos."

"Raoul must love it."

Schuyler shrugged. "Raoul is a very well-seasoned maître d', he knows when to keep his nose to himself, and he knows how to make discretion pay."

"What about the house?"

"One day I calculated the man's daily bill. Then I multiplied this by two hundred and fifty-five, which is the number of business days in a year, allowing for a few holidays. The Bullfrog spends better than a quarter-million dollars a year on lunch. For this kind of trade, even the Four Seasons is not going to fuss about a brown-bagger. Especially one who comes early. That way, practically nobody ever sees the mess he hauls in with him."

"The bagels and catsup you mean, not the bimbos."

"Check."

"So, no questions asked."

"Ask? Nobody speaks, apart from the Bullfrog and somebody on the other end of that dork phone of his. Raoul seats this guy and his bevy at the same table every day. Then he takes the bag out to the kitchen. He holds it with

two fingers, out away from him, like there's something in there that's just died. A couple of minutes later, one of the assistant chefs comes out in his long white apron and toque and he's got the bagels sliced up and slathered in catsup—all on a covered silver tray. The Bullfrog's happy, and practically nobody with a decent palate is the wiser."

"The Bullfrog and his guests, they really eat this?"

"For starters. But like I say, he also buys a lot of lunch."

A waiter materialized. He set down two plates of pâté de foie gras and a baguette, sliced thin. Schuyler dug in. Ruby preferred to drink.

"You've spent a lot of time studying the scene here, haven't you, Jay?"

"Nowhere near a quarter million a year's worth. But yes, I know the room. In this line, you should be a student of rooms."

"Speaking of which, you mentioned how you wanted me aboard?"

"Of course." Schuyler smiled, and it was deadly. He added, "After all, you're a genius."

"You told me that before."

"See how you remember the good old days?"

"You used to say there were two kinds of people who mattered. Smart people and geniuses."

"Quite so. And do you remember the difference?"

"Smart people know what smart people want, geniuses know what stupid people want."

"Check."

"So on that score, things are exactly the same in the advertising dodge?"

"Yes, folks, she's still a genius." Schuyler paused and leaned close to add, "And she has remained gorgeous."

"Steady, Jay. Let's stick to business."

"Plenty of time for that. There's a rumor in the street that you got married last spring."

"It's true."

"To a policeman?"

"Also true."

"Jesus, Ruby." He waited a moment, but Ruby said nothing. Schuyler sighed, and this was the closest thing to personal defeat that Ruby had ever heard or seen in him. Then he said, "Well, you know what this means."

"No, I don't think so."

"The chase is over. I don't fool with married women. You're finally safe from me." Schuyler gazed in the direction of the pool, specifically the Bullfrog's table. Ruby followed his gaze. Schuyler said, "Also, I don't sit over there anymore."

"What's the connection?"

A waiter glided up to the table, whisked away the pâté de foie gras and the baguette and poured out another round of champagne. He suggested that the king salmon and the milk-fed veal were especially good that day, as each had been flown in that morning from Alaska and Japan, respectively.

"Very good," Schuyler said. The waiter raised his hand and clicked his fingers softly; in a moment the wine steward appeared, to suggest a bottle of light Bordeaux to complement both entrées. "Very good," Schuyler repeated.

When the waiter and steward were gone, Schuyler asked Ruby, "Now, you wanted to get down to business?"

"First tell me about the pool and married ladies."

"It happened before you came to the agency. Also before Margot."

"How is your wife, by the way?"

"Still writing, still doing good works for the opera crowd."

"Anyway, about the pool?"

"I was once crazy for a certain blonde actress. She was half-Swedish and half-Polish and so beautiful she made you want to go bite something. We used her for the old Erik cigar spots, back when you could still advertise tobacco on the tube. You know, the Scandinavian chick on the deck of the Viking ship as it sailed into the New York harbor?"

"The blonde smoking the little cigar? Very tasty."

"She was that."

"Married, too?"

"Not that you'd notice."

"Somebody usually does."

"You have a point there." Schuyler shook his head in the slow, involuntary way a man will when remembering something especially stupid and embarrassing from his past.

It was more a wince than a shake. "Seems like only last week. But my God, it's been so damn long ago." Schuyler sighed, this time the way a man will when remembering a lost youth for better or for worse. "I don't suppose you ever heard of Earl Wilson."

"Sure, and I heard about the dinosaur age, too. Even though I wasn't here at the time."

"Wilson was the last mastodon of yuk and titter journalism. And still around when it happened."

"*It?*"

"One day, late in the afternoon, we're sitting over there." Schuyler nodded in the general direction of the pool. "Two tables this side of where the Bullfrog is right now."

"*We,* meaning . . . ?"

"Blondie and me. We're just about to slip off to my place when somebody comes by to nix the plan. Take a guess who."

"Mr. Blondie?"

"Check. And he's a big guy. Built like a wall that learned how to walk."

"What did he do to you?"

"Not what you'd think. He just walks over and smiles down at us for a couple of seconds that seem like a couple of weeks. Then first he says to me, 'It's not your fault, my friend.' "

"Then what?"

"He picks up the missus right out of her chair and heaves her into the pool. So this lovely fracas, it naturally becomes one of Earl's pearls."

"In his *Mirror* column."

"But that's not the half of it."

"The Erik people were not amused?"

"Lost the account."

"You've led a harrowing life, Jay."

The salmon and the veal and the wine arrived. Ruby spent the next hour eating, and catching up on two years' worth of Madison Avenue gossip. She also had enough Bordeaux to feel a pleasant buzz. Which made her feel guilty, considering where her husband the alcoholic cop was.

Schuyler would occasionally ask her something about the struggling theatrical company she had started up with all the money she had earned from being a genius at what she used to do. But it seemed to Ruby as if he somehow already knew all the answers. Oh yes, he had done his homework.

The waiter materialized with tiny glasses on a crystal tray, the usual treatment. Two stingers. Ruby sipped hers, and the little buzz saw inside her head began sounding like a jackhammer. At times, she barely heard Schuyler talking.

He was saying, "Sorry, you'll have to work with Crosby. After all, Crosby's the one who brought in the business—"

Ruby interrupted. "Oh God, Jay!"

"But let's look on the bright side."

"What's bright about it?"

"You get a big retainer up front on a consultancy contract, and then a nice paycheck every week like a regular person. Plus, you'll be helping me out. You know we keep a thin staff. There's nobody I can put onto a new project without looking to the outside. Might as well be you, kiddo. You should come in from the cold for a while. Don't lie, this is something you've been dreaming about for months. You can't pay your bills with that theater of yours, can you?"

"Well ..."

"Look, I've had people go down there."

"Market research?"

"Check. Your best night, maybe there's twenty paying customers. Otherwise, you paper the house. So you're flying by the seat of your pants. You need money for either one of two things: to live like a human being, or else to toss it down your arty rat hole."

"You sweet talker."

Schuyler smiled. "Sure, and here's how I'll make it even sweeter. You get Sandy, the best secretary we've hired in years. Also you get southeast corner office on the thirty-fifth floor."

"I thought Foster was in there."

"He retired."

"You fired him."

"I persuaded him."

Ruby rubbed her temples. There were now at least two jackhammers at work. It was all she could do to ask, "What kind of trade did you say this was? I don't think I can get excited about the discovery of yet another body part that needs deodorizing."

Obviously, this was the cue for a silver pot of coffee and the pastry cart. Ruby declined the pastry.

"This business you're going to love. I promise, it's a long, long way from package goods." Schuyler smiled and watched Ruby drink down a cup of black coffee. "Tomorrow morning, nine sharp. We'll all be waiting for you in your new office."

"All—?"

"Sandy Malreaux, that's your secretary. Crosby and me. Also the Likhanov brothers."

"The who?"

Schuyler waved a manicured hand. "For now, just think new world order." He looked at his Cartier tank watch, then rose from the table, and said, "Got to scoot."

Ruby finished her coffee and stood. And the two of them left the Pool Room. At the Four Seasons, nobody but Jay Schuyler ever said *check*. The bill would be in the mail, and Uncle Sam would eventually be the sport. And it was back to the salt mines for Ruby Flagg.

There were two limos waiting outside. One for Ruby, one for the man with the alligator smile.

Schuyler kissed Ruby on both cheeks. She felt heat.

Schuyler said, "I want to meet this policeman of yours. He's a good guy?"

"He's got his problems. But yes, he's good. He's very good."

2

MANY OTHER TIMES IN MY LIFE I HAVE BEEN WITHOUT IT. No big deal. But then one day I had no choice in the matter. And this felt very different, like I was walking around naked in a bad dream.

Seven weeks ago, Inspector Tomassino Neglio, my so-called friend, put me on restricted duty, which is what regular cops know as the bow-and-arrow squad. He said what they always say: *It's for your own good.* Ruby even said that.

Right away, all the regular cops saw how the bulge was gone out of my jacket. Or else when I was not wearing a jacket they saw how the leather clip on my belt was empty. They would then have themselves a snorty laugh and say to me, "So, they take it away from you?"

A week of this and I started having quite a lot of blue flu. Then, thanks to my old rabbi and former so-called drinking buddy, Davy Mogaill, the body snatchers came and got me.

Short of my having to go back to wearing the bag after all my plainclothes years, I used to think the bow-and-arrow squad was as bad as it gets. But I have recently discovered that the worst of it all—short of being canceled out in the line of duty—is the body snatchers. When I complain about this where I am lately, the only commiseration I hear is this same line, over and over, *"Take it one day at a time."*

Lately, I am obliged to live in an ugly red brick building on the wrong side of the river. During the Prohibition years, a temperamental gentleman from the Bronx named Arthur Flegenheimer, who was better known as Dutch Schultz, ran a brewery in this ugly building over here in Paterson, New Jersey. Right here at the intersection of Straight and Narrow streets. Check out the map, I am not making this up.

Everywhere I go inside the Straight and Narrow I am surrounded by pissbums from New York, a sorry and tiresome lot of humanity. It is assumed here that I myself, Detective Neil Hockaday, am likewise a pissbum. Why else would anybody go to Paterson, New Jersey?

Right now I am sitting in the day room with fifteen or twenty pissbums. This room is called Cheers, which is somebody's bad idea of a joke. There is no radio or television set here, there are no books or magazines or newspapers. On the other hand, there are a couple of hundred different AA pamphlets, most of which I have read about ten times each.

God forbid a pissbum might see one of those slick ads for Dewar's White Label in *Newsweek* or someplace, or Billy Dee Williams singing about Colt 45 malt liquor on the idiot box, or even a sweaty bottle of Budweiser painted on an outfield fence if he should want to tune in the World Series like I myself want to do. Naturally, he would go nuts from thirst.

Here at Cheers—ha-ha!—there is not even a Holy Bible. According to the priests who run the place, the Holy Bible is risky, since it contains quite a lot of parts where people drink wine, including Jesus Christ. I suppose the good fathers should know. Maybe pissbum priests sometimes get the alky sweats from reading the consecrated word.

There are only two reasonable diversions allowed in here: pencils and steno pads. So instead of reading some AA tract for the eleventh time, or maybe playing dominos with the pissbums over in the corner, I pass the time by writing in a pad. I wish I could draw. I would draw a picture of a guy having himself a nice big double of Scotch and soda at some great bar and show it to all the pissbums and watch them go berserk.

This is how mad I am. Knowing that I am allowed to talk

to Ruby on the telephone at six o'clock—which is approximately three hours, twelve minutes, eight and one-half seconds from now—is the only thing that prevents me from strangling somebody. If I hear the word *denial* one more time today, I will set somebody's hair on fire.

However, I would not deny that my life has come to a godawful pass. Somehow.

Oh, but I know very well how. *How* is what I have been telling these chowderheads at the Straight and Narrow for six long weeks. And all they do is toss back slogans. So I do not want to go into all that. Maybe later. But since I now have about three hours, ten minutes, and four seconds to kill, I should at least get down in this steno notebook two things that happened to me recently: the morning with the department chaplain, and the night of the body snatchers.

It was Inspector Neglio who sent me to the chaplain. This was when he called me downtown to his office at One Police Plaza at nine o'clock on a Tuesday morning. Actually, he wanted me there on Monday. But I was slightly under the weather on account of a long Sunday night in a neighborhood bar and grill by the name of Angelo's Ebb Tide. So we had to reschedule. This did not make the inspector happy.

Anyhow, it was a Tuesday morning when he took my gun away from me. For my own good. After which he told me I was all of a sudden supposed to temporarily stop working as a street detective and sit around some office typing crime statistics into some kind of computer I never heard of. Without my gun. This did not make me happy.

"Okay, the chaplain's expecting you now," he said to me after all that. "That'd be Father Sheehan." Inspector Neglio could no longer look me in the eye. He pressed a buzzer on his desk, and this freckle-faced uniform about the age of twelve walked in, breathing through his mouth. "Officer Neuman here, he'll make sure you get to the counseling unit, down on the sixth floor. Good luck and get well soon, Hock."

Go ahead, put the shackles and bracelets on me, too, why don't you? I thought this, I did not say it. Neuman came up and took hold of my elbow with his fingertips. I hate that.

18

I thought about shaking him off, but I know the drill. Any trouble and a lot more Neumans were likely to show up. So I went along peaceably.

Down in counseling, I was offered a seat on a cracked orange plastic chair outside the police chaplain's cubicle. The chair pinched the left side of my fanny whenever I shifted around. I had to wait ten minutes in that chair until this Father Sheehan was through yakking with somebody over the telephone about who was bringing what to some ordination reception for some new Jesuit priest. Neuman put a stick of spearmint gum in his mouth and stood around saying nothing with his arms crossed over his chest. I could have used another vodka and grapefruit juice eye-opener like the one I'd had about half-past seven.

Finally, this short fat-cheeked guy in a black cassock stepped out from the cubicle. He had a creamy face, a black beard that tried to hide his dimples, thick bifocals, thinning black hair with a couple of gray streaks running through it, and eyes the color of baker's chocolate. He sounded happy enough with his pal on the telephone when the subject was carrot cake and cold cuts and strawberry punch, but talking to me his voice had all the joy of a gravedigger.

"Come in, son," he said, sticking out a small, soft hand for me to shake. "I'm John Sheehan."

Another plastic seat I got. This time it gave me troubles in my right-hand backside. For himself, the father had a nice padded chair behind a wooden desk loaded down with all kinds of paper. He was holding some of this paper in his hands and reading, and scowling.

"These muster reports, I just don't know," he said, shaking his head. He stared at me over the tops of some heavy silver-framed glasses. "You've been out sick. A lot. What's the problem, Detective Hockaday?"

"Flu's going around."

"Really."

"My stomach, it's whacked."

Now he was staring at where my jacket did not bulge anymore. He said, "So, they take it away from you?"

This was not the sort of question where I had to give an answer. The silence hung there between us for several seconds. I could hear Neuman's breathing and chewing behind me, just outside the cubicle.

"You know what it means when they do that?" Sheehan asked, looking away from me. He inspected his fingernails.

"I guess I do."

"But you never thought it applied to you, did you, son?"

"Does anybody?"

Sheehan laughed. He sounded like an old horse the way the air whinnied through his nose.

"I heard about what happened last April," he said. He pulled a nail clipper from a pocket and started trimming. Little crescent moons of calcium snips spilled over his desk.

"Yeah, well it made all the papers."

The father was referring to what I do not care to elaborate on right now, since all the time I have before I can talk to Ruby is about two hours, fifty-one minutes, and seven seconds. Briefly for the record, though, Sheehan had in mind the case of a priest friend of mine by the name of Father Timothy Kelly who had blown his brains out one Sunday only this past April in the confessional at Holy Cross Church in my own neighborhood of Hell's Kitchen, and how my rabbi Davy Mogaill's house out in Queens had blown up from a bomb right around this same time, and how this had led me overseas to Dublin and a lot of related Irish murder and treachery. Which led to my seeing my old man for the first time in my whole life, and having him and his clay feet die in my arms. All of it definitely made the papers. And I only wish it was a great load of whiskey under the bridge because that would be the kind of drinking I might have been able to forget. As it is, the whole bloody thing is still creeping my dreams.

"*Made the papers!*" Sheehan whinnied again. "It's good to know you have a sense of humor."

"Why is that?"

"Because humor is emotional chaos remembered in tranquility, my son. Because humor can cure what ails you."

"This day I don't see as particularly funny."

"Correct. Nobody's cracking jokes with you, Detective Hockaday. Today is your official warning."

"That's how this bow-and-arrow thing works?"

"Captain Mogaill and Inspector Neglio, they told me you catch on very quick."

"Did they?"

"Which is why I recommended temporary reassignment. So you can get yourself together. Which you'd better do, since I have taken a personal interest in your case." Sheehan brushed dead fingernails off the end of his desk. Then he gave me one of those disgusted looks I used to get from the priests and brothers when I was a kid in short pants at Holy Cross and I was the one they suspected of slipping a condom into the collection plate at morning mass.

"I always wanted someone to watch over me," I said with my smart mouth.

"Screw up the deal, Hockaday, and you've probably heard what comes next."

"Yeah, I've heard."

I did not right away get myself together. Meaning that during my month-long sentence typing crime stats in an office, I drank a lot of funny coffee. When I showed up, that is. So then, sure as the sun and the moon, the next thing came: the night of the body snatchers.

This occurred not at Angelo's Ebb Tide, where I sometimes take Ruby and where I generally imbibe like a gentleman. No, the night of the body snatchers took place at the Flanders Bar. Which is located on the nether side of my neighborhood, and where sometimes my evil twin drinks.

The Flanders is the sort of place that takes full advantage of the New York State laws governing drinking hours. Meaning it stays awake until four in the morning, goes to sleep for a hundred-twenty minutes, then reopens at six o'clock in the very same A.M. with about twenty-five pre-poured jiggers lined up on the bar for those with the shakes.

When the body snatchers got me, I was slurring my pearls before swine. By which I mean a room full of boyos who drink stuporous amounts of whiskey; after which they tell lies about their ill usage of love-starved, compliant female beauties; after which they generally engage in a lot of manly vomiting. They also for some reason spend a lot of their time complaining about *faggots,* which was the topic that particular night. Just to be sociable, I was regaling the house with a living legend by the name of Joe Kowalski, scourge of *faggots* and thus a keeper of the sort of cop justice that generally sends me straight into the warm red arms of Mr. Johnnie Walker.

"Everybody knows what to do when you need some special advance justice done," I was saying. "Take for instance the case of some rich ballerina with a secret mean streak who falls in love with an altar boy, say, and does what he has to do. You want to run the risk of losing this creep when he's let go on his own recognizance and his uptown lawyer takes over? No. You take the creep to Kowalski ..."

I proceeded to explain.

Joseph Kowalski is the desk sergeant on the overnight trick down at the Manhattan Sex Crimes Squad. He is a man of formidable appearance. King Kong Kowalski they call him.

He has a square, packing crate body, skin with the sweaty color of pale oleomargarine, a face that looks like a shaved mastiff hound, and enormous hands with thick fingers all the same size. Those fingers of his are like rolled quarters, they do not bend. He is a few inches shy of six feet and he is pushing three hundred pounds. Because his weight is well over the department limit, Sergeant Kowalski hides in the locker room showers whenever an Internal Affairs Division snap inspection team shows up at his unit. Working the freak shift makes life easier for him, since IAD types usually have enough seniority to be home by a decent hour.

The sergeant is a member in good standing of the Holy Name Society of his Queens parish, Our Lady of the Blessed Agony. He observes certain of the more severe police devotionals as well.

For instance, Kowalski reserves the traditional desk sergeant's privilege of judging certain of the hundreds of miscreants he sees each night especially odious due to what he considers their sins against nature. On such occasions, he will step away from the desk and whatever he is eating at the moment (a Blimpie sandwich, a box of Russell Stover chocolates, Chicago-style pizza, maybe a carton of pork fried rice) to personally handle the booking and printing details.

For these private sessions, Kowalski maintains a small, sparsely furnished room beneath the central staircase of the squad station house. Actually, this is a large supply closet that he long ago commandeered from the janitor. There is a strong overhead light in this room, no windows, one chair, and a small two-drawer desk. On top of the desk is an inked stamp pad and standard FBI fingerprint forms.

Sergeant Kowalski introduces himself to the sinner by jamming a couple of his thick fingers down the back of the unfortunate's belt, after which he bounces him up and down like he was a yo-yo. Kowalski then persuades him to come along to the special room with a hearty, "Okay, turd, it's show time!" The cops hanging around the desk laugh, and then King Kong Kowalski goes and does what he has to do.

In the special room, Kowalski switches on the light, locks the door, and orders the now heavily perspiring perp to stand next to the desk. Sergeant Kowalski sits down in the chair behind the desk and slowly checks through the drawers. He finds the forms he needs, and he says, "We got to take your prints now. All of them. That okay by you?"

What can he say? The poor bastard goes along. Kowalski takes his left hand, inks down each fingertip and rolls them nice and easy, one at a time, into the different squares on the form. This does not seem so bad, and the guy relaxes some. Then the right hand gets it. While he is carefully inking the fingers, Kowalski will once in a while ask gently, "I'm not hurting you now, am I?"

Eventually, Kowalski gives him a paper towel to wipe his hands. Then he says, "Off with the pants."

The poor bastard is confused. Also he starts sweating again.

"Drop the freaking pants," Kowalski repeats, not gently. The mastiff hound's eyes narrow, the jowls shake. It looks as if King Kong has gone without food for three days. He growls, "The skivvies, too."

"What for?" the guy asks. He is naturally suspicious.

"For the dickprint."

"The dick what—?"

"You heard me. We got to be able to identify the salami on all you freaking pillow biters. It's these new health department rules that just come down. What are you going to do?" Kowalski takes a pair of latex gloves from one of the desk drawers, stretches them out, pulls them on. "Come on now, turd. You think I like this any more than you? Leave us quit stalling. Drop trou and flop your lolly-johnson up here on the desk."

The perp obviously does not like the idea. At this point, he will usually say something about a lawyer. But it is impressed upon him how it is the middle of the night and how he is in a locked room with an armed, three-hundred-pound pious Catholic cop from Queens—a man who was having a lovely snack that was interrupted on account of an alleged disgusting crime, and furthermore a sin against nature. The perp listens to reason.

"Yeah, that's it," Sergeant Kowalski says encouragingly as the perp complies by bellying up to the desk, as it were. "Lay it out there right on the ink pad, big and proud."

The guy by this time is anything but proud. He seems to be melting, like he was a cake left out in the rain. Usually he will start crying right about now. His nose snots up and he wails away like he was a kid again with his very first skinned knee. And so Sergeant Kowalski advises, suddenly in his most paternal tone, "Take it easy, son. Go ahead and shut your eyes if you want."

Then while the guy has his eyes shut, Kowalski rummages around through the other desk drawer. He takes his time, and he says, "Let's see now, where did I put the dickprint forms . . . ?"

Kowalski soon enough finds what he is after. Which as it turns out is not a standard FBI dickprint form, since there is of course no such thing. It is instead a foot-long braided leather sap that will do its job without leaving any bruises.

Eyes hot and righteous red, King Kong Kowalski now slowly raises the sap with his powerful right arm. The perp's teary eyes flutter open just as King Kong shouts, "Beware, my terrible swift sword!"

And then the sap comes hurtling down, smashing the lolly-johnson on the ink pad.

The perp screams.

All the cops laugh.

And when I finished telling this story, I myself cried.

Maybe if I had groaned and held my crotch like everybody else who was drunk that night, maybe if I had laughed like a loon at the legend of King Kong Kowalski, it would have been all right. But no. I, Detective Neil Hockaday, blubbered like the softhearted sentry at the gate to the Emerald City when Dorothy told him about the cyclone and her poor old Auntie Em and how she needed to see the great and powerful Oz in order to find her way back home.

My face fell to the beer-sopped bar. I covered my head with my hands, and I cried for every poor miserable twisted perp who Joe Kowalski had ever called *turd*. The fat hump. Then I cried for all the other miserable twisted things I have known as a cop for all these years. Then I cried for bloody Ireland, and for my dead Irish daddo. And then I cried this mournful catechism all over again, starting back with Kowalski's victims.

Then I cried again, and again.

The fat hump!

I could have sworn at the time I was only screaming this inside my head. Later, though, they told me I was hollering out loud and scaring the boyos so bad they vomited twice the usual volume.

The fat hump!

So this was the way I was carrying on when Davy Mogaill, reformed drunk, walked into the Flanders Bar with three uniforms. That damn Neuman was one of them.

People were already moving away from me, the nodders and the whores and the loudmouths. Especially the loudmouths. I was left alone at the middle of the bar, my foot hooked over the rail. Mogaill and the uniforms surrounded me, and started grabbing hold, one man per limb.

"What the hell is this?" I naturally shouted.

"Did you never hear of us body snatchers?" Mogaill answered, struggling with my flailing left arm and its impotent fist.

They cuffed me, hands and ankles. Then they lugged me out to the street, and jammed me into the backseat of an unmarked patrol car. I screamed inside my head, *Daddo ... Daddo!* They had little trouble with me, for I was limp with shame.

We rode in the dark of a rainy night, through the city and its water-stained colors rolling by outside the car windows. I screamed so nobody but me could hear, *Ruby ... Ruby!*

Then over the wide black Hudson River to Jersey and the Straight and Narrow.

Looking back on it, and with the charity of six sober weeks in my soul, I would say a good time was had by none.

"It's six o'clock. Do you know where your pissbums are?"

"Hello, Hock. I love you."

"You do? So how come you went and told Davy where to find me that night?"

"Give it a rest. I told you already."

"You said it was for my own good."

"That ought to be good enough."

"It's not."

"Miss your Ruby?"

"You want to change the subject? Okay, so I miss you. Also I forgive you."

"God, Hock—I miss you so."

"You sound like a girl I once took to a school dance."

"When you come home, maybe we'll go dancing."

"You'd be too much for me."

"We'll take it easy."

"So long as we take it."

"Tomorrow, Detective."

"Right. Tomorrow when I finally go over the wall. Will you be here to pick me up?"

"You know I want to, Hock."

"What's that mean?"

"Don't be upset. I've got a job I'm starting in the morning, nine sharp."

"That thing you told me about? With your old boss, the penthouse guy with the hots for you?"

"Don't worry about Jay. He took me to lunch today."

"Yeah, where?"

"The Four Seasons."

"What do you need with a job offer from a place like that?"

"Money. Besides, it might be interesting."

"How so?"

"I can't say yet, I honestly don't know myself. Why don't you tell me about your day?"

"Davy sent me a Hallmark."

"Not another one of those twelve-step cards?"

"What else?"

"So what was it this time?"

"A mountain sunset on the cover, right? I open it up and it reads, 'In this dysfunctional world, it's nice to know I have someone to feel functional with.' "

"I can't stand it."

"You can't say the man hasn't got religion."

"That I wouldn't deny."

"Please, don't say *deny*."

3

MADISON AVENUE. *MAD*, AS SHE USED TO CALL IT. THE TIMES she had here. Old home week. So what?

Such was Ruby's drab mood—weather inspired—at twenty minutes before nine o'clock on a sunless, windless morning. She disliked such a day's beginning, when the air was so heavy and still under a lowering sky; air with nowhere to go, and nothing to do but cause trouble. Down home in New Orleans, this was hurricane weather. Up here in New York, it was the kind of weather that went as naturally with ambivalence as lox with a bagel.

Ruby held the collar of her raincoat tight against her neck as she walked up the avenue from her bus stop. She felt vaguely cold and damp, as if she were passing through a long, narrow room lined in wet wool.

At the corner of East Fifty-third Street, Ruby left the Mad parade to enter a sleek building. Five-dozen storeys of glazed concrete trimmed in chrome, and what appeared to be giant wraparound Ray-Ban sunglasses. She crossed through the lobby, her own freshly waxed pumps joining the chorus of determined feet marching across a vast expanse of corporate marble. She took her place in the anonymous crowd at the bank of elevators and waited, eyes fixed on the dials above the doors like everybody else.

An elevator car opened with a soft ding-ding sound. Ruby

stepped inside, then whooshed one-eighth of a mile up into the Manhattan sky, to the world headquarters of Schuyler, Foster and Crosby, Inc.

The first new sight of her old stamping grounds did nothing to improve her mood.

Half the reception area was occupied by a glossy herd of actresses hoping to be hired for parts in TV commercials or magazine layouts. The cattle call. Everybody had dewy lips and long legs to cross. Most female brands were represented, although the group was weighted on the side of the American pie type.

Ruby knew the routine. And liked it much less than before.

The actresses were there to be seen for nonexistent jobs. Every afternoon, Frederick Crosby had his secretary phone the talent agencies and order up a morning gaggle of sugar snaps, one of Crosby's more courteous terms for women. This was in accordance with one of Crosby's philosophies of interior decor. "The office should be lousy with tail every morning," he once explained to Ruby Flagg, unwisely. "It stimulates the creatives, and it's a kick for the clients."

Whereupon, Ruby smacked him in the face. Which surprised Ruby far more than it did Crosby. She was rarely impulsive and had not struck anyone since back home, where she and her sister, Janice, tussled on a daily basis. Certainly she had never struck an adult; most certainly never a pencil-neck like Frederick Crosby, who reminded her of a bandy-legged rooster named Charlie she kept as a childhood pet. Ruby was shaking with embarrassed fear after walloping a partner of the firm, no less, but Crosby never noticed that.

Hand covering a reddened cheek, he laughed at Ruby, again unwisely. "You don't like me calling them tail? Give me a break. I've come a long way, baby. You don't hear me calling you girls babes or gashes anymore, do you?"

"I don't like you talking, period," Ruby said, looking at his sneer. Embarrassment and fear turned to anger now; she decided that slugging a runty misogynist had been for a good cause after all. She added, "I don't like the dumb lifts in your shoes, either. Or your padded shoulders, or your puffed-up hair, or the way you eat your cuticles."

"You don't have to get personal." Crosby moved on her, like maybe he was going to hit her one back.

"Get out of my face, weenie."

"What are you *saying?*" Crosby screeched. To Ruby, he sounded like Janice caught in a half nelson back behind the house on Gibson Street, hollering like blazes for Mama to come save her. Crosby screeched some more, "I want your apology right here, right now!"

Apologize to this peckerwood? Maybe if she were a man, maybe if she were white; maybe if she were of her mother's generation. But she would not—she could not—say she was sorry. An apology would only be held against her. For the likes of Ruby Flagg in the time and place she lived, the only option was audacity. *Bodacity,* as it was said in Louisiana.

"You're fired, Freddy," she said, bodaciously inspired.

"The name is Frederick. Or Fred." Crosby touched blood trickling from a nostril of his long, delicate nose. His voice was now wounded, too. "Just what's got into you, Ruby? What are you thinking? You can't fire me, I'm a partner around here. Hell, I'm your goddamn boss!"

"Who cares, Freddy? You're history. I'm giving you one hour to clean out your desk and split."

"You crazy black-assed—!"

Whereupon, Ruby clouted both his ears. Blood flowed.

"Jesus Christ! I'm going in to see Jay—right now. Then I'm calling up my lawyer."

"You'll need a lawyer because I'll be calling the New York City Human Rights Department, the United States Office of Equal Employment Opportunity, the NAACP, the advertising trade press of New York, and the national news media. When I'm through talking to them, I'll be ringing up the performers' unions to tell them how you're treating actors like they're potted plants for your lobby with these phony audition calls. Which means the unions won't let you hire talent anymore—which means you're out of business."

"You—!"

"Don't say it, Freddy, I'm warning you. Just answer me yes or no. You still want to talk to Jay?"

"No."

"That's funny, I do. I'm going in to tell Mr. Schuyler

exactly what just happened here, word for word. Want to come along with me?"

"No."

"You mean yes, Freddy."

"Yes."

"Good boy."

"Scary bitch!"

Ruby kicked his shins, very hard. Crosby staggered along beside Ruby as she steamed into Jay Schuyler's office. When Schuyler finished listening, he promoted Ruby Flagg to a vice-presidency. It was further agreed that sham auditions would be eliminated at SF&C. Frederick Crosby, since he was a partner, could keep his job.

"I think that's fair, don't you, Freddy?" Schuyler asked him.

"Goddamn it, Jay—it's Frederick, or Fred!"

That all happened twelve years ago.

For the past two years, Ruby had been free of Mad Avenue. Free of moronic clients and useless products, free of the office politics, free of the fool Crosby. That part was easy. The hard part was that she was also free of her old Mad Avenue salary.

But now here she was again. Back to where she started a dozen years ago, back to Jay Schuyler.

Back. Only to find that some things never change, starting with the reception area. Where was Freddy, that scrawny ofay?

Ruby slipped the raincoat off her shoulders and folded it over an arm. Underneath she wore a drapy cream-colored silk suit and a topaz-brown crêpe blouse. She walked through the buzz of actresses toward the reception desk. Eyes vacant of much more than mascara, tinted contacts, and jealousy followed her every step of the way.

"I'm Ruby Flagg," she announced.

The receptionist placed a caller on hold, glanced up at Ruby, then consulted a piece of paper with names on it. She was wearing an expensive pair of tortoiseshell glasses. They were big as welder's goggles, the kind of glasses favored by society matrons and ladies of a certain age who lived uptown before they were widowed and then became midtown office receptionists. Which was the type addressing Ruby now.

31

"Let's see, dear," she said. "Are you the one with William Morris?"

"No, I'm the one all by myself."

"Oh, my. Would you like to take a seat?"

"Is Freddy in yet?" Ruby heard hissing sounds behind her.

"My goodness. Do you mean Mr. Crosby, dear?"

"Dear Freddy, yes."

The sounds Ruby now heard behind her were of an elevator sliding open, a confident man striding across a tile floor, an affable, well-bred voice, and rustling skirts as legs coyly crossed. The receptionist started to say something when Ruby turned.

"Ruby! Sunshine! Buttercup!" Jay Schuyler, chairman of the board, approached from the elevator in his pinstripes, arms open to embrace Ruby. One of the actresses muttered, "Bitch." There was no telling who.

"So here I am, boss, early on the job," Ruby said, smiling. Her teeth were white as sugar, lips lightly rouged in maroon.

Schuyler said to the receptionist, "Arlene, I'd like you to meet Ruby Flagg, our new genius. She'll be on the Likhanov business."

Arlene sputtered, "I didn't realize . . . I'm so sorry, Miss Flagg."

"Don't worry about it," Ruby said.

"Mr. Schuyler?" Arlene said, nervously adjusting her goggles and consulting a nest of telephone messages. "Miss Malreaux is in with the Russian gentlemen."

"Check. The Likhanov brothers."

"Yes. Miss Malreaux has escorted them to Mr. Foster's old office."

"Good. Ruby here will be taking over that office."

"Oh, my."

Schuyler looked appreciatively at the cluster of hopeful actresses, then took Ruby's arm, and said to Arlene, "We're on our way there now, in fact. To Ruby's office. No calls there for the next hour."

"Very good, Mr. Schuyler. Oh, but, sir—one more thing."

"Yes?"

"Mr. Crosby called in sick."

"Today? When we've got the Russians here? This account, it's Freddy's baby!" Schuyler slapped his forehead. Only seconds ago he was pumped and fresh, now he looked as if he had spent the afternoon rush hour on the D train to the Bronx in mid-August. Wilted, he asked, "What's the matter with him?"

"His wife didn't say."

"Wife? Freddy's a bachelor."

"Oh, my." Arlene's face flushed scarlet. She patted her hair nervously. "Nevertheless, it *was* a woman who telephoned. Perhaps a housekeeper?"

Schuyler shrugged, a gesture now of annoyance at the news of his partner's absence. He turned to leave. Ruby followed him.

They walked down a wide corridor with money-colored green carpet and glazed gold walls full of Clio Award certificates and grabby magazine ads that were nicely matted and framed. Heads of various rank bobbed up from desks or out of doors along the way, and greetings were offered according to station. "Good morning, Mr. Schuyler" . . . "Hiya, Jay, how's it hanging?" . . . "Morning, sir" . . . "Morning" . . . "Let's do lunch, how about it . . . ?" Schuyler responded to each greeting with a noncommittal "Check."

"I have an old bone to pick with that dog," Ruby said as they walked.

"Who—Freddy?"

"I thought the sugar snaps number was all over."

"It is."

"So what's with the debutante ball back in reception?"

"That's legit. They're here for the Likhanov account."

"Freddy's idea?"

"Look," Schuyler said, touching Ruby's arm, "I'd like it if you could go easy on poor Freddy."

They stopped for a moment outside Ruby's new office. She could tell it was hers because there was a new brass plate on the door that read RUBY FLAGG. The oval-shaped secretarial station just outside the door contained creamed coffee gone cold in a Spode cup and saucer, a flickering desktop computer, a black leather appointments calendar, an impressive telephone console, and a vase filled with a dozen red roses. The secretarial chair held a cardigan sweater, but no secretary.

Voices could be heard from inside Hiram Foster's—Ruby Flagg's—private office. Off to the side of the closed door was a three-by-four-foot window that the doddering Hiram Foster had had cut into his office wall. Old Foster thought it was democratic to allow the help to peer at him through glass. To Ruby, it was beyond democratic; she used to say it looked like a window at a drive-up pizzeria. She looked now through the pizza window of her new office at the scene inside: two wide-backed men in wrinkled suits drinking coffee and being charmed by a tall young black woman.

Ruby turned back to Schuyler, and said, mockingly, "Poor Freddy?"

"He's been having his troubles lately."

"What a shame. Maybe he'll go the way of Hiram Foster?"

"Not office troubles. Personal."

"What would you know about that, Jay? I thought outside Mad Avenue the two of you had nothing to do with each other."

"True. But you work with a man for years and like it or not you get to know his rhythms. This calling in sick, it's all out of step. Freddy's the first one here in the morning, and most days he's the last to go at night. Like he's got no life. I've seen him here when he's had pneumonia."

"You saw him yesterday?"

"Sure, and he was in the pink, all excited about the Russians. You know how he gets."

"I remember him sleeping over here in the office every night before a big presentation. He'd keep on a team of creatives on overtime—at least one writer, an art director, a studio guy. Three or four secretaries, too. And he'd work them just about to death. The Dawn Patrol we used to call it."

"Check. That's what I mean about rhythms. Yesterday he's all jazzed about this meeting we're about to have. So what does he do? He goes home at five in the afternoon. From this and other little things lately, I can tell the guy's having serious problems."

"How serious?"

"Enough for me to wonder. Who likes to wonder when it comes to partners?"

"Hiram never did. Guess what he used to say about you, Jay."

"I don't like guessing."

"The day you take on a partner is the last night you sleep."

"Enough." Schuyler waved a hand. "Hiram's an idle rich man now. I should feel sorry? He should feel sorry for his two ex-partners."

"The ones who muscled him out of the picture."

"Persuaded."

"Shouldn't we be talking to the Russkis?"

"Check."

Schuyler picked up the phone on the secretary's desk and rang reception. "Arlene, see if you can raise Freddy at home," he said. "Put him through to Ruby's private line and I'll pick up."

Then Schuyler held open the door with Ruby's name on it. He smiled like an alligator, and said, "Welcome to your web."

Ruby strode into familiar space. On frazzled days, she sought refuge here. She and old Foster would have tea. Hiram would repeat a few of his stories about Madison Avenue in the days before "all these goddamn ass-kissing MBAs went and mucked everything up," and Ruby would soothe herself by listening. On good days, she would enjoy the grand view. The majestic Chrysler Building out the downtown windows, and far beyond, clear south to the Brooklyn Bridge. The crosstown windows showed her Roosevelt Island in the mist of the barges and tugboats floating along the slate gray East River, and Beekman Place, and Sutton Place. And all the other places most colored girls from Louisiana would never see ...

"Ms. Flagg?"

The tall young black woman flashed about thirty teeth and stepped away from the two Russians to greet Ruby, one hand outstretched, the other fingering a pearl button on her blouse. She was perhaps twenty-five years old and moved quickly and smoothly, like a dancer. She wore an African print skirt and her hair was sculpted in a high fade. Her skin was radiant and dark—the color of buffed mahogany, darker and redder than Ruby's. The young woman trailed the cool scent of an expensive cologne. Schuyler had said it well at yesterday's lunch: *So beautiful she made you want to go bite something.*

"Ms. Flagg, hello. I'll be your assistant."

The women shook hands as Schuyler formalized the introduction. "Sandy Malreaux, Ruby Flagg." Then he moved to the Russians, and the men took their turns shaking hands. "Alexis, Vasily," Schuyler said, grabbing each one in turn, giving them bear hugs. "How are you this wonderful morning?"

The brothers Likhanov crinkled identically tiny blue eyes, smiled, and said "Goot" in unison. Four Slavic lips curled to reveal gapped rows of yellow teeth. The brothers were dressed in off-the-rack navy blue suits that strained against their bread-and-cheese bulk, white shirts, and red neckties with fat Windsor knots. They looked like middle-aged cops in church, Ruby decided. They had twin fringes of close-cropped gray hair, pug noses, pink faces the shade of Canadian bacon, and fleshy moles under their eyes, one apiece. Ruby wondered how long it would take her to tell who was who.

"Alexis, say hello to our resident genius, Ruby Flagg," Schuyler said, standing now between the brothers. He tapped the shoulder of the Likhanov with the mole under his right eye. The other one had the mole under his left. Grateful for this, Ruby made quick mental notes. Alexis, right mole. Vasily, left mole.

"I'm so pleased to meet you, Mr. Likhanov," Ruby said, taking Alexis's soft, furry-knuckled hand. "Welcome to the United States." She said the same to his brother when Schuyler introduced Vasily. Both Likhanovs kissed the back of her hand, leaving it very moist.

Each of the brothers said "Goot" once again, remaining pleasantly mysterious men of few English words, or at least words that sounded English. Ruby looked at Schuyler with arched eyebrows, since she had not the slightest idea what to say next. Sandy Malreaux broke the awkward silence by saying, "Well now, Mr. Crosby should be along any moment."

"No," Schuyler told her. "Freddy's called in sick."

"Sick? Mr. Crosby?"

"So Arlene tells me." Schuyler turned to the Likhanovs, and added, "Sorry about that."

"No goot?" asked the brothers.

"Don't worry. We'll get Freddy on the speakerphone. It'll be just like he's here with us."

"Only better since he's not," Ruby said, shooting a sorority glance at her secretary and fellow *tail*. Sandy did not return the knowing look. Maybe she had yet to be treated to Crosby's piggery.

"Ms. Flagg, gentlemen, I've set out coffee and Danish over here," said Sandy, in a distracted manner. She led the way to the corner bay of windows, where leather club chairs were circled around a glass-topped conference table that also held notepads with the SF&C logo and ballpoint pens and a telephone console. Sandy moved a bit clumsily now, as if her dancer's arched feet had suddenly gone flat. When Ruby and Schuyler and the Russians were seated, Sandy left them with a toneless, "I'll be just outside . . . whenever you need me."

"Here's the way I like to do it in the advertising business," Schuyler said, directing himself to the Russians as Sandy closed the door behind her. The patented Schuyler smoothy talk, Ruby thought. He poured coffee for everyone from a silver pot that gleamed as brilliantly as his cuff links. "First impressions are important. That's why Ruby is completely in the dark about what you gentlemen are up to. We want to get her absolutely unvarnished first reactions. Check?"

The Russians looked at each other. They seemed impressed by what Schuyler had said, although slightly confused. *Czech?*

"Ruby, I want you to just blurt out the first thing that comes to mind as you begin to learn this project," Schuyler said. "Can I count on your being honest?"

"Brutally," Ruby said.

"Now then," Schuyler said, turning back to the Russians, "suppose we begin things with a simply stated overview."

"A fine idea for the uninitiated," Ruby said.

"Check. Vasily, how about bringing Ruby up to speed?"

After a nod to his brother, the left mole leaned toward Ruby and addressed her with a flourish of self-satisfaction, as if he had recently invented electricity: "In Russia, is ready to be making the goot times roll." Vasily Likhanov now concentrated his most enthusiastic smile on Ruby. His teeth made Ruby think of yellow moons over Lake Pontchartrain in the late summertime.

"Get it, Ruby?" Schuyler asked. "When Vasily first said that to me, right away I thought of you for this job."

"I don't get it, Jay."

"*Laissez le bon temps rouler?* Let the good times roll? Mardis Gras and all that? Get it?"

"You want to make Mardi Gras in Moscow?"

"Is *genius* Mardi Gras in Moscow!" Alexis Likhanov said. He walloped the conference table with a fist, spilling some coffee. Ruby thought of Nikita Khrushchev banging his shoe at the UN back in the fifties.

"Well, all right, maybe not Mardi Gras exactly, but very spectacular," Schuyler said. "Alexis and Vasily here, they're sitting on something bigger than Disney World."

Her voice dripping sarcasm, Ruby suggested, "Bigger than big?"

"Is goot big genius!" chimed the Brothers Likhanov.

Ruby sighed. "Jay, this is the new world order? Bright lights and shiny objects for weary old Mother Russia? Disney World? You want to turn Moscow into Orlando?"

"Not Orlando exactly. But I am talking bread and circus. And megabucks," Schuyler said. The Likhanovs' beady eyes danced at the mention of *bucks*. "Think Bolshevik revolution, okay?"

"I'm thinking."

"Bankrupt farmers, jobless factory workers, resentment against the Japanese, frustrated intellectuals, persecuted minorities . . ."

"Like Yogi Berra said, déjà vu all over again."

"Check."

"Is *genius!*"

"I knew you'd get it, Ruby."

"I don't get it, Jay."

"Picture the angry masses, picture Tsar Nicholas in the Winter Palace complaining about how the peasants are revolting . . . Never mind the Mel Brooks bit."

"I'm picturing."

"Okay. Now suppose you have a place where all these pictures, they actually come to life . . ." Schuyler paused. "Freddy really ought to be here to talk about this part. It's his baby, what with the actors and all."

"Jay, what are you saying? Political passion plays?"

38

"Not exactly—"

"But you are talking tourist trap."

"Don't be a snob. Tourists might have soft heads, but they carry hard currency. Get the idea?"

"*Goot* idea!"

Ruby smiled patiently at the Russians. She said to Schuyler, "I saw some of Freddy's other ideas lounging around reception when I first came in."

"Maybe you heard, cheesecake sells."

"Russia you want to sell? With cheesecake? Who wants to go to godforsaken Russia?"

"That's what they used to say about a godforsaken town in the Nevada desert. Bugsy Siegel, he saw things differently."

"Now you're talking gangsters? Vegas by the Volga?"

"Like I said, it's ironic."

"Is genius!" The Likhanovs clapped their hands together.

The telephone pulsed gently, Ruby's private line. "Aha!" Schuyler said, picking up the receiver from the console. "Ready Freddy."

"Mr. Schuyler?"

"Yes, Arlene?"

"I've got Mr. Crosby's apartment," Arlene said. "But something's ... Oh, my! Something's terribly—"

A man cut her off with a raspy, "Who's this?"

The interloping voice did not belong to Frederick Crosby, who had learned to speak at Dalton, Andover, and Yale. This voice had been forged in outer borough New York maybe fifty years ago, the voice of an elemental man accustomed to getting fast answers to blunt questions.

"Bradford J. Schuyler here. To whom am I speaking?"

"You'd be, what—Crosby's boss?"

"His partner."

"Yeah? What kind of freaking business you in?"

"Arlene," Schuyler said, "are you still on the line?"

"Yes, sir."

"Just who the devil is this?"

"Oh, my. A policeman, sir."

The outer borough voice broke in again.

"This here's Sergeant Kowalski, pally. Manhattan Sex Crimes."

4

DAWNED THE DAY OF MY JERSEY BUST-OUT.

According to the calendar, the skinny trees lining the streets of Paterson should still have been wearing October colors, especially the sugar maples. But there was a viscous haze that morning that made everything out the window look to be floating in dirty water. The streets were dark as subway platforms. Leaves that were supposed to be red and orange and yellow were wet and gray instead, like stones in the cemetery lane.

Cemetery.

Days like this, I used to think about my mother in her grave over in Queens. Days like this, I used to get drunk early.

Since breakfast I had been sitting around in the Saloon waiting for Davy Mogaill to come take me away from all this. I was willing to forgive Davy for putting me there in the first place, but if he brought Neuman along again I could change my mind. My suitcase had been packed since yesterday afternoon, and it sat on the floor beside me.

There was a new pissbum across the way trying to play solitaire, a guy about my own age. Ten days now he had been in the Straight and Narrow, and it took him until last night's meeting to finally speak up. *"Hi, my name's Phil and*

40

I work domestic crimes out of the Bronx, the four-four precinct. Okay. So I guess I'm a drunk."

After the serenity prayer he seemed steady enough, but this morning he was having the dry troubles. He kept wiping his lips with a hand that seemed to be holding an invisible lowball glass, and every so often his head dropped to the table with a loud bang, and then he would sob and shake for a couple of minutes and mess up his cards. There was a janitor who was busy at work near Phil, tossing down colored sawdust over something on the floor that did not smell right and then mopping it all up.

Okay. So I guess maybe six weeks ago this was more or less the very picture of myself. But now here I was sitting like a gentleman by the window, sober as a Shi'ite, looking at my watch and drinking black coffee out of a lettered mug that said EASY DOES IT. Also I was calculating how once I stepped inside Davy's car, it would take forty-five minutes, tops, before I was back home in Hell's Kitchen where I belonged, and all these pathetic pissbums would be history.

A rude angel poked me in the neck, and sneered, "You're one of us, Hock. One of us, one of us . . ."

This I ignored. If I kept staring out the window into the soupy air, I figured the sneering angel would eventually get lost.

It was hard to see through the soup, so it helped to know what I was looking for. A big boxy Plymouth I knew to be cop blue rounded the corner and angled into a curbside parking spot. A big Irish-born ex-cop I knew to be Davy Mogaill got out. He was alone, plodding along now like some Celtic war god come to my rescue.

My suitcase and I were not long in getting downstairs to the lobby to meet him. With a shudder, I hurried past Phil and the janitor, then clean out of the Saloon to the main corridor, then down the central staircase to where Mogaill waited.

I was likewise unsentimental about parting company with the rest of the place. The priests and the pissbums—these past six weeks my keepers and fellow inmates, respectively—were generous with the hails and farewells. I returned their affections by hustling past them like I was crossing a blazing bridge. Some of these guys were actually all right. I could have taken the time to say some proper good-byes. But no. Shitheel that I am, all I could think about was how I absolutely did not want to be *one of us, one of us . . .*

Mogaill saw how I needed to get out of there fast. So he and I did not make a big production of greeting each other. He signed some papers one of the priests had waiting for him down in the lobby office and that was that.

Now, once again, I was free to walk in the sunshine. Only of course there was no sun.

We got in the Plymouth, with Mogaill at the wheel. He started up the engine and we drove off with nothing much passed between us beyond "Top o' morning, Hock, how you feeling?" and "Fine, fine, let's roll." Four blocks later, with the Straight and Narrow safely slipped from view and me reclining in the passenger seat with my eyes shut in order to worry about the pretty wife I had not seen in six long weeks, Mogaill popped an old question. "How about after we cross the G.W. we stop up to Nugent's for a couple of jars? Just to welcome you home."

Nugent's would be the fine and murky pub at the heart of an Hibernian enclave called Inwood at the northernmost tip of Manhattan. This is one of many establishments around the city where New York's Irish gather to compound the crime of human folly, principally by means of Scotch whiskey. Davy and I met at Nugent's when both our worlds were young. I was then a rookie cop, painfully at sea with a pair of harsh mysteries: the ways of the department, and a first marriage sinking into flames. Mogaill was older by a dozen years, wiser by more; he was then a precinct detective who subsumed his widower's grief in work and books. He was as fine a cop as he was a literate drunk. For better and for worse, I am the man I am today due in large measure to my rabbi.

I closed my eyes. In back of my lids, I saw those old drinking days as plainly as if I was looking at photographs. There was Davy holding court at the bar, his curly red hair wild, waving stout arms as he talked and talked, his voice in fullest Irish cadence, the forever amber shot glass comically small in his peasant's paw, telling us fellow compounders of crime what he considered to be the central, infuriating fact of mortality: "Why shouldn't things be largely absurd, futile and transitory? They are so, and we are so, and they and we go very well together."

And in back of my eyelids, too, there was the newest snapshot in the album of my life: Phil the pissbum from the Bronx forty-fourth wiping his miserable lips, dropping his head, slopping his solitaire cards.

So I turned to Mogaill, and said, "Are you barking nuts, Davy?"

Mogaill laughed, as darkly as the day. "I'm as sane as the next man," he said, "meaning to cause you no alarm. Testing your resolve with an invitation to the bad old days, that's all I'm doing."

"Busting my chops is more like it. How come, Davy? Once upon a time, you yourself could have been put in the trap with the pissbums back there. When you were running Central Homicide, how many times did I see you tip from the bottle in your desk?"

"Many was the time, I grant your point. I was head of homicide in a homicidal town. Naturally, I drank."

"Naturally. And did I ever rat you out to what's-his-name, the chaplain?"

"Father John Sheehan."

"Tell me when I ratted on you to Sheehan."

"Such a silence as yours, Neil, did you never imagine it was a great and unmerciful failing?"

"Didn't think about it."

"Most people would sooner die than think. In fact, they do."

"It's peachy riding along with you like this, Davy."

Mogaill grunted. Unspoken resentments flooded the car. I was used to this surly mood, having just spent all these weeks in a house full of drunks; in the innocence of new sobriety, I was surprised that a sour old fog would not simply lift itself. But—had I not been warned of this very phenomenon in one of the meetings? Mogaill read my thoughts.

"There's something you mustn't forget, Neil," he said. "While you're in a meeting soaking up all the grand advice, your problem's out in the hallway doing push-ups."

I grunted this time.

Then, at last, the George Washington Bridge came into view. The huge pillars and cables and the double deck of suspended traffic promised that very soon I would be back in my briar patch. Ordinarily, the sight of this was reassuring. But not this morning, not in this cemetery weather I could no longer drink away. Now everything that was old had to be made new again. Which for a man such as myself, somewhere in the middle of his age, is somewhat overwhelming.

Davy stretched an open-palmed hand across the seat and asked, "Have you four bucks handy? For the bridge toll."

"You're the one who snatched me over. You pay it."

"It's your party now, boyo, is that not so?" Mogaill waggled his fingers. "Come on, come on, let's have it."

"One day at a time, you call that a party?"

With a growl, Mogaill cut the steering wheel hard to the right, his upper body listing with the effort. His feet pumping alternately at the brake and accelerator pedals, he then took the Plymouth on a wild ride—half-skidding, half-swerving through four lanes of eastbound bridge traffic. All the while, he was oblivious to a riot of fist waving, cursing, and horn honking.

When he finally landed all four wheels on the narrow asphalt shoulder, he slammed on the power brakes so violently he killed the engine. The Plymouth screeched to a stop. In the days before seat belts, I would have lurched through the windshield with my skull full of glass, maybe shot halfway across the river. Instead, the straps clamped over my waist and chest like a vinyl spider's web held me in place. Also they cinched the breath out of me.

I could not even whisper, I had so little air left. Mogaill had plenty enough for us both.

"Look here now, apart from being a cheap hump, you're showing yourself to be an insufferable ingrate." Mogaill's face was full of heat. He turned in his driver's seat and raised a hammy arm. He wanted to clout me, but changed his mind. Which was very lucky for me. "I have just saved your life's bacon. Do you know what I'm talking about?"

I rolled down a window, hoping it would help restore my breathing. Mogaill railed on.

"Good rabbi that I am, I have bumped you off a debilitating road. One that only leads straight to my own awful fate in the department. Loyal friend of the family that I am, I have done no less than to have salvaged your marriage."

I turned from the window and shot him a murderous look. Which only confirmed Mogaill's accusations, stated and otherwise. Yes, I was ungrateful. Yes, my Problem was still lurking in the hallway shadows, like a lazy mugger waiting for the same victim he took down yesterday. Yes, I would have to find some way to keep from being beaten down all over again.

And, yes . . . yes. I had not undergone an exorcism, only six weeks at the Straight and Narrow. After which the priests had signed a document, certifying to whom it may concern that upon this day I was merely lucid. The rest of it was up to me.

"And your poor, poor Ruby . . ." Mogaill's voice and his tsk-tsking seemed so distant, though he was removed by only a dangerous arm's length. "Bad enough she should love a cop. Are you thinking for one minute a fine one like Ruby should weather a life with the drunken wretch I found six weeks back? Nae, unless you're an arrogant pig as well as an ingrate . . ."

Here I allowed myself a drunkard's fugitive thought: of stepping out of the car and crossing the river under my own power. Often as a drunk, after all, I had walked the city's bridges when the black dog of alcoholic depression had me in his jaws. Any good, high bridge provided a reliably grand view, and there was always the option to jump into the gloom below and be done with it. Mogaill, not hearing these thoughts of mine, kept sternly on his course.

". . . What paltry respect do I request for troubling over your Irish bum? Two wee things: that you consider my blessings, and that you hand over the four bucks toll." Again, he waggled his fingers.

I made no sudden move toward my wallet. Instead, I listened idly to the rumble of cars and trucks to the side of us, and stared at the distant, lumpen scenery beyond the haze. We were now close enough to the city to see the familiar thickets of Manhattan. Ruby would be at work in one of those tall buildings.

Ruby. A cop's wife, I had made her; a drunk's wife, too. Shame on me. Memories of whiskey and waste, deep and black as the river below, flooded my head. Davy was remembering bottom days of his own.

"I've noticed there are only so many chances in life," he said. "It's the brainless amongst us who let them all run out before showing a little thanks to those who might be helpful. You've got a brain near as I can see, Neil."

"Thanks," I said, sarcastically. Mogaill remained unwithered.

"Use your head, start appreciating us helpful sorts. Otherwise, the world that matters will soon be whizzing by you, much as this traffic. Now that includes me. And even Ruby, too. Said from one drunk to another, here's your choice: You can see that I'm telling you right, or else lose yourself in the wicked jape that taunts our Irish manhood."

I did not have to ask. Mogaill pushed on with the ancient, awful joke.

"What's an Irish homosexual, hey, Neil?" Mogaill provided the answer when I passed. "He's a mick who prefers women over whiskey."

I laughed a sad laugh. Knowing how mankind relies on its simplest stock characters for an understanding of itself makes me laugh; knowing that in all of history there has never been a shortage of volunteer stereotypes saddens me.

"Are we arguing, Davy?"

"We are."

"About what?"

"Unresolved sorrows, Neil. It's natural. Surely they told you."

So they did. In meeting after meeting, the priests warned us: *"When you leave here—sober—the world will be uncomfortable in ways you never knew."*

"They told me a lot of things," I said. "Who told you?"

Mogaill shrugged. He looked out the windshield now as he answered me. "I drank 'til it was too late. I used up my chances by slipping once too often. So they retired me. When the hammer finally come down, there I was all alone. A man loses balance in the department when he's alone."

"You had friends. You had me."

"Pissbum friends. Fat lot of good you were."

Mogaill stared out the windshield at nothing. He gripped the steering wheel with both hands, squeezing it until his pink knuckles went to white. I opened my wallet and drew out four dollars, and held them out for Mogaill.

"It had to be complicated, drying out on your own."

"Bloody hard, but not so complicated." Mogaill took the singles and started up the car again. We eased back into traffic heading for the toll booths. I was beginning to feel some of the old reassurance. Then Mogaill said, "Consider how we drink, Neil."

"How's that?"

"Like whores we are to the bottle. Ask yourself, Do you love drinking any more than a whore loves shagging?"

"Never thought about it . . ."

But now I did. I thought about a Coney Island prostitute who helped me on a case a few years ago. Her name, of all names, was Chastity. I once asked her if she actually enjoyed her work. *"Honey, I don't like it and I don't dislike it. I'm just used to it."*

"One day, like a wise old whore," Mogaill said, "I woke up in my soiled bed to see that half my life was stolen away by the vice I confused with having a good and easy time. Sure, but I done the vice night after night, telling myself the days of regret would never fall due. And isn't your story much the same?"

"Something pathetic like that."

The bridge traffic was not heavy. We made it over to Manhattan in a couple of minutes and were then soon cruising downtown along the equally uncrowded West Side Highway. Davy glanced my way.

"Now'd be the right time to tell you the truest thing I know," he said. "Here it goes, blunt as a pig's snout: What you are is no better than me, a pissbum. The day you forget this truth is the day you surrender to the fact. By which I am referring to the *fact* of your being the way you were one certain night six weeks ago. Drooling drunk and your gut so bloaty from booze and bar grub you could be tied up in ropes and floated in Macy's parade. It'll serve you well to recollect that night you went to the Straight and Narrow, the night—"

"You and that goddamn Neuman. What's his angle on me anyhow?"

"He's someone to watch over you, Hock. Though not so sweet as myself. Officer Neuman's official-like."

"You're saying he's my leper?"

"Aye, he comes on the orders of your Inspector Neglio."

"My luck."

"Had devil luck graced me like he did you, there'd not be the one big difference between us two pissbums."

"And what would that be?"

"If somebody'd put a leper onto me, maybe I wouldn't have bollixed it up like I done. Maybe I'd be with the department still, same as you." Mogaill swerved from the left lane to the right to avoid running over the lump of a dead mongrel dog. It was just as well, we were coming up on the exit to Forty-second Street. Davy looked now like a thousand other cops I have seen in my time, feeling sorry for himself over a lonesome drink. He asked, bitterly, "What do you think's the darkest line a man ever wrote?"

"You tell me."

"I'd say it's a bit from a most unlikely source—Karl Marx. Now, he wasn't writing about politics. He was writing about human history, and how certain of us go around this old world twice. 'The first time as tragedy, the second time as farce,' as he put it. Oh, but he could have been writing about my own damn life."

"Come on, how bad can it be? You're in business for yourself."

"You can say it plain, Neil. I'm a peep. And right now, I'm working the best job I've had since hanging out the private-eye shingle."

"Who's the client?"

"A certain poshy hotel on the East Side suddenly infested with whores not of the genteel sort. Management tried working with the Public Morals Squad, but maybe you know how that tune goes."

Early in my career, I did a turn with Public Morals. I had neither the stomach nor greed for it. Eventually, I put in for duty that still suits me: assignment to the plainclothes Street Crimes Unit—Manhattan, more fittingly known as the SCUM Patrol. But I still remember the enterprising drills from Public Morals days. I recited one of them now for Mogaill.

"The cops make a splashy show about running in the girls," I said. "The hotel yelps about what the noise and publicity is now doing to its reputation. So one of these vice cops in a bad suit gets a bright idea and puts it to the hotel manager, You want discreet, maybe we should go off the books to control the hubbub?"

"Aye, the old story."

"I never met a vice cop who wasn't carrying a tin cup."

Mogaill shook his head in sorry agreement. "But here's a wholly new tale for where I'm working—the Harmony Arms by name. In an age that was decent, Audrey Hepburn was a regular guest of the house whenever she come to New York. So bloody different now, it is. Self-respecting mice and cockroaches keep to themselves in the old walls, piqued as they are by the sight of the two-legged vermin now crawling around the place."

"Hookers and vice cops."

"Them and a certain ilk of guests."

"Bad for trade, at least the old kind."

"Sure it is. The hotel one day finally counted up the money they was paying to the vicers to stay the hell out of the place. They saw it was cheaper to hire my services."

"So what do you do?"

"When I see one of the guests with a hooker, I get on the elevator with the two of them, and during the ride upstairs I give her a look so she'll know I'm wise. Then I get off the elevator with them, follow them down the hall, and note the time and the room number in my little book. Two reasons for doing this: first, to let the hooker know she's being watched; second, to cover myself. Usually what happens is the john wakes up in the morning and finds his money gone."

"He's plenty mad."

"Sure he is. He's only observing the code of the offended mark."

"By looking for somebody besides himself to blame."

"Of course. Right away, he calls up the management to complain he's been robbed. This is where I step in. I ask him if he's had any guests in his room. The answer's always no, followed by his accusing the bellhop or maybe the poor chambermaid. I then pull out the book and tell him exactly when he went up to his room and exactly who was on his arm, and I invite him to try again with an answer to my question."

"Then what?"

"Always the same thing he says, 'Forget I called.' Now, Hock, I ask you, is it not a shameful trade of mine?"

"It's a living."

"Don't be gassing me. It's farce, I'm telling you." Mogaill sighed. I am just old enough to sympathize with the corrosive regret behind such a sigh. He added, "It's not like in days past."

"Nothing is."

"That's right, nothing's seemly anymore. Not even the bad guys. Do you remember when thugs were thugs?"

"I remember a time when it was easier being a cop."

"Sure, that's what I'm talking about," Mogaill said. "The thugs these days, they're mostly corporate weasels."

Mogaill laughed at his own remark, and this lightened his mood considerably. We drove along for a few more minutes without saying anything, then Mogaill turned off the highway. In a couple of minutes more he had us pulled up alongside my apartment house—a walk-up at the corner of Forty-third and Tenth Avenue.

We parked in front of a bus shelter with the Plexiglas bashed out of it. Mogaill hunched forward in the driver's seat. His eyes combed up over the slanty west wall of my tenement, with its soot-stained bricks and window ledges thickened by a hundred years of pigeon dung. Davy's improved mood vanished.

"A shame you've not a fit place for homecoming," he said. "You're living in a house that'll soon be gone with the wind. It's not right for you and a fine new wife. Shame, too, how you're alone in the flat your first day of return."

I picked up my bag from the backseat and opened the passenger door. A moist breeze swept into the car, bringing with it memories of moist old times; all those times when three comrades would sit up in my place together after rough days—Davy Mogaill, Johnnie Walker and me. Davy knew what I was thinking.

"One day at a time, Hock. If need be, one minute at a time. Know that I'll be in touch."

Slogans I felt I did not need from a man not much healthier than myself. Nor did I care to hear further slander about where I happen to live. So I left Davy that morning with, "Thanks for the lift, I'll give your love to Ruby."

"Do that, please."

I stepped out from the Plymouth to the street and closed the heavy door. Davy touched a couple of blunt fingers to his forehead, gave me a short wave, and drove off. I thought about what he had to do with the rest of his day, riding up hotel elevators full of pross and weasels, and felt sorry for him. Sorry for myself as well, I headed into my building.

In the vestibule, I collected mail from the half-jimmied-open box marked 3-R. Twenty-four hours a day, the vestibule is bathed in a light bright enough for surgery. This is thanks to a circular tube of humming fluorescence dangling from the pressed tin ceiling, which in New York is known as a landlord's halo. Because of the glare, I had to squint at the mail, which only turned out to be an uninspiring collection of second and third notices from various commercial institutions. I filed the mess in a nearby rubbish can, rousing a well-fed rodent from his nap.

Then I took the dusty stairs to the rear apartment on the third floor, rooms I only so recently shared with whiskey dreams of family ghosts. I have now faced down the ghosts, and though I often dreamed of tasting it, I have not drunk whiskey in six long weeks. And now at the heart of my old bachelor home, as unlikely as it seemed only a season ago, here lives my wife and the new, dry me.

I turned the key in the lock and entered. Davy was right, this old dump was no fit place for Ruby. Bless her, though, she has not once complained. In fact, it was Ruby who decided after the wedding that we should make our home in my apartment—temporarily anyhow. She had good reasons, one of them sentimental. I could not easily live outside my briar patch, she claimed, and this was true. Besides which, we would see considerably more money every month by subletting her place.

I tossed my bag into the bedroom, then stepped to the dim parlor and collapsed in the big easy chair by the fireplace. It looks warm and inviting, but I cannot put a light to the hearth, as it is plugged up with cinder blocks. People burned coal in this fireplace back in the days before landlords were required by law to install proper steam heat in the tenements of Hell's Kitchen. As for the chair, it came from the place where I buy all my furniture, the Salvation Army over on West Forty-sixth Street. It cost me fifty bucks and was covered in battered green brocade with fringe around the bottom. I like to think some charitable madame of a neighborhood whorehouse donated it to Sally's.

Sitting in my whorehouse chair, the rest of the crowded room does not seem so bad. There is the kitchen alcove by the door to the hall, next to this a little bathroom complete with a clawfoot tub. The parlor is furnished with a rocking chair, two walls full of books, a table at my side for the telephone and newspapers, and a corduroy-covered couch under the windows where Ruby sits to read, with her legs tucked up under her.

There is an oak sideboard, too, directly opposite my chair. On top of the sideboard is a black-and-white Philco TV set from Sally's and a fine Grundig radio I bought brand-new. Also on the sideboard on this homecoming day was the reminder of my desolate past: a sealed liter of Johnnie Walker red. It sat there on a silver tray, surrounded by a matched set of lowball glasses. I broke into an all-over sweat staring at the bottle and the glasses.

God help me. *One day at a time, Hock. If necessary, one minute at a time . . .*

I looked away. I thought of Yankees' games up in the Bronx on muggy August nights and southern fried chicken at Sylvia's restaurant in Harlem and ham and eggs in my neighborhood spoon and Ruby sleeping beside me later that night. Then I looked back and the booze on the silver tray was still there, going no place, still crowding my uplifting thoughts.

I was furious with Ruby for leaving the bottle out. For busting my chops, like Davy with his invitation to Nugent's bar. *Testing your resolve is all . . .*

I reached for the telephone. I should call up my hardworking wife and tell her off. Good idea! No! Better idea, I should ask her out to lunch somewhere nice.

The instant my perspiring hand touched the receiver, the telephone rang. My body jerked and twisted, like I was the condemned man being fried in an electric chair. Neglio was on the line.

I said hello and my voice cracked for the first time since the age of twelve. Neglio naturally asked, "What's the matter now?"

"Just glad to hear from you, Inspector."

"That all?"

"Also, since I've done my bow-and-arrow time, not to mention the Straight and Narrow, I'm wondering about a new post."

"What's the big hurry?"

"Six weeks I've been out of it, but the paychecks keep coming. You think I like being a burden on society?"

"We got domed buildings full of society's burdens down in Washington. You think you should be any better than a Congressman? Take the money, Hock. Sleep late in the morning with your bride, take strolls up in the park, see some nice Broadway shows. Like you're on the honeymoon you never had."

"What are you saying?"

"You're on extended leave."

"Six weeks in Jersey, that's not enough downtime?"

"You've now got a psych sheet in your file, okay? So now the chaplain's got to clear you for active duty, then IAD. Sorry, Hock. Regulation."

"Completely out of your hands."

"That's right."

"So what I'm talking to here is just another round-ass bureau hump who can't read anything besides the department handbook?"

Neglio started to say something about insubordination, which I was in no more mood to hear than Mogaill's unpleasant remarks about Hell's Kitchen. So I cut off the inspector by accidentally slamming the receiver in his ear on purpose.

Again I looked at Johnnie, and felt the sweat trickling down into my shorts. On my soaking back, I could grow rice.

I picked up the phone again, dialed information for the number at Ruby's ad agency, and called it. A lady who sounded like she wanted to faint came on the line.

"Good morning. Schuyler, Foster and Crosby. Oh, my. I should say, Schuyler, Foster and the late . . . Oh, my!"

"Ruby Flagg, please."

"My—!"

There were a lot of scratchy switchboard noises, then Ruby's voice.

"Yes?"

"How about lunch? Someplace with a canopy out front."

"God!"

"Way off. It's only me, babe."

"Right now, I sort of can't talk . . ." Ruby said, her words trailing off, as if she was distracted by something. I heard pounding in the background, and a couple of different guys hollering something in foreign accents, and then an American guy saying "check" in between everything the two excited foreign guys were saying. Ruby whispered, and again her words trailed off, "We've got something serious here, something awful . . ."

"I got a clue from your receptionist."

"She's upset. She's not used to talking with cops."

"Cops? What cops?"

"Kowalski. I think he said he was a sergeant."

"Jesus—*Joe* Kowalski?"

"I guess. There's been a murder."

"Kowalski's in sex crimes."

"He said that, too."

"He works graveyard. Besides which, the guy never leaves the shop. You should get a load of him, and I mean *load*. What was he doing at your place?"

"He wasn't here. He was on the phone."

"I don't follow."

"He was with the body . . ."

5

THE BUCK-NAKED, MASKED DEAD GUY WAS SPREAD-EAGLED on his back in the middle of the kitchen floor. Blood was streaked everywhere across a checkerboard of otherwise tidy blue and yellow tiles. Most of it had gone tacky, but here and there were puddles that remained brightly wet. The body was nearly empty of fluids and white as Elmer's glue. But still, tiny streams of blood dribbled from spike wounds at the hands and feet. The guy had been nailed down to the floor. There was also a little blood still spurting out from below his deflated hips. I could see the curved handle of a crowbar between his upper thighs. From the looks of things, someone had rammed the steel rod up the poor bastard's backside.

Maybe I have come across grislier scenes in my career, but probably not many. On this occasion, as on all the others, I was saved from going squirrelly by the general irreverence all cops who are mentally sound will exhibit when confronted by what is darkly known as permanent violence. Cops' minds will wander a little off the track at such times. Also cops can become as chatty and colorful as a Dixie senator, as if filibustering against the kind of sudden death they know is the occupational hazard we share with the bad guys.

My luck, I walked into a glob of red and slopped my

trouser cuffs. A forensics guy with rubber gloves barked at me, "Watch it with the goddamn big feet, or get the hell out of my kitchen." Civilians are under the false impression that cops are meticulous about little things like crime scenes. But cops are as sloppy as everybody else in America. Which is a big part of the reason so many bad guys are running around loose in the country.

I carefully sidestepped the body over to the counter and used a handful of Bounty paper towels to clean off the sweet-smelling slime, putting me in mind of a television jingle about this particular brand being the quicker picker-upper. After all, the dead guy was an advertising executive. Maybe he even wrote the Bounty jingle.

Meanwhile, the guy who had chewed me out was kneeling over the corpse and using a pair of tin snips to cut away a black leather mask. The mask was one of those full-headed models found in certain downtown sex shops, with sturdy zippers over the mouth, nose, and eye holes. I remembered a line from some Hemingway novel, Papa's view of the sour side of human endearments: *Love is something that hangs up behind the bathroom door and smells of Lysol.*

The kitchen could have used a few gallons of Lysol to kill the ripe odors of fresh homicide: clotting blood, urine, feces, intestinal gas. Instead, we had cigars. One of the detectives from the Nineteenth Precinct Detective Unit was passing around a box of White Owls. I took one myself and lit up.

For a second or two I wondered if maybe I had done the wrong thing by asking Ruby for the dead guy's name and address, then rushing over to the scene to see what on earth King Kong Kowalski was doing there. The feeling passed. Doubts did not exactly float away, but I have grown accustomed to my basic meddlesome character.

Anyway, the dead guy was a forty-three-year-old Caucasian named Frederick Laurence Crosby. He had lived and died in one of those Upper East Side apartment houses that come with teakwood and marble lobbies and intimidating doormen. In this case, a burly white-haired guy named Otto who spoke with a German accent and wore black boots to the knees, an olive-brown belted greatcoat with epaulets, braided gloves, and a crested hat with a stiff leather brim. Usually I do not see outfits like this unless I am watching old films of torchlight parades in prewar Berlin. Big rents are paid to live in buildings where an escaped Nazi commands the lobby. Tenants who have the wherewithal thus believe themselves immune to low-rent unpleasantries they read about in the tabloids. They are certain that money buys shelter from the storm, and they trust innocently in rich appearances amongst their own kind. They are reliably shocked to the core when they learn a fact of modern life: Vileness has become very democratic, and more often than not horror dwells in the basement of propriety.

Otto had certainly wised up. For years, maybe he thought he had a fine retirement gig in a building full of respectable types, mostly Aryans. When I passed him in the lobby, though, he was a sorry sight: crumpled into a spindly antique lobby couch that probably nobody had ever sat in before, an ungloved hand covering his palpitating heart, his command duties having been assumed by a detail of uniformed cops, mostly non-Aryans.

Upstairs in apartment 5-C, meanwhile, I had a few minutes earlier badged my way into Crosby's place. Right away I had to go skidding in some of Crosby's blood. King Kong Kowalski had laughed at this comic move on a bleak stage. But now, in all seriousness, here was the meaty sergeant: leaning on a table, smoking a panatela, and holding forth on the cruel ironies of life, death, and a variety of sex not likely countenanced by his fellow parishioners of Our Lady of the Blessed Agony.

"Here we got the case of a mixed-up boy named Fredericka. He played like the bachelorette, now he's paid for it like they do nine times out of ten." Kowalski pointed his cigar down at the splayed, malodorous corpse. "Got himself toasted good and weird."

I was the only one actually listening to him. This was because Kowalski and I were not busy with any real tasks, since neither of us had any real business being there. Others had plenty of the usual work to do. The forensics crew was bustling all around the place, since time is of the essence in their specialty. They photographed Crosby's leaky remains, dusted for prints, and picked up various motes and hairs with tweezers. A PDU detail was busy interrogating the super in a bedroom with a walk-in closet containing enough gowns, wigs, and unmentionables to stock a ladies' boutique.

Kowalski was shaking his mastiff head as he now stepped over toward the corpse with me off to the side of it. The sergeant wore an especially uncharitable expression, with his features all pinched up along the lower one-tenth of his facial plane. If he lost the cigar and slipped a black-and-white cowl over his head, he could have been a nun from my schoolboy days: Sister Bertice, who used to bash me over the head with chalkboard erasers if I seemed bored when reciting the Baltimore catechism. Plump ashes now fell from Kowalski's panatela, landing on the late Frederick Crosby's stomach and lying there like baked feathers.

Kowalski turned to me and I could feel his breath, like hot beef broth. "Tell me something," he said, taking on a pious look. "You think it's possible for a freaking rump-hugging sinner to take Christ the Lord into his heart?"

This is the kind of question I am forever hearing from people who are enormously pleased to tell me they have been born-again. Usually, I respond with something like, Sorry about the brain damage during your rebirth. But in the interest of cop fraternity, I changed the spirit of my answer to Sergeant Kowalski.

"I don't know, Joe," I said. "I think maybe whatever anybody does, God's going to forgive them, since that's the main purpose of being God."

Kowalski scowled, very much like Sister Bertice. I halfway expected an eraser to come crashing down on my head.

"So you're saying what? It don't mean a rat's fanny when a guy don't act like a right guy? Ob-la-di, ob-la-da, life goes on? That's what you think?"

"Let's skip the philosophy, Sergeant, all right? How about telling me why you're up and around so early in the morning. It's not your style."

Kowalski did not say anything. Somebody from in back of me did, however.

"Detective Hockaday, I've been meaning to ask you the same thing."

I turned to face a dayside lieutenant of my slight acquaintance. He was a short, crew cut, messy guy named Schecter who did not look like he belonged with the Nineteenth.

Plainclothes detectives will mostly try to dress like the neighborhood civilians while on the job. On the Upper East Side of Manhattan, this means trying to look like stockbrokers who pay around eighty bucks for a haircut. I have seen detectives in the Nineteenth wearing French-cuffed shirts and tasseled loafers. But here now was Schecter wearing a brown polyester suit, a clip-on tie, and a schmeer of Butch wax. He looked like a clerk in a Brooklyn linoleum shop.

"My wife told me about this murder," I said to him.

"Yeah, who's she? And what's your wife got going with this here dead faggot?" Schecter took a pad from his pocket and clicked a ballpoint pen into action. I was suddenly put in mind of my disagreeable conversation with Inspector Neglio, and how my extended leave could become even more extended if I made a wrong move.

"Her name is Ruby Flagg," I said, deciding to play my part straight, at least for a while. "She's working at the advertising agency where the dearly departed happened to be a partner. I called her up this morning to ask her out to lunch, right when everybody found out why Crosby here never showed at the office."

"You got nothing better to do on your day off than hang around some case that's not yours to catch?"

"No, he don't, Lieutenant," Kowalski said, butting in. "I hear Detective Hockaday's fresh back from a little breather over to Jersey."

"Straight and Narrow?" Schecter asked. He looked me up and down and decided the answer was yes. "Been cleared for return yet?"

Not wanting to take too much time with an answer, I blurted out the first plausible thing that came to mind: "I'm working as a peep, sort of part-time. Keeps me occupied while I'm on furlough."

"Who you working for?"

"Davy Mogaill."

Schecter and Kowalski looked at each other.

"He's licensed," I said. "You can look it up."

"Why? I don't got a reason to doubt that." Schecter made a note in his book, then put it away.

Kowalski decided to antagonize me some more. He jabbed a thumb in my direction and complained to Schecter,

"Being a peep don't make him prince of the city. He still ain't told you any good reason for being here."

"Which reminds me," I said to Kowalski, "you never answered that question yourself. I see there's maybe a sex crime someplace here, but since when do you do field work?"

Kowalski lifted an arm, waving me off. "I don't got to explain nothing to a peep."

Nevertheless, Kowalski proceeded to explain a great deal. About the nuts and bolts of Crosby's murder anyway. Of his own motivations for being on the case, he kept his mouth shut.

With a lot of huffing and puffing, Kowalski lowered himself to one knee for a close look at the body. "Look here at the backside of his johnson," he said, using his cigar to lift up Crosby's forever wilted penis. "There's freaking lipstick traces. See? Right before somebody does this pillow biter for good, they tickled his pickle."

"If he got off, I guess they'll find that in the autopsy," Schecter said. He took his pad out again and made another note, probably about the lipstick. Kowalski turned his attentions to the spikes. Schecter asked, "What do you make from them big ugly nails, Sergeant?"

Kowalski gave a noncommittal grunt. He had his own question for Schecter: "Anything besides queen frocks in the closets?"

"Such as what do you mean?"

"Pecker pumps, whips, nipple clamps—maybe them little chains and pins the pervo boys like to clip onto their hairy nuts. Like that kind of stuff."

I wanted to ask Kowalski about his expertise in exotic sexual merchandise, but restrained the impulse. Later, I told myself.

"None of that. There's two closets back in the bedroom actually. The walk-in with the lady's stuff. And then the other one, with pretty much the usual junk you find in regular guys' closets. Regular shoes, regular clothes, mothballs, sweaters in plastic boxes. Just regular." Schecter used his pen to scratch his crew cut head. This helped him remember something. "Oh, yeah—also there was a pair of cowboy chaps, purple leather with a lot of brass and fringes."

Kowalski grunted again.

Schecter laughed slightly and asked us, "You guys got dust all over your closets like I got at my own house? Me, I got dust bunnies the size of Pennsylvania."

Kowalski and I admitted to dust.

"Well, there's none of that in none of the closets here," Schecter said. "These fags, they're neat, I'll give them that."

"Some are," Kowalski allowed. "Some of the pain girls, they can be real pigs, though."

"That's what Crosby was?" Schecter wanted to know.

Kowalski was now looking into Crosby's face, which was flattened out and rust colored, like a big hamburger patty ready for the barbecue grill. "Naw," he said, as if he was a doctor making his diagnosis. "Fredericka here ain't a pain girl. He don't look one bit happy about what happened to him the last time he felt anything."

Kowalski stood up again, which was a great relief to his trouser seams. He did not take his eyes off the body nailed to the floor. He rocked on his heels and shook his head and stared at Crosby's remains.

I myself had no trouble turning my eyes away. I puffed on my White Owl and occasionally glanced down through the smoke at poor Crosby and what the forensic cops were now doing to him. My eyes did not have to linger over the vision of Crosby's hamburger face to understand why tin snips were being used to take away the mask. I relied on Kowalski's commentary.

"What a freaking mess! Looks like they went and hammered his schnozz down to pulp after he pulled on the mask. Or probably after somebody zipped him into it. Either way, the result's as good as glue—one hell of a lot of blood and mucus and busted cartilage. It's all over him and the inside of the mask, too. See?"

"What's all the frilly crap in his mouth?" Schecter asked. I realized that Schecter had not cared to look at the body much more than I had, likewise trusting the graphics of Kowalski's play-by-play for the official write-up.

"They crammed his yap full of nylon stockings and ladies' scanties," Kowalski said. "The perfect muffler for a nice, quiet job."

"Sure, elsewise there'd be the racket of Crosby screaming

when they run that crowbar clear up his bum," Schecter said.

Kowalski stamped the kitchen floor with his size twelve Thom McAn brogans. In my place down in Hell's Kitchen, this would have made the lights flicker and the windows fall shut. But nothing shook loose in this upper East Side room. However, the toe of Kowalski's left shoe splashed up some more wet blood on my soiled trouser cuffs.

The forensic guy with the gloves hollered again. "Would you for Christ's sake give me a break with the goddamn feet already?"

Kowalski apologized to him. Then he said to Schecter, "The floors in these big old dumps, they're solid as the Wollman ice rink. When they nailed down Fredericka and made him a steel-reinforced butt, I bet in the place underneath of here it only sounded like maybe somebody was tacking down a loose rug."

I needed air.

"Mind if I talk to the super you got in the other room?" I asked Schecter.

"How come?"

"Like I said, I'm moonlighting."

"Oh, yeah, for that pissbum Mogaill."

"Ex–pissbum."

"You ought to know."

"That's right."

"Who's the client?" Schecter took out his notebook again. I had to think fast.

"The firm," I said. "Schuyler, Foster and Crosby."

"Minus Crosby."

"Which begs the question, see?"

"I see that fine." Schecter made his notation, and shrugged. "Go on, be my guest, Detective Hockaday. You want to peep around for somebody on Madison Avenue, no skin off my butt."

I left Schecter and the grunting Kowalski in the kitchen, taking care to steer clear of any more blood stains on my way to the bedroom. Inside of which was a pair of young detectives well dressed for duty in the Nineteenth. They were finishing up what sounded to be a standard interrogation.

The subject of the questioning was the building superintendent, a Latino in starched khakis, a T-shirt with rolled-up sleeves, and a Saint Christopher medal hanging on the outside. He was trim and his movements were light and quick, like a bantamweight. He sat on the edge of Crosby's bed and chain-smoked Pall Malls without benefit of an ashtray. Raul was his name, he was ten years too old for the ring anymore.

The two detectives in their nice uptown suits were the irritating type. They had smirks on their faces, the kind worn by an unfortunate new generation of cop: New York's suburban occupation force. They were not born in my city, they have never lived in any of the five boroughs of my city, and they never will. Also they will never understand why somebody like me—meaning white, English-speaking, and not rich—chooses to live in the city where he was born. They consider their union dues well spent on an army of lobbyists that keeps the legislators up in Albany from including them in a law that says if you draw your paycheck from the City of New York you ought to live there. The president of this union lives so far out on Long Island he should be a lighthouse keeper.

I produced my gold shield for the smirking young detective in the blue suit and told him Schecter sent me in to ask anything I wanted. He looked over the shield with my name on it and nodded to his partner in charcoal gray that I was all right. Blue Suit asked the super, "Okay, Raul, let's run it down one more time. Tell Detective Hockaday here where you were all night long."

"Working the lobby besides all the other stuff I do around the building." The way Raul looked at me, he was trying to size me up. Maybe he liked it that I was wearing chinos and sneakers and a raincoat instead of a suit. "I could've called up the agency for some temps. But Christmas is coming, you know, man?"

Charcoal Gray filled in the blanks. "Raul's one very ambitious little beaner. The house has got twenty-four-hour doorman service, right? The guy on the weekday afternoon shift and also the midnight guy, they're Raul's cousins, right? These two other beaners, they're on vacation down in Puerto

Rico. So Raul here pops some uppers and pinch-hits for a couple of nice extra paychecks."

Besides being paid-in-full members of the Suburban Occupation Force, these two were the type who proved something about cheap men and good suits. There are so many of both that it is only logical they will sometimes get mixed up together. Hence, a guy can look like a million dollars in a really good wool worsted and still he uses a word like *beaner*. When he opens his mouth, he might as well be wearing white socks.

"Ambitious." I said that without expression.

Blue asked the super, "And who came calling on poor Mr. Crosby last night?"

Raul stood up and reached into his back pocket for two sheets of paper. These he handed over to me. The sheets were lined, with rows of visitor names and their call times listed down the left margins. Pleased with himself, Raul said, "I already showed these other two guys my logs, man. The one for the four-to-midnight shift, okay? Then the other one, the freak shift."

"That would be midnight until eight this morning?" I asked. Kowalski's very own schedule at the Sex Crimes Squad, I thought. I checked my watch. Raul and King Kong Kowalski had both been off the clock for about three hours.

"Yeah," Raul answered. He watched, tapping his foot impatiently, as I scanned through the logs without benefit of my reading glasses. "Hey, man," he said, "you don't got to make it hard on you. Just run your finger down the right-hand column, stop at number 5-C and then look back across the page for what you need." This I did while Raul snubbed out yet another Pall Mall on the bottom of his shoe, dropping the butt on the floor with the others.

I started with last night's four-to-midnight log, which recorded the perfectly ordinary comings and goings of Frederick Crosby's bachelor apartment. At ten past seven, somebody from Park Avenue Valet came by to pick up his laundry. A messenger was sent up at eight o'clock with a package from the office. "That's pretty routine every night," Raul informed me when I asked. At half-past nine, Crosby took delivery on a Szechuan dinner from a Second Avenue joint called Hsin-Yu.

That was all yesterday. Today's postmidnight log told the

more interesting story. Shortly after 1 A.M., somebody called Veronique Unique signed the register. There was no sign-out time. I looked at Raul and he read the obvious question on my face. He shrugged, and said, "The fancy lady, she go up. But she never come down."

Never came down? I wondered about this as I tried to picture somebody named Veronique Unique. I asked, "Fancy lady—?"

Gray piped up. "He says this Veronique broad was a showgirl, so to speak." He laughed and so did his partner, their blended haw-haws sounding like a pair of yahoos all dressed up in their Budweiser shorts. "Like the ones with the fruit baskets on their heads shaking their black booties on spic TV. Know what I'm talking about, Raul?"

Raul kept his mouth closed and his hands open. In my time, I have seen a lot of men all too quick with their fists and mouths. But Raul had thrown enough punches in his life to know that when you have a dirty fight on your hands your best chance of winning is to pick the time and place. Maybe under more balanced circumstances—late at night in a dark street, say—he would not be obliged to listen gently to some commuter cop's notions about *las bailarinas Latinas negras.* So my guess was that Raul wanted to slug the suits as much as I did. This was not actually much of a guess. Nor was it any great shakes to divine that sooner or later Gray would get his. I hoped it was sooner.

Meanwhile, here was this super named Raul with a solid lead in the murder—the question of one Veronique Unique. Raul seemed willing enough to cooperate with investigating cops, but what did he draw? These two smirkers. More and more, I am finding myself in the middle of exactly this sort of stupid situation.

Which is why I said to Raul, *"No les prestes ninguna atención a estos hijos de la chingada."* In a very large part of the Western Hemisphere, this would be an advisory to ignore somebody born to a sullied woman. It is something I often hear in the streets of my neighborhood, which is called *La Cocina del Infierno* about as often nowadays as it is Hell's Kitchen. Out where the smirkers live everybody talks, like, you know, regular American.

Raul's hands loosened and he gave me a nice big conspiratorial smile before answering, *"Oye, hombre, contigo sí hablo, pero a estos hijos de la chingada no les digo nada. Lo que pasa aquí es mucha mierda. ¿Okey?"*

"Okey," I said.

Our conversation was beginning to seriously disturb *los hijos de la chingada.* Blue's face was red and he wanted to know, "What's with the *español* jabber, Hockaday?"

"You're very close to strike three, Detective." I halfway wanted to see Raul jump off the bed and cold-cock the two of them. But he just sat there with his calm hands, enjoying this unexpected show of squabbling cops.

"So who's counting?" Charcoal asked this, speaking on behalf of himself, his partner, and their entire ilk. Then he and Blue stepped up close to me with their chests all puffy. I noticed they smelled like a couple of magazine cologne strips.

"For now it's only me counting," I said. "Either one of you says one more charming thing like *spic* or *beaner* and I'll let the Human Rights Commission take over."

"Wait a minute, I thought Lieutenant Schec—"

"On second thought, don't say anything at all," I interrupted. Raul was smart enough to keep quiet. I allowed a few seconds to pass, enough time for the ruffled plumage to settle. Then I said to my steamed colleagues, "See what a nice guy I am, giving you fair warning about your mouths? You owe me."

"Owe you what, Hockaday?" asked Blue. He tried sounding brassy, but then he wiped the back of his neck with a shaky hand. This gave me the reasonable hunch that he was nervous about his personnel file, which no doubt contained more than the usual number of complaints from New Yorkers of unglamorous races. Gray looked none too comfortable either.

"Answers to questions maybe nobody's going to be asking but me."

The suits tossed a couple of apprehensive looks back and forth. Gray spoke to me like I was no better than Neuman the leper. "You want to say something, say it."

"I know a kick when I see one."

"What do you think you're seeing?"

"The two of you going through the motions with Raul here. Along with your looey out in the kitchen trying to lay off a PDU homicide onto Sex Crimes."

"You say you got eyes. Take a look around this flaming fruit bowl." Gray walked over to the closet with the mostly

66

ordinary menswear and pulled out the exception that proved the rule: a black leather jumpsuit on a hanger. Schecter had not mentioned this garment, but it was next to the cowboy chaps. He twisted the jumpsuit around to show me a steel mesh codpiece on the front and a pair of rear cheek cutouts. He laughed darkly, and said, "Now here lived a man who might've made the acquaintance of the mighty King Kong."

"Could be. Who caught on this call?"

Blue said he did.

It seems a porter was running a vacuum cleaner down the fifth-floor hallway and spotted a lot of blood dripping off the outside doorknob of Number 5-C. That was a little past nine o'clock. The porter summoned Raul, who was back in his super's apartment off the basement laundry room having himself a beer after finishing up the overnight lobby watch. Raul came running. He used his passkey after pounding on Crosby's door. He came across the mess in the kitchen, and telephoned 911.

"Like I thought, the call was routed through regular precinct," I said. I looked at my watch. "It's not even lunchtime and already you want to kick the case. This is what I don't quite get, Detective. You could put some effort into a collar on this kind of swell homicide, you've got a chance at glory."

"Obviously you never worked the Nineteenth," said Blue.

"What's that mean?"

"Remember the movie where Jack Nicholson played the LA peep back in the thirties called Jake Gittes, and Faye Dunaway had this daughter maybe eighteen, nineteen? And John Huston played the grandfather, an evil old rich bastard?"

They make a lot of movies about detectives, private and otherwise. This is probably because in real life a good detective becomes a kind of nosy actor in the stories people hand him. As a result, detectives are very big movie fans.

I said I remembered that one.

"There's this one scene where Jake slaps Faye around," Blue said. "And then his disgusting secret about her daughter and her old man comes out . . ."

She's my daughter, she's my sister . . . She's my daughter, she's my sister. I thought, Who could forget?

". . . And then Jake's cop pal says to him—you know, in that voice like an old cop on an overnight stakeout in the rain—*Forget it, Jake, it's Chinatown.*"

Blue waited, but the dawn did not come quickly to me.

"Question—how many Chinese in that movie?" In his own way, Blue was striving to illuminate. Which he eventually did. "Answer—chinks don't matter. See, the movie is saying there's all different kinds of Chinatowns."

"And you're saying even the old silk stocking district of Manhattan's got its Chinatown."

"Not that anybody wants to notice, since they all got their snouts in the caviar. The Upper East Side here, it's got more money than God. Also more clout."

"Making things delicate when crime comes cheap."

"You said it. Any other precinct in the city, you get wet dreams about some nice sweet glory case rolling your way."

"Say like this splashy Crosby murder you caught?"

Blue nodded. "The game's different here. A pouf like Crosby's connected to all sorts of rich big shots. He comes to a bad end, suddenly the big shots don't want to know about it. And they sure as hell don't want their regular station house cops working their hearts out to find the chinks in their dream world. They know how to write letters in this precinct, and they got a hundred other ways of squawking that can definitely bring career trouble. See? A glory case comes rolling at you here in the Nineteenth, you don't want to pick it up right away."

"It might be too delicate."

"Delicate like a pipe bomb."

"I see why you look for some way to kick."

Not only are cops as sloppy as everybody else, they are every bit as cynical. Meaning that I myself am as capable of stumbling over blood stains as I am in sometimes knowing the answers before I ask the questions.

"Before the Nineteenth," I asked Blue, "where were you posted?"

"Sex Crimes."

"That's how you know about King Kong?"

"Lots of people know him."

"Maybe you heard of Crosby, too. Maybe one night your friend Kowalski took a dickprint off poor Crosby?"

"He might of."

"So this morning you're catching for the PDU. It comes in that Crosby gets dusted, and you can see from Looey's

reaction that maybe the case is one of your pipe bombs.
Then it comes to you. You've got an ace in the hole by the
name of King Kong Kowalski."

"You know how it is. Maybe this type of murder, it's not
for the PDU. Maybe it's for a specialized squad."

"So, you've got your kick. What did you do, call up King
Kong wherever he drinks after tour?"

"I might of."

"You know you can get Kowalski hopped up because this
sorry mess is very much his meat."

"So to speak."

Raul had been quietly enjoying my interrogation. Now he
was laughing lightly and shaking his head. He rolled his eyes
at me, and said, *"¡Sí sí, aquí es mucha mierda!"*

Blue and Gray expected a translation. I said nothing,
though. Instead I pulled a notebook out from my pocket and
wrote down a few ticks for my later consideration: Frederick
Crosby's rap sheet downtown at Sex Crimes, Kowalski's special interest in his demise, and the matter of one Veronique
Unique. Gray ran out of patience. He sputtered, "What the
hell'd he jibber, Hockaday?"

"Raul? He says never mind about this neighborhood,
it's Chinatown."

I said my good-byes in English and Spanish and left the
bedroom. Before returning to the corpse that had drawn us
all here this day, I took a quick survey of Crosby's parlor,
a bookless room full of expensive mauve and beige mini-
malist junk that I would not want to sit on and besides which
told me nothing. Back in the kitchen, though, Kowalski still
had plenty to say.

The kitchen was quite a lot bloodier than before. The photographers had finished their work, so the forensic cops had
finally pulled up the spikes from the floor, the ones that had
nailed down Crosby's hands and feet. They had also flopped
the body over and pulled the crowbar out of Crosby's rectum,
accounting for most of the fresh spillage of blood.

Schecter was off to the side of the room, greeting the
arrival of an autopsy crew of four guys in rubber boots,
gauze masks, a stretcher, and the kind of green body bag I
used to see in Quang Tri province back when they told me
that gag about making the world safe for democracy.

Kowalski, not Schecter, was clearly the man in charge. He stood next to a forensics cop sealing up the blood-streaked crowbar in a plastic evidence pouch. He had removed his sergeant's jacket, rolled up his sleeves, and slipped on a pair of surgeon's gloves. And now he was unfolding something as I carefully navigated the slick floor.

"What's that?" I asked Kowalski. He flattened out a piece of paper, about the size of a sheet from my own pocket-size notebook. At his feet was a plastic sandwich bag and three rubber bands. They were soaked in blood and some other kinds of bodily effluvia I did not care to know about in any detail.

Kowalski held the paper in one hand and squinted at it through the waning smoke of his nearly extinct panatela. His other hand was busy pulling a Snickers bar from out of his shirt pocket. Kowalski spat the cigar from his mouth, the butt landing in a puddle of red. Then he tore open the candy wrapper with his teeth and bit off chunks of chocolate and caramel and nougat while he read some words typed on the paper.

When he finally managed to bulge the whole candy bar into his mouth, he snorted and motioned toward the plastic bag and the rubber bands with a foot, finally answering me with a muffled, "Found a little present wrapped around exhibit A in this mess here. A rude message from the pervo who gave Crosby the crowbar enema."

"What's it read?" I took out my Bic and my pad.

"It sure as hell ain't a nice fortune inside of some cookie you get for dessert down on Mott Street." The sergeant laughed, causing some of the masticated Snickers bar to bubble up from the corners of his mouth. The cop next to him curled his lips in disgust and walked off. Kowalski sniffed, adding, "No, it sure ain't that."

"Come on, Sergeant."

"Oh, let's just say somebody wrote the perfect epitaph for a freaking fanny-packer."

"Let's don't tempt me to call up dayside IAD about your weight."

"All right, all right." Kowalski looked at the note in his hands. He snorted again. "It says here, and I quote, 'Such is an evildoer's end: death is the just reward for a misspent life.'"

6

AS IT HAPPENED, I DID MAKE A CALL BEFORE I LEFT THE apartment. But not to Internal Affairs. There was a telephone in the foyer, and I decided that since Crosby would not object I could save myself a quarter. The phone was one of those ebony and ivory French boudoir models like Mae West used in the movies. I used it to check in with Ruby at the agency.

"Please tell me you haven't got yourself involved in this case." Ruby picked up on my call and just started talking like that, without even a *Hello* to start things off, which reminded me of Sister Bertice all over again. She knew it was me on the phone because I had had to go through the edgy receptionist again, and also through some nervous secretary named Sandy who was diligent about clearing my call with her boss lady.

"Not quite, I'm—"

"Wait, my other line's flashing," Ruby cut in, adding a little frantic note to her exasperation. And why not? It had been quite a morning at the firm of Schuyler, Foster and Crosby, minus Crosby. "Oh God, I'd better pick up. Hold on, will you?"

I did not mind the interruption. It gave me the chance to finally ask myself, Well now—am I on this unholy mess of a case—or what?

Or what. Whenever a cop such as myself, fully laden with the various sad learnings that come with my job and my age, happens on a crime of some complexity he right away makes a number of personal calculations. Starting always with the question, How much of my beat-up heart is likely to break in seeing this through to the end?

Here now lay the bloody complication of one Frederick Laurence Crosby. And here was I, consulting my heart for the first time in many years without the assistance of my old dear friend and colleague, Johnnie Walker.

Of course, I was intrigued by the homicidal questions playing leapfrog all around me. This was only natural, only professional. Also, God help me, I was now for the first time in so many years peering stone cold sober into the contrarian well of my soul.

What I saw most clearly were the very personal motives for poaching in the Nineteenth Precinct. To begin, there was King Kong Kowalski. He was the last thing on my mind when the body snatchers caught me weeping in a bar; now here he was again for unexplained reasons of his own. Then there was Inspector Neglio's motion of no confidence, in the form his putting me on additional furlough. And then Ruby, who just a second ago seconded this terrible motion before she had even said hello.

But most of all, there was my own obstinacy. Maybe I had to prove something—to Neglio and Ruby and Davy Mogaill and King Kong Kowalski and Lieutenant Schecter and Father Sheehan and Neuman the leper and everybody else in the department, including myself. Which is, ex—pissbums can still hack it.

On behalf of ex–pissbums everywhere I naturally decided I was in on the case. Right then and there on the phone, waiting through the Muzak. I did not even say hello to Ruby when she came back on the line.

"Sorry, babe. As it turns out, I've got no time for lunch today."

"Did I ask about food? No. I asked about you and this Freddy Crosby thing. You dodged the question, which I guess pretty much gives me the answer I don't want to hear." Ruby stopped to take a breath. "Anyway, I can't see you now either. I'm doing lunch with somebody else."

"Doing? One day back on Mad Avenue and already you're *doing* lunch? What, again with the boss man?"

"His name's Jay, and he's not exactly my boss. And no, it's not with him. It's his wife. That was her on the other line. I'm taking lunch with Margot Schuyler."

"Nobody *has* lunch anymore? They *do*, they *take*—?"

"Your wife needs you bad, Hock, but she doesn't need you to be a nudzh. The day's bad enough as it is with this Crosby thing, and the Russians . . . and now I have to go and see Jay's wife . . ."

"Russians—?"

"Later about them. Tell me where you're going now, since you don't have time for lunch, and who you're going to be seeing."

"Davy Mogaill."

"Didn't you already see him? Didn't he pick you up from Jersey this morning?"

"Sure. But now I have to go see him about something."

"Oh." Ruby sounded relieved. She did not say what she really meant, which was, *Good, it's okay you're seeing Mogaill because he's not drinking anymore.* Instead, she said, "Well, good. He's not with the department anymore."

"He doesn't see it that way."

"How do you mean?"

"In Davy's life, things get lost. His wife died young. I knew her a long time ago. She was a great beauty from Kildare. Then he lost his career, which he loved like only a widower can love his work. Now the poor guy doesn't even drink. He's still got his books, but is that enough?"

"We'll talk about it."

"Okay, that and some more things. For instance, your Russians. Also this guy Fred Crosby—"

"Oh, God!"

"Maybe not Crosby right away tonight."

"Hock . . ." Ruby stopped herself, probably from telling me how she would be worried about my being alone for the whole afternoon in a city with thousands of bars, about half of which I knew in varying degrees of intimacy. The priests back at the Straight and Narrow warned us about moments like this, how we might resent these pregnant pauses. "I'll see you later then, Hock?"

"It'll all be like before," I said. "Just you and me, Ruby. And the movies. Let's rent some videos. Anything in black and white."

"I know. And especially anything with John Garfield. What about dinner?"

"Suddenly I've got this craving for chow mein. Meet me at the China Bowl on West Forty-fourth, seven o'clock."

"After all these weeks. Some craving, lover man."

"Later on at home, wear something satin."

Leaving us with satiny thoughts of evening, I hung up the phone and rode the elevator down from Crosby's apartment to the lobby. Otto the doorman was back on the job, standing in the gray light of the doorway, gazing out at foggy shapes passing by on the street. His black shiny boots and his braided uniform were as stiff as ever, but the man inside seemed to have shriveled one size smaller. His face was bleached as a butter bean and his bottom lip trembled some, like a codger trying to remember the taste of food he was not allowed to eat anymore.

Again I showed him my gold shield and said I had a few questions, beginning with, "What time did you get here this morning?"

"Seven forty-five."

"I bet that's on the dot."

Otto responded with a slight tilt of his shoulders and some listless heel clicking. Not worthy of his days in the Shutzstäffel. The old boy was truly shaken.

"First, I enjoyed my coffee," he said, motioning to a folding chair just inside the entryway, next to a doorman's desk. On the desk was a thermos and mug. There was also the book to log the arrivals and departures of visitors. And on the chair, a copy of the tabloid *New York Post,* stained red from a jelly doughnut. The screamer on the cover read, VILLAGE GAYS HAVE BEEF WITH COP "PANSIES." Otto said, "Eight o'clock, it is time I start work. On the dot, *ja?*"

"Finished with this?" I asked, picking up the paper. I did not wait for the answer I knew would come anyway. I rolled up the *Post* into a cylinder and slipped it into my coat pocket to read later.

"I make gift to you."

74

"Why, thanks, Otto. Now help me with something else, okay?"

Otto gave me a worried *ja* while I scanned the top sheet of his logbook, not finding the name Veronique Unique. So I put it to him, "Sometime on your watch a visitor came down from 5-C. A woman. Not the type who lives in the neighborhood."

I turned the log so Otto could inspect it for himself. He passed a white gloved finger across the top page, then said, "No, nobody comes out Mr. Crosby's apartment—except Mr. Crosby. Now you."

"What are you talking about Crosby coming out? Crosby's upstairs and he's very dead."

"*Ja*, that I know. But this morning ..." Otto's words trailed off into unpleasant thoughts.

"You saw him?"

"The man walked past, right here." Otto motioned to the floor in front of him, then raised his arm and pointed to the door. "Frederick Crosby—in a trenchcoat, and a hat."

"Did he say anything?"

"No, he never talk in the morning."

"He says nothing, he's wearing a hat and coat. How do you know it was Crosby?"

"I say, '*Guten morgen*, Herr Crosby.' He wave to me, like this." Otto snapped off a salute. "Every day, it is like this between us. I greet him in the Deutsch, Herr Crosby wave to me."

"What time was your little act this morning?"

"Same time. Every day, Mr. Crosby leave for his work fifteen minutes after I start my work."

"Lots of the tenants down here in the lobby around eight-fifteen?"

"Yah."

"Thanks again for the paper, Otto."

I headed out the door and turned east to Lexington Avenue. Then downtown for several wet, gray blocks toward the Harmony Arms Hotel.

As I walked, it struck me that I had trouble seeing much beyond a half-block in front of me. Maybe my visibility was constricted to the ugly tableaux I had just left behind: Fred Crosby's corpse, naked but for a zippered leather mask; Joe

Kowalski gnawing on a Snickers bar, with the stink of murder all around him.

Or was I having trouble seeing because the skies had gone even gloomier? Had this bloody day now delivered a darkness at noon? But not exactly darkness. The fog had merely lifted some, giving way to a dull luminescence. There was light, but no shadows. I felt like I was walking around inside an ice cube.

In a lot of police movies, there is the stock scene where a perp is hauled into a room by a couple of impatient detectives and made to sit down in a chair and answer questions with big lamps turned around to glare into his scared puss. I have been a detective for a number of years, so long that one sweet day I will collect a pension for my services—assuming, please God, that I get out of this job alive. Yet in all my time carrying the gold shield, I have never myself witnessed this Hollywood scene with the bright lights.

The fact is, detectives do not need much light at all. Detectives look for shadows, for it is the things that live in shadows we are after.

"My Lord . . . Ruby! You don't say! Back at the agency? Well, now that's too . . . Anyway, grand to hear your voice. Really—grand! Here I thought you'd gone and died."

"Why would you think that?"

"Nasty thing to say, isn't it? Makes you wonder what in hell people must think you look like. Right?"

"I guess so, Hiram."

"Don't worry, doll. I bet you look swell as a sweet young thing in a prom dress waiting for some pimple-faced boy to pin a gardenia someplace on your spaghetti straps while he cops a peek down your front. Speaking of such, I bet that horny bastard Schuyler has already tried playing hide-the-salami with you half a dozen times at least."

"I can handle Jay."

"Bet he'd love *that!*"

"Hiram—you thought I *died?*"

"Course not. It only popped into mind because it's what everybody says to me all the damn time. Whenever I go down to the city and stop by one of the old hangouts, some prick comes up and says, *I thought you died.* Man, I'd like to just deck him. But I can't because of my damn arthritis. I tell you what this retirement jazz is, Ruby honey. It's the shits."

"Of all days to be talking about dying."

"Well, why not? I always say sleep's lovely, but death's better—and not to have been born in the first damn place, that's the miracle."

Hiram Foster laughed. He expected Ruby would, too. In the old days she always laughed at his epigrams.

"You're not laughing, Ruby. That's one of my best gags."

"You haven't heard?"

"About what?"

"Freddy."

"Who—Crosby?"

"He's dead."

"What happen? The fruit got himself bumped off?"

"Fruit?"

"Sure, I knew he'd get it sooner or later."

There was commotion outside Ruby's office. She wanted to question Hiram Foster but had to put the telephone aside when Jay Schuyler popped his head in the door, and said, "See you in a minute, Ruby—please?" There were lines of perspiration on his patrician forehead. Behind him, Alexis and Vasily bellowed something in Russian. She could see them through the pizza window, their pudgy hands bouncing, fists smacking into palms. Schuyler pulled his head with the silver wings back into the outer room.

"Hiram, listen," Ruby said, returning to the telephone, infected with Schuyler's uncharacteristic panic. "Crosby was murdered. There's a cop over at his apartment right now, from the Sex Crimes Squad."

"Sex. What'd I tell you?"

"I'd like to talk to you about it, Hiram . . ."

"Sure you would. I heard you married a cop."

". . . But I'm tied up now."

"So, come on up and see me in the country someday, why don't you? Gawk at the pretty autumn foliage. Bring along the cop husband."

"Thanks. I'll call you, Hiram."

"Anytime, doll."

Ruby hung up. *Fruit?* Crosby?

Outside, she heard Schuyler's desperate voice. First perspiration, now desperation. Murder does strange things to people.

"Come on, Alexis . . . Vasily," Schuyler whined. Ruby saw their two chubby, blue-suited bodies turn defiantly, then stalk out of sight. She heard one of them say, "Is no goot!" And Schuyler in pursuit, pleading, "Come on—we can talk about this . . ."

7

FOR THE SECOND TIME IN AS MANY DAYS, SHE FOUND HERSELF in the Pool Room of the Four Seasons. Once again, in this palace of tax-deductible luncheons, she was struck by starkly contrasting thoughts of home. And how the St. Bernard Project was slowly but surely becoming the most faraway place she knew.

The sidewalks up and down Gibson Street broken by sinewy oak roots, thick smells of chinaberry blossoms and sour beer and Creole cooking, always full of black women scrubbing pails full of laundry brought home from white ladies' houses.

Mama Violet, and all the tired weary ones like her. Their angry men and their skinny kids, too. All of them back home, nestled in the bosom of their sweet warm ghetto, television in the front room blinkering endless visions of unattainable comfort and joy, red beans and rice for supper on the kitchen table. All of them back home, being told again and again throughout their lives, This is America, boy—where there's no such thing as a free lunch! And little Ruby Flagg with her cat-eye spectacles and her plastic-wrapped library books, suspecting otherwise . . .

She spotted the Bullfrog ensconced in his usual lily pad, surrounded by a whole new bevy of *tail*, as Freddy Crosby would say. The Bullfrog grunted into his cellular phone as Ruby passed, on her way to table eighty-nine. She turned, caught him staring at the sway of her hips and shot him a look to shrivel his bowels. Mama taught her that.

From across the pool, Margot Schuyler caught the rare sight of a brown-skinned woman wading confidently through a sea of pale, powerful men. Margot arched delicate eyebrows as a sign of her recognition, flickered a smile and raised iced fingers, ever so slightly, to wave. Her mama taught her that.

"So glad you could make it, dear," Margot said when Ruby joined her at the table. She stood and took Ruby's hands in her own, as if she were attending a funeral and consoling a bereaved relative of the dearly departed, then said, "Dreadful circumstances for our little get-together, don't you think?" Without waiting for an answer, Margot kissed air on both sides of Ruby's cheeks and the two of them sat down.

"Yes, well of course . . ." Ruby said, allowing her conflicting thoughts to fade as a waiter approached. She told him, "Just soda and lime, thanks," after which she noticed the half-gone martini on Margot's side of the table. She had a scribble of worry that maybe her own drink order might not be quite sociable.

"Absolutely horrible about Frederick! Have you heard anything?"

"Details, you mean?"

"Yes."

"No. Have you?"

"Only what Jay told me when he called to cancel our lunch. Frederick's been murdered in his own home, poor thing, and some policeman named Kowalski says it's all about sex. Gads! Policemen are *so* disgusting." Margot picked up her martini and sipped. A square-cut diamond on her ring finger refracted light in several brilliant shades of blue, yellow, and red. "Jay is positively up to his ears with the scandal of it all, don't you know. Be that as it may, I told him there's really no sense in letting a perfectly good table reservation go to waste, and so when I heard that you were back with the agency, Ruby, I—"

"My husband's a policeman by the way."

"Oh ... No offense, dear."

"As a matter of fact, I think he might end up working the Crosby homicide."

"I see ... Well, so you're married now. To a policeman. How wonderful. Is that what they call it—the *Crosby homicide?* How exciting." Margot, speaking breathlessly, had probably not expected Ruby's response. She raised some fingers again, ever so slightly. This time, a waiter obliged her by laying out menus. "Shall we think about ordering?"

Ruby unfolded her menu and ignored the diet bill of fare, a near-starvation regimen provided for customers recently returned from California's Golden Door health spa, where half the masters of corporate America have at one time or another paid thousands weekly to skip rope, eat nuts and beans five times a day, and crave forbidden booze. Ruby concentrated instead on the calorie-laden entrées of the day: smoked salmon quiche, lamb curry crêpes, *arrosto girato alla florentina,* pheasant with grapes and walnuts, *lapin à la moutarde.* Nothing was priced, of course, because price was nobody's concern. A meal at the Four Seasons is merely a matter of trading money with the government.

Ruby thought again of rice and beans, kitchen tables and droning television sets, and how Mad Avenue had delivered her from all that. Then, all in a very few seconds, she dreamed a subversive dream: the shooting script for a satirical TV commercial.

MUSIC:	Classical strings *(baroque).*
SFX:	Subdued café chatter, tinkle of plates & glasses.
PAN UP:	Large, elegant restaurant. Diners in formal wear.
ANNCR VO:	"Ladies and gentlemen, today we're at the legendary Four Seasons restaurant, where the movers and shakers of Manhattan are accustomed only to the very, very best ..."

ZOOM IN: Champagne flowing into glasses; caviar being spread on crustless bread; bustling waiters carrying silver trays— of suckling pigs.

ANNCR VO: "And where you, the tuna fish sandwich set, pay the tab! That's right, folks. Thanks to your government, big-time corporate meals like these are tax write-offs! And nothing's too good for the people who own your government . . ."

ZOOM OUT: (Slowly, from waist up) Businessmen diners in tuxedoes—(then: VISUAL PUNCH LINE)—with heads of grinning, drooling hogs.

& SFX: Hog grunts & squeals.

ANNCR VO: "No such thing as a free lunch?"

FADE OUT

Ruby settled quickly on the salmon quiche but kept the large menu fanned open in front of her, as if she were carefully studying the luncheon options. She needed her screen. Ruby did not want Margot Schuyler to be able to read her face as she considered the meaning of this invitation to the Four Seasons.

In the best of the old times, the relationship between Ruby and Margot was cordial. In the worst of those times, when Ruby happened to be the desired object of Jay Schuyler's notoriously roving eye, Margot could be socially dangerous. Nothing overt, of course. Ladies like Margot Schuyler were bred to believe in certain holy principles such as owning seven pairs of lace gloves, one for each day; low-toned, lockjaw elocution; and in making one's personal objections obliquely known.

There was, for example, the agency Christmas bash of 1984. Margot took full charge of the event that year, to ensure against a repeat of 1983, when Jay made his first pass at Ruby. Thus did Margot attend to all the choreographic details, including table assignments. Ruby the rising agency genius and her date, a thoroughly forgettable senior copywriter who went on in life to become somebody's first husband, were seated in Siberia. Their only tablemates were the Hambleys: doddering old insanely wealthy Harrison and his grumbling wife, Leola.

Hambley owned a few skyscrapers around town and some other real estate and had retained Schuyler, Foster and Crosby to promote a luxury hotel venture he had created to keep Leola occupied. Leola was slowly but surely becoming an embarrassment to the agency, as the star of her own heavy-handed advertising campaign. In those years, Johnny Carson was making jokes every night about that ad campaign and everybody in Mad Avenue was laughing, save for SF&C. Nonetheless, the Hambley money was good and plentiful, and paid on time, and so they had been duly invited to the agency bash. Leola was not the type to be excluded. Only nobody wanted to sit with her, which perfectly served Margot's oblique purposes.

As Margot surely knew they would, Harrison Hambley nodded idiotically through the night, agreeing with everything his wife said; Leola Hambley mostly nattered at length on the glorious reelection victory of Ronald Reagan. Which was at least an improvement over her opening remarks. On meeting Ruby, Leola had said, "Well, Margot told me you were a pretty one. Harrison, don't you think Miss Flagg's real pretty, for a colored girl?"

What Margot may not have foreseen about the outcome of that ghastly evening was that Ruby established a certain peculiar respect for her hostess, because of and despite the Siberian table. Margot had insulted Ruby with fullest equity, after all. In all her time as a black woman living and working in a white world and making mistakes like everybody else, nobody ever seemed to have a cross word for Ruby. Except for Freddy, who hardly counted, then or now. Margot was one of those rare white ladies in whose company, for better or worse, Ruby was not subtly and forever reminded of her race.

Over the years, when they were thrown together at other

agency-related social occasions, Ruby's respect for Margot only grew. Whenever Ruby was around, the group conversation would take an inevitable turn. Suddenly racial injustice in South Africa was the issue that raptly interested one and all, or the pity of welfare mothers in Harlem, or the plight of America's inner cities. But whenever Margot was around, Ruby was sure of being spared. "Oh, please—*inner cities?*" Margot once intervened. "How tiresome. Let's talk about the outer cities."

Margot Schuyler was a natural woman, unaffected by and unapologetic for her wealth. She threw gobs of money at worthy causes and unworthy people; her idea of the perfect summer evening at the Oyster Bay house was to have the butler set up dinner on the beach; in her Fifth Avenue triplex, Margot had an English architect design her writer's study, at a cost that thus far still exceeded the combined earnings of her four published mystery novels; and Margot gave heart, soul, and maybe half her pocketbook to the Metropolitan Opera.

Most of all, Margot Schuyler was the kind of well-born woman that Mama Violet appreciated. *"Least she ain't one of them ones from the uppity class be wanting to help out us poor unfortunate Negroes by slapping down some kind of urban renewal in our part of town that nobody 'round here want ... Least she ain't just another one of them white ladies trying to have herself a problem."* Ruby listened, hidden behind the fan of her menu as her mother's sentiments, which she had heard applied to a few certain rich white ladies in New Orleans, now ran through her head; she could almost see Mama sitting at her kitchen table, shelling peas into a bowl, dishing with the neighbor women from up and down the alley on a lazy, humid New Orleans afternoon ... *tearing up some air,* as Mama would put it. And Ruby realized how her mother's long-ago words now shaped her own standard of respect for Margot Schuyler and ladies like her.

But nothing Mama ever said answered the question of why Margot had asked her here today. Even the notoriously generous Margot was not in the habit of treating rivals for her husband's affections to pricey luncheons.

Ruby put down the menu and told the waiter about the salmon quiche. He had already taken Margot's order for the pheasant, and now he drifted off, leaving the women alone. Ruby remarked on this when she could think of nothing else to say.

"In all the years I've known you, Margot, it's never been just the two of us like this."

"Sweet luck, then. It's high time."

"Not so lucky for Freddy."

"I didn't mean that. Gads!"

"Oh, I know."

"I suppose the *Post* will have the gory details in the morning. I must buy a copy, wherever one buys the *Post.*"

"Resource material for your next book?"

"My dear, I hardly write about that sort of thing."

Ruby felt herself flush. She had never actually read a Margot Schuyler novel, although she had certainly seen them, and knew they were mysteries of a sort. There always seemed to be some swarthy brute on the covers with his hairy hands around the creamy neck of some big-bosomed career girl. All the secretaries at the agency read them. Ruby would see the paperback editions tucked inside canvas tote bags of the secretarial pool, along with earnest salads in Tupperware containers and sneakers for when it was time to shuck off the high heels and head for the subway.

"You *do* write about murder—?"

"Murder, of course. Very entertaining. But the sex lives of my friends? Well, I should say not. Unless I should need the money someday." Margot smiled sweetly, then became thoughtful. She finished the martini. A waiter leaped to her rescue with another. Ruby looked across the pool and saw that the Bullfrog was having an extremely energetic phone conversation, complete with fist pounding. He happened to pound on the upturned tines of a fork, flipping it neatly into the décolletage of a blonde guest. Margot, oblivious to events at any other table, said, "Besides, poor Frederick was one of our supers. I wouldn't like this squalorous murder of his to reflect on the Met."

"Freddy was a building superintendent?"

"No, dear. *Super*—as in supernumerary. You know, a spear carrier."

"Oh. Like a movie extra."

"Exactly."

"When in the world was Freddy a spear carrier?"

"Let's see now." Margot looked up at the ceiling, tracing her chin with a forefinger. "I introduced him to our house manager, Norman. Three, four years ago, I guess it's been. Norman Applebaum. Frederick was thinking about an opera theme for some ad campaign. I've forgotten which one. Anyway, it was love at first sight with Norman and Frederick. Among other things, Norman sponsored Frederick for the Boys Club."

"Boys Club? What's that?"

"It's what the supers call themselves. Maybe I'm making it sound more formal than it really is." Margot took a sip of her martini, her third. "Although, they do have their little rules. It's not as if they have bylaws and dues and all. But one simply *must* be body beautiful, don't you know. You and I should have such bodies ... Well, I suppose *you* do, dear."

A vaguely hostile spirit had crept into Margot's tone, something new to Ruby's ears. Jay Schuyler could sweat in desperation, Margot Schuyler could be reduced to common jealousy. What next? Ruby took a deep breath and decided to clear some air. What was to lose?

"Let's not be like this."

"Like what?"

"The way women are, letting men intrude on their friendships. And ready or not, you're my friend, Margot. Your husband's my boss—period. No matter what he thinks, no matter what he may have said, that's all it's ever been. I'm no threat to you. Nor to any other woman married to an attractive man."

"No, dear." Margot's eyes misted, and Ruby dreaded what might come next. Something maudlin. Ruby disliked that about women, too. But Margot said, coldly, "You're right, you're not the threat."

The arrival of the salmon quiche and the pheasant could not have been more timely; the conversation took a merciful turn. Each dish was pronounced delicious, respective nibbles were ritually traded, and much to Ruby's relief Margot had something to do with her hands besides lift a martini glass. The conversation eventually got back to the topic of the Metropolitan Opera, pleasantly so at first.

"I don't suppose Jay's told you about my latest project at the Met?" Margot asked.

"There's hardly been a moment . . ."

"Are you familiar with the Opera Club?"

"Is it connected with the Met?"

"I should say so. You're clubable if you can donate ten thousand a year. We have our own special room, just off the dress circle. All very brocade and gold leaf. These days it's a lounge for between acts and for receptions where we meet the cast—things like that. I don't suppose you can guess what it used to be."

"Probably not."

"Were you aware that women weren't allowed as members in the Opera Club until 1975?" Margot's thin eyebrows danced a suggestive two-step. "Before that, it was restricted."

"Restricted. To the usual suspects?"

"In this case, the Opera Club was for rich men and their mistresses."

"How convenient."

"Quite. You'd think the old boys would have built a little powder room, though."

"They never did? Where did their mistresses go?"

"The same place the wives do today. Two flights up, in our heels. So—that's why I'm endowing a ladies' room."

"Good for you."

"For all that I've spent on the Met over the years, I've got my name in precious few places. But this time, I want a big brass plate on that Opera Club powder room. I shall have it read, The Margot Schuyler Memorial Ladies' Loo."

They had a laugh, like a couple of college girls. Then came the dessert tray. Margot and Ruby ordered a pair of forks, a single serving of a simple *tourte aux blettes* and two glasses of chilled rosé.

As she ate and drank with her lady friend, a troublesome man intruded on Ruby's thoughts: Hock. When would the worry go away? Had not Davy Mogaill said to her, *You'll no doubt see it's one day at a time for you, too.*

So long as Hock was there in her head, Ruby decided, she might as well be a helpmate. Hock was bound to involve himself somehow in the Crosby homicide. And there, sitting across from her, was maybe somebody with a lead.

"Margot, I have to tell you, I'm surprised to find out Freddy Crosby was a homosexual."

"You weren't supposed to know." Margot finished off the last morsel of their shared dessert.

"How many people did know? At the agency, I mean."

"Nobody."

"Not even Jay? Or Hiram?"

"If they knew, or suspected, it wasn't because of me. I can keep a confidence." Margot's eyes grew wet again, and she added, "Poor, poor Frederick. You don't have to be happy to be gay."

8

It was not difficult to find Davy in the lobby of the Harmony Arms Hotel, since there he was plopped right down in the middle of it. He sat in an overstuffed purple chair with his head up against a stained doily on the seat back, one thick leg crossed over another with lots of bare white calf exposed. He wore sunglasses and smoked a cigar. Judging by its aroma, I would guess the cigar cost him half what he paid for the newspaper in his lap.

All around him various rich guys and playboys breezed by. They carried thousand-dollar briefcases or else those men's purses they make in Italy and wore dark suits pinched at the waist and haircuts like movie stars get from barbers with only one name. The women in the lobby all looked like they just sashayed through the red door of the Elizabeth Arden shop on Fifth Avenue. There was a concierge in a wing collar and gray cutaway talking French with one of the guests. Off to the side of the lobby was a small and inviting zinc-topped bar with big flower arrangements at either end. On the stools were a couple of long-legged good-time blondes and four well-tailored out-of-towners, the kind who eat steak dinners a lot. This bar crowd was laughing quietly at nothing especially funny and pulling down the kind of drinks where the glasses come with stems.

I decided the Harmony Arms appealed to me. The hotel

had a fine sense of a lost, rakish elegance from between the world wars. The Duke of Windsor would have fit the place. Scott and Zelda, certainly. And Robert Benchley and Myrna Loy and Preston Sturges and S. J. Perelman. Davy Mogaill, on the other hand, fit like a cockroach on a plate of soufflé.

He dumped some cigar ash onto the floor and took off the shades when he saw me walking toward him. "Hock," he said, looking around him like somehow he was embarrassed to be associated with me, "what are you doing?"

"I got a big favor to ask."

"I'm working here."

"Good. This is about work." I glanced over at the inviting bar.

The good-timers, the expensive kind since they were gorgeous, did not interest me. Neither did the flowers or the beef eaters. But that smoky, blue-tinted mirror up behind the bar did; so, too, all the pretty bottles in their rows. The bartender gave me a friendly smile as he wiped a glass with a linen towel. He was a round-shouldered black guy of about sixty years with a frizz of gray hair and a face full of lines deep enough to hold rainwater.

Mogaill saw what I was looking at. "Somehow I doubt it's work on your mind," he said.

"It's important, Davy. Give me a couple of minutes to lay it out."

"All right, all right." He hoisted himself up, shaking his thick legs and sending his trouser cuffs back down toward his ankles where they belonged. He folded his paper and left it behind in the deep, warm recess he had left in the purple chair. With a nod at the bar, he said, "We'll take ourselves over there. It's as good a time as any for you to be seeing and believing there's more to a bar than whiskey."

Mogaill took his cigar along, I brought the morning *Post* I had borrowed from Otto the doorman. A porter with a whisk broom and dustpan cleaned up around where Davy had sat.

"Gentlemen?" the bartender asked in a raspy voice.

I had no memory of the few seconds it took to walk with Davy over to the bar. I must have been in a trance. But now here I was with my elbows on mahogany, sitting two stools from a pot full of flowers next to Mogaill. On the other side of me sat one of the curvy blondes. I noted the slit up the thigh of her silk dress and that her hair smelled of jasmine.

"Seltzer with lime, Moses," Mogaill said to the bartender. He jerked a thumb at me. "My newlywed friend, he'll be having the same delicious libation."

I nodded agreement and tried not to think of Scotch. I thought about Ruby instead. Which only made me consider what a rotten proposition she had accepted in me, beginning with Ireland last April.

The intention of that fateful trip, irrespective of the murderous violence that dogged us, was to begin our new life together; we were in search of joy, not an Irish family tragedy. It seemed so simple as we took off from JFK to Dublin: Ruby would meet my ailing Uncle Liam; I would find out something of the mysteries of my parents; Ruby and I would be married, and live happily ever after. And indeed, we returned to New York as husband and wife—married in a tinkers' camp, the same as my own mother and dad. In the early weeks back at home, this was joy enough. But I had come back sadder and wiser, and as shadowed by the troubles I found as by the curse of Davy Mogaill's ominous bon voyage. *"Sorry to say, Hock, there'll be no easy sleep under your Irish roof."* And so I would walk my black dog walks through the Manhattan streets, with fallen angels riding my shoulders, popping the old question, "A wee jar?" Some new life. I decided Ruby and I would have a big talk about all this. Sober, for once in my life . . .

"Tell me now," Mogaill said, interrupting these thoughts of a new life. Some new life, I thought. Mogaill asked, "What's it about with you today, Neil?"

"I need a job."

"That you've already got. You're a copper, my son, a touchstone of democracy in the city we love."

"You sound like a damn priest." I now thought about Sheehan and how I had to submit to his clearance for my return to active duty. "Priests aren't on my hit parade right now."

"A crisis of faith?"

"You could say that."

"Always love Jesus, son. He's the world's only successful anarchist."

The drinks, such as they were, arrived. Moses the bartender set them down with a grin I would have liked better if it came with Scotch, which I was still trying not to think about.

"*Sláinte,*" Mogaill said, raising his glass. I tapped mine against his.

"Two shots of seltzer," I complained. "The clink doesn't sound right."

"No, that it doesn't. But I'll say this for the awful stuff: You're able to state your business plain while drinking it. So why don't you get on with yours?"

"Inspector Neglio, he's not taking me back on. At least not until the chaplain gives his okay, after which there's the IAD." I had turned away from Mogaill while admitting this, feeling suddenly as naked as when my service revolver was first confiscated. I looked up to see Davy shaking his head. "You probably know all about that," I said. "Like you know about Neuman and the body snatchers."

"You can't be taking this personal."

"I remember them telling us that about a thousand years ago at Police Academy. I ignored it. I always take everything personal."

"Aye, and it's the noble flaw in your personal code. I'll forever remember you fondly for one other particular rule of yours."

"That being?"

"Neil Hockaday will put the collar on no poor man, unless absolutely forced."

"Poor men are arrested every day. But by the end of the year the crime rate's always up. So I just don't see the percentage, that's all."

"Your head's full of more stars than you know." Mogaill took a final puff of his cheap cigar, then mashed it out in an ashtray. One of the beef eaters waved a garnet-ringed hand under his nose and sniffed a cokehead's sniff. We ignored him. Mogaill said, "Small wonder you're having it rough with the department. I mean aside from your being a pissbum like myself."

"Us pissbums have to stick together."

"Aye."

"So hire me, Davy."

"Malarky! It's no good your being a peep. Besides, there'd be the matter of your wages. I tell you, all I've got's a license and this here job as house snoop."

"Give me back the four dollars you made me pay on the bridge this morning."

"Why should I?"

"It's the only wages I'll take until I bring around some new business. Deal?"

"So that's what it is. You've got yourself a moneybank case. But under the circumstances, you can't do anything about it?"

"More like a can of worms case. There was a murder this morning, Davy. A real hack job. Something tells me there's more to come."

"Such as?"

I spread out the *Post* on the bar. On the way over to the Harmony Arms, I had read the story under the screamer for myself. I now wanted Mogaill's reaction. He looked over the cover photograph first: an angry young man wearing a bandana and a nose ring throwing something at a disgusted cop with a big belly. Then Mogaill turned back the cover and read:

Village Gays
Have Beef With Cop "Pansies"

by William T. Slattery

Cops who can't or won't protect homosexuals from violent, sometimes fatal assault in Greenwich Village are "pansies."

That was the mocking message shouted at officers of the Sixth Precinct last night as some 500 homosexual activists demonstrated outside the station house on West 10th Street. Burly cops were also pelted with thousands of lavender Kleenexes the demonstrators had fashioned into paper flowers.

"They're pansies, just like the NYPD," said the demonstration leader of the paper flowers—and, figuratively, of New York's Finest. The leader would identify himself only as "Sly." He said further, "Real cops go after real crime. Well, we've got one hell of a crime wave going. What are the cops doing about it? Zip! They're sitting around eating doughnuts and showing their true colors—pansy colors."

The "crime wave" referred to by Sly is both the current epidemic of gay-bashing along Sixth Avenue, chiefly between Eighth and Houston streets—and what police say is a series of unrelated violent deaths at, or in the vicinity of, homosexual nightclubs along West Street near Christopher Street.

Two nights ago, a young man dressed flamboyantly in women's clothing was found dead on the nearby Hudson River piers. According to patrons of a nearby homosexual bar called the Ladies Auxiliary, he was a popular transvestite prostitute. The dead man, still officially unidentified, had a bullet hole in the side of his head. Police discovered a .22 caliber pistol nearby. Sixth Precinct detectives have tentatively labeled the case a suicide. Sly suspects otherwise.

"That's the third so-called suicide of a drag queen in the past month," Sly noted. "Just wait until Halloween when we have our parade. There'll be a wholesale slaughter of queers!" (On the night of September 28th, a gay man was found dead by gunshot wound in a toilet stall of the Ladies Auxiliary. A week later, a gay man initially thought to be a woman was found hanged from a street lamp nearby the same club. Both these cases were also labeled suicides.)

"And I don't know how many times we've had these gangs of suburban punks drive in to jump queers and beat them," he added. "The cops have a way of not taking these cases seri-

94

ously. Their attitude is, murdering queers can be ignored, beating queers can be ignored. Well, let me tell you something about us queers—we may be many things, but we ain't going to be ignored! Tell you something else—this crime wave, it's going to spread uptown, baby. Way uptown!"

Spokesmen for the Sixth Precinct and One Police Plaza would say only that in all cases of death and violence mentioned by last night's demonstrators, whether bias-related or otherwise, standard investigative procedures were followed by officers and detectives involved.

Some officers on hand at the demonstration were willing to make statements to the press, on the condition that their names not be used. Most of these officers described the demonstrators— and homosexuals in general—in terms impossible to publish in a family newspaper.

But one officer who spoke openly to the press was Sergeant Joseph Kowalski of the Manhattan Sex Crimes Squad, which is housed within the Sixth Precinct station house. He grounded his comments in Christian scripture.

"These gay boys, maybe they got a right to be paranoid," Sgt. Kowalski said. "After all, you got a lot of people who read their Holy Bibles, even in godforsaken New York City. In the Bible it says a man lying down with another man is an abomination to our Heavenly Father. So, God Almighty Himself hates homosexuals . . ."

Mogaill stopped reading. He got the point, and there were only a few more paragraphs anyway. His face dark and bloody as a cube steak ready for the skillet, he asked me, "Would this case of yours be having anything to do with Joe Kowalski?"

I nodded. Then I briefed him on the morning's uptown murder, how Frederick Crosby had led a double life: solid citizen of Madison Avenue by day, Barbie Doll by night. I mentioned the elusive visitor, Veronique Unique, and the rudely lyrical epitaph rammed up Crosby's nether side. "Nobody's going to be calling Frederick Crosby a suicide," I said.

"No, you're right," Mogaill agreed. "But what connects the Crosby murder with his dead sisters downtown, you should pardon the expression?"

"One big thing. The lesser stuff we're going to get paid to find out."

"First question: What's the big thing?"

"King Kong Kowalski. He's hanging around last night's demonstration outside the Sixth Precinct, now he just so happens to show up in the Nineteenth while the forensics crew is working over Frederick Crosby's corpse. He's got no particular business at either place, so it's either coincidence or the sergeant's heart and soul is with the gay-bashers, like he says to the reporters. I ask around, and it turns out Kowalski did his legendary dickprint number on Crosby. You know the drill here?"

"The sick hump . . ." Mogaill rubbed his forehead.

"I'm guessing he did it to Crosby not long ago," I said. "Anyhow, it gets Crosby physically down into Kowalski's bailiwick."

"Which is where the queens are getting theirs."

"Right."

"Next question: Why would we be getting paid to open up this particular can of worms? Make that bucket of snakes."

"Crosby was a partner in the advertising agency where Ruby works. Which is my next stop, by the way." I checked my watch. Ruby would still be at lunch. "I'm going to chat with the boss, somebody named Schuyler. I've been wanting to meet him. And he wants to hire us, to conduct a discreet investigation."

"He does?"

"Sure, as soon as I help him decide he does."

"Okay. And what's Inspector Neglio going to say about your extracurricular activity?"

"If he doesn't like it," I said, ripping the article about the demonstration out of the *Post* and slipping it into my side pocket, "then maybe I should call up my old reporter buddy Slattery. Slats might be real interested in an item about how the brass hats don't want even so much as a furloughed pissbum asking questions about cops who don't mind it when unpopular citizens get canceled out."

"Meaning it's Kowalski you're gunning for?"

"For starters. I wouldn't mind agitating the department some either."

"I'm with you. What do you want me to do?"

"Back me up when I tell people I'm working for you. Which like I said will cost you four bucks until I get the agency to pony up a retainer."

"Two dollars, Hock. In consideration of the fact I come to fetch you up all the way over to Jersey."

"Three."

"Deal."

Mogaill reached for his wallet and slowly picked out the bills, like he was an old lady in babushka shopping Ninth Avenue for the best price on haddock. I took his three bucks and also left him with the tab for the seltzers. And he left me with a possible starting point for my snake hunt: the name of Officer William Lenihan of the Sixth Precinct.

"Lenihan's got a motive for being helpful," Davy said. "He used to work for me at Central Homicide. They call him Three Dollar Bill. Follow?"

I said I did.

Then Davy gave me a useful warning.

"Steady on, Neil. You're now a cop going up against other cops. Meaning you're much like the man wearing pork chop pants in a room full of starving hounds."

The closest I ever came to having an office was when I worked a long assignment out of the Midtown-North station house. I was given an upstairs corner of the PDU, boxed in by a couple of rows of beat-up filing cabinets. In the middle of this box was a beige steel desk the city bought at a military surplus auction sometime between Korea and Vietnam, and a window. I could not see out the window because the glass was painted over in government green, which was just as well, since the view would have been an airshaft. The telephone on the desk sometimes worked. The manual typewriter was missing the letters *k*, *m*, and *d*, making it impossible for me to adequately include the words *sucker, mark,* or *dip* in my daily reports.

So it was not much, this office of mine. But the memory of it all came to mind now as a secretary guided me into the hushed sanctum sanctorum of a Madison Avenue mogul with Roman numerals after his name.

Funny enough, I thought, but my little old dump at Midtown-North had it all over this poshy refuge belonging to Bradford Jason Schuyler III. In my own shabby office, I always felt a sense of order and purpose and authority. But here now, in a great huge expensive room that looked more like a private men's club than a business office, was a man having as bad a case of the shakes as anything I had seen at the Straight and Narrow.

"Detective Hockaday, yes?" he asked. This was not so much a question as it was a greeting, the kind I have heard before from people who went to good schools. Schuyler stood in his cuff-linked shirtsleeves with his back to me at a wall of windows with a commanding view of the city. Given the day's bleak weather and the shock of Crosby's murder hanging around the agency like mildew, maybe it was a good thing the windows were the type that do not actually open.

The secretary left me waiting for Schuyler to say something more, or to at least turn around and face me. I watched a blimp advertising Fuji film float by in the Manhattan sky. I heard ice rattling in the fat lowball glass that Schuyler held in his unsteady hand. There was a trace of an amber something in that glass that I tried not to think about, despite the fact that an open bottle of that same something sat on the edge of his desk, which was big enough and clear enough to land a Lear jet. With his free arm, Schuyler made a hospitable circling motion. Still with his back to me, he said, "Sit down, why don't you? I'm drinking early. Care to join me?"

But then he spun around, spilling ice cubes from his glass and embarrassed apologies from his lips. "Oh, Christ, I'm sorry. I heard that you . . . I mean, Ruby says . . . Look, would you like a cup of coffee, a soda—"

"Don't worry about it, Mr. Schuyler, I'm not thirsty." I sat down in the nearest place I could, a leather club chair about half a dozen paces away. It was part of a semicircle of chairs grouped democratically around a mahogany coffee table. The table was sedately set out in silver, china, and crystal, and fresh copies of *Advertising Age* and *The Wall Street Journal.* In case Schuyler had not seen it yet, I flattened out the clipping from the *Post,* with the cover shot of the fat cop versus the rough trade with the nose ring.

"Please, call me Jay." He walked toward me, damp hand outstretched. We shook, he sat down.

Walking over from the Harmony Arms and thinking about this guy Schuyler and how he probably used to hit on my Ruby all the time, I imagined him several different ways, none too flattering. But I did not figure him for the jumpy type. And yet here he was in his shirtsleeves—meaning a custom-made number with stripes and a snowy white collar and cuffs, along with a silk tie and fancy braces, probably all of it from London—and the way he was twitching inside of those pricey clothes was not so different from a thousand shackled perps I have interrogated in my time.

It did not square. Not in this incredible office—with the enormous desk and the credenza, ten- or twenty-grand worth of leather chairs, a forest of potted date palms, Oriental rugs, fireplace, built-in bar, a wall full of Moroccan-bound books, a video screen half the size of a squash court, adjoining bath and shower. Most people I know, including myself, do not have apartments this good.

"Nice of you to see me on short notice," I said.

"Anything for New York's Finest."

I smiled. *Anything for New York's Finest.* Whenever I have heard that phrase—and I have heard it, spoken exactly so, hundreds of times over the years—I know I can count on the opposite, especially when it comes from a guy as tense as Schuyler. Not that I would ever complain. Lies are as good as shadows in my job; when a detective seeks truth, an ounce of evasion is worth a ton of candor.

"Could I ask you something personal?"

"I don't know why not."

"Hard day for you, sir?"

"Check." Schuyler shuddered, and drained his glass. "Mind if I have another one?" I shrugged my shoulders and he walked over to his desk for a refill. This took a little time, since the enormous desk was so far away from the circle of club chairs. I wondered if Schuyler ever got weary from just walking around his office. He sat down with me again and tried being cheerful by saying, "I'm happy to finally meet you, Detective Hockaday."

"You are?"

"Well, yes . . . Your wife's told me lots about you. Ruby's a genius, you know."

"Like Einstein?"

"Well, in a manner of speaking."

"All his life, Albert Einstein was never able to tie his own shoes. I read that once in a book."

"I didn't know that."

"Sure, I can read books."

"No—of course you can read, Detective Hockaday." He put his glass with the iced amber up to his forehead. This seemed to soothe him, enough so that his voice dropped to a lower pitch. I looked down at Schuyler's pinstriped trousers with the knife crease and his gleaming, hand-cobbled brogans as he added, "What I meant was, I didn't know about Einstein and the shoelaces."

"Everybody calls me Hock. Did the genius remember to tell you that?"

"You mean Ruby?"

"I guess. So far as I know, Einstein died in 1955 without ever knowing I'm called Hock."

"So, Hock . . ." Schuyler now paused for an impatient cough. Somebody who was not trying to hide something from me might have laughed instead. Then Schuyler looked at his wristwatch, which is something I have noticed that guys in striped pants are always doing when it happens I am around them. So, I did the same. Whereas Schuyler's watch was one of those big Rolex jobs that cost about two months of my salary, my own brand, which also ends with the letter x, cost what I earn in roughly two hours. Schuyler coughed again, and asked, "So . . . you'll be investigating this dreadful murder?"

"Yes, I will. So will the cops."

"Policemen . . . besides you—?" Confusion flickered in Schuyler's boozed eyes.

"The cops have their case, which is public interest," I explained. "You and me, our interest is private."

"Sorry, I've had a few drinks. I'm afraid you've got the advantage of me."

"Never mind. Is your handshake your bond, sir?"

"Indeed."

"I was hoping."

"What's my handshake got to do with this?"

"We'll get to that by and by, sir. I hear you talked to Sergeant Kowalski this morning. From the Sex Crimes Squad. Not much of a gentleman, is he?" Schuyler shook his head no, shuddered, and then took a big swallow of his fresh drink. I asked, "You want him poking around this case all by himself?"

"God, no!"

"That's why I'm here for you on this sorry day, sir. To help my wife's friends and colleagues. To help you protect the agency."

"Protect the agency . . . ?" Schuyler glanced at the *Post* clipping. I could almost hear him thinking about boardroom whispers all over town. In Schuyler's world, little whispers have a way of losing big money.

"Your late partner led one hell of a double life."

"Let's just say Fred had problems."

"That's putting it mild. What do you suppose the trouble was?"

"As I was telling Ruby this morning, poor Crosby was under some kind of stress lately."

"Why?"

"Crosby and I were partners, not pals. I didn't know anything about his personal affairs. I don't think anybody here did. He was a loner. He was good at what he did—here at work, I mean. He wasn't interested in socializing with anybody. Actually, nobody much liked him anyway." Schuyler thought a moment. "You know," he added, "I've never been up to his apartment for a drink."

"I wouldn't drop by now if I were you."

Schuyler's face whitened.

"This I'm afraid I have to ask, sir. Did you know Crosby liked to dress up in women's clothes?"

"It crossed my mind that Fred was homosexual. Not that it was ever an issue. Not that I cared."

"Sure, who cares these days?"

"Check."

"I could be gay and *you* wouldn't care."

"Check."

"You could be gay and *I* wouldn't care."

"I'm not gay."

"Who cares, sir?"

"Look here, Detective Hockaday, I'm not accustomed—"

"What about Crosby's associates? Know any of them? Wheaties or Fruit Loops, not that we care."

"No—nobody."

"Actually, if you think about it, sir, that's a lie. You and Crosby knew all kinds of the same people. The people who work here, for instance. See what I mean?"

"You're twisting my words. I'm not a liar—sir."

"I tell you, Jay, in my line of work you get funny ideas about truth versus lies. Same as in the advertising dodge, come to think of it."

"Funny you're not."

"Want to know what I think of the truth?"

"Not really."

"Truth is a steel rafter in a house of cards. Think about it."

"No, I'm not going to think about it. And I've had just about enough of this!"

"I bet Crosby said something like that. Did you hear how he got it?"

"No . . ."

"Somebody nailed your partner down on the floor, buck naked except for a pervo black leather mask. Then they ran big spikes through his hands and feet. Then they hammered his head to a pulp with a crowbar. Then they took the crowbar and rammed it up his backside."

"Sweet Jesus—!"

"Nothing sweet about it, sir."

"The violence, my Lord . . . !" Schuyler fumbled the wet glass in his hand and it crashed down on the coffee table, then fell to the floor in a pool of Scotch and perfect little ice cube squares. And then Schuyler became urgently sick. He managed to catch most of his sickness in his hands as he trotted off to the private bathroom way down at the far end of his sanctum sanctorum. I heard him retching in there, then a lot of toilet flushing, then water splashing in the sink. He emerged a few minutes later, smelling of spearmint and apologizing for the upset.

"Think nothing of it," I said.

"Have you quite all you need from me today, Detective Hockaday?"

"Sorry I had to give it to you straight and rough. But you think it's sickening now, wait until you see the crime scene photos. Sooner or later, Kowalski's going to want to come around and show you pictures. He loves that part of the job. Believe me, you're not going to want to eat red meat for a couple of weeks. And that's just from the sight of Kowalski."

"I don't want . . . !" Schuyler's voice trailed off into a fog of worry.

"Of course not, sir. Would you mind if I asked you something personal?"

"Why stop now?"

"If the government wanted to audit your taxes, would you just leave everything up to the IRS accountants?"

"No."

"You'd sleep easier if you hired your own guys—accountants, lawyers. You need somebody watching your interests in such a sensitive matter. Right?"

"Check."

"Same thing here. Your partner's been murdered, the cops have to make an audit. That's all fine and well. But do you want it all riding on the likes of Joe Kowalski?"

"No!" Schuyler looked like he might be nauseated again. I moved my chair back from him a little.

"Of course not. You want your own guy on the case. Doesn't mean you're not a public-spirited, cooperative citizen. Just that you have one or two special interests you don't want trampled by clumsy cops." I opened the *Post* to the inside page with Slattery's story on the demonstration outside the Sixth Precinct, and pointed out the section where Kowalski was quoted. "Not to mention cops who shoot off their mouths to reporters."

"Oh, Lord . . . !"

"Jay, remember I said we'd get back to your nice honest handshake?" I stuck out my hand now. Schuyler grabbed it like he was going down for the third time and I had just tossed him a lifesaver. As we pumped, I said, "Nice to be working for you while I'm on furlough from the department."

"What—?"

"Now that you got me on the payroll, here's the deal: You stop worrying, I start. My partner will be calling your secretary about fees and expenses and all. Do I hear a *check?*"

"Check . . ."

"You're doing the right thing."

"Maybe. But, I want you to know . . ."

Schuyler broke down. I waited for almost a minute while he sat with his silvery head in his hands, whimpering. I felt sorry for him, even though I had only done what had to be done. When Schuyler finally collected himself, he said something I would later put at the top of my case list of shadows: "It doesn't add up. There's something else here, something coming from way out in left field . . ."

He put his head in his hands again, and I left him there with something that was easy for me to say, "Machines add up, people don't."

9

I found Ruby waiting for me outside the restaurant. The place was closed. Six lousy weeks I was gone to Jersey and during that time they killed off yet another one of my favorite Times Square joints.

The front doors were propped open with bricks, and I could see a wrecking crew inside, banging away under fluorescent light filtered through plaster dust. Big-shouldered guys with pick-axes and pry bars were tearing apart the red Naugahyde booths. The planter full of plastic geraniums was still there in the front, the time-stained blossoms jouncing bravely through all the commotion. The little café curtains were still up. But they, too, would soon fall.

Dented pots and banged-up colanders had been tossed into a dumpster at the curb, like bodies piled on the dead wagons in Vietnam after some village was firebombed so America could be safe from Commies. One of the dead pots rolled around in the stale evening breeze, banging over the other dead pots. This was the death knell of the China Bowl.

Ruby stood by one of the propped-open doors. I had not seen her since the body snatchers stole me off to the Straight and Narrow that night I was in my cups at the Flanders Bar, all on about King Kong Kowalski. And here I was now, practically blubbering again. Not from missing Ruby—which

105

I did, like she was one of my limbs—but because they were tearing down my China Bowl, throwing her away like she was old chop suey.

It doesn't add up ... Bradford Jason Schuyler III had just told me that. Of all people.

Like so many joints in the New York of regular people like me who have only a couple of names and no numbers, the China Bowl was a place of memory and culinary innocence. The greasy walls of the China Bowl had heard much that remains important to me. Conversations with Mairead Fitzgerald Hockaday, for instance—my mother.

Until I was drafted and dispatched to 'Nam with the rest of the suckers, Mama and I had dinner together at the China Bowl every Sunday night. Sometimes one of the parish priests from Holy Cross would be our guest. In the Eisenhower years, the place was exotic, especially for a harp kid from Hell's Kitchen. The chow mein was glutinous; the crisp, bland noodles were perfect for stuffing into the egg drop soup; everything came sweet-and-sour, and swimming in MSG. Chinese was Chinese, nobody knew from Hunan or Szechuan.

People like us went to the China Bowl because it was cheap but not dirt cheap. As a kid, I liked the way the waiters in their white jackets ran around jabbering like lunatics making a run over the wall. I also liked watching the mysterious, ageless, sloe-eyed hostess with her blue-black hair and her shimmering, high-collared *chongsam*. Mama liked the fringed silk lanterns that kept the place dim. A classy touch.

"What are you thinking about, Irish?" Ruby asked me. She held her arms open, there were tears in her big hazel eyes.

"How I forgot you were so beautiful..." And my God, she was beautiful. Her black hair held in it the evening mist. Her raincoat, belted around her slim waist and draped down to midcalf, was beaded. I pictured Ruby in our bathtub, reading a book. And I kept on babbling, "I'm thinking how dumb I am . . . How I'm so awful sorry about—every-thing..." And how I did not deserve Ruby, which I did not dare to say out loud.

I pulled my bride against me, hard, and the two of us

stood clutched together on West Forty-fourth Street for a long time, rocking gently on our feet, hanging on for dear life as the pick-axes thudded and the dead pots banged. Then Ruby said softly to her big dumb cop husband, "It's all right now, Hock, it's all right . . . all right."

I kissed her a lot of times, and felt her soft body yield to mine. "We have to talk," I said. "About so many important things. Damn me for wasting our time."

"Time we've got, Hock, don't you worry. An ocean of time. Tonight, let's just sleep on it."

So we broke the embrace and headed toward home, holding hands, with thoughts of bed in mind.

Damn me! I could not dispatch other thoughts: the corpse of Frederick Crosby, the loathsome spectacle of King Kong Kowalski, the unaccountably jumpy Jay Schuyler . . . and his excellent Scotch, poured over perfect ice cubes.

I shook my head and tried thinking of something light and sophisticated to say. All my lonesome nights of imagined conversations at home with my wife—those Nick and Nora chats, only bravely minus the martinis—failed me now. I could not remember a single one of those fantasies. And maybe Ruby's lonely dreams failed her, too, for we were as short on small talk as a pair of deaf nuns.

Finally, I thought of telling Ruby about her boss retaining my services as a peep. But before I could say anything, Ruby spoke up herself.

"Hungry?" She made this sound lascivious.

"Only a couple of different ways."

"Well then, you'll need your strength."

"So let's stop by the Mexican joint on Ninth Avenue. Great colors in my dreams when I eat Mexican. We'll get a couple of chimichangas."

"Fine with me. The videos I've got already. One apiece."

"What are we seeing?"

"For you, *They Made Me a Criminal*. That's with your man Garfield. For me it's *Lover Come Back*. Doris Day, Rock Hudson, Tony Randall. Your nice, light comedy romp—about Madison Avenue."

"No sense in getting away from it all."

This bright remark I made as we stood on the east side of Eighth Avenue waiting for traffic to clear. Ruby never heard me, though. She was distracted by the shock of seeing somebody she knew from some respectable place suddenly right there in front of her in this unsavory place.

"Look at her, she's standing around like she's waiting for somebody," Ruby said, pinching my arm. Ruby pointed across the way, in the direction of the Bijou Boy Cinema.

Beneath the peeling marquee stood a tall black woman, impatiently tapping a toe on the sidewalk and looking around through a pair of high-priced sunglasses. She was well groomed and well dressed and had a cultivated look about her, none of which fit the surroundings. Eighth Avenue is as cheap as a toupee with a chin strap. On the marquee above her was a twin bill of features in red block letters, DANNY DOES DENVER and FOAMING FANNIES. The pavement at her feet was gummy with cold spit, spilled beer, and the latex refuse of debauched love. Skels and junkies and beggars and near-naked hookers with sores on their thin legs were either screaming or sleeping in scabby doorways.

"Who is she?"

"My new secretary. At least I think so."

We crossed the avenue and Ruby made sure.

"Sandy . . . ?"

"Oh, my goodness! Miss Flagg!" Sandy removed the shades, hardly necessary in the waning light of a rainy October day. Nervous fingers flew to her slender neck. "I'm meeting somebody . . ."

"Neil," said Ruby, turning to me with question marks playing over her face, "I'd like you to meet Sandy Malreaux." To Sandy, she said, "My husband, Detective Neil Hockaday."

"Everybody calls me Hock," I said, taking Sandy's hand. It was clammy. She withdrew it quickly. "We've met, sort of. Over the telephone."

"Oh, yes . . . Well, really, Detective Hockaday, I've got a perfectly legitimate purpose for being here—"

"He's not on duty," Ruby said, interrupting. Then she laughed, as if she had just made a joke, and this put Sandy at some ease. Ruby told her, "You can't help being on this nasty street any more than we can. We live a couple of blocks away."

"I'm meeting a producer," Sandy said, her voice rushed.

108

The sunglasses went back on. "I'm an actress, you know. Well, no—I guess you wouldn't know that. We haven't had much time to get acquainted. Not today, not with ... what happened."

"The murder," I said.

Sandy clasped her elbows in her hands. "I don't even want to think about it," she said.

"What kind of acting have you done?" Ruby asked her. "I'm in the theater myself."

"In fact, Ruby owns her own playhouse," I said, butting in. "Down on South Street."

"Maybe not for long," Ruby said. "It's a very big money loser and I hate writing grant proposals, so I don't. Not that there's all that much money floating around for Off-Off Broadway houses."

Sandy scanned the Eighth Avenue traffic, both the sidewalk shuffle and the cars and taxis whizzing their way uptown. "Actually, I haven't done much stage work," she said. "This guy I'm meeting, he makes films you never heard of unless you watch cable. It's a start I guess."

"Break a leg," I said.

"Interviewing for a good part?" Ruby asked.

"Yes, I think so. And it's the final step I hope. I went through an audition with the director, then four callbacks. Now this producer's taking me to dinner. So, if I make a good impression tonight ..."

"You're saying maybe I should look for a new secretary?"

Sandy Malreaux sighed the kind of sigh that actresses understand. Her voice went low. "Sister, you were in the business. How many times some man want to take you out to dinner so he can listen to himself tell you how he's going to make you a big star?"

"I had my share of the type," Ruby said.

"You listen to the man, maybe one fine day he's a prince instead of a frog. Meantime, you best hang on to your day job."

"Okay, I won't shop secretaries."

"Thanks."

"Maybe tonight you'll meet a prince."

Sandy looked me over like she was a government meat inspector, then said to Ruby, "I see you surely met yours."

"Hock here's been called a lot of things," Ruby said, taking my arm sharply, as a sign we should be moving along. "Prince isn't one of them."

"Have a real fine evening," Sandy said, waving some fingers at us as we stepped away.

"You, too," Ruby told her. "See you in the morning. I want to hear all about your dinner."

When we turned the corner at Forty-third Street, Ruby asked, "Did something seem odd?"

"Your secretary you mean? What's-a-nice-girl-like-her-doing-in-a-place-like-this?"

"Something like that."

"There's no figuring show business," I said. "It's the story of human nature in comedy and tragedy. So it's only natural, there's no figuring actors."

"Oh?"

"Sure. Who else but an aspiring actress would hang around a grind house on Eighth Avenue waiting to kiss yet another frog?"

"There's another thing. The way she was talking there at the end. *Sister* and *you best . . .*"

"Homegirl talk. She's off duty."

"I wonder what Freddy Crosby sounded like when he was off duty."

Words do not come much more discouraging than those said by a woman to the man lying beside her in bed, "All right, what's the matter now?"

These were Ruby's very own midnight words to me.

What's the matter now? What matters is the weight of time, the fact I am no kid anymore.

Last year I had to buy a pair of bifocals from an optometrist who is younger than me. I needed the specs if I ever wanted to read another book or watch another movie. The year before that, a chiropractor who is younger than me made me a pair of orthotics to slip into my shoes so that walking around on my flat feet will no longer throw my back out. My barber, who is younger than me, says he can no longer find a way to cover up the Friar Tuck bald spot on the back of my head.

This was my flurry of sorrowful thoughts of lost youth as

Ruby popped her horrible question. But then, our homecoming was not entirely a washout.

We ate *las chimichangas* for dinner, we watched the videos, I stayed sober. And finally, we talked.

"Like I said, I'm sorry for all this, Ruby."

"All what?"

"The irony."

"Six weeks in Jersey to think about everything and all you come up with is one word—*irony?* Come on, Irish. I've listened to you talk before. Hours I've listened. You can do better."

"When I was drinking, I'd talk 'til the purple dawn."

"Not exactly. You'd spend the whole night filling your glass to the brim, hoping your troubles would dim. It took a good amount of speaking. But I wouldn't call it talk."

"So this now, what we're doing—this is talk?"

"Ironic, isn't it?"

There are times I think about giving my wife a nickname. The tag "Nails" generally comes to mind. I had not yet actually mentioned this to Nails . . .

"Let me start over."

"Good idea."

"Ruby, I've been a cop for a long time. It's a culture that shuts out everything else."

"If you let it."

"Sometimes it's like I'm living that Peggy Lee song, you know?"

" 'Is That All There Is?' "

"That's it. But when you came along, I suddenly got the idea I should have a personal life. Which, as you know, hasn't been easy."

"I'm worth it. Besides which, you shouldn't think of me or what we have together as a struggle. You have to start enjoying your personal life, and pretty damn soon—before you're too old to find the energy."

Too old . . . What's the matter now?

"Incidentally, dear, you're letting more than cop culture get in your way."

"The drinking. I know, I *know!* I can't spend the rest of my years saying I'm sorry for all I drank."

"When did I ever ask for an apology?"

"Okay, you never did."

"Listen to me good and close now, Detective Hockaday. Life heaves crap all over you. There's no sense in your adding to the stinking mess."

"You sweet-talker, you."

"And by the way, it's also more than boozing that's holding you down."

"From what?"

"Deciding what it means to be a good husband to me and a good cop for the city. And what it means to be a man—a different man from Aidan Hockaday."

My father, God rest. *Daddo . . . Daddo!*

"You think a little vacation at the Straight and Narrow wins you power over yourself—or marrying me?" Ruby paused to draw some breath. "You think that does it for you? Think again."

"What? I don't know—"

"Sure you do, Hock. You know exactly what you have to do. You can't fool yourself with the booze anymore, or with fool talk from your old drinking buddies. And you certainly can't fool me."

"Yes, Nails dear."

"What—?"

For dessert, in a manner of speaking, there was Ruby in satin. Twice. This is not so bad for a man somewhere in the middle of his age. I thought about saying this to Ruby now, by way of an answer to her horrible question. But all that came out of my mouth was an extension of discouraging pillow talk.

"What do you mean, what's the matter?"

Ruby lifted her smooth, warm thigh off mine. "You're gone away someplace, you haven't heard a dirty word I've said." Her voice was low, her breath sweet. I could almost see her in the darkness of the bedroom, almond skin against the white sheets. "Your first night home to your loving wife, and you're obsessed with this Crosby case."

"Come on, I'm—"

"Don't deny it. Just tell me, why can't you ever go off the clock? Let crime take a holiday?"

"It's lonesome off the clock."

"Which is what you are officially, I might point out."

"But that's no good for me, Ruby. There's an old Irish saying—"

"Isn't there always?"

"Contention is better than loneliness."

"Let me try another question. How do you expect to work a homicide case when you've been ordered onto furlough?"

"What do you know about my furlough? You've been talking around about me."

"I had six weeks to kill."

"So you had some lovely chats with Neglio?"

"And with Davy Mogaill. And with Father Sheehan. And Angelo, too. What of it?"

Nothing, I thought. *Angelo? My own favorite bartender?* Six weeks ago, the last time Ruby had seen me up to this night, I was a slobbering drunk. I should expect somehow that all is forgiven and forgotten?

"Skip it," I said.

"All right. But you didn't answer me."

"I got a job today," I said. "I'm a consultant."

"Who consults you?"

"I had a lovely chat of my own. With Jay Schuyler. He hired me to nose around the messy circumstances of one of his partners dying of unnatural causes."

"He did?"

"That's right. I'll be moonlighting for a while. As a peep— in association with Davy Mogaill, duly licensed by the state and city of New York to conduct private investigations."

"Damn him!"

"Please, we're colleagues."

"I knew you couldn't stay away from this."

"Neither can Davy. So don't be complaining about him. This case is more than Crosby."

"What are you talking about?"

"Kowalski from Sex Crimes for one thing."

"The one who spoke with Jay on the phone?"

"King Kong Kowalski they call him."

"You'll have to tell me all about it. But if you don't mind, not tonight. Tell me how it went with Jay instead."

"You talked to him about me, too."

"Not really."

"Then how did he know I'm a drunk?"

"He did?" Ruby propped herself up with her arms. "You're a recovering alcoholic, not a drunk."

"Whatever. So you never told him?"

"No. Jay makes it his business to know things about people."

"Why me?"

"He wanted me on this casino account with some Russians. So I suppose he asked around about my circumstances, of which you're one. Jay does his homework."

"I wonder why." I thought for a moment about another nosy tycoon, a character down in Texas with big ears and a billion dollars and an army of snoops on his payroll. "Anyway, what's this about Russians?"

"Alexis and Vasily Likhanov, the new Moscow elite. They're twins. They look like the metal shop teacher from everybody's high school."

"They've got a casino?"

"Big plans so far as I know. Bigger than big." Ruby snorted. "Picture this: Six Flags Adventure Park, Las Vegas, and Disney World—rolled up into one big, tacky package. Now move it all to Mother Russia."

"Maybe in Russia these days it makes sense."

"As much as anything."

"You had lunch today with a Margot Schuyler. That would be the boss's wife?"

"It would."

"How did that go?"

"It was strange," Ruby said, sighing. "And why not? Everything's been strange today."

Ruby was then very forthcoming in telling me about her uneasy relationship with Margot Schuyler and how Jay Schuyler was the reason for it. She also told me what she had learned from Margot at lunch: about Crosby's involvement with the so-called Boys Club at the Metropolitan Opera—and about Norman Applebaum, the house manager.

Then she fell asleep.

I lay awake, letting all these tumultuous events of my first day back home swim through my brain. Ordinarily, a little Scotch would be swimming along with the pictures. I started getting thirsty.

I rose from the bed, crept into the parlor and sat down by the telephone just like they had taught me to do at the Straight and Narrow. I was three digits into Davy Mogaill's number when I changed my mind, hung up, and dialed the Sixth Precinct instead.

"Detective Neil Hockaday, SCUM patrol," I said to a desk sergeant named Schneider. "I want to know if Officer Lenihan happens to be on your overnight muster."

The sergeant laughed when I said Lenihan.

"You think Irish names are funny?"

"Bill Lenihan's a funny Irishman, that's all I think."

"I'll bet it is."

"What's that supposed to mean?"

"Nothing. Lenihan on the muster now?"

"No, he's down for the afternoon sheet, all month."

"Where's your nineteenth hole these days?"

"Joint up in the Tenth Precinct called Buster's."

"I know the place. Thanks." I hung up.

My next call was to Buster's bar on West Thirty-first Street, back behind the Morgan station postal freight office. My luck was good, and Lenihan was winding down there with some of the others from his shift.

"Detective Neil Hockaday," I said when he took the phone from the bartender. "I'm a friend of Davy Mogaill."

"What can I do for you, Detective?"

"Stay right there. I need to talk to you."

"About what?"

"The demonstration outside the Sixth the other day, with the pansies and all ... King Kong Kowalski ..."

"I'll be waiting."

Quietly as I could, I went back to the bedroom and rounded up sneakers, chinos, a shirt and sweater. Back out in the parlor, I wrote down in my casebook what Ruby had told me before I forgot it. Also I read Slattery's piece in the *Post* again, and made a couple of more entries into the casebook. I tore out a clean page and left a note for Ruby in the event she woke up before I returned.

Wind rattled the parlor window, so I took along a corduroy coat as I left. I flagged down a taxi crossing West Forty-second Street.

The hour was a tiny one. And I was on my way to a cop bar. Just like the bad old days.

But now, with the sudden vision of Bradford Jason Schuyler puking up booze into his hands, I was very unthirsty.

And when she woke to find me gone, I hoped that Ruby would understand that I was out doing exactly what I knew I had to do.

ᜥ 10 ᜥ

WHAT MAKES BUSTER'S POPULAR WITH MIDDLE-AGED, wound-licking cops such as myself is the soothing imbalance of time in the place. This is every bit as palpable as the yeasty aroma of whiskey and beer and the clouds of tobacco smoke. Thus in the warmth of Buster's, fond remembrances of the past will rise to the mind, overlapping a frequently despairing present.

The music comes by way of WQEW-AM radio, which plays American standards. The framed snapshot of some-body's long-deceased mutt dog named Buster is the lone wall adornment. There are no waitresses, pretty or other-wise. There is nothing in the place to say that the night belongs to the present any more than it does to the past. Buster's offers reliable delivery on a subtle promise: time frozen in the year of one's choice.

My own frozen choice is typical of the clientele. I conjure up some year of my past when life was free of ridicule, depravity, and pity. Sure, sure—that would be the year that never was. No matter, there are nights when a cop is very tired to the bone, when fictive memory is a fine balm for the awful sight of truth. Maybe I had seen too much cop truth in my time. Like the truth of poor Crosby.

... Or was it some kind of terrible fear I was mixing up

with truth? And what was it the Irish nuns of my youth called such a confusion? *Peaca súil*—sins of the eyes ...

Buster's occupies a street-level niche in a squatty brick warehouse with a lot of broken windows on a needle-and-condom-strewn back street off Eleventh Avenue. There are no working street lamps at this nether end of Hell's Kitchen. One naked, hundred-watt lightbulb hanging over the corrugated steel door to Buster's is the only sign of life after dark, save for slumbering junkies here and there on the street, and hookers of indeterminate sex.

A few years ago, somebody opened a nightclub on the block. This was one of those clubs where beautiful people crowd up on line behind velvet ropes in hopes of getting inside in order to damage their hearing from the music, sniff cocaine in toilet stalls, and swap business cards. The place went under in about two weeks flat when the cops from Buster's kept coming over to make dope collars among these new undesirables. The pross and the street junkies they left alone, of course, since this old bunch knew how to keep themselves peaceable and quiet. Besides which, the pross and junkies were not car owners competing for the good parking spaces.

It had been a while since I was last in the place. Six weeks since I had last been in any bar. And now, in the small hours of a black morning, I walked through the homely steel door into Buster's.

Working the bar was a barrel-chested guy with a dented face and a red pompadour by the name of Ken Bauman. He used to be a professional wrestler in the fifties, when he went by the ring name Kenny the Crusher. It somehow made sense that Gogi Grant was singing a fifties tune called "The Wayward Wind" from inside the battered, pine-cased radio that sat on the ledge of the only window in the house, shrouded in a tangle of venetian blinds that had not opened in anybody's recent memory. The place smelled like it always smelled, a mix of booze, Pine Sol, and cigarettes.

I found a place to stand at the bar, near the cash register. Bauman came over to say, "Long time no see, Hock. What'll it be?"

"You know of a cop here called Lenihan?"

A cop in chinos and a sweater like my own looked up

when I said this name. I had never seen him before, not at Buster's or any other cop bar in Manhattan. He had been debating the merits of various beer brands with another cop; in other words, forgetting all about the department and the street for a few blessed hours. So I naturally figured he belonged.

But now he started smirking like some teenage mall brat, reminding me of my irritation with Blue Suit and Brown Suit from the Suburban Occupation Force. I looked at Bauman, and it was clear by the reaction on his face that he did not care for this one any more than I did. I looked over at the smirker again and asked myself, Did this guy ever bounce a spaldeen against a tenement stoop in the good old New York summertime? And if Buster's bar now now serves cops who do not know from spaldeens, I had to further ask myself, What is the world of my city coming to?

"Who the hell are you, pal, one of Three Dollar Bill's little friends?" This the smirker asked me. The cop next to him finished off a beer, dipped his nose into the glass, and belched. Then the mouthy one flicked his fingers at me, and added, "Looking for a little pixie dust?"

Kenny the Crusher grabbed the mouth's arm with one of his burly claws, in much the same way as a two-ton wrecking ball goes at the side of a vacant building. Everybody was getting a load of us by this time. Kenny growled softly at my detractor, "Shut up that canned ham you call a face."

I said to Bauman, loud enough so the mouth could be aggravated by what he heard, "Why, I could just kiss you."

Not altogether repentant, despite the red bruises rising on his arm, the mouth hissed at me, "Faggot!"

And now, for the benefit of a house I knew was disposed to laugh off the likes of this one, I said, "Don't get your panties in a bunch, Officer."

The tactic had the desired effect. The mouth was shot down by a chorus of hoots. Even the belcher slapped his back, and said to him, "Oh Gawd, that was rich!"

I was having a good laugh myself until somebody clamped a hand around the nape of my neck and yanked me away from the bar. This is practically the first maneuver they teach at Police Academy. Nothing persuades a man to back off a heated situation in a big hurry so much as a cop's knowing fingers dug firmly into the cords of his neck. I have seen lady cops little more than a hundred pounds practically lift a man off his feet this way.

"Let's just step away, nice and friendly," my persuader said from behind. There was no excitement in his voice and he had me well hooked. So instead of arguing, I walked backward as he dragged me away from the bar. We stopped when we reached a booth along the far wall. Turning me around and releasing my aching neck ever so slowly, he asked, "Everything all right now?"

I faced a man almost a head shorter than me and maybe ten years my junior. He had short, dark blond hair and a matching mustache, and looked like he spent regular time in a gym, which I myself do not. He smiled, and said, "I'm Patrolman Lenihan. You would be Detective Hockaday?" I shook his hand and we sat down together in the booth.

"Lenihan," I said, rubbing my sore neck, "you're very good with the basic come-along."

"Sorry if I hurt you, but I didn't want the situation to get any worse. I went by the book, figuring you were the one I should pull out of the fracas."

"For once the book's right. You don't want to isolate the hothead if you see a chance the crowd might cool him down for you, so you grab the other guy. That jerk, who was he anyhow?"

"His name's Porter. He's been coming in here a lot lately."

"How lately?"

"Couple of weeks, I guess. He's a transfer from Queens, I don't know where. You see for yourself I'm not his type, so we never talked."

"He's got a bad attitude to be working the Sixth."

"Porter's not with the precinct. He's at Sex Crimes."

"One of Kowalski's lovelies. I see."

"Do you?"

Bauman walked up to our booth with a tray. He put down a long-necked bottle of Rolling Rock with a glass for Lenihan, and a lowball of Scotch on the rocks for me. "Johnnie Walker red. Right, Hock?"

Before I could say anything, Lenihan asked, "What's all this, Kenny?"

To which I added, "Never in my life did I ever think I'd see table service at Buster's."

"You guys can use a belt," Bauman said. "It ain't on the house. This is Porter's treat, which I informed him while I was taking from his dough laid out on the bar. That was just before I informed him that he was eighty-sixed the hell out of here."

"Thanks, but no," I said. I picked up the Scotch and put it back on Bauman's tray. It was easier than I thought it would be.

"Come on, Hock. Porter's a kookamunga, so who cares? I seen you take free drinks from lots worse."

"You didn't get the word yet. I'm not drinking anymore."

"You? What's the joke?"

"No kidding, Kenny. I had to join the choir."

"With the first-names-only and all that crapola?"

"The whole megillah."

"You want I should bring a seltzer?"

"No, but do me a favor."

"Whatever."

"Don't feel sorry for me."

Kenny the Crusher shrugged and ambled back to the bar. He seemed a little dazed, like a referee just gave him a three-count after a flying scissors hold and then a double-crab armlock came at him out of nowhere.

"Funny, it's easier for a pissbum," Lenihan said, sipping his beer.

"Easier than what?"

"It takes something for a cop to admit he's a drunk. It takes a whole lot more to admit he's queer."

"That's what you go around calling yourself?"

"It cuts to the chase. Let's us do the same, Detective. As a queer cop, how can I help you?"

"There's a very bad homicide in the Nineteenth that I'm working. I'll tell you right off, it's not for the department. I'm on furlough, working a private investigation, along with our mutual friend Davy Mogaill."

"Why not stay the hell off duty?"

"That's what my wife wants to know. Anyhow, about this uptown murder. King Kong Kowalski's taking a special interest."

"Kowalski doesn't work field."

"Makes you wonder, doesn't it?"

"This homicide. Would it be that closet queen somebody whacked out by nailing him down on the floor? Big advertising exec?"

"Frederick Crosby, that's right. His agency hired us. Know anything about him?"

"Only what I heard on the TV news. What's Kowalski's angle?"

"That I don't know, yet. But here's how it plays. Crosby gets the business, and right away a couple of PDU suits up in the one-nine who just so happened to have worked in Sex Crimes once upon a time ring up Kowalski. Then Kowalski comes running up to the scene while he's off the clock. I've got reason to believe that one night shortly before he died, Crosby got the famous dickprint routine from Kowalski."

"What's your reason?"

"I had a word with the PDU suits, a couple of suburban dorks like Porter. You know about Kowalski and his dickprints?"

"The legend's familiar."

"Kowalski might have done his number on Crosby right around the time of these deaths down around West Street."

"The ones the Sixth Precinct are officially calling suicides?"

"Right. Which got the activists out the other day throwing the Kleenex pansies at you."

"I read Kowalski's choice comments in the paper."

In my coat pocket were bifocals and Slattery's piece from the *Post*. I pulled them both out, put on the specs, and spread out the article on the table between us.

Lenihan thumped the last paragraph in the story, Kowalski's printed remarks, and asked, "You got an opinion on this?"

"The usual low one of people who claim God's on their side," I said. Lenihan was gauging me, which I could appreciate. It helps a cop to know if another cop is simpatico. I decided to let him know I was. "Kowalski puts me in mind of the boyos screaming about gays in the Saint Paddy's parade."

"How so?"

"Maybe real Irishmen shouldn't be wasting time yelling about fags on Fifth Avenue. Maybe they should be fighting the Brits in Ulster."

A smile crawled over Lenihan's face as he said, "Now these big brave ones, they're screaming about queers in the military. As usual, they've got it backward."

"Backward?"

"They shouldn't ban homosexuals from the service, they should ban *hetero*sexuals. Nobody of either persuasion would have to worry about taking showers anymore. And if America went to war, we'd be protected by the most powerful force on earth—an army of enraged queens."

"You should write the president."

"I have. He hasn't written back."

"Meanwhile, maybe you can help me out."

"Maybe." Lenihan sipped his beer. "Let me understand something. You're saying this wormy stuff connects? The uptown murder, queers down in the Village supposedly canceling themselves out—and King Kong Kowalski?"

"I'm saying it all makes me wonder."

"About what?"

"Read this part," I said, my hand now on the newspaper article. "The part where a guy called Sly is quoted. He cuts to the chase, like you."

Lenihan read aloud, " 'I don't know how many times we've had these gangs of suburban punks drive in to jump queers and beat them . . . The cops have a way of not taking these cases seriously. Their attitude is, murdering queers can be ignored, beating queers can be ignored. Well, let me tell you something about us queers—we may be many things, but we ain't going to be ignored! Tell you something else— this crime wave, it's going to spread uptown, baby. Way uptown!' "

"So what do you think?" I asked.

"You're asking me as a queer?"

"Who happens to be a cop. Give me a break here, Lenihan. Yes—I'm asking."

"Straight or bent, it's no secret to any cop in the city that when some queer dies—especially some lowlife you find on West Street—it's nothing but a nine-to-five job."

"If you can blow it off as suicide, all the better."

"That's right. The department's full of Kowalskis and Porters. At least they've got the decency to wear their phobias out where you can see them. There's a lot more hiding their hatred. I'm not telling you anything you don't already know."

"You know this guy Sly?"

"I know of him."

"He makes some very serious implications."

"Such as suburban punks driving into the Village to beat up queers? Serious, but no surprise. A queer murder spree spreading uptown? You might be reading too much into coincidence."

"Maybe. Tell me about Sly."

"He's the type of queer who makes my type embarrassed."

"Your type?"

"I'm with the so-to-speak silent majority. We don't think there's much mystery to the gay life. It's a fact of nature, period. Like a fine spring rain, only less fearsome."

"And Sly's type?"

"Noisy, self-indulgent, makes every decision based on his sexual urges. You see him around in some of the clubs."

"What about this club called the Ladies Auxiliary?"

"I hear it's practically his headquarters these days. He likes hanging with the drag queens. Not my scene, but I've been there for laughs."

"Laughs. That sounds nice."

"What are you saying, you want a date?"

"As a cop, yes."

Lenihan was only marginally more comfortable in the place than I was. He kept looking at his watch, and then the front door, then back at his watch again. "I'll stick with you until Sly comes around, then I'm out of here," he said more than once.

The room was dim and airless, heavy with the aroma of hair spray and perfume and cigarettes. The walls were plastered with thousands of fashion pages torn from glossy women's magazines, the fantasy images of supple young models with perfect hair and blazing white teeth and pouty red lips.

Down the middle of the room were tables reserved for what Lenihan called the dress-up crowd, and a little dance floor off to the side. The tables all had soft pink lights on top, and the chairs were mostly turned toward a grand piano and a small runway stage down at the end. According to Lenihan, the ones seated here were a very mixed bunch: femmes, butches, even a few genuine women.

"Fruit flies, that's what they call actual females who show up in a place like this," Lenihan said, explaining the finer points of the Ladies Auxiliary. He nodded in the direction of a customer seated at a table, a femme in a platinum wig and Cleopatra eyes and four inches of Barbara Bush pearl strands. She looked like a cross between Tina Turner and Margaret Thatcher. "Now that one over there, she's what you call an ultra-real."

Huddled around a side bar were young drag queens of every size, shape, and style. "Over there's what we call the real girls," Lenihan said. "Sugar and spice and everything nice."

We watched the real girls trying to drum up commerce with the stand-up crowd of average-looking guys in dreary business suits. Lenihan and I were the two average-looking guys in chinos and jackets, standing at the end of the bar with no-sale written all over our Irish pugs. Appearance was everything here. A hundred pairs of mascara-caked eyes knew us in an instant as voyeurs—maybe cops even—and we were left alone.

Lenihan ordered a beer when the bartender finally paid attention to us. I asked for a Seven-Up with plenty of ice and had to pay five bucks for the thrill of it.

Try as I might, and notwithstanding the memory of scolding nuns, I could not take my eyes off the real girls flocked around us. Lenihan saw very well how I was gawking, despite my discomfort.

"What do you make of the show?" he asked.

"Strange. And sad, I think." My answer was honest, reflecting my immediate impressions.

"I agree. Does that surprise you?"

"I don't know."

"All the young, strange creatures . . ." Lenihan paused, and looked around at the girls. He shook his head sympathetically. "Their lives are dedicated to the pursuit of a certain kind of beauty. Butcher beauty. Beauty that comes with hormone injections, breast implants, electrolysis, and tracheal surgery."

A tall Latina in a slinky green dress chatted up a bald-headed accountant with a wedding ring on his finger and pens in his shirt pocket. A blonde beauty in a black body stocking reached inside a salesman's suitcoat, stroked his tie and his flabby chest with her red Press-On nails. A ginger-haired girl in a long, shimmery dress cut open in the back to reveal her thong-riven cheeks slipped a delicate knee between the pinstriped legs of a stockbroker.

I stared and stared until I finally understood the root of my fascination: the shock of recognition. What I saw all around me were my adolescent fantasies, never quite forgotten and previously available only in fevered dreams.

Now I wanted a real drink. I closed my eyes and thought about nuns.

When I opened up, it was not a nun that I saw standing in front of me. It was instead a three-hundred-pounder in a foot-length magenta gown with rhinestone spaghetti straps and a beehive the size of a bread box. She was shimmying up to Lenihan, who she seemed to know. "Billy, dear?" she asked. "Can it be?"

"Irma!" Lenihan said. "How's tricks?"

She took Lenihan's shoulders, pulled him close, and air-kissed him. He planted genuine smacks on both her chalk white cheeks.

"Oh, Billy," she said, patting down her powdery face, "tricks are for kids. I'm too old and gray under all these feathers to be wicked anymore."

Lenihan turned, rolled his eyes, and made the introductions. "Detective Hockaday, the incomparable Big Irma. She owns the place."

"Enchanted," Irma said, extending a hand encased in a lace and rhinestone glove. "Do tell me, are you boys here professionally or are you just relaxing?"

"Has Sly been around tonight?" Lenihan asked.

"He's very late, but I do expect to see him by and by," Irma answered. Then to me, "A few detectives came around during our recent misfortunes. You weren't one of them. I would have remembered you."

"Misfortunes," Lenihan said to me, "as in the so-called suicides."

I told Irma I was new on the case.

"Well, well. Is that what the department's calling it these days? We're an actual *case?*"

"Not yet, and maybe never," Lenihan told her. "My friend Hockaday's working this freelance while he's on a furlough. He's investigating that murder uptown, the advertising big shot who dressed up in secret."

"Oh!" Irma fluttered some fingers in front of her face.

"Detective Hockaday seems to think there might be some connections to what's been happening down here."

"Is that so?" Irma scratched seductively between her shaved male bosoms. She asked me, "What's that in your hand?"

"Soda."

"May I buy you a real drink, dear Detective Hockaday?"

"I'd like that, but I'll pass."

"Why—the very words we're all using in these days of the almighty shadow. AIDS, don't you know, it's making us all pass." Irma sighed and arched an enormous eyebrow, in deference to plague. "Even I have to worry. I've had such a torrid past. All I am now's a VCR queen, if you know what I'm saying."

"You don't have to give the VCR any breakfast," I said. Irma's laughter was not the delicate tinkling kind. She sounded like a longshoreman. When she was through laughing, I asked, "So what's with all the high-risk trade I see going on around your very own bar?"

"My dear man, these children must still turn tricks. Or starve. You see how life goes on? Even under the almighty shadow?"

"I see."

"You and me, we're lucky. We came up in the days when schools still educated and factories still hired. But you know it's a new world, honey. And not a very brave one when it comes to minding anybody's children."

"So I've noticed."

"The oldest profession is still the easiest, even though some say it's a one-way street leading to a bad end."

"You could say that about a lot of the polite careers."

Irma turned to Lenihan, winked at him, and said, "I surely do like your friend, Billy. I've got a feeling he will see us through our troubled waters." Irma turned back to me to say, "These are frightful times, you know."

"Aren't they all."

"I'm trying to hang on, I really am. But it's damnably discouraging. The hate these days! It's like oxygen to some people. Sometimes I want to just run away from it all, buy myself a one-way ticket to Miami Beach and live out my days in the sunshine. With air-conditioning and bonbons, of course. I'm no fool." Big Irma cracked her knuckles and looked wistfully around the bar at all the busy young things nuzzling the suits for drinkies. "But then, what would I do about the children? They're beautiful in their way. Don't you think so, Detective Hockaday?"

"In their way."

"They've nowhere to go, not even home. Their mamas and papas disowned them because of what God made them. Now, wouldn't you say that's a sin?"

"I'm a cop. Not a priest."

"Either way, sin's your bread and butter, isn't it? So you should answer the question."

"I don't think it's a sin to be born," I said. "I've noticed the world pretty much disagrees with me."

"They don't eat right, these poor beautiful children. They all sleep on the piers, one time or another. I can't bear it sometimes." Big Irma paused for a look at the real girls. She quickly turned back to me. "Like I say, sometimes I want to run away. But I can't. Somebody has to watch the children in these awful times. Somebody has to give them dreams before they die. Do you believe in dreams, Detective Hockaday?"

"Only that everything's made from dreams," I said. "And nightmares."

"Irma, you're a regular institution," Lenihan said. His tone was not sarcastic, but there was a tiredness to it, as if he had talked of sad conundrums too many times.

"An institution! I do believe I am. Let me tell you why that is. You should understand, Billy. And even though your friend is straight as a string, which I am most truly sorry to observe, I believe he'll see it, too ..." Irma searched my face. Maybe she expected a smirk.

"Tell us," I said.

"Big Irma has tended a little patch of humanity living behind

God's back," she said, flicking a tear from her eye with a meaty finger. She took a deep breath. "Right here in this unlikely place, I have preserved a little beauty, however perverse or fanciful it may seem. Above all, I have helped these poor children in a victory of imagination over poverty."

Big Irma's head dropped. She pulled a handkerchief from the sleeve of her gown and used it to wipe her face and blow her nose. I put a hand on her soft shoulder and felt sorrow deep in her skin.

"Forgive me," she said. She composed herself, and looked up. "Why, sir, just look how you've got me positively carried away. Is my face presentable?"

"You look peachy," I said.

"Praise the Lord." She tossed back her head. "Stick around for the floor show and see all my beautiful children. I do a little patter up at the piano first." Irma turned, girlishly, heading up toward the stage. *"Ciao-ciao,"* she said, waving at Lenihan and me.

She snaked her way through the tables, saying hello here and there. She was remarkably agile for her size. Customers would reach out to touch her in greeting; to love her, for she was an institution and beautiful in her way. Dancers released each other when the taped music was shut down, and everybody took their seats for Irma's show.

A blue light spotted her as she neared the piano. She sat down and ran through two minutes of a fierce boogie-woogie to work up the crowd. Then she stopped abruptly, and picked up the microphone clamped to the piano.

"A little song . . . a little dance . . ."

The crowd joined in on the last line of this signature opening of the late floor show at the Ladies Auxiliary. A hundred voices said as one:

". . . a little seltzer down the pants!"

When the crowd settled, she continued.

"Before we bring out the girls, boys and girls, Big Irma's got a little story for you. My dears—you do want to hear my story, don't you?"

Irma cupped a hand to her ear and cocked her bewigged head. The crowd stamped their feet, roared yes.

"Well then, goody. It seems that one day Sherlock Holmes and Dr. Watson entertained a most perplexing case.

It began with a strong suspicion that the friendship developed during all their years together might have grown to something more! And so, the two lifelong bachelors went to a fine French restaurant that very night to discuss the matter. It was a very good dinner they had, with all the proper wines, although they skipped dessert, for Mrs. Hudson, their faithful housekeeper, had left a fresh-baked lemon pie in the parlor for their return. And return they did, hurrying home to Baker Street in a most jolly and romantic mood. The two of them walked into Holmes's bedchamber, hand in hand. Dr. Watson stripped off his clothes and leaped upon Holmes's bed, assuming the position. Holmes excused himself for a moment, and left the room. When he returned, he carried with him the lemon pie dessert. Holmes walked toward the bed and then, standing a few paces behind the uplifted rear end of Dr. Watson, hurled the lemon pie at him. The pie reached the bull's-eye of Holmes's target, splattering all over Watson's great pink posterior. Watson, stunned, asked, 'Holmes, old boy, why on earth did you smash Mrs. Hudson's lemon pie against my arse?' Said Holmes, 'Lemon entry, my dear Watson—lemon entry.' "

There were groans here and there in the crowd, but mostly high-pitched laughter. Big Irma picked up a glass from the piano and drank, winking at friends in the audience and waiting for quiet to return.

Lenihan touched my arm. "Look at the guy who just walked in," he said. "That's your man."

"Sly?"

I watched as a tall, sallow-faced man about forty years old strode in through the door. He was wearing jeans, a khaki bush jacket, and a red bandana on his head. He stopped at the opposite end of the bar and scanned the tables full of drinking and laughter. He was looking for someone he knew.

A waving hand shot up from the crowd. It was clear up front, belonging to somebody with a glittering ring and a ball of yellow hair. Sly waved back, then started through the pack of tables.

"Okay," Lenihan said, moving away from the bar. "I brought you this far on your maiden voyage. Think you'll be all right now?"

"Sure. Take off if you want."

"Easy does it, Detective." Lenihan looked at my half-gone glass of Seven-Up. I rattled the ice cubes. "If you catch my drift."

"Like a tidal wave. Go home, sleep tight and don't worry about me."

"My regards to Mogaill. Nighty-night."

Lenihan was out the door when the crowd quieted. I turned around and stole a look at all the pretty bottles lined up against the back of the bar, searching for my old friends Johnnie.

There they were. One labeled in black, the other in red. Now all the sounds of the room went away for a while, save for the clink of ice against glass. For one whirling moment, the whole world had no sharp edges and the only color was amber. I felt as if I were falling, falling. And the sounds of the people were miles away . . .

Big Irma breathed heavily into her microphone, then boomed, "All right now, boys and girls! Pay attention, pay attention!"

The bartender asked me, "What'll it be?"

All I could say was, "Troubled waters."

I turned my back to the bar, closed my eyes and thought this time of Ruby. I hoped she was sleeping still. I wanted to be home, even more than I wanted a drink. Again, I heard Nails tell me, *You know exactly what you have to do. You can't fool yourself with the booze anymore, or with fool talk from your old drinking buddies. And you certainly can't fool me.*

I opened my eyes. I looked through the crowd for the yellow ball of hair up front, and the red bandana that would be sitting beside it.

Up on the runway stage was a trio of Irma's children striking poses, as if they were in a fashion show at Saks. A saucy-looking Latina with spit curls wore a lacy wedding gown and threw petals to the crowd from her bridal nosegay; a curvaceous black diva in a white body stocking, white patent-leather boots, and a flouncy jacket pranced around to the beat of whatever she was listening to on her Walkman radio; a young Liz Taylor type, in a sleeveless dress with a waistband and full skirt in a shade of royal blue, combed her black hair into a long bun.

I spotted the yellow hair and the red bandana.

And heard the shot.

~ 11 ~

FOURTH OF JULY FIRECRACKERS. THE THWACK OF HORSEHIDE at Yankee Stadium on a muggy August afternoon. Satchmo's singing. Brace Beemer in black mask and pearl-handled six-guns, calling from high atop his raring palomino, "Hi-yo, Silver—away!"

We know these sounds so very well. They are as American as apple pie. We pause when we hear them, comforted by their meaning: continuum through all the other things we hear, for better or worse.

There is another sound that gives pause. And this is often the softest of all apple pie sounds. An irony, for it is this sound that steals away our comforts: a bullet fired somewhere in the predawn of an American city.

At half-past two in the morning at the Ladies Auxiliary came such a soft, popping sound. In the midst of Big Irma's longshoreman laughter—and the bumping chairs and tables and the catcalls and boozy cheers from a roomful of drag queens out for a good time—all stopped as they heard the sound, all knowing what it was.

The room and everything in it was motionless for one terrible, communal instant in time. As if everybody was holding still for a group photograph.

My cop training instructs me to know and value this instant, to make use of it; to watch for the casual toss-down

132

of a murder weapon, to keep my head while all about me are losing theirs, to watch the exits. But none of these lessons seemed to apply in a place as alien to my experience as the Ladies Auxiliary.

On monkey island at the Bronx Zoo at feeding time I have heard less shrieking than I now heard in this crowd gone berserk with fear. At basement cockfights in East Harlem tenements there is less clawing and hissing and pummeling than that which I now fought on my way to the front of the room.

Minutes passed before I was able to break through the screaming stampede, from the bar to the ringside table where the shot had been fired. With each minute, there fell another heavy curtain between the fleeing assailant and me.

There was a calm around Sly's body, a circle of space respected by panic. He lay on his back on the tiled floor, untrampled. Nearby were an overturned table and two chairs. Sly's arms and legs flopped in violent spasms. His eyes were wide, he had been taken by surprise; his mouth was open, as if he were trying to make sounds. A crumpled, taxi yellow fright wig covered his chest, soaked with blood as red as the bandana the shooter had worn.

I straddled Sly's body, lowering myself over him, using my haunches to still his flailing legs and my hands to steady the twisting arms. Sly would need all available energy if he was to live.

"Oh my God! Jesus, Mary and Joseph! Oh, my dear God in heaven ...!"

I recognized Big Irma's voice.

Turning from my struggle with Sly's spastic limbs, I looked up at her. She held her big head with both hands, shouting her prayer to the ceiling, "Dear God, dear God, dear God ...!"

I pleaded not to God, but to Irma, "Help me!"

It was as if I had slapped her. Big Irma stopped her useless prayer, and said flatly, "Tell me what to do."

"Get someone to call up 911. You stay here with me. Be sure to have the caller say the words *officer in trouble*. Then ask for a *mobile emergency unit*. Those words exactly. Understand?"

Irma nodded yes. She glanced around at the scattering crowd. She reached out, grabbed a muscular butch queen, barked orders at him. "There's a phone just backstage. Understand?" He leaped up onto the stage, and disappeared.

"What now?" Irma asked.

"Get down here with me."

Irma moved next to me, then her huge body folded until she was kneeling on one knee. I asked her, "Would you have a kerchief or something?" She pulled a yard of lavender from her sleeve. "Good," I said, and then gave her orders. "Tear it in half, put one piece over my face, like a mask. Don't cover my eyes . . . tie it up in back so it stays put."

Then when Irma had the mask in place, I said, "I need your hand now. But first, cover it with the other half of the kerchief. Be careful you don't get any fluids on your exposed skin, all right? Now I want you to pull open his lips, use your fingers to clear out any blood in his mouth and nostrils."

"My God . . . !"

"Do it!"

Irma did it. She looked away as she worked her covered fingers between Sly's whitening lips, scooping out blood. Then the same with his nostrils. As she worked, I spotted the bullet wound. The assailant had jammed a gun up under Sly's jaw, firing straight upward. I could not see an exit wound anywhere. I managed to touch his wrist, and felt a weak pulse.

"All right," I said when Irma had done all she could. "Put your hand in back of his neck, cradle his head. Hold him steady. I'm going to give him mouth-to-mouth."

"But . . . !" Irma began weeping. Her tears fell on Sly's stony, terrified face. "Aren't you afraid . . . of the almighty shadow?"

I was. I said only, "The wig's in my way. Be careful of the blood."

Irma plucked the wig off Sly's chest. There was a small knife underneath, plunged into Sly's breast, just over his heart. A sheet of paper was impaled by the blade.

"Don't touch the knife," I said to Irma.

"No problem . . ."

I stretched forward over Sly's jerking body. I put my face to his. "Steady!" I said to Irma as I covered his lips with my mask.

I puffed twice into his mouth, paused and puffed again. I felt only dead heat and hollowness. I repeated the process. Nothing. I tried again.

Someone behind me shouted, "I got through, I got through . . . !"

Irma could see how I could not turn from what I was doing. She knew what I needed to hear. "He called 911, the cops are on their way," she said.

Time and sound were now irrelevant, as were the odds of Sly's life. I did what a cop has to do. Furloughed or not, I puffed . . . and puffed.

Mercifully, my mind wandered during the awful mechanics. I thought about Ruby and how beautiful she was, and if she would forgive my leaving our bed this first night back together again; I thought about Davy Mogaill, and what he would have to say when I told him all that had happened since we talked in the lobby bar of the Harmony Arms; I thought about Scotch pouring over shaved ice and lemon twists; I thought about God, and decided He had a wicked streak.

I had no idea of how or when I came to be removed from my cop duty. Or how I came to rest on a purple brocade divan in a small back room of the Ladies Auxiliary, my forehead swathed in a cold, wet rag and Big Irma sitting next to me with a basin of soap and water in her lap, sponging blood off my face and hands.

And King Kong Kowalski looming over me with a cigar between his grinning lips.

"Swell freaking place you picked out to celebrate," Kowalski said, shaking his head. He was still on duty and dressed in his sergeant's uniform. His shirt was unbuttoned at the top due to the fatness of his neck, his food-stained tie was a limp and sloppy mess. "First night home from the Straight and Narrow and this here's the company you keep. I'm starting to wonder about you, Hockaday."

"On Sunday you can say a prayer for me, Kowalski. Right now, just give me the facts."

"There's one less corn-holer in the world, that's what."

"Sergeant, really!" Irma said, swabbing a final bit of blood from my hands. She explained to me, "The paramedics, they said Sly was pretty much already dead when you gave him mouth-to-mouth. They said sometimes you can't tell right away if a shooting victim's really dead because—"

"Same as when you cut off a toad's head," Kowalski cut in. He dumped ash from his cigar onto the rug. "Freaking reptiles, they keep hopping around for a while like they can't figure out how to die."

"Have a care!" Irma complained, looking down at Kowalski's spilled ash. "I entertain in this parlor."

"I bet you do, sister," Kowalski said. He dumped more ash on the floor, mashing it into the rug with his foot. He laughed in Irma's face, then said to me, "First you badge your way up into Crosby's dump, now you're down here, johnny-on-the-spot when what's-his-name gets his."

"Sly," said Irma.

"Yeah, well, for the record it's Sylvester Harrington," Kowalski said. He asked me, "Can't you never get enough of these here canceled-out beautiful people?" Kowalski pronounced it *beauty*-ful.

"I told you, I'm on a peep job."

"Oh, that's right. You and Private Eye Mogaill. So, what—the both of you think some rich fairy uptown connects with this here downtown faggot scumbag?"

"We keep meeting in all the same places, Sergeant. You tell me."

"I don't got to tell you nothing."

"That's very true." I decided to break a fundamental rule of the detective trade and accuse Kowalski of something I could not completely back up with firsthand knowledge, not at the moment anyway. "Likewise, I don't have to tell Slattery down at the *Post* about your dickprint routine, or how you ran it on poor Crosby and Sly—and now just look how they wound up."

"You threatening me?"

Kowalski got my meaning, all right. I gave him my best choirboy look and said nothing.

"You don't rattle me none," Kowalski said. "Slattery can't run with that kind of crap, not even in that rag of his."

"Don't be too sure. Slattery's the kind of reporter that if he died late in the afternoon, he'd have a bulletin from hell for the bulldog edition."

"I should cram a ferret in your mouth and staple your lips, you pissbum you."

"Very Christian of you, Sergeant."

"Boys, boys . . . !" said Big Irma. She stood up and placed her imposing bulk between Kowalski and me. "Oh, for the love of God, I'll never in a thousand years understand testosterone."

"Don't be talking about God, you sick bastard!" Kowalski snarled at Irma, his face turning righteous red. "Any man who's thinking of homosexuality is thinking of disease and wrongdoing! So sayeth the cardinal himself! God Almighty despises all you freaking fruitcakes!"

I got up off the divan. Everything ached, but I felt another duty, this one to Big Irma. So I jabbed a finger into Kowalski's fleshy chest, and asked him, "What makes you think you know what's on God's mind?"

Kowalski made a sound with his lips, like a slack-jawed dog.

"I don't go much for your kind of religion, Kowalski, and I'm going to tell you why. It's not polite. When you're rude to God, it's a sin. A venial sin, but anyhow a sin."

"You getting a load of this down here, Lord?" Kowalski addressed the ceiling, hands palm side up in front of him. He laughed an especially corrosive and nasty laugh while speaking with the Lord. "I got to be in Tinkerbell's powder room, on account of it's part of the crime scene you know, and here's Hockaday the pissbum going churchy on me."

I turned to Irma, and said, "How do you like that? The sergeant not only reads God's mind, also he kvetches to the Creator of heaven and earth."

"Watch your freaking step, Hockaday!" Kowalski snapped. Happily, I had offended him. Kowalski's arms dropped back to his sides like a pair of giant hamburgers.

"Good advice, Sergeant. Here's some for yourself: He who is without sin, let him cast the first stone. That's a direct quote from God Almighty. You can look it up."

Kowalski sputtered for a couple of seconds. He looked like he wanted to eat something fast.

"For some strange reason of your own," I said to him, taking advantage of Kowalski's imbalance, "you're not very forthcoming."

"I don't got to be!"

"Right. So later on this afternoon maybe I'll have that little chat with Slattery about how come a certain fat desk sergeant is suddenly hopping all over town to make all the gay murder scenes. It ought to make for good reading at IAD." I walked over to the door leading out of Irma's parlor and put my hand on the knob. "Meanwhile, I'm going out where the uniforms and the forensics boys can help me out on a couple of questions. Maybe I should start with how come you're on this call."

Kowalski grumbled, "You got something to ask, Hockaday, you freaking ask me."

"Fair enough, for now." I put aside the matter of Kowalski's presence in the interest of some greater immediate curiosities. After all, neither Kowalski nor any other officer in the club was obliged to tell me anything, since I was on furlough. So I had to ask while the asking was good. "In Sly Harrington's chest, there was a knife . . ."

"A little shiv. That ain't what did him in."

"No, I didn't think so. But it was pinning something in place, right?"

"Remember your boy uptown? The little epitaph they crammed up his butt?"

"Another message?"

Kowalski fished out a glassine evidence bag from his shirt pocket. This he handled with tweezers. "It's kind of bloody as all hell," he said, "but you can still read it okay."

Which I did, through the glassine: THERE IS NO LOVE HERE. WE GO FROM JUDGMENT TO JUDGMENT. I found my casebook and made a note of this, then asked, "So what's your take on the shooter?"

"Nothing with meat to it." Kowalski nodded at the door. "The PDU guys and also a crew from Sex Crimes, they're still interrogating out there. They ain't turning up diddly on who the blondie was that done it."

"Weapon?"

"Didn't find no toss-down."

"Ruling out a pro."

"Probably, yeah. My guess, it was one of them sweet little automatics easy enough for a fruitcake to slip it into his purse, like maybe a .32."

"So you never found a slug?"

"Probably still in the stiff's skull."

"Forensics' got the wig?"

"Yeah, for whatever good it's going to do."

I said to Irma, "Sly and the blonde, they were sitting right up front. You must have seen them."

"Of course I did."

"Well, did you recognize Sly's date?"

"They asked me that already. I never saw the bitch in my life." Irma was still sitting holding her swabs and her basin of blood-tinted water. She set them down on a table covered with doilies and magazines. "What a mess!"

"Was Sly in the habit of showing up here with strangers?"

"I'd have to say yes. But they wouldn't be strangers for long."

"Freaking sick bastard sinners!"

"Shut up, Kowalski. Tell me, Irma—when Lenihan was still with me and you told him you were expecting Sly to-night, what did that mean?"

Again Kowalski butted in. "Lenihan? You're talking Three Dollar Bill Lenihan? You come here with that fruit cop, Hockaday?"

Irma winked. "He says you're real hunky, Sergeant."

Kowalski's fists doubled up, but he thought twice. A vein in his neck throbbed, and his face went red again. Big Irma went red, too, clear through all the makeup. She thought twice, too, then said to me, "Sly and yours truly . . . Well, let's just say our flames used to burn as one. That was a long time ago."

"Jesus H. Christ!" Kowalski said. "Pardon me all over the place, but now I got to go puke."

"That'd be nice," I told him. "Before you go, tell me one more thing. Whatever happened to the shooter?"

"Nobody seen nothing. This here place, it was one mass hissy-fit soon's the gun went off. So in the middle of it all, the shooter he just run out, with nobody the wiser."

"That part of it sounds pro."

"Or just lucky."

"What about once he hit West Street? Somebody must have seen a guy running for it."

"No, we got zip."

"One thing you do have, Sergeant."

"What's that?"

"A bona fide murder. You can't call this one a suicide."

Kowalski raised a dismissive paw and said, with disgust, "Aw, there ain't no use to dealing with you, Hockaday. You're swallowing all this fruitcake propaganda—hook, line, and sinker."

"Go pray for me why don't you?"

Kowalski stalked out of Irma's parlor. I saw through the door that the cleanup was pretty much complete. The bar and the stage area were empty, except for the forensic crew and some other plainclothes types about to file through the main entrance, which was covered in yellow crime-scene tape.

I looked at my wristwatch. How had all this time passed? It was shortly past seven o'clock in the morning. Sly Harrington's body must have been removed hours ago. Shifts would be changing at the Sixth Precinct. New faces would be back in about an hour, to fine-comb it through the Ladies Auxiliary.

Ruby would be awake by now, and worried.

"Come on out here with me," I said to Irma.

She followed me through the parlor door. We walked to where Sly's body had been. Now there was only the chalk outline. Big Irma, with her thick fingers laced together, began weeping softly. "My poor, poor children. They only want to turn the laughter around. That's what it means to be gay, Detective Hockaday. Did you know that?"

"I hadn't thought about it."

"Not many people do. Nor do they think of the opposite."

"Laughter turned around from what?"

"From Sergeant Kowalski's diabolical laugh." Irma looked up at the ceiling. "The wounds of cruel laughter are frequently salved by murder."

"That I have to remember." I took out my casebook and wrote down Irma's dark philosophy, plus a few things I remembered Lenihan telling me. I then asked Irma something of a practical nature. "Besides the main entrance from West Street, what are the other doors here?"

"Just the fire door."

"Show me."

I followed Irma around to the side of the runway, then two steps up to the stage. Another few steps and there we were backstage, at a gray metal door under a sign that read EMERGENCY EXIT ONLY.

I pushed this open. There was a short cast-iron staircase down to a twisting, cobblestoned alleyway between West Street and Charles Lane. Access to the West Street side was blocked by a ten-foot Cyclone fence. The Charles Lane side was clear. The morning sky was brightening some, but the alleyway remained nearly as black as night. And it smelled of something dead and wet, like rotted chicken.

"So this was the getaway route," Irma said, taking a guess. She was standing behind me, on the top landing of the cast-iron stairs, daubing her teary cheeks with Kleenex.

"Probably it was. What's this alley used for?"

"To satisfy the fire code, that's about it."

"Your children, they ever take their tricks back here?"

"Oh, a long time ago." I turned and looked at Irma's face. She wore a newly pained expression. "But not for years now."

"What happened?"

"My dears would come back with their ankles full of rat bites. The gentlemen callers didn't much like it down there either."

I decided against a stroll through the alley.

"I'm going home now," I told Irma, stepping back into the stage area.

Irma saw me out the main entrance.

"Take care," I told her.

"Honey, that's all I been doing with my sorry life. So much so I don't know anymore about taking or caring."

Outside, the sun was trying to break through a thinning layer of low-hanging gray clouds, leftovers from yesterday. I could see a patch of blue—*Big enough to make a pair of dungarees for Patsy's pig,* as my mother used to say of a day that came with the promise of a clearing in the weather.

West Street, absent its night crowd of the variously forbidden lovelorn, was as innocent at this hour as it is ever likely to be. Off in the near distance, on the choppy Hudson River, a pair of sailboats skipped along upstream. Not a care in the world. Ashore, the early commuter traffic was doubtless the same. A freshly shaved crowd of drivers whizzing by with their Jersey plates was blissfully ignorant of what had happened a few hours ago inside the squat, nondescript building behind me.

I headed for the next block, where I could flag an uptown taxi. I had a decision to make. Should I go right on home, or first drop by a hospital clinic for a blood test? Was it too soon for a test? Wait a second ... What about sampling Harrington's blood? Might that be the better test, with the quicker results? The age of the almighty shadow.

Walking along thinking all this over, I noticed something about the Cyclone fence blocking the alleyway, something that escaped my attention a few minutes earlier. The fence was topped with coiled razor wire, and somehow an old kitchen chair was tangled in the vicious loops.

It troubles my New York heart to see a neighborhood gone so bad even the furniture is trying to make a break for it.

12

"NEIL HOCKADAY, YOU WILL SIT YOUR SORRY ASS DOWN AND shut your mouth. I'm not in the mood for any of your pretty damn words, or your old Irish damn chestnuts. No, sir. You're going to listen to me! And you'd best listen hard because I'm only going to say this once..." She paused, waiting for me to react.

"What's that?" I duly asked.

"I'm going to tell you about the kind of woman you married, big guy ..."

I thought in my own defense, Had I not come home stone sober? Had I not first stopped at St. Vincent's Hospital for a blood test? And arranged for the morgue to sample Harrington's blood? Had I not then come home and showered, and soaked my shirt in ammonia? What did she think, that those stains on my collar were lipstick?

None of that mattered, for clearly the worst had happened. Ruby had awakened to find me gone. Over the hours, she had waited helplessly in the parlor. Her concern had crumbled into fury. All patience had long gone, banished by strong black coffee. Now there were hands on hips; now there was glaring, as if Ruby had the shotgun drop on the Grand Wizard himself.

Her yellow dress, still in plastic from the dry cleaner's, was draped over the back of the green whorehouse chair.

On the floor nearby were her mahogany brown pumps and matching handbag. Her face and hair, too, were ready for a day in Mad Avenue. All that remained before she would finally stamp off for the office was a few minutes' rant.

So there stood Ruby in a sheer white slip, one more thing to do before leaving me. I could see through her slip how she was wearing the hosiery I like, the kind with little ribbons woven into elastic thighs. And there stood I, with the blessing of sexual desire and the curse of bad timing.

And the blood test results to come!

My knees were saggy as a bed in a Times Square hotel, delayed shock from all I had been through. Wifely harangue or no, it would now be the greatest luxury to sit down in my own house.

I sat. Ruby ranted.

"Let me guess. You were in a bar."

"Well, I had to—"

"How much did you drink?"

"Christ, Ruby—nothing. Can't you tell?"

"A little something on the side?"

"Give me a break."

"Do you know what it means to leave me in the middle of the night?"

"I'm sorry."

"Who do you think I am, buster? Some little white bread Suzie-Q?"

"I said I'm—"

"Sorry doesn't cut it, Hock. I've been sitting here for hours since you left me, wondering about all the things you might have to say for yourself. Don't you think I already imagined your dragging your butt in here to tell me how awful sorry you are?"

"Forget I ever mentioned sorry."

"You're thinking you made a big mistake marrying me. Is that what this is about?"

"Oh, for the love of God . . ."

"After all, I'm not the kind of wife most men want."

"What kind is that?"

"Clever enough to grasp her husband's cleverness, stupid enough to admire it." Ruby snapped her fingers in front of her face.

"Did you work up that punch line just for me?"

Ruby let her scowl do the answering. She picked up her dress and made a noisy show of ripping through the plastic and throwing the hanger on the floor. She slipped the dress over her head and used her hands to smooth down yellow fabric over her bust and waist. Then she sat down in the chair and put on her shoes. I watched the dark plum shadows between her legs as she crossed them.

"One more thing I want to say to you this morning." Ruby rose from the chair and crossed the parlor to the doorway. She took her raincoat from a peg, placed it over her shoulders, and said, cool as could be, "Mister man, no matter what—don't you ever, *ever* treat me like this again. For I am unlike any nigger woman you ever met in your whole damn life."

"Jesus, Ruby!"

"You piss in my face, I call it piss. I will not call it rain. Deal with it."

She snapped her fingers again. Twice this time. Then Nails was gone with the wind of a hard-slammed door.

Alone at half-past nine o'clock in her thirty-fifth-floor office—the one where she and Hiram Foster would have tea and commiseration on the darkest of the old days—Ruby Flagg taped torn strips of *The New York Times* over the glass on her side of the pizza window. She then sat down behind her desk and made a note for Sandy on a memo pad: *Please have building maintenance come close up the stupid hole in my wall—permanently.*

She pressed the receptionist button on the telephone console. Arlene answered, "Yes, Mrs. Flagg?"

Mama?

"Actually, it's *Ms.* Flagg," Ruby said. Certainly not Missus Hockaday, she thought.

We're married, so I've been telling myself since April. In our eyes, we're married? Are we, really and truly? What about the law?

"Oh, my, I'm so sorry."

"Please, don't be sorry. Has Jay come in yet?"

"Well, Mr. Schuyler generally arrives at ten, at the earliest. Eleven if he's had a busy night."

145

"Please tell him to see me right away."

"Oh, my. Yes, of course."

"And Sandy. What times does she usually show up?"

"Nine-thirty, always. Miss Malreaux is as punctual as she is beautiful. Oh, we all just love her so. And we know you two are going to work so well together . . ." Arlene paused to allow Ms. Flagg's response. Ruby kept an uncharitable thought to herself. *Ruby and Sandy, a couple of grown-up pickaninnies—why, of course they'll be a good team.* An awkward silence was ended with Arlene's nervous throat clearing and goggle adjustment, and then, "But if you'd like some coffee now, Ms. Flagg, I'd be happy—"

"Thank you, no."

"Very well, dear."

Great. Some killer mood you're in. First you treat your husband like yesterday's crap. Then you come to the office and pull the bitch-boss routine on the poor receptionist.

Ruby leaned back in her chair, bumping the credenza. She sighed a long sigh. Then she sat forward again and ran her hands over the top of her desk. Which was empty save for the telephone board and a memo pad with the SF&C agency logo, a Montblanc pen set also with the logo, and a crystal vase full of lilies. There was a card attached to the flowers that read WELCOME TO THE SALT MINES—SMACKS, JAY.

So—when did he have time to write that?

Wondering about this, Ruby drummed her fingers on the desk. There was little else to do. Except maybe to darkly calculate the shortened life span of the Likhanov account in view of Freddy Crosby's sordid departure. Which led to some pressing personal questions.

How in the world am I going to make money to pay my bills? How am I going to hang on to the theater? How am I going to hang on to Hock when I say such ugly, horrible things and storm out of the house? And dear God—how am I ever, ever going to tell Mama about this man of mine?

Which led to tears.

Fifteen minutes passed before the tide of Ruby's weeping crested. She pulled a wad of tissues from a box on the credenza and wiped her wet face with a fury. What would Jay think if he popped his head through the door right now? Or Sandy?

But Ruby's private sorrows were not interrupted. She was able to take several deep breaths, and eventually dry up. When she had collected herself, she pulled a mirror, lipstick, a brush and mascara from her handbag and quickly retouched her face and hair. *Oh—I'll have to ask Sandy how it went at dinner last night.* She looked at her watch. It was closing in on ten o'clock.

Ruby took a few final pokes at her hair with a finger before returning the grooming things to her handbag. She stood up, crossed an expanse of maroon carpet and opened her door, expecting to see Sandy sitting there at her secretarial station.

There was the Spode cup and saucer on her desk that she had noticed yesterday, the leather appointments calendar, the computer. But no Sandy. *Miss Malreaux—late? But what will Arlene say? Oh, my!*

Ruby lingered in the doorway of her private office, watching the agency come to life. It was either that or maybe taking a crack at the *Times* crossword puzzle. She had bought the *Times* in the lobby newsstand, but had not yet so much as glanced at the front page.

The early ranks of the SF&C secretarial fleet had already filed in for the most part, and now the stragglers were arriving. They were capable-looking suburban women for the most part, padding along with their jumbo tote bags and tennis shoes that would be switched for high heels as soon as desk drawers were unlocked. There were a few men among this group, of two basic kinds: recent college graduates on career paths, and middle-agers who looked like they might have been interesting back in the sixties. The women smelled of rosewater, the young men of Paco Rabanne; the middle-aged guys trailed the vague aroma of neighborhood taverns.

Next came the parade of vice presidents in their blue or gray pinstripes, male or female cut. Of the veeps pushing sixty, all were men; they carried boxy briefcases and looked like they could all use a nap. The younger ones, men and women alike, carried slim attachés in one hand and lunchtime squash racquets in the other. They cast envious looks at Ruby standing idly in the doorway of a coveted corner office.

The creatives, a team that Freddy had always liked to see feuding, were already at it hammer and tongs down the corridor in the studio. During Ruby's last tenure, the same argument—featuring nearly always the same words—was bellowed almost daily, as it was now:

"Idiot! What, you call this an illustration? This doesn't rate a matchbook cover!"

"Clear out of my goddamn studio, you Philistine putz!"

This, Hiram Foster told Ruby once upon a time, was the eternal battle of artistic souls doomed to spinning the rude and plodding wheel of commerce. All up and down Mad Avenue such routine squabbles were occurring, and being routinely ignored by all those in other ways doomed to their corporate tasks.

But then Ruby heard another pair of familiar sounds, dependably pleasant ones: the squeaking wheels of a mailroom cart, and Albert Caulkins's breathy singing. This morning the tune was Art Pepper's "Blues for Blanche."

Albert finally came into view. He was tall and slender, and looked to be all of his sixty-eight years only upon closest inspection. His smooth face was exactly as Ruby remembered—open, nut brown, threatening at any moment to break into laughter; a face much like her father's own, in the years before it was twisted by a pain and delirium so bad he would forget Ruby's name before he died. Albert's step remained syncopated, too, and he still had the air of an amused gentleman in spite of his humble labors.

There was a big difference in the way Albert dressed, though. Ruby had always seen him in khaki pants, sweater or shirt—and always the tweed cap, worn indoors and out year-round. Now capless, Albert was these days resplendent in a navy wool blazer and charcoal gray trousers, white shirt, red necktie.

"Bring us a little sweetness over here, handsome," Ruby said, arms open.

Albert dropped the mail he was holding back into the neat bundles he had arranged in the cart. He bounded over to Ruby, gave her a gentle bear hug, and said, "Girl, I heard all about how you was coming back to us. Now you know I been dying to see you!" He stepped back and looked Ruby up and down, and said, "Well, you're still easy on an old fool's eyes."

"Darling, you can look. But mind, I'm married now. Since last April."

"Oh, that's beautiful." Albert hugged Ruby again. "I'm so happy for you." He noticed Sandy's empty desk, checked his wristwatch, and asked, "Where's Miss Thing?"

"Late."

"Well, I guess there's always a first time." Albert shrugged. He took a quick look around him to see that no one could overhear, and whispered, "Say, why do you suppose they stashed all the bubbling brown sugar over here in this one little corner?"

"I don't know, Albert. No more than I know why you're decked out in the coat and tie."

"Oh—this?" Albert moved his hands up and down the lapels of his blazer. "The three cheeses one day decides everybody got to be upscale. Freddy, he sends me down to Saks with his very own personal charge plate. So Albert don't mind looking fine."

"Three cheeses . . . ?"

"As in *big cheese*. The partners, see? The three cheeses. Schuyler, Foster . . . and poor dead Freddy."

"Speak of the devil."

"Not me, sister. I like to talk about anything else but that unholy mess." Albert screwed up his face and shook his head. Ruby saw the boy he must have been, protesting a spoonful of cod-liver oil. Albert the man brightened, and said, "I know—tell me about this husband of yours."

"Sure. Come on in here with me, sit down a minute." Ruby stepped back into her private quarters, motioning for Albert to follow.

"Don't look much different in here since old man Foster took his money and run," Albert said after he had stepped inside. He held his hands on his hips and let his eyes sweep over the office. "What do you plan in the way of personal renovations?"

"I haven't thought that far ahead." Ruby walked to the desk and sat down. Albert settled into a leather side chair.

"Just look at you now, sitting up here in this fine office and all." Albert beamed at Ruby, as if he were her own daddy. *He's the right age . . . Mama's age.* "Girl, I'm real proud of you."

"I'll tell you a secret, Albert. They could keep me here 'til the weekend's come and gone, and I still wouldn't know why."

"They're paying you good, aren't they?"

"Real good."

"Seems like *why* enough to me."

"You have a point, I guess." Ruby slicked her hands over the empty desktop again. She thought about how nice it would be getting her first paycheck, and working down her stack of bills. Then, again, she felt a pang of regret for the hurt she had left that morning in Hock's tired face. "Even so, I'd like to have some clear idea what I'm supposed to be doing for the money."

"That'll come, by and by," Albert said. "All's I know, the head cheese's been yakking weeks on end about you. Ruby this and Ruby that, and how he's missed you so much, and how he's going to grab you back in here to work on some really big deal."

Bigger than big.

Ruby asked, "Schuyler's been talking like that?"

"Well, you know Mr. Jay. When he wants something, he puts it right on his sleeve so's everybody can see."

"Freddy couldn't have liked seeing me there."

"Shoo, that was nothing compared to Mrs. Head Cheese."

"Margot Schuyler?"

"You know that's who I'm talking about. If you want, go right ahead and say, Shut up your old magpie mouth, Albert. But I tell you something, girl, everybody 'round here thinks you and Mr. Jay got some thing going on."

"Margot, too?"

"Well, I do notice she's touchy on the subject of you."

"And what do you think about all the gossip, Albert?"

"Don't change my notions none. All my life, I heard white folks say the only way us black folks make it's because of some trifling reason or other. No way they want to know about any black brains. You know what I'm saying—?"

The intercom button on Ruby's telephone console lit up. She picked up the receiver.

"Oh my, Ms. Flagg ... Well, Mr. Schuyler has finally arrived. I told him you wanted to see him right away."

"Thank you, Arlene."

"He's in his office. He asks that you come by in fifteen minutes."

"All right." Ruby started to hang up, then asked, "Arlene, has anyone thought about calling Sandy's home?"

"I called myself. There's no answer, I'm afraid. I suppose that means she's on her way."

"Yes, I suppose." Ruby hung up, and said to Albert, "You seem to have your ear to the ground. I'm told everybody loves this Sandy Malreaux. What do you know about her?"

"Cool and beautiful, mostly cool. I'm no use to her ambitions, so we don't speak much." Albert paused, clearly wanting an end to talk of Sandy Malreaux. "Who cares about her? Why don't you tell me about this man you took without even inviting me to the wedding?"

"Oh, I wish I'd had you there!" Ruby brushed a tear from her eye before Albert could see it. She thought back to last April, and her Irish wedding day.

A tinker camp in the countryside just north of the grim end of Dublin. Ruby and Hock on a rare sunny day, returned from the southwest, beyond the brooding Wicklow mountains, where Hock had finally met his father—and learned the worst.

The tinkers all ringed around them: The men in suit coats and hats; the women dressed in colorful skirts; a hundred children scrubbed clean, holding hands over laughing faces. And the camp leader, old Sister Sullivan, pronouncing them husband and wife.

Ruby with flowers in her hair. Hock promising they would make it legal once they were back home in New York, then forgetting his pledge with all that he drank.

"Could have been the one to give away the bride," Albert said, chiding her gently. "Could have been best man. Anyhow, something."

"His name is Neil Hockaday," Ruby said. *It's so complicated. What's Albert going to think ... ?* "He's a policeman."

"Shoo, you married a po-lice?"

"He's older than me. Twelve years."

"Nothing wrong about a man who appreciates sweet and young when he meets up with it. He treats you right and one fine day he'll come to appreciate sweet and old."

"He was married once before."

"What year you stuck in, girl? You think anybody gets snorty about divorce these days?"

"He's a recovering alcoholic."

"Well, so long's he don't re-*dis*cover."

"He's white."

Albert's eyes flickered some, but did not betray judgment. He considered his next words carefully. "There's all kinds of white folks. Some are good. Others, they're like the white you see on top of chicken doody. What kind's your police husband?"

"He's pretty good, Albert."

"Well then, that's all right."

"I haven't told my mama."

"Hold on. You was married *when?*"

"Last April."

"That's what I thought you said. Well, here it is October, girl. Why you be keeping this from your mama?"

I don't know. Yes, she did. But Ruby said nothing.

"Ain't worthy of you, Ruby. Ain't fair to your mama, and it ain't fair to your man neither."

"I know."

"Long's you know, you best get to work on it." He looked at his watch again, stood, and turned toward the open door. "Time for Albert to make the rounds."

"Wait." Ruby got up and took his arm. When they reached the door, she stood on her tiptoes and kissed his cheek. "Thank you, Albert."

"What for?"

"For being a dear, for listening. You know my daddy passed young."

"Yes, you told me."

"A girl who grows up without her daddy needs men like you all through her life. You're one of my old dearhearts, Albert. Did you know that?"

"Shoo . . ." Albert laughed as he stepped away from Ruby to his mail cart. He picked out a bundle of letters and dropped them on Sandy's desk. He said to Ruby, "You're

152

a true magnolia, girl. You best remind your new husband every day." Then he moved on down the corridor, picking up right where he left off with "Blues for Blanche."

Ruby went back inside her office and decided there might be enough time before her meeting with Schuyler to act beautifully, like a magnolia. So she held her breath and phoned home.

"God, I'm so sorry, babe." Ruby said this as soon as her husband answered "Hello," interrupting him in fact. Hock said nothing when it was his turn to speak. And so Ruby asked, "What are you doing right now?"

"You know us pissbums. Any little thing is likely to set us off." His voice dripped with sarcasm. "Let's say that a pissbum's wife implies he's some kind of redneck. Right away, he's going to run off and get drunk."

"I said I'm sorry. Don't call yourself a pissbum. Or a redneck."

"I've been called worse."

"Not by anybody who matters. Tell me what you're doing."

"Rinsing out my clothes, mother, and otherwise recovering from last night."

"What—?"

"You haven't read the papers, have you?"

"No, and I don't know if I want to."

"Maybe you should."

"Before you get in deep—"

"Too late."

"Damn you!" Ruby slapped her desk. "We need to make time for ourselves, Hock. Please. This is not just your wife asking. Inspector Neglio and Father Sheehan, they're saying the same thing."

"I promise, Ruby, after—"

"I've heard your promises."

"What do you want from me?"

"I want to get out of town for a while. I want to go home, Hock."

"Home?"

"Promise we'll go to New Orleans."

"Sure, I'd like to. But the bills—"

"I dream about it all the time. About sitting on my old

back porch with a moon pie, and seeing Lake Pontchartrain on a clear night, and listening to zydeco at Tipitina's, and having coffee and beignets and reading the *Times-Picayune* at six in the morning at Café DuMonde ..." Ruby stopped, only briefly to catch her breath.

"I want to see my mama! I want Mama to see you, Hock. I want to be around my family, and a whole lot of other black folks—black faces everywhere I turn. I want to eat Creole daube in red gravy and a big old Muffuletta sandwich and boiled crawfish and filé gumbo—and all that kind of good food, cooked by colored people."

"Jesus, Ruby. Okay."

"Promise!"

"I do, I do."

"I'm holding you to this one, Irish. When are we going?"

"Ruby, I'm right in the middle of something here, which you'd see if you read the papers. And isn't your own plate full? With the Russians? What can I tell you?"

"Think of something quick."

"You're a little manic today. And your feet are big. But I love you, Ruby."

Ruby did not want to laugh, but she did. "I love you, too, Irish. Stick around the house tonight and I'll show you how much."

"Promise?"

I was bone tired and wanted to sleep for a long time. So after I hung up from Ruby I thought about taking the phone off the hook and drifting away.

Then I thought twice. I considered the way things work in New York.

Right about this time of the morning the mayor's press secretary, a nervous guy by the name of Ben Peterson, would be pretty much convinced the sky was falling. This is because when he rode in his limo down to work at City Hall he would have read the tabloids.

Unlike Ruby, Peterson would have noticed from headlines as thick as his wrist that something awful had happened overnight. Namely, a certain furloughed detective—a piss-bum—happened to be nosing around a downtown drag joint with a recent reputation for its clientele dropping dead in and around the premises. All suicides, so the cops were alleging.

But this time the deceased was murdered, with an audience to prove it. And this time the victim was more than some no-name the cops could forget about. This time the deceased just so happened to be the same guy who made the big splash in yesterday's tabs: Sylvester Harrington aka Sly, who threw pansies at a precinct full of cops because he claimed they were doing nothing to stop the strange and untimely deaths of homosexuals like himself.

Ben Peterson riding in his limo and reading these ironic things would sweat. This was generally his first reaction to bad public relations. Unless it was a story and picture of his boss cutting a ribbon someplace in the city with a lot of cute kids, Peterson saw just about everything in the papers as bad PR. And since the gay vote happened to be a significant constituency, Sly's murder at the Ladies Auxiliary (again!) was not merely bad PR. It was far more serious, it could cost his boss the next election!

Anything that weighty and that political made Ben Peterson sweat about twice his usual outflow. He probably had to change shirts before the morning press briefing in room nine of City Hall. And he had probably taken the reporters' fraternal insults unsportingly.

Which meant that after the briefing Peterson had scurried into the mayor's office and frightened Hizzoner. Which meant that the mayor had called up his police commissioner to find out the name of this certain furloughed pissbum's commanding officer. Which meant that Neglio had been called onto the mayor's carpet.

Which meant that any minute now, Neglio would be wanting to ring me up at home and chew me out, at the least. And if he kept getting a busy signal, he had other means of making things unpleasant. Namely, he could send Neuman the leper after me. Or maybe another squad of body snatchers if his mind worked like Ruby's and he figured I had to be drinking just because I was in a bar and having a private little rhapsody about all this stuff, the way Ruby was dreaming about New Orleans.

So I stayed put in the green whorehouse chair next to the phone stand, yawning and waiting for Neglio's call. To take my mind off my troubles, I tried picturing New Orleans from the way Ruby was running on about her southern briar patch.

The only time I have ever been in the South was when the army sent me off to boot camp in Georgia. I remember heat and Spanish moss hanging in the trees and big-bellied cops with mirrored sunglasses and snarling dogs who thought it was hilarious to say Jew York instead of New York. I had to believe it was better in Louisiana.

But what in the world was a moon pie?

The telephone did ring, of course. I picked up, and said, "Good morning, Inspector."

"Yeah, small freaking wonder you figured Neglio."

"Who's this?" As if I did not know.

"A little birdy out of Manhattan Sex Crimes. Okay, a big birdy."

"You're making me some kind of habit, Kowalski?"

"Steady, pal. Don't be disagreeable. Sounds like you could use a drink, hey?" The way he said this, and now the way he was laughing, Kowalski reminded me of all the hilarious cops I used to know in Georgia.

"What do you want, you fat hump?"

"Birdy's got a song to sing."

"What did I do to deserve hearing it?"

"You better just listen to me, Hockaday. 'Cause we got another one, and it's a real freaking beaut."

"Another murder?"

"This scene you ain't going to believe, my friend."

"Where are you?" I picked up a pencil and pad.

"A joint called Devil's Heaven."

13

THERE ARE TWO THINGS I KNOW JUST AS SURELY AS A NUN knows her beads. One is, I shall go to heaven when I die.

This would only be right, since turnabout is fair play, and a halfway honest career with the New York Police Department is deserving of a get-out-of-hell-free card. Especially my career, as I am the long-suffering type. Not by choice, as I recently learned the hard way, but by the accident of Irish birth.

I enjoy neither comfort nor pride in seeing a company of angels at the far pass. Many people and most Catholics would classify this as ingratitude and spiting God the Father, and therefore a cardinal sin. But I do not feel sin. Instead, I feel a sad patience. For I know this, too: Before I die, the world will have broken my heart many times over.

Not many would recognize a great patience in me. Most people would call it something else. Foolish maybe.

Some years ago, for instance, way back in the days before the body snatchers got me, Inspector Neglio and I were out drinking the night away someplace. The occasion was a celebration of my taking down some penniless nonentity who went off his nut and eliminated a quantity of his fellow New Yorkers.

"The poor sod," I said. I was naturally blue at the end of the great chase. And feeling charitable, too, as I always do after bagging somebody the whole city imagines to be a stone crazy monster man. This one was a little squeak of a guy. They usually are. "He'll spend the rest of his life up in Attica with the mentals, for what that's worth to us. No belt, no shoelaces, his food all cut up on the plate for him."

"Better the lousy dirtbag should croak. If we had justice in this state, he'd be on death row wearing slippers every day until one cold morning it's time to do the shuffle-shuffle down the dance hall for a sit-down on Old Sparky." Inspector Neglio, since he is a man of the bureau instead of the street, said this with the same abstract savagery that allows politicians and other such deep thinkers to compare the hardships of the poor with the unhappiness of the rich.

"That you call justice?"

"You don't, Hock?"

"No, I don't. Justice is when you try and figure out what's gone so wrong that people get hurt, and when you try to figure out what everybody concerned is going to do about it. This squeak, he killed some people. And then, in the name of the people, what did we do? We collared him, then the judge sent him up."

"What's the problem?"

"It's too easy. So easy it's going to happen all over again. Tomorrow some other squeak out there nobody ever heard of is going to kill somebody else, and he'll get busted and sent up. And then the day after tomorrow the same thing will happen. Then the tomorrows will keep on coming—and so will the squeaks. And all we'll have to show for this is a whole lot of squeaks on the inside with no belts or shoelaces and their food cut up in little pieces. So what?" By now I was well into my cups. Maybe I was waving my hands around as I spoke. "All the cops in the world, and all the prisons, and all the poor sods vegetating in all the cells— the devil with it. Some justice, Inspector. How is your idea of justice trying to find the answer?"

"To what question?"

"Where do all the damn squeaks come from?"

"Hockaday, you remind me of a certain bleeding-heart priest of my youth," Neglio said. As I recall, Neglio was shaking his head. "He was a fool and a soft touch—"

"Thanks. I love you, too, Inspector."

"You didn't let me finish." The inspector smiled. "You let on to anybody it was me saying what I want to tell you now, and I'll say Neil Hockaday's a goddamn liar ..."

"Spill it, Inspector."

"What this country needs is an army of fools."

Not fools, no. I would have said an army of patient men and women. But I loved the inspector all the same. In his way, he was trying.

A patient army. That is my idea of a good police department. Since this sentiment is not widely shared, I do not expect to be named New York's police commissioner anytime soon. And so I do what I can on my own.

For instance, I try to be patient with the despised. By which I mean the winos and howlers and dopers—the lost souls, the skels, the seekers of refuge who somehow find their way to my city. I understand that these men and women and children are angry, and vulgar; why should they not be so?

Over the years as the streets have grown clogged with the luckless and loveless, as the comfortable have grown ever more heartless, I have felt obliged as a cop to be a good host to the unwelcome. I make no claim to nobility. It just strikes me that we live in fragile times, and it behooves us all to be familiar with the gutter. That way, when we fall we will know the way.

The old smokes who have proceeded us to the gutter know me as a soft touch, as Neglio rightly puts it. They smile at me, or else they curse; for my part, I try to make no distinctions. They routinely bum change from me. Sometimes, when the day seems bright, we trade our respective war stories. If the day goes sourly, we at least nod at one another.

But today was like no other. My mind was unaided by the balm of Johnnie Walker, and burning up about many terrible things: the argument with Ruby, the furlough and my missing gun, the kitchen floor mess of the late Frederick Crosby, the shooting of one Sylvester Harrington aka "Sly" right in front of my face, the blood test ...

... the discovery of my unresolved Irish sorrows; the unkept promises of April, made to Ruby as we married in a tinkers' camp.

159

Today, may heaven forgive, I lost patience.

Racing through my mind at the very moment I lost it was the meat-breath visage of King Kong Kowalski, awaiting my arrival at the scene of fresh murder. Seeing nothing but Kowalski's big salami face, I accidentally stepped on somebody's hand. Down at my feet came a quiet scream, followed by a gross lie concerning my anatomy and sexual habits.

"Pussydick motherfucker!"

"What the . . . ?"

Sprawled in the gutter just outside my tenement house, dressed in his customary stained rags, was an emaciated crackhead of my acquaintance. His street name is "Shitty." Somebody told me his actual name is Smith, that friends back in his respectable days called him "Smitty," that he used to be a typesetter for one of the old neighborhood print shops gone bankrupt.

"What'd you say, Smitty?"

"You heard me." Shitty picked himself up and regally patted down his rags, like some tailor in Savile Row had cut and sewn the filthy things. The stench and the dust made me cough. This seemed to enrage Shitty. He said, "Now get out my face!"

He then spat out a huge looge in my direction, and this enraged me. My mind clouded by all the terrible things concerning me and my hands spread open like claws, I lunged for Shitty's crusty gray neck. Shitty dodged my grab and took off down Forty-third Street like his pants were on fire. Unlike heroin nodders, crackheads are fleet. I chased after Shitty all the way to Ninth Avenue, then up and around the corner to Forty-fourth and back over to Tenth Avenue—winding up exactly where I began this mindless hot pursuit.

Shitty turned at one point to see me slowing up. So he shot into the double door of a supermarket and probably ran clear through to the rear and out into Forty-second Street. At least I assume he did. I cannot be sure because I myself was completely out of steam. All I could do was stand there on my flat feet shaking with anger, all sweaty and empty-handed. And thinking just like anybody else, If I could only just get my hands on the dirtbag and wring his lousy neck . . .

By this time, I had taken notice of several more of Shitty's fraternity loitering in the gutter. Apparently, they had witnessed the entire entertainment. Most were pointing and laughing at me. But then one of the more respectful old smokes came up and touched my shoulder in an understanding way, and said, "Score one for the assholes, my friend. Your day will come."

I mumbled thanks and started walking off. Not only had I lost patience with the likes of Shitty, I had run myself around in a sweaty circle—again. First in Ireland last April, now on this October day in my own street in Hell's Kitchen. And again, there was little to show for my effort besides a kind of defeat.

Aware of rheumy eyes on my back, I headed for the Tenth Avenue bus shelter to wait for the uptown M-11. And as I waited, alone, I thought, Maybe I never should have gone to bloody Ireland.

How many times have I wondered this since my drunken return? How many times now have I asked myself, What did I expect to inherit from Irish ghosts but the weariness I already know as the memory of my mother's face? And what business did I have bringing sweet Ruby Flagg into all this drunken, cursed codswallop of guilt and regret?

"Sorry to say, Hock, there'll be no easy sleep under your Irish roof." No, and certainly not now—now that I know what my father, Aidan, was. And how it was that while she lived I understood almost nothing of my mother, Mairead, save for her nearly constant fatigue.

An absent parent may easily be a god. So it was with Aidan Hockaday, who I met only last April, in Ireland. So, too, it is now with Mairead Fitzgerald Hockaday as she rests in peace. Six weeks ago, when I was still drunk, I would visit her grave on rainy days. I would touch the letters of her name carved in the rose marble headstone, and whisper to the mound of earth that formed her blanket, "You're my hero."

Private First Class Aidan Hockaday of the United States Army did not return home to New York from the war against Hitler and Tojo. All I had of the man—until April's fate—was a stiffly handsome soldier's portrait in black and white, and a stern sense from earliest boyhood that the subject of this absent god was never a proper one for family discussion. Through all her life as an immigrant working woman raising a boy alone in a Manhattan slum, my mother kept her husband—my father—consigned to some deeply private memory. Which I accepted but never understood, and considered it a theft. But which I did not dare disturb, until April.

I found in Ireland an old dog of the war that has raged for some eight hundred years now, without the decency of forgiveness or forgetfulness; a war made endless by, among others, the drunks and great haters who have plagued Irish history. Though I had not journeyed to Ireland with Ruby for any such purpose, I discovered my own daddo's role in this long, drunken farrago of hating and fighting. And the knowledge shamed me to the bone. For I found that my own daddo was a part of the plague, a man whose hate came of a dirty dream planted in Irish soul by fanatical ancestors who betrayed him by robbing him of natural kindness.

The world at war between the years 1939 and 1945 provided cover for Irish haters rallied to a classic tactical opportunity: the enemy of my enemy is my friend. Thus did a shadowy movement of Irishmen use the convenience of war between Nazi Germany and England: a soldier named Aidan Hockaday, steeped in fiercest Irish hatred and armed with the advantage of his American uniform, led a campaign of Irish sabotage against the ancient enemy in London.

Aidan Hockaday and his associates in this underground enterprise were financed and equipped by the old conspiracy of haters in Dublin, willing agents of Nazis in Berlin. He was blind and decrepit when I found him, living in his final Irish hiding place, protected by the conspiracy that has outlived him. We spoke only twice, he and I, which was all I could stomach.

My father said he was a patriot, claiming for himself a central role in the holy purpose of Irish history. By the lights of many still he was a martyred fugitive, a man who sacrificed a life of comfort and safety in New York with his wife and boy for the interests of a grand national cause. By my lights, an absent god had become a disgrace and a traitor— to his adopted country, to my mother, to me.

The mystery of my father was only half the abandoned

sorrow discovered in Ireland. Over there, too, the reason for my mother's silence on the subject of Aidan Hockaday became clear: determined to break the chain of hatred, she would keep her son and his father at total remove. And so she had, until April.

My father died in my arms there in Ireland. I did not weep. Instead, I returned to New York and got drunk.

Drunkenness absorbed me, protected me from my duties and promises as a cop and a husband and a man. Booze protected me from all this, the way Aidan Hockaday's patriotism protected him.

Then they got me—Davy Mogaill and Inspector Neglio and Father Sheehan and Neuman the leper and the body snatchers and the priests at the Straight and Narrow. And now I am officially sober, and thinking, So why has the darkness not yet cleared?

"You know exactly what you have to do ..."

Oh yes, I know exactly—and how much. For am I not in the business of seeing justice done?

Step number one: King Kong Kowalski was waiting for me at a place called Devil's Heaven.

I decided to take a taxi. I was in a hurry.

14

"LET'S GET SOMETHING STRAIGHT BETWEEN US, JAY."

"Don't tease me." Schuyler attempted a lewd alligator smile. Ruby looked at him like he was something that lived under a sink.

"That crack I'll let go. The next one you should think about because maybe I'll suddenly be in a bad mood. You know how women are." Ruby was standing, having declined the offer of a chair. She knew better than to sit. Jay Schuyler had his office arranged to his fullest advantage, with his own chair set higher than all others. "Maybe I'll get it into my silly little female head to file sexual harassment charges with the Human Rights Commission, and then maybe I'll have to repeat your oh-so-funny remarks in front of an adjudicator."

"Lighten up, Ruby."

"Easy for you to say."

"Check."

"I hear you've been spreading it around about us."

"What *us?*"

"Exactly. There's no such thing. So lose the innuendo whenever you're talking around the shop here about me and the Likhanov project. I don't appreciate the gossip. Do yourself a favor and knock it off at home, too."

Girl, now you're really on a tear! And why not? You work and you work, and what have you got to show for it? A

164

basketful of bills for troubling yourself in the wonderful world of stage. A husband who goes on a four-month drunk after your gypsy wedding, and then the first night home from the tank he leaves your bed to chase after killers. A boss who would have his jealous wife and everybody at the office think you're his little chocolate bonbon. And you haven't seen your family in years!

Jay Schuyler leaned forward over his desk and rested his chin in his hands. His fresh Egyptian cotton shirt with bold blue stripes rustled with his movement. He looked worn and tired, though, as if he would be more comfortable in pajamas.

"Yesterday morning I came to work and learned my partner was murdered," Schuyler said. His voice was as tired as his appearance. "That afternoon, I met your new husband—Hock. Quite a guy. Before I know what's happening, somehow he's on staff here as a private investigator. Now then, first thing this morning I'm under attack by my favorite executive—for being a pig. Oh, did I say *favorite?* No offense intended, ma'am."

"None taken. And please consider the attack, as you call it, over. I said what I had to say, and you heard me. Check?"

"Is that about all?"

"Not quite. I'd like to know about the Russians."

"That makes two of us." Schuyler rubbed his silver temples. "I tried calling their office today. All I get is a recording that says the line's been disconnected. How do you like that?"

"What—?"

"You know the business, Ruby. Every so often, you get these blue-sky types who come in, get you all lathered up, and then do the old skip-to-my-Lou."

So there go your big plans for paying off the bills!

"Freddy brought in this account?" Ruby asked.

"Hook, line, and sinker you might say."

"Do the Russians owe money?"

"Is there anybody who doesn't owe big these days?"

"That could be a problem. But you've Hock on the payroll. So at least you have somebody to run down these guys—Alexis and Vasily."

"Not a bad idea. I thought about that myself."

"Meanwhile, I guess I'm out of a job."

"What makes you say that?"

"Unless the Russkis materialize, there's no Vegas on the Volga. So what am I supposed to be doing around here in the way of gainful employment?"

"That I've been thinking about, too. Your husband's busy with Freddy's murder. So why don't *you* take the Likhanov case?"

"Me?"

"Ruby . . ." Schuyler stopped after saying her name and slumped back, swiveling around in his chair to face the south windows of his office. He sat quietly for several seconds, taking in the sweep of Manhattan. Jay Schuyler in the foreground, sitting in his elegant shirtsleeves, looked oddly diminished. And when he finally spoke again, his voice was someplace faraway, dying in the distance. "Have you ever gone diving? Not just snorkeling around some nice coral reef in the Bahamas or someplace. I mean deep sea diving."

"No, and also I've never skied a mountainside."

"There's a certain ocean level that even the strongest sunlight never pierces. It's black down there like you wouldn't believe, blacker than any night you've ever known. You bump into things down deep, and things bump into you. Your diver's torch is useless. Oh, sure—you've got maybe a four- or five-foot arc of smudgy light. But you see, light is irrelevant."

Ruby felt something crawling on the back of her neck. She raised a hand to brush it away, whatever it was. Only to discover there was nothing there.

Schuyler swiveled in his chair to face Ruby and continued. "Everything that lives in such an unbelievable blackness has learned to live without light. And so along you come with your diver's torch. Which means nothing. Not any more than if you found yourself in some village in the Amazon rain forest and tried speaking your English to the pygmies. Do you understand?"

"Like you said, light is irrelevant."

"Yes, but there's sound. It's sound that you must learn to see. That's the only way I can explain it."

"Please—what are you trying to tell me, Jay?"

He held up his hand, a request for Ruby's patience. "But

there's a trick. In the black ocean depths, the *sound* is something you can't believe—sound that has no timing."

"No timing."

"Which requires a reaction from you that's completely opposite from the way you've always reacted to sound."

"I see ..."

"Check. Let's say you're sitting in a room with the door open to a corridor. Somebody in the corridor is coming toward you. You can't see him, but you can hear the footsteps, right?"

"Of course."

"And the sound of the footsteps gives you an idea of how long it will be before this unseen guy walks through your doorway. If he's a long way off, the footsteps will be soft—and vice versa."

"That's timing."

"Check. Down deep in the ocean, though, time has no relevance to sound. You hear some clanking noise, and you think it's within your reach. You shine your torch in the direction of the noise. Nothing. What you're hearing might be half a mile away. Or, just as easily, six feet away."

"So, things go bump."

"If you can't see the sound, yes. That's what I'm trying to say." Schuyler got up from his chair and crossed the room to the bar. Ruby saw him age ten years as he passed, as if, truly and completely, time no longer had fair meaning to the man. He poured a finger of Scotch into a glass for himself, swirled it around, and said to Ruby, turning question to statement, "You don't want to join me."

"In a drink?"

Schuyler nodded.

"Thanks, but not now."

"I'm drinking around the clock because I don't know what's around the bend."

Two of them on my hands now!

"I don't follow you, Jay."

"Something's out there ..." Schuyler's words died off again as he returned to the window. He put back his drink. "I can hear it, but I don't know how close it is."

"Jay—"

"I need someone I can trust," he said, turning back to Ruby, interrupting her. "Please won't you stay?"

They'll never believe this back home. Little Ruby Flagg from the St. Bernard Projects, the one and only true-blue friend of Bradford Jason Schuyler III of New York City. Shoo ...

"Yes."

"Thanks."

Schuyler turned his back to Ruby, and looked down into the depths of Manhattan. He said nothing more. Ruby left his office, feeling somehow the weight of the whole agency was on her shoulders. It was a burden she might have wanted once, years ago in her serious career days. She certainly did not want it now. But just as certainly, Jay Schuyler was not up to the job.

Her thoughts were interrupted at the reception desk.

Arlene waved a handful of red fingernails, stopping Ruby with, "Ms. Flagg, there's a call that's come in for you." She then fumbled through a stack of telephone message slips in front of her, finding Ruby's and handing it to her.

"Sandy called?" Ruby asked before she had a chance to look at the name Arlene had written down on the message slip.

"No. And my, but I just don't know what to think about Miss Malreaux today."

Ruby looked at the slip and forgot about Sandy. She said, "Oh, good—one of my dearhearts called."

At this remark, Arlene's eyebrows popped up like two slices of burnt pumpernickel flying out from a toaster. Ruby laughed to herself as she walked back toward her corner office. It was partly a lie she had told the boss; she did not necessarily mind office gossip, not so long as she created it herself.

She sat down at her desk and dialed the number on the call slip. It was busy. She tried again, with no more success.

She thought about calling Hock, but decided first to look through the *Times*. Maybe, like he said, there was something in the paper to explain his whereabouts last night. She found it on the cover of the local section, in a story with no byline that raised more questions than it answered.

DEVIL'S HEAVEN

Murder of "Gay" Activist
Has Police Wondering
About Possible Serial Killer

An activist in "gay" causes was murdered at 2:30 this morning in a Greenwich Village nightclub, prompting police to acknowledge the possibility of a serial killer or killers behind a recent spate of deaths in New York's homosexual community.

The dead man was identified as Sylvester "Sly" Harrington, 40. Mr. Harrington was among the audience for a floor show performed by transvestite dancers at the Ladies Auxiliary club on West Street.

In full view of horrified patrons—and in view of an off-duty New York Police Department detective—Mr. Harrington was shot to death. His assailant, described by witnesses as a person of indeterminate gender wearing a blonde female wig, escaped during the several minutes of pandemonium following the killing.

The unnamed police detective attempted but failed to resuscitate the shooting victim. Mr. Harrington was later pronounced dead on arrival at St. Vincent's Hospital.

Only yesterday, Mr. Harrington led a demonstration against police officers of the Sixth Precinct station house on West 10th Street. Mr. Harrington and a few hundred followers protested the alleged lack of police concern over a number of violent deaths in recent days at—or in the immediate vicinity of—the Ladies Auxiliary. He expressed concern for the possibility of a "wholesale slaughter of queers" on Halloween night, a significant date on the homosexual calendar.

Command officers at the Sixth Precinct declined comment on the coincidence of Mr. Harrington's protest, followed by his murder. A spokesman for police department headquarters, though, said that in the ensuing days a special task force might be assigned to assess possible links among Mr. Harrington's murder and other untimely deaths. Meanwhile, no police spokesmen would identify the detective who tried to save Mr. Harrington's life, or suggest a reason for the detective's presence at the nightclub.

However, Sgt. Joseph Kowalski of the Manhattan Sex Crimes specialized unit, who was among police officers responding to the Harrington slaying, offered some explanation. He, too, refused to identify the detective, but said: "He was on furlough from the department and told me he was working some private job having to do with the consequences of ungodly lifestyles. So probably that's how come he was down in this West Street club snooping around. Well, he come to the right place for ungodly."

According to the owner of the Ladies Auxiliary, a transvestite singer and pianist who gave the name "Big Irma," the off-duty detective performed bravely in his attempt to save Mr. Harrington's life. "That detective was a sweet man and a guardian angel, and I do believe he's the only policeman in this city capable of solving this horrible, hateful murder spree," Mr. Irma said. "Unfortunately, this hero is off-duty. Even more unfortunately, the police department wants to call a murder spree a mass suicide. Well, they sure can't get away with that lie any longer. Not when everybody was here to see poor Sly get killed."

Others who have died thus far include . . .

Ruby stopped reading when the intercom on her telephone console rang. It was Arlene.

"Oh, Ms. Flagg, your dearheart's called again."

"Put him through."

"Hiram?" Ruby said. "I tried calling you back, your line was busy."

"It's been ōne of those mornings," Foster said. "Anyway, I'm coming down to the city today. I want to see you."

He did not sound like himself, Ruby thought. *It's sound that you must learn to see.*

"Good. Come on up to your old office. I need your advice."

"Not at the agency, for God's sake."

"We could have lunch."

"And not at any of the regular watering holes. Better we should skip the whole East Side."

"All right, there's a place on Ninth Avenue at West Forty-fifth called Angelo's Ebb Tide. They have booths in the back."

"That's the stuff. See you at one."

Foster clicked off. Ruby held the telephone receiver in her hand and stared at it for a few seconds, as if it might provide some clue to Foster's urgency, his concern for privacy.

She then dialed home. She had a lot to say. Twenty-five rings and she hung up.

Where are you, Irish . . . ?

☙ 15 ❧

WHY I AM FOREVER IN SUCH A BIG DAMN RUSH TO GET TO the scene of a homicide, I will never know. The dead person has got nothing to do but wait for me.

The call to meet Kowalski was only twenty-some blocks uptown. And so there I was in a smelly taxicab instead of a nice bus.

I do not like taking taxis. This is for the simple reason that pretty much everybody the FBI arrests nowadays for conspiring to blow up Manhattan with terrorist bombs turns out to make his living driving a cab. Even when the driver's hobby is not mass destruction, an innocent bystanding passenger runs the risk of a loopy conversation. Which is what happened to me this time.

"Hiya there, pal, and welcome aboard," said the driver as I slid into the litter-strewn backseat of his cab. I settled into a well-worn dip in the cracked Naugahyde and rolled down a window to clear out a blue cloud of cigarette smoke. The driver stared at me cheerfully through the pocked shield of Plexiglas dividing us, a safety precaution whereby all taxi fares are democratically presumed to be armed bandits. The driver's remaining teeth were the same color green as his eyes, his wispy orange hair the shade of spoiled carrots, his face sallow and blotchy. He said, "Here's your thought for the day: laugh hard at the absurdly evil."

172

"Thanks, I'll take that under advisement," I said. "How about right now you take me up to Amsterdam and Sixty-eighth? Near corner, right-hand side."

The orange head laughed, wetly. He turned around and drove for two blocks. Then he started up all over again with the loopy chatter.

"For instance, that's what Charlie Chaplin did," he said, craning his neck to look at me while he spoke. "Laughed his ass off at Adolf Hitler, that evil bastard, by making a film called *The Great Dictator*. If you'd ever of seen that picture, you'd know what I'm saying."

"I saw it." I was immediately sorry I responded.

"What'd you think, hey?"

"An artistic masterpiece. Also a classic of unfortunate timing, since nobody called it a masterpiece until Chaplin was practically dead."

"Yeah, maybe I get what you mean. When the picture first come out, a lot of people maybe didn't think Hitler was such a funny guy."

"Maybe not. Maybe you'd better watch the traffic?"

The driver turned so he could see out the windshield, and I was grateful. He lit up a cigarette and said, "Satire's tricky, ain't it? You want to dish up some good, stiff rum punch like people need sometimes and if you ain't careful you wind up accidentally serving it to them in a dribble glass."

"Mind if I ask a personal question?"

"Like most people, it's my favorite kind."

"What do you do besides drive this cab?"

"I'm a collector of great thoughts, my friend. Which I nobly give away to peasants who climb into this here beat-up yellow taxicab every day. What'd you think—all I am's a grunt with a hack license and hemorrhoids?"

"Not at all. By the way, you just ran the red light."

"So what? You want to call a cop?"

"Cops aren't my kind of people these days."

"All right then. Just remember what I told you."

"About laughing hard."

"That's right."

"Speaking of absurdly evil, that's my corner you just passed."

"What are you talking—that one back there that's all lousy with cop cars?"

"Yes, please."

The Collector of Great Thoughts pulled over to the left-hand side of Amsterdam Avenue at Seventy-first Street and came to a stop by softly colliding with a mailbox. He swiveled around in his seat and squinted past me through the back window to a flock of squad cars back down at Sixty-eighth, then said, "Watch out for yourself. Got us some trouble today, it looks like."

"Nothing I can't handle." I waved off the change of a fiver and stepped out from the cab.

"Say, thanks a lot for the tip," the driver said, his orange head lolling out the window. "Here's a little tip for you: Money buys absolutely everything. The peasants, though, they been trained to believe otherwise, so don't pay them no attention."

"Okay."

"Money buys the stuff that dreams are made of."

"I'll keep it in mind."

"You do that, friend." The driver crinkled his face into one of those pained smiles I have seen on people staring at contortion artists out at Coney Island. Then he laughed, loudly and more wetly than the last time, and jeered, "Hey, you—you want to buy a second chance? Want to buy forgiveness for your sins? Want to buy a piece of the American dream? Want to buy something for nothing?"

Again he laughed. And before driving off, he left me with a final something to think about, "Hey, you—want to buy an alibi?"

Wondering if I might ever get into a taxi again in my life, I jaywalked across Amsterdam and headed down three blocks to the tenement house address that Kowalski had given me over the phone. Besides the squad cars outside, there was a forensics unit vehicle and a meat wagon from the Manhattan medical examiner's office. Nobody had bothered about calling out an ambulance.

The house was maybe the last remaining tenement in the vicinity of Lincoln Center. Which is where people in expensive clothes go to hear the opera and the symphony nowadays since the old neighborhood was cleaned out of Puerto

Rican life that gave the area much livelier music once upon a time. Not to mention the inspiration for a Broadway musical called *West Side Story*.

I badged my way past the usual phalanx of uniforms giving vague answers to the usual types found buzzing around a New York crime scene, neighborhood geezers and gawkers and lawyers out of nowhere. From the officers, I heard the standard chorus of "I-really-don't-know-ma'am" and "The-detectives-inside-they-don't-ever-tell-us-nothing" and "Show's-over-folks."

A yenta in the parlor floor window with her hair in rollers and her big dimpled elbows cushioned by a sill full of pillows kibitzed with the sergeant in command.

"Sure as hell took your sweet time getting here," she said, wagging a plump finger in disapproval.

"Well, we finally made it, dear," the sergeant said from his post at the entrance door. He tried gently to laugh her off, but this only agitated her.

"A month we been complaining to the city about what goes on down in the cellar with these artsy-fartsy types coming around all hours. Not a peep do we hear out of you cops, and nobody else neither. Now you come like the Cossacks. What happened—some richy-rich blow the whistle? You think just because the house's poor we ain't decent people living here?"

The sergeant rocked on his heels, hands in his gunbelt. He glanced at my badge and let me past. After a fraternal wink to me, he said to her, "All's I do is what they tell me, lady. You got a political gripe, you got to deal with the mayor."

In the narrow, ground-floor hallway was another detail of uniforms, this one to double-check credentials of incoming detectives and plainclothes officers—and to conduct preliminary interviews with the tenants. After making my way through this second gauntlet, one of the uniforms showed me to the back of the central staircase, where there was an open door leading down to the cellar.

From down below in the dark, I could hear the shuffling of dozens of cop feet, and Kowalski's sentiments, hearty as ever, although muffled some by the heavy dank of basement air: "You evil freaking fairy bastard! Holy Mother of God, you got more than hell to pay here, boy! You got Sergeant Joe Kowalski to answer to, hear?"

The uniform next to me pointed nervously at the stairway, and said, "The party's down there." He looked to be a rookie. His hair was still cropped close on the back and along the sides, academy style. Also it was not difficult to guess that the normal complexion of his face could not be nearly so white as it was now.

I further guessed that this was the rookie's first "unusual" call, as it is daintily known in the trade. I remembered my own maiden voyage, so many years ago up in Morningside Heights, where I first met Davy Mogaill. This was the case of a woman who disemboweled her frail husband with the help of their hulking son. First, she knocked the old man to the kitchen floor with the blunt side of a ten-pound meat tenderizer. Then she had the boy, a sumo wrestler type, sit on his father's skinny chest. And as he howled, and bled considerably, the lady of the house sliced open her husband's belly with a carving knife and ladled out his intestines. The old man lived, thanks to the prompt attention of rescuers roused by his unearthly screaming.

"Been down yet yourself?" I asked the rookie. I wiped my mouth with my hand, remembering, too, how I drank away the night after my own first unusual.

"No thanks, man."

I proceeded downstairs alone. Five black wooden signs with pink lettering lined the staircase, each lit with its own tiny fluorescent tube, as if they were museum-quality paintings. Each was progressively more disturbing: IT'S EMBARRASSING TO BE CAUGHT & KILLED FOR STUPID REASONS ... HIDING YOUR MOTIVES IS DESPICABLE ... SLIPPING INTO MADNESS IS GOOD FOR THE SAKE OF COMPARISON ... DEVIANTS ARE SACRIFICED TO INCREASE GROUP SOLIDARITY ... MURDER HAS ITS SEXUAL SIDE.

"Looky who's here—Neil Hockaday. Long time no see, Detective."

Kowalski's voice boomed up at me from the dark. I was only three risers away from him at the bottom of the stairs, but my eyes were not yet accustomed to the gloom. A uniformed officer with a flashlight walked by, behind Kowalski. The officer's flashlight shone briefly on Kowalski's ripplesoled oxblood shoes with the laces unable to close fully around his two fat feet.

"What now, Sergeant?" I asked. I rubbed my eyes. This did not help me see as much as I wanted in the dim entryway to the cellar, although I did notice that Kowalski had a choke hold on somebody's slender neck.

"This dump down in the basement, it's the sickest freaking thing there is in New York City, which is saying a lot," Kowalski said. "You should maybe of brought a crucifix and a wooden stake with you, it couldn't hurt."

"Who's the perp?" I asked.

"Make the acquaintance of my friend Roberto," Kowalski said. Roberto was hauled up close to me. Realizing I could not make out the face, Kowalski barked at the uniform behind him with the flashlight, "Shine him up here so's Detective Hockaday can see the face of a mortal sinner."

"Anybody read you your rights, Roberto?" I asked him. Roberto's small, oval face was a mass of rising bruises. The black hair over his right temple was matted in place with blood.

Roberto tried answering me, but his tongue was too thick to make any understandable sound.

Kowalski, offended, said, "I already give the Miranda to this sick freaking bastard. In English and Spanish both. You want I should tell him in Polish, I can do that, too."

"You got a first-degree collar on him?"

"Oh, it ain't anywhere near as clean and normal as all that. Like I told you, this one's a beaut."

"There a body someplace down here?"

"'Course there is. Don't worry, Hockaday, we'll get to that. First I want you to square something with me."

"Don't be irritating, Sergeant. I'm very tired."

"Think I'm pretty hard on all these fairy boys, hey?" Kowalski let loose of Roberto's neck. Roberto's body folded, then slumped to the floor.

"I think you've got a certain reputation."

"Come on here with me," Kowalski said. "I want you to see something really choice. Maybe it'll soften your opinion of me and my reputation." He said to the heap at his feet, "How's about you stay right here and wait for us, Roberto."

Kowalski headed down a short corridor, and I followed

behind his wide back. We both had to lower our heads to keep from banging into the grids of duct work up on the ceiling. There was the rancid smell of rats from that ceiling, and the sound of their claws scurrying along the sweaty pipes.

At the end of the corridor was a half-open door, with a lot of smoke and red light behind it. Over the portal was another black wooden sign with bright pink lettering. This one read: DEVIL'S HEAVEN.

Kowalski shoved open the door with a foot. Then he opened up his tunic and removed a pair of cigars from his shirt pocket, one for each of us. "It's definitely going to require one of these," he said, handing me mine. We lit up, and then Kowalski, motioning for me to go through the doorway first, said, "After you."

I stepped onto a steel mesh catwalk surrounding a sunken boiler room. Left or right, my choice, I could walk down steel stairways to the main floor.

What I thought to be smoke was actually only the ordinary steam of an ordinary tenement house boiler room. I stood there on the catwalk deck looking down at the swirl of forensics officers working yet another homicide scene—hands covered tightly in rubber gloves, gauze masks covering their mouths and noses as they moved through the steam. The forensics officers seemed to be searching for something—something besides the ordinary motes and fingerprints of their trade. I began to realize that steam would be the only ordinary thing about the place.

The concrete floor was painted tomato red. Scattered over it were clusters of sofas and loveseats and easy chairs, all chintzed and overstuffed and laden with doilies. The walls—even the boiler and auxiliary tanks—were painted with red-toned murals of male homosexual congress. The ceiling was strung with red strobes, the only source of illumination other than flashlights.

And the ceiling had a single, unified mural of its own: a legion of black-bearded imps and demons happily clustered around a great horned devil with a long protruding tongue, blood red and shaped like a penis.

I looked quickly away from the overhead tableau, as well as the murals on the walls, once again struck by the memory of boyhood nuns. *Peaca súil!* And once again, I was struck for a loop by a conversation with a taxi driver. *Laugh hard at the absurdly evil!*

There was a focal point to the floor, a sort of stage that I had been ignoring on some sort of instinct. Each grouping of furniture had been carefully arranged with a view to what I now took in for myself.

In the middle of a raised platform the size and shape of a twin bed, and covered in red satin, was a nude black man. He lay on his side, motionless. A pillow, encased in the same shade of red satin as the sheet beneath his body, rested uselessly over his shaved head.

"Dead?" I asked Kowalski, pointlessly. The whole place smelled like a butcher shop full of rotting poultry. I puffed hard on my cigar. So did Kowalski.

"Yeah," he said. "Dead as tits on a boar."

"Anything more I have to learn down there?"

"Well, you're the detective now, ain't you?"

At Crosby's place yesterday, Kowalski had been glad enough to deliver an exuberant lecture on the nasty particulars. Now he wanted me to learn directly.

I headed down a stairway, crossed the tomato floor and came up to the dead man from behind. I felt Kowalski close at my heels, puffing, smelling of cigar and nougat-filled candy bars.

A forensics examiner with an optiscope banded on his forehead stood on the opposite side of the platform from me, shoving a two-pronged plastic insert into the dead man's mouth. When he had the lips pried open and holding firm, he bent over to show the optiscope light into the dead mouth. From behind me, King Kong Kowalski explained, "That's so's the medics can scoop out any semen he ain't swallowed down yet."

The examiner looked up over the body, the beam of light from his optiscope blinding me. He said, in agreement with Kowalski, "We like to have our own fresh samples. Otherwise, we got to wait until after they open up the stomach down at the morgue."

I thought again about that first time drinking away the night. Whiskey could be a fond memory, like a first kiss. No matter what the earnest priests would say over at the

Straight and Narrow—no matter what reformed drunks like Davy Mogaill would advise, and certainly no matter the sloppy sentiments served up by writers of twelve-step greeting cards—this shall forever be true for me.

While I was thinking all this—and, God help me then and there in that devil's heaven with all its scarlet, thinking also of Johnnie Walker red in a chunky glass of ice—Kowalski waved over another forensics officer. This one came to the foot of the platform, where he spread out a foot-square sheet of plastic, on top of which he used tweezers to flatten a two-inch-square bit of bloodied paper.

I looked at the dead man's buttocks, resting lifelessly in crusted stains of rust and milky white. My knees shook, with disgust; I made a promise to myself to go to confession that very day, for I knew in that instant the same rage that possessed Kowalski.

Then, like a bad angel perched on my shoulder, Kowalski gave me a tap, and said, "Go ahead, why don't you? Take a look for yourself what we picked out of this one's bum, wrapped in an empty olive bottle."

The one with the tweezers tried to be helpful. "It's some writing," he said brightly.

"That I already figured," I told him.

I stepped down to where the message was—the as-yet-to-be-publicized coup de grâce of New York City's newest serial murderer. Slattery himself might kill for the scoop. This time the message read: WHY DON'T YOU HAVE THEM KILLED, THE WAY YOU DID OUR CZAREVITCH? I pulled my casebook out from my back pocket and noted this, along with a brief description of the boiler room and the dead man and a few other impressions I had.

"You couldn't have just told me?" I asked Kowalski. "Like you did yesterday at Crosby's place?" I happened to look up to the other end of the body then and saw the guy with the optiscope hauling out globs of something from the dead man's mouth, and placing these globs between the kind of lens plates used for microscopic viewing.

"You ain't been listening careful to me," Kowalski said, regaining my attention. "I told you, this time it ain't clean and normal."

"No ..." I tried thinking of something besides the whiskey and the chunky glass of ice, but it did not work.

Kowalski now walked over to the guy with the tweezers. "Go on, Earl," he said to him, jabbing a dead brown thigh with the burning end of his cigar, "tell the detective the same as you told me about this here African queen."

A squad of photographers flocked around the platform and took another several dozen flash pictures while Officer Earl slowly put the tweezers back in his pocket, then the paper message back in its glassine bag. The olive bottle I never saw. Earl consulted a small notebook before saying, tentatively and very carefully, "This is hardly what you'd call official—"

Kowalski interrupted. "Well, hell, Earl, neither is Detective Hockaday here."

"Neither are you," I growled at Kowalski.

"All the better." Kowalski shrugged his beefy shoulders and found a Three Musketeers bar in his pants pocket. "So, Earl, let's give it up already."

Officer Earl cleared his throat. "Well, all right. But anything I say has to be confirmed with the medical examiner ..."

"Earl, we ain't got all freaking day."

"It would appear that the deceased was the object of a massive amount of sexual penetration." Earl coughed. "But this was neither the cause of, nor a contribution to his demise ..."

"Sounds like he's doing an audition for one of those lawyer TV shows, don't it?" Kowalski asked me.

I ignored Kowalski, and asked Officer Earl, "So how did he die?"

"That, I don't know, since there aren't any obvious signs. He might have had a massive coronary ... embolism ... epileptic seizure ... something medical like that. How's a forensic man going to tell that without the help of a doctor? See what I mean?"

"But that ain't the real question," Kowalski said. He was excited now, impatient for some awful punch line he had in store for me. Some chocolate dribbled out from the side of his mouth. "The real question is *when* did this here freaking bum-boy die?"

"Okay," I said to Officer Earl, closing my eyes in anticipation, "when?"

"This man died several hours before penetration."

"You mean, he was already dead when . . . ?" My knees felt like sponges.

"Like the hippies used to say . . ." Kowalski said. He paused to polish off the Three Musketeers and mash his cigar back into his mouth. "Different strokes for different folks, hey?"

I asked Officer Earl, "How do you know he was dead—before?"

"This is just purely on the basis of the available physical signs, you understand . . ."

"Out with it, Earl." It was no longer Kowalski hectoring Officer Earl, it was me.

"Well, it's just that the muscular system has radically different resistance quotients to various types of activity. Like exercise, stress, aggravation—"

"Like murder?" I asked, myself aggravated with Earl.

"We don't know that this man was necessarily murdered," Earl said. I was sorry to have got him off on a tangent. "We might assume murder, given the fact he was young and looked to have a perfectly healthy physique," Earl said. "But the sergeant was quite right in saying the question of how he died is not the one for me to answer."

"Okay, okay. Back to the point about the different muscles."

"The resistance quotients, yes indeed. On the one hand, you see, this man has had the standard reaction to death itself. With even the most passive, natural manner of death, there is a general resistance, leading logically to rigor mortis—or stiffening of the entire muscular structure . . ."

"We know from rigor mortis," I said for both Kowalski and myself.

"Of course. Then you gentlemen can touch him yourselves, just about anywhere. You'll see he's in the first stage."

"We'll take your word," I said. Kowalski seemed to agree with me on that.

"On the other hand, there is still another telltale muscular resistance pattern in the instance of unremitting sexual intercourse. Which in this man's case, we need not assume. His body is positively overloaded with solid forensic evidence of that . . ."

"Meaning the toasted queer got creamed in the end, but good," Kowalski said.

One of the photographers heard this remark from Kowalski and staggered away, holding his stomach. This would be the first time in my career that I have ever beheld a police photographer sickened by anything.

"I don't know that I follow you exactly," I said to Earl.

"You see, the sphincters are particularly sensitive to assault. As this man was repeatedly . . . well, ah . . ."

"Rear-ended!" Kowalski said, sputtering with laughter.

"As it were, yes," Earl said, nodding to the sergeant. He continued, addressing me, "The sphincter muscles will mount a furious resistance to intrusion. If, however, the intrusion continues, the sphincters are quick to spend themselves in fighting—to the point of complete surrender."

"So you're saying what?"

"That given two things—the extraordinary number of times we estimate this man's rectum and throat were perforated, versus a reasonable guess of when this man died—there's a clue that leads a trained eye to an obvious conclusion."

"And that clue is?"

"If this man was alive at any time during the onslaught he obviously experienced, then the sphincters should be almost totally relaxed—even now in death, and regardless of the stage of rigor mortis in any other part of his body. As it happens, though, the overall stage of rigor mortis in this corpse is evenly dispersed. Thus, the sphincter muscles were never engaged . . ."

"Thus, we may reasonably conclude . . ." Kowalski paused to belch, after which he tossed the Three Musketeers wrapper to the floor. He then scorched the body with his cigar again. "This one here was dog food way before his admirers got to him. What'd I tell you, Hockaday? A beaut, hey?"

"This place . . ." I was becoming more than a little woozy. I had to hang on to the side of the platform to keep from falling down. As soon as I could, I pulled my hands off the platform and wiped them off on my chinos. I made a mental note to burn the chinos later. Recovered somewhat, I said to Kowalski, "My God, who comes to this place?"

"Probably you got the same idea as me," Kowalski said. "You want to hear somebody else say it, okay then. This here club's a previously discreet little joint for necrophiliacs of the faggot persuasion."

"No—I can't believe . . ."

"Hey, come on down to earth with the rest of us, choirboy."

Kowalski laughed out loud at me now, and so did Officer Earl, despite all he did to hold back. Anyway, it was true about my being a choirboy, back in the fifties at Holy Cross Church. Slattery had printed that little fact quite a number of times in the *Post*. The item stuck well in the minds of certain cops, these usually being cops who had yet to see their own names in the press.

"Get real, Hockaday. You never heard of Jeffery Dahmer out west there in Milwaukee? Christ, that freaking maniac did them one better than this bunch of New York necros. Dahmer, now there was your regular triple threat of a psycho fruitcake. First he'd go kill some guy, then he'd fuck him—then he'd have him for tomorrow's lunch."

"Begging your pardon, Sergeant," Earl said, walking around the platform. He snugged on a fresh pair of rubber gloves and nudged the body, rolling it over so that now the dead man lay flat on his back. "But actually, there is perhaps something here to suggest that Jeffery Dahmer's got nothing on our local boys after all."

"Say—I guess that's right," Kowalski said, looking down at the dead man, then beaming back at me. He asked, "Okay, Detective Hockaday, so what do you suppose is missing from this lovely picture?"

I looked at the shaved head first, at a scalp as brown as Kowalski's candy bar. Then the broad face, with glazed eyes half concealed by their hooded lids, staring deadly up to the devil's obscene heaven that was the boiler room's ceiling.

Where had I seen that face before?

I looked from the face downward. It did not take me long to see that the dead man used to have a penis. Half of it was missing now.

"Where's the rest of him?" I stupidly asked.

"If we knew that," Kowalski said, "you wouldn't be seeing half the forensic cops in New York searching the freaking place, now, would you?"

"No, I guess not." I had to sit down someplace, and fast. *Where had I seen that face?*

I staggered over to a couch with Kowalski's cigar in my mouth slowly dying out. I sank down deep into one end of the couch, as if I weighed about twice what I actually do. My head felt like the corner bell at a prizefight, my neck and forehead were sweating. Kowalski following me over and plopping down in the chair next to me did not help matters. I turned away from him and spat out my cigar. The butt landed between two of the seat cushions and I did not much care if I caused a fire; I even thought it might be a fitting gesture.

Meanwhile, all around me, forensic cops hunted for half a dead man's penis. Soon, I thought, I would be telling Davy Mogaill all about this place—Devil's Heaven. And as he listened to me, maybe Mogaill would be asking himself how many drinks I might have had.

"Roberto . . ." I said to Kowalski. I stopped when my breath came up short and I thought I might vomit. I waited a moment, then asked, "What's the collar on him?"

"For the time being, simple accessory. He'll keep. He's only the towel boy around here, and he's soft in the head."

"So I noticed. You did a real hammer job on him."

"Hey, what—you think I beat on that spic? No way. Whatever's dented on the little guy, my bet's the necros did it."

"Speaking of the clientele, where are they?"

"They had time to scatter before I got the tip. Probably they lit out of this place like gerbils fleeing a downtown bar."

"Fleeing what?"

"Gerbils, choirboy, gerbils. Ain't you never heard of the latest fag passion?"

"I don't get around like you, Kowalski."

"The fags, they take these cute little rodents and snip off their claws and grease them with Vaseline and then shove them up their butts. Every so often, one of the gerbils takes a wild detour up the large intestine. Guess what happens then?"

"I don't want to guess."

"The fag . . ." Kowalski broke up, wiping tears of laughter from his eyes with his fists. "He winds up at St. Vincent's . . . for a *gerbilectomy.*"

I waited until Kowalski had collected himself, then asked, "So you were tipped to this?"

"What can I tell you?" Kowalski grinned. I wanted to rip off his face. "Sometimes, it just falls into your freaking lap."

"Not that it's anywhere near as much fun as your Holy Name Society functions, Sergeant—but you're having a real good time here this morning, aren't you?"

"Shut up."

"Who was the first one here to this house, Sergeant? You?"

"Shut up, I said!"

"There's a lady hanging out in her window on the parlor floor. She seems to know a lot about what goes on around here. You don't want to tell me, maybe I could ask her."

"I done you a big favor by bringing you into this, Hockaday. Now I'm telling you for the last time—shut up that yap of yours!"

"There's a sign I saw today with your name on it, Sergeant. Did you know that?"

"Everybody's got some sort of a sign, my big-mouthed friend."

"Yours I saw hanging on a wall—coming downstairs here."

"What are you talking, you pissbum?"

"It says, 'Hiding your motives is despicable.' Now isn't that just you all over? You should talk to your priest over at Holy Agony about this."

Kowalski's jowly, mastiff hound face now turned to terrifying expression, bursting into the color of bruises—charred and pulpy red, streaked with yellow. The smell of his meat breath matched the foul aroma of the boiler room steam. A long blue vein in his forehead pulsed. I suddenly realized I was not carrying a weapon. I imagined that the face I was now seeing was the same one seen by King Kong Kowalski's dickprint victims, among them the late Frederick Crosby.

"I done you a big freaking favor," Kowalski growled.

"Don't do me any more."

I had made Kowalski burn, and again it seemed the appropriate gesture. The seat cushions where the cigar butt smoldered began to smoke.

I stood up to leave . . .

. . . and then suddenly, I remembered.

That face. It belonged to a man I knew.

☙ 16 ☙

RUBY SAT IN A BACK BOOTH AT ANGELO'S EBB TIDE. SHE WAS early for her lunch date with Hiram Foster by forty-five minutes, but she did not mind the wait. She needed to escape the agency and all that was making her sick to her stomach that morning: the walking ghost of Jay Schuyler; the anxiety about Sandy Malreaux; the impossible mission of finding motives in the behavior of the deadbeats Alex and Vasily Likhanov.

And so it grimly goes, she told herself. It could be that way from now on, day in and day out, because she had promised for richer or poorer, in sickness and in health. Ruby hated to be so starkly practical in her thinking; she hated herself for now asking, What exactly can I count on from Hock?

But, oh—she loved him so.

Ruby asked the waiter for a glass of burgundy. Which only reminded her of home. She concealed her thoughts by raising a paper napkin to cover her humid eyes. The French Quarter...La Vieux Carré...Burgundy Street, pronounced Burgundy by everybody but the tourists.

She tried consoling herself with the idea she was by no means alone. Far from it. She was in lockstep with all the others far away from home.

Rise up, girl. Oyez, rise up so early in the morning! Bravely

187

set forth—and spin the wheel of commerce. Pay no mind to those people you left behind. Why, they're so mighty proud of you all dressed up in your fine wheel-spinning regalia ... natural fibers, too. Look at you—you're a big wheel rolling, girl ... You must know something ... Don't you just keep rolling along now?

Had it not been for Angelo dropping by her booth, the big wheel might have taken it into her head to roll on off into the deep, cold Hudson. She remembered Hock telling her that very such random and unholy thought, and how he had such on certain of his darker days when he would go to see the undulating river, whose grimy water beckoned as a final solution to his destructive thirst.

Ruby shook herself.

"Darling, are you all right?" Angelo asked her. He reached a hand to her chin, and chucked it.

"Oh—Angelo! I think you just saved my life. Sit down with me, talk to me. Please?"

"Ten minutes I can give you, maybe fifteen but that's tops." Angelo sat. "My chef's throwing a tantrum. Meanwhile, the new bartender's skimming the house blind."

In a way, and although there was certainly nothing sitting across from her that in the least way physically resembled Mama Violet, this was Ruby's absent mother: Angelo Cifelli. He was unmistakably Italian, six feet tall and sturdily padded from top to bottom with his own fine Tuscan cooking. He had only black fringes of hair left on the sides of his head, an olive moon face, and a classic Roman nose. Mama was slight of build and light skinned like the Creoles, although she had a broad African nose. Her hair was red, and nappy like Ruby's own, but Mama conked it.

What would Ruby have done without either one of them? Mama to tell her it was no good hanging around New Orleans wasting herself on trifling men. Angelo to calm her through troubled waters all these months since she and Hock returned from Ireland—married, so they said.

And was that not grand irony? Angelo's Ebb Tide was Hock's own snug in Hock's own briar patch of Hell's Kitchen. Its proprietor, after all, was Hock's friend and bartender of long-standing.

See, girl, you never know.

Hock would be off somewhere unknown to Ruby. Salving his Irish sorrows in private, she supposed. Maybe uptown, all the way to Inwood and Nugent's bar, where he and Davy Mogaill used to drink together. Or maybe at the low-down Flanders Bar—where his evil twin went to drink, so he joked. Ha-ha. Or maybe somewhere else, with a woman who would have no concern for the way he was killing himself? Ruby was helpless against such thoughts, even of her choirboy. Whatever, Ruby now had a place to turn. And a home, in a way. And another dearheart. More than that, she had in Angelo Cifelli a mother-man.

"Yesterday—"

Angelo interrupted her. "I forgot all about yesterday. Hock's back home!"

"I thought it would be . . . Oh, you'll laugh."

"No I won't."

"I just thought once he was back home we'd start all over."

"Jesus—don't tell me he's drinking again."

"No. Angelo, you don't read the newspapers, do you?" That was something Hock would say, she thought. Every day he bought all the papers. Reading the daily line of cod-swallop, he called it.

"I swore off newspapers years ago. All they ever seem to do is quote the opinions of the uneducated and the uninformed. So why should I buy a paper? I've got problems enough with ignorance of my own."

"You've heard the expression 'I love man, I hate mankind'?"

"It's my middle name."

"Likewise, you can still love the reporters—at least the ones who sometimes get good things through. Hock is wild about this guy Slattery at the *Post,* I happen to like Susan Harrigan at *Newsday.* We both like Maureen Dowd at the *Times.* The papers we don't love."

"Well, that makes sense, Ruby. But I'm slow at being sensible. So I don't know that I'll be rushing out to the newsstands anytime soon."

"Well, if a newspaper should happen to fall in front of your face today and you manage to read between the lines, you'll see Hock's name all over a certain big story."

Ruby rummaged through her handbag until she found the page from the *Times* she had torn out, the page with the story of Hock's exploits at the Ladies Auxiliary. This she allowed to fall in front of Angelo's face.

"So it's not that he's back drinking," Angelo said when he was through reading the piece. "It's worse than that. He's back working."

"As a peep," Ruby sighed.

"A what—?"

"It's what the cops call a private investigator."

"Peep. It doesn't sound polite."

"Whatever, it's his job now."

"I don't get it. He's got a job, with the department."

"They put him on furlough, soon as he came home. But do you think he could just rest, and spend his time with me—who he hasn't seen in six weeks since they took him away to dry out?"

"Hock's not the loafing type."

"No. And God help us, he's found a way to work this case."

"That's why he went to West Street last night." Angelo folded the newspaper page and gave it back to Ruby. He shook his large head and looked down at his hands, then said, "Forgive me, darling, but I'm glad Hock's on the case."

"What are you saying?"

"Let me tell you a little story about how it was growing up in an Italian family in a guinea neighborhood of Trenton, New Jersey . . ."

What are you saying, Angelo?

"I went to Our Lady of Sorrows School for Boys the first eight years of my life. Everybody there was just like me. Maybe not Italian, but all-boy. Anyway, this is what Mama and Papa liked to think. Especially Papa. He was very old country, you know what I'm saying?"

"Yes."

"Papa's pals down at the neighborhood bar called him Chooch, and I was Little Chooch—and my papa spent all the time he could with me, taking me everywhere with him. I loved him. I loved Mama too. They were good and beautiful. To my way of thinking, when you are blessed with good and beautiful parents you should never do anything that

190

might break their hearts. So, how could I tell Chooch I felt different from the other Sorrows boys?"

"When did you know?"

"It's probably not like you're thinking."

"Tell me, Angelo."

"One day at school, the nuns arranged a special entertainment. I suppose you're too young to have ever heard of the Great Rubinoff. He was on the radio—as a regular on the 'Eddie Cantor Show' and the "Chase and Sanborn Hour.'"

"Before my time."

"And a little before mine. But kids like me growing up at the tail end of radio's heyday, we knew about Rubinoff being famous back in the thirties and forties. Well, now it's way past Rubinoff's best days, that's for sure. Radio's on its last legs for one thing. For another, Rubinoff's style is too schmaltzy for the modern times. The guy's pretty soon flat out of work."

"So the Great Rubinoff and his violin wind up playing school concerts for kids?"

"Yeah, which you'd think is really sinking low."

"People could look at it that way."

"Most people could, not all."

"How's that?"

"Listen, you'll see," Angelo said, waving his hand. "So there we are in the auditorium this one day at Sorrows. I don't know . . . I must have been eight or nine thereabouts, third or fourth grade. Now understand, this is a big, big day for me."

"Because of the Great Rubinoff."

"Of course. Papa always made it his business to know what was going on at school. He told me that morning at the breakfast table, 'Little Chooch, today you see a wonderful man play the violin sweet as your dreams on Christmas Eve. It don't matter he's not Italian, this man he's my favorite of all violinists. Your mama and me, we always listen on radio for the Great Rubinoff. Pay extra attention, my little Chooch. Music is true language of the soul.'"

"And you heard your soul?"

"I got a seat in the front row, so I could pay extra close attention. Rubinoff wore a tuxedo. I remember it was too big, as if he'd lost weight, and that it needed pressing.

Mother Superior got his name all wrong when she introduced him. What did she care about music? She was half
deaf anyways. The boys down front started a joke around
about Rubinoff's flapping tuxedo, how the geezer with the
fiddle was dressed sort of like a nun."

"At a certain age, I suppose boys get a big laugh at that
sort of thing."

"They did that day."

"How did Rubinoff take it?"

"Like a trouper. He goes straight ahead with the act.
Which was pretty lame if I stop and analyze it. Here's a
bunch of fidgety boys in a hot auditorium, and this guy in
a bad tuxedo is playing what is practically old granny music
on his violin. Stuff like 'I'll Be with You in Apple Blossom
Time.' Come on already, it's the age of Elvis the Pelvis!
Anyhow, you can't even hear half this junk way in the back
of the auditorium, which is why Rubinoff's got his own little
fold-up speakers. God, I remember him kicking the things
to get them started up."

"The Great Rubinoff hasn't exactly got them eating out
of his hand."

"Well, he's got me. I'm sitting there in my seat, fascinated.
I'm wondering how this guy can keep going on, how he finds
the courage to play for us ignorant snots. You should have
seen them—holding their noses, wriggling around, pumping
their armpits and making with the disgusting whoopee blasts.
Know what I mean?"

"I've seen little boys in auditoriums before. It had to be
like that whatever school the poor guy played."

"Sure. But the Great Rubinoff kept on."

"A trouper."

"Then came the schmaltziest tune of his medley that day.
That's when I knew. About my soul I mean."

"What was the tune?"

Angelo gave his impatient wave again. Ruby contented
herself to listen.

"The whole auditorium is horsing around, really giving
him the business. And I mean some of the nuns are in on
the act, too. Sisters are not necessarily angels."

"So I've heard."

"Anyways, the little snots have got the howl on now.

They're turning the event into one more humiliation for this guy who was a very big star in his day, and still has obviously got his pride."

"What about Mother Superior? Couldn't she stop it?"

"She's half deaf at least, like I said. She thinks everybody's loving the geezer."

"What a nightmare for Rubinoff."

"Sure it was. And right at the worst of it, Rubinoff starts playing something he had to know was going to kill him off for good with the crowd. He steps back, he closes his eyes, and he plays 'Ah, Sweet Mystery of Life.' "

"It bombed, of course."

"Big-time. But Rubinoff goes on. And I pay extra close attention. I notice two things. While he's playing, there's tears falling from Rubinoff's eyes—and I'm crying, too. Can you understand why?"

"Tell me."

"I'm crying because this to me is real, even though it's only a joke to everybody else. This Rubinoff the violinist, this is the kind of man *I'm* going to become."

"A different man."

"Different." Angelo laughed at the word. Ruby had no idea what the Great Rubinoff looked like. So instead she pictured Angelo Cifelli in a worn tuxedo manfully playing schmaltzy violin tunes for an assembly of brats.

Ruby asked him, "Have you ever told this to Hock?"

"I've never told anybody who's ever come into my place, until now."

"Not even Hock. Why?"

"Maybe because *different* isn't all that different." Angelo shrugged, then tried to explain himself better. "Every man has his closet. And maybe that's all right, since every man has secrets, and at least one thing he's afraid of."

"You all keep back something of yourselves, don't you?"

"Yes. But when I think of my own secret, I like to imagine that Hock somehow knows. It's what makes him a good detective."

"Once he told me how he knows when he's doing his job right—when he feels he can see what people are doing, even when he's not there."

"And you, darling—can you see what I mean?"

"About what?"

"Hock, dear. About him being the best cop for this case they're talking about in your newspapers."

"These days, he's only a peep."

"Don't sell him short. You're married to a cop, you've got some idea of the department politics."

"Some."

"In this city, you can count on about two thousand murders every year. You don't think that means you can count on two thousand murderers being locked up every year, do you?"

"No."

"No, they got priorities on murder cases. You don't have to believe me. Ask you husband's pal, Mogaill. He's been in here plenty of times telling us the score. Meaning priorities, see?"

"Yes, I think I do."

"When it comes to us *different* types, darling, the regular cops are just like those snots back at Sorrows honking gas out of their armpits. And if a Rubinoff should die in all the ruckus—well then, who cares?"

"Hock does. I'm crying, Angelo."

"So am I."

Angelo left the booth in a hurry when an argument erupted out in the kitchen, in English and Spanish. The argument was accompanied by a clamorous though unseen battle, the weaponry being plates and pots and pans. Angelo shouted as he ran toward the swinging double doorway to the galley, "*¡Por el amor de Dios!* ... Just let me get there before they start with the knives!"

Ruby sat back, dumbfounded. She was looking at the double doorway, where she could see various cooking utensils in flight, but she was not seeing as well as she might. Not with all that was on her mind. She managed to hear Angelo's voice over the others as the fight volume lowered some.

She wiped her eyes. In the flood of emotions that was crowding logic from her head at the moment, she wished for the laws of time and physics to change so that her day could begin all over again, only more to her liking. With a perfect first cup of coffee, then a long hot shower; some cheerful words spoken to her husband, without the slightest thought of his drinking problem; a completed *Times* puzzle on her lap by the time she got off the crosstown bus on her way to the agency; a smiling secretary with a bud vase of roses on her desk awaiting her arrival, and—*check!*—Jay Schuyler's old bracing confidence permeating the shop; and maybe an early dinner with Hock at the Ebb Tide. The way it used to be, with everything about closets still left unsaid.

But most of all in that discomforting moment, Ruby wanted Hock. *Damn, I should have gone straight to the apartment instead of showing up so early at the Ebb Tide!* She had tried calling first, though, and Hock was gone—or not answering the telephone. She did not want to be by herself in the apartment just then, not with her unpleasant and stormy words from earlier that morning being the last things she had left said in the place.

Ruby decided to try calling home once more. Or at least she ought to ring Arlene at the agency, to let her know where she was in case Hock called her.

But there was no time for any of that. Not with her dear-heart approaching.

With the far light of the Ebb Tide doorway behind him, Hiram Foster looked to be much like his former partner Jay Schuyler, another modern classic of the Manhattan patroon: tall, slender, silver-haired, well tailored, sixtyish and fit. On first sight, he looked to have lost his way and wandered into a Ninth Avenue bar and grill quite by mistake. Now someone would have to set him on the right course, see to it that he made it back to the East Side for his half-hour set of squash at the University Club, followed by his luncheon of watercress salad and pâté with tomatoes.

Up close, however, the resemblance to Schuyler abruptly ended. Appearances, like advertising, are deceiving.

Foster was half a generation older than his recent partner, winter to Schuyler's autumn. Schuyler smiled like an alligator, whether pleased or otherwise; Foster only smiled when he was genuinely happy, and looked like a cocker spaniel when he did so. There was also the matter of hands.

Whereas Jay Schuyler's hands seldom performed any more vigorous functions than shuffling the occasional deck of cards or popping the frequent bottle of champagne,

Hiram Foster's hands were a complete betrayal of life beyond Mad Avenue. His nails were often soiled from working in his garden; he frequently sported small cuts and bruises, this from performing his own carpentry; and he had the calloused palms and fingers of a sailboat owner.

Smiling like a cocker, his natty green and brown tweed jacket smelling of apples and pipe tobacco, Foster bent and kissed Ruby's cheeks before he sat down across from her at the table. He glanced over toward the kitchen when a man in chef's whites burst through the door, powered by a large foot that had thumped rudely into his buttocks, knocking the toque clear off his head.

The foot belonged to Angelo Cifelli, whose farewell line to a fast-moving, disgruntled employee was, "So see if I care!" He picked up the toque, put it on his own head, and reassured a roomful of startled customers, "Don't anybody worry, you'll all get your lunches just like you ordered." He winked at Ruby and disappeared into the kitchen.

Foster said to Ruby, "Remember during the eighties when you didn't dare offend a chef?"

"Times are changing," Ruby said. "Maybe for the better."

"Let's hope so. How about you, Ruby? How have you changed?" The cocker spaniel smile went away.

"I married . . ."

"A policeman, I know."

"Yes . . . well, and I went back to the agency. I've got your old office, which you also know. I had them fill in the pizza window I never liked . . ." Ruby paused when Foster laughed at this. She put a hand to her throat, and continued. "I went abroad last April . . . to Ireland, with my husband. His family comes from there, you know . . ."

"No, I didn't know that about him either."

Do you know it was a gypsy wedding, Hiram? That we've yet to be legally married? Do you know I've been waiting ever since we got back from Ireland for my husband to make good on his promise that we would, only he's probably forgotten all about that, since he got drunk on the flight home and stayed drunk until the department couldn't stand it anymore and put him on bow-and-arrow duty—and then he still kept boozing? Do you know Hock's just back from six weeks in a drunk tank? Do you know how much I worry about

Hock when he's away from me? And how much I ache for
the sight of my mother ... and how much pressure's on me?

"I'm having some money troubles ..."

"That's why you're back with the agency?"

"Just temporarily, until I finish a project ..."

A waitress who was not also an actress came by to take
their lunch orders. "No problem about whatever you want
off the menu," she said, holding her pad and pencil in one
hand and smoothing out a twisted brassiere strap with the
other. "Actually, the owner's a whole lot better cook than
that jerk he just canned."

Ruby chose brook trout, string beans, and new potatoes.
And another glass of wine. Foster ordered an immediate
double bourbon. "Be a dear and put a wiggle on, will you?"
When the waitress returned, Foster happily ordered the
grilled sirloin and frites.

"Back to what you were saying," Foster said, "about your
temporary project."

"It seems it's more temporary than anyone ever imagined." Ruby felt a rush of relief wash through her, catharsis
in simply telling her old dearheart the strange story of the
Likhanov brothers, yesterday and today.

Foster sipped at his bourbon. And carefully watched
Ruby's facial expressions as she talked.

Ruby recounted Jay Schuyler's offering her the hush-hush
"bigger than big" consultant job over one of his patented
Four Seasons luncheons; the disagreeable surprise of Freddy
Crosby's involvement in the new assignment, followed by
the repellent details of the business itself—and the even
more odious details of Freddy's murder, now the subject
of her husband's private investigation on behalf of Foster,
Schuyler and Crosby; then finally, the morning's announcement that Ruby was now the executive in charge of tracking
down the missing Likhanov brothers—this assignment given
to her by an eerily pensive Schuyler.

"The two Russians backing out like I guess they've done,
that I can handle," Ruby said, winding up her story. "It's
Jay who's got me really thrown here."

"Why is that?"

"He's drinking, Hiram—and it's very bad. I've never seen
him *booze* like this. I mean the first thing this morning, Jay's

drinking—right after he shows up at the office. While he's telling me about diving in the deep, dark sea and how the Russians skipped town."

"Jay Schuyler's a man blessed with a charmed life, he's always had things come to him smooth and easy. Certainly he drank, but like you say—he never boozed. Jay never really had any reason for that brand of desperation." Foster sipped some more of his bourbon. Ruby had the feeling he was picking his words carefully. He said, "Now it would seem he does."

"What with all that's going on you mean?"

"From what you've told me, yes. All that and something else, too."

"Such as?"

"Such as why I retired, such as what Jay's doing to himself."

"Jay said he persuaded you to retire."

"Persuaded."

"Jay's word."

"It wouldn't be the word I'd use."

"So, this is why you wanted to see me? To give me the real lowdown on your retirement? Here—away from the agency?"

"I like this place of yours," Foster said, looking around, ignoring Ruby's question. The back dining room held six booths along opposite walls with some tables for two in between. The colors were soothing, brown and dark rose; the lights were low, the menu was short and to the point. "Yes, I like it. People come here to eat and talk, not to be seen."

"Nobody comes to Hell's Kitchen to be seen. Go ahead, Hiram, say what you have to say."

"Well, but also I came to eat." Right then, the waitress returned to the booth with their meals. Her brassiere straps were still twisting on her. She walked away, adjusting herself. Foster knifed off a bit of steak and slipped it into his mouth. He asked Ruby, "How are you getting on with Jay's wife?"

"Fine, I guess. We had a nice lunch yesterday, at table eighty-nine. We have an understanding."

"Excellent. If you want to pick up your career again, you'll have to keep on Margot's good side."

"I'm not making it a career. I told you, Jay wants me around during all this . . . this flux, for lack of a better explanation."

"Someone he can trust. Is that how you put it?"

"It's how Jay put it."

"So, you're what—the new vice president in charge of being trusted?"

Ruby had only just cut into her trout. But now she laid down her knife and fork, and said, "Look, Hiram—if you could be the one person in my life these days who could be uncomplicated, I would very much appreciate it."

"All right." Foster picked up his glass and drank down the rest of his bourbon. Then he waved it around in the air so the waitress could see he wanted another one. And then he said to Ruby, "I'll say my piece as soon as I get another drink. I'll tell you why and how Jay Schuyler sold me out, and who the bastard's in bed with now . . ."

~ 17 ~

BEFORE CLEARING OUT OF DEVIL'S HEAVEN FOR SOME OF God's fresh air—and doing the main thing that had to be done next—I stopped at the yenta's apartment up on the parlor floor. I wanted a word with her, and also I had to make a couple of important telephone calls.

"Well, sure, why not?" she said to me after I badged her and asked about the phone. She smiled at me and patted her hair rollers and said her name was Mrs. Pinsk but that I should call her Lottie. She pointed to a couch full of magazines and cats. "The phone's one of them portable jobs, but it don't give you that much static. It's over there someplace where I left it while I was chatting with my girlfriend Shelly. She lives up in the Bronx."

Mrs. Pinsk went ahead of me. She slugged some of the cats out of the way so I could have a place to sit, and then turned the volume down on a television show where some women were being interviewed about platonic love affairs with imprisoned sex offenders. "So talk," she said. "It's no bother while I got the TV down low."

I thanked her and dialed the operator for long-distance information, for the number of the New Orleans Police Department. "Don't worry, Mrs. Pinsk—"

She held up a finger, reminding me with a little trill in her voice, "Lottie."

"I've got a caller credit card for this, Lottie."

"No bother."

The young woman who answered on the New Orleans end put me through to a duty captain, even though I said she could help me with what I needed every bit as well. I said as much to the captain, too, but he told me, "Hey, it's no bother."

"Can you tell me what a moon pie is?" I asked him.

"Y'all mean the cookie?"

"Oh, it's a cookie?"

"Well, sure. Marshmallows inside of a baked sugar crust, wrapped in cellophane. You buy them 'round here just about any old place, all the way from the supermarket to the jot-'em-down store. Taste real good, too. Comes in three flavors: chocolate, vanilla, and banana. I'm partial to banana."

"Thanks, Captain."

"Anytime."

I hung up the telephone. Mrs. Pinsk asked me, "Cookies you're talking? There's some kind of murder and God-knows-what-all dirty business down in my cellar, which is right here in New York City, and you got to call up cops on the other side of the world?"

"Believe it or not, it's an important clue, Mrs. Pinsk—Lottie."

That was a big fat lie.

Up until six weeks ago, whenever I would come across something as horrible as what I had just seen in the bowels of Lottie Pinsk's house, I would cure the bad pictures in my head with a lot of Johnnie Walker. Which crossed my mind only a couple of minutes ago. And so I tried to think of something besides booze—or the dead guy I happened to know in that malignant place downstairs, and how King Kong Kowalski was leading the search for his missing penis. Maybe it sounds ridiculous, but what I thought of was Ruby carrying on about some kind of New Orleans food called moon pies. So I made a long-distance telephone call, maybe instead of tying one on.

And then I lied to Lottie Pinsk. In court when I am under oath, I almost never lie. But otherwise, if it suits my needs, I speak as honestly as the average member of Congress.

"Crime works in mysterious ways, like the Lord," Mrs. Pinsk said. She thought about that, and added, "That don't sound so nice."

"Never mind, Lottie. I'm sure you're a little upset about what's happened. We all are. That's why I'm here, to help you talk it through."

"That's swell of you."

"No bother. First, I have to make one more call."

Mrs. Pinsk sighed and turned her attention to something a jailed sex offender on TV was saying about pinup photos his girlfriend on the outside was sending him, and how he traded these to the guards for cigarettes. I dialed the blood clinic at St. Vincent's Hospital, where I had so recently learned from Kowalski there was a procedure called gerbilectomy. And as I waited for an answer, I thought, You got to love this country.

"Outpatient screening," somebody answered. It sounded like a young woman.

"Hello. My name is Hockaday, and I had a sample taken."

"Blood, you're talking?"

"Yes."

"The HIV test?"

"Yes. Are the results up yet?"

"I can't give you anything over the phone, Mr. Hockaday. Not without the ID number. They tell you that?"

"Yes, just a minute." I went into my wallet and pulled out an identification number, which I read off.

"Hold on a sec."

Maybe in real time it was actually only a minute I had to wait. But in terms of drinking, I imagined enough time for a pair of reds over shaved ice. But still I was waiting. So I tried thinking of something wholesome that must have happened to me at some point in my life. First communion at Holy Cross! *Me in my black pants, long ones at last, and new black Buster Browns and a white shirt and a bolo tie the guy at the dime store said was made by the Navajos. A gold-plated cross pinned to my shirt collar. And Mama and her friends from the pub where she worked giving me gifts— a missal, a rosary, a scapular ...*

"You still there?" the young woman asked.

I said I was.

"All right, I've got your whole file here now. I see it's *Detective* Hockaday." She riffled some paper. "Well, Detective, I've got both reports here, ours and the medical examiner's—and mostly good news."

"What do you mean? There's bad, too?"

"We can't know that right now. You might as well let me give you the good stuff."

"I guess."

"First, *you* read negative—"

I interrupted, "Thank God!" My blood pressure had been on a roller-coaster ride, which I had not enjoyed until now that things seemed to be on an even track. I asked, "What about the other test?"

"Okay, according to the morgue's sample of . . ." Her voice faded, some more papers riffled. "Let's see, the party's name was Harrington, Sylvester . . ."

"Come on, come on!" The roller coaster was heading downhill on me.

"Well, Harrington also tests clean."

"Thank God!"

"But the thing is, you need periodic tests over the next six months," the young woman said. "Would this one be your first one?"

"Yes."

"The virus doesn't always show in the bloodstream on a first sampling. Since this Mr. Harrington is dead, we can't ask him if he's been tested before."

"Maybe he was, maybe there are records . . ."

"Yes, maybe. Know anything about him?"

"Only what I read in the papers."

"What do you mean by that?"

"He led that big demonstration against the Sixth Precinct cops the other day."

"Oh, sure, that one. So he's an activist?"

"Yes."

"So maybe you're in luck, Detective Hockaday. Chances are, he's gone through the drill."

"Drill?"

"These activists, they've organized a regular testing program right here at St. Vincent's. If you want, I could run his name through the computer when I get a chance."

"Yes, that's what I want." I wanted to kiss her.

"Call me in an hour or so, same number. Ask for Betty."

"Thanks, Betty." I hung up the telephone. And decided that not only would I go to confession today, I would also fill up the poor box with everything in my pocket.

Lottie Pinsk turned toward me and smiled, and the world seemed new again.

"Tell me, Lottie," I said, trying not to count the seconds before I could check in with Betty, "where's the super of this building?"

"You got to be joking. We ain't had a super since President Johnson."

"I came across a little guy in the cellar called Roberto. Who's he?"

"That's his name? He's just some junkie come around here one night with the artsy-fartsies, and he stayed put."

"You want to tell me about the artsy-fartsies?"

"All of a sudden, about a month ago, these fancy men start showing up here at midnight. Some of them, I'm telling you, they're prettier than any woman you ever seen. Every night we got anywheres from ten to twenty of them. And all of them are hopped up on dope and liquor—and snarling at us if we even look at them sideways."

"You've called the cops?"

"For what good that does. The cops come over a couple of times, and I show them where the fancy boys go downstairs. The cops go down, and they come right back up and say it's only a bunch of fags hanging out doing nothing."

"Have you seen what's down there yourself?"

"The whole story I don't want to know."

"Do you know the owner of the building?"

"Here you are with the jokes again. You could be a regular panic up in the Catskills."

"So how do you pay your rent?"

"A couple of men come around the first of the month. They don't take no checks."

"Do you know their names?"

"Mr. Policeman, please—you're going to make me laugh myself to death. These men, they don't talk to me or nobody else. They ain't nice like you with a couple of minutes to listen to an old lady. All they do, they walk up and down the stairs, they knock on the doors, and they say, 'You got money?' "

"People here, they're afraid of these guys?"

"They're lying if they say they ain't."

"How about you, Lottie? Are you afraid?"

"I got to say yes, a little bit. But still, they should come sit down with me sometime. I don't mind putting out tea."

"They don't sound like the talkative type."

"With me they could talk. And not in English neither, which all they know anyhow is 'You got money?' Did I mention these two men, they're Russians?"

"You speak Russian?"

"A name like Pinsk, you think maybe I grew up talking Portuguese?"

Lottie Pinsk told me a lot of other things over the next twenty minutes or so, not a lot of it particularly useful. I asked her about the other tenants still hanging on to apartments in her mostly warehoused building. There were four other ancient mariner types, and nothing she said about them inspired any suspicions. So I listened and nodded, and made a break for it as soon as I could.

This turned out to be not quite soon enough. I was just nicely out on the stoop when Inspector Neglio himself rolled up in front of the place in the armor-plated black Chrysler the city provides for him, along with a driver who carries a little flasher he can stick on the roof when the boss is in a rush someplace such as an emergency cocktail reception up at Gracie Mansion.

"They said I'd find you here," Neglio said. He opened his own door and stepped out from the backseat. There was a vague snarl to his voice. "Come here, you hump, I want to talk to you. I've been trying your phone all goddamn morning."

I walked down from the stoop, and then kept walking east on Sixty-eighth, paying Neglio no mind at all.

"Where the hell do you think you're going?" Neglio squawked, falling into step with me. I started moving faster, which was easier for me in my tennis shoes than it was for Neglio in his Guccis.

"You're talking to me?" I asked the inspector.

"What the hell is this, Hock?"

"My furlough. I'm going for a walk in the park, like you told me I should."

"Don't be cute. I don't like you working a case through the back door like I see you're doing. It's no good for your career, I can tell you that."

"Worry about your front door, Inspector. It's wide open and King Kong Kowalski's walking through. Go on down to the basement of that house back there and see for yourself. Meanwhile, since you've got me cooling off from the department, why not let me worry about my new career as a peep?"

I decided not to mention to the inspector the fact that I happened to know the dead man in the boiler room. It would be good to have a small jump on the police. And right after I thought that, it struck me as to how I had just thrown down the glove by withholding the advantage of this information; how I was now fully engaged in an investigative competition—myself and Davy Mogaill as the misfits, the pissbum peeps, versus the department of Neglio and Kowalski. It felt good to have one up.

Neglio did not reply in a sporting manner. In fact, he said a number of rude things to me as he followed me down the street. Out of his frustration, which I could understand, the inspector made abundant use of an ancient Anglo-Saxon vulgarism that may at various times be a noun or a verb or an adjective or an adverb, and which is a word we could not have won World War II without. So I shrugged this off and kept heading in the direction of Central Park, reminding Neglio that unless he wanted to return my department-issue .38 and put me back on active duty there was not much relevance to our conversation.

Pretty soon he left me to walk alone. I slipped into Central Park without looking back at him.

I entered the park grounds near Tavern on the Green, which is an expensive restaurant with a lot of glass and chrome inside of it and which is popular with out-of-towners because the food is familiar, easy to pronounce, and reliably spiceless. Once I got through the restaurant parking lot and the hansom cabs disgorging tourists for their midday feeding, I was soon passing through the succession of hushed glades full of pines and maples and lindens and oaks, slowly making my way over to the East Side—and trying to make out some shape, and sense, to the deadly events of the past two days.

Although I am not the outdoorsman type, I have all my life enjoyed Central Park. I especially like the quiet that falls over me like a fine blanket in those first few minutes I walk into the park, leaving far behind me the clang and the frenzy of Manhattan streets, making everything in the world seem softer and simpler, and easier to understand.

I like all the buskers who work their various acts in the warm months; I like crunching through the first snow of the winter up around Dog Hill and the lagoon at West 103rd Street; I like watching grown men and women acting like kids as they pilot radio-controlled model ships over the shallow waters of the boat pond; I like watching the Dominicans playing softball, old Italian gents tossing the boccie, girls in jodhpurs riding palominos through the bridle paths, boys from the West Indies playing cricket, nannies pushing strollers near the Dairy Barn, bikers and roller-bladers whizzing along the roadways. And most of all I like the Central Park Zoo, where I remember sitting down one day with Ruby to tell her I thought I might be in love with her.

About once a year, unfortunately, some kind of sociopath discovers his personal far side in the park. This starts up about a weeklong flood of bad press from coast to coast because there is nothing people like more than confirmation of their blind prejudice against New York City, and everybody in the media knows that. Never mind about all those stories the rest of the year about crazed good old boys out in those nice, neat rectangular states blowing away customers while they are innocently standing on line waiting for McDonald's hamburgers.

Today as I walked through the park—thinking over my case, scuffing through the acorns and fallen leaves—I spotted a pair of hawks on the hunt. This I could not help, since they swooped down together onto a spot of open ground about fifty yards ahead of me. One hooked a mouse with its talons, the other grabbed up a piece of old cardboard in its beak. I watched the hawks turn and fly back up over the treeline, soaring easterly to their perch—the steel-spiked ledge of a stately limestone apartment house on Fifth Avenue, where I happen to know Woody Allen lives. The mouse was lunch, I imagined; the cardboard I figured was something like a linoleum floor in hawk life.

And in this moment, I was struck with a pair of thoughts. The first was the unremarkable recognition of an ecological dependence between the quiet of Central Park and the noisome city streets surrounding it. The second was the bright idea that maybe I should look at these street crimes I had to solve like a biologist looks at Mother Nature; maybe I should think about the effects of environment on organisms, and vice versa; maybe crime, like nature, has an ecology.

In these ruminations on God's laws and man's crimes, echoes of my Holy Cross schooldays sounded in my head. I could almost hear the nuns discoursing on the proper methods of detection for a right and good Catholic policeman.

What of the spiritual nature of crime? If there exists the good and beautiful heart of the city, the green and leafy and life-nurturing Central Park, the realm of the Heavenly Father—surely there also beats the dark pulse of another and opposite life force. The depths of hell! Could a dank, evil cellar called by a blasphemous name be this wellspring of serial murder?

A panhandler with stains on his pants and a friendly grin loped up to me, interrupting my thoughts. He asked, "Say there, Mr. Rockefeller, tell me now—what's the best nation in the whole, wide world?" I said I was not in a political mood. He shook his Styrofoam beggar's cup, and said, "A donation, my man, a *doe*-nation." I gave him a dollar. He gave me a little salute of thanks, and loped on.

I left the park through the Seventy-second Street gate on Fifth Avenue, not far from Woody Allen's place, where a couple of hawks up in their aerie were having themselves a mouse feast. Down below there were two human beings slumped together along the inside of the gate, huddled close and nearly out of sight in a wad of rubbish and the prickly branches of some dense shrubbery.

They were young, a man and a woman, hibernating for the day with the help of what they had probably drained from a discarded bottle of Duggan's Dew not far from their feet. They shared a blanket, on which they had pinned a paper sign to suggest an idea for anyone with the eyes to see, and a heart to care: GO WHERE PEOPLE ARE SLEEPING AND SEE IF THEY'RE SAFE.

Today's date on the newspaper that Davy Mogaill was holding appeared to be the only difference between what I saw in front of me now and what I remembered seeing yesterday in the lobby of the Harmony Arms Hotel. Which was then, as now, Mogaill sitting in his overstuffed purple chair smoking a cigar with the ashes falling down around him.

Yesterday, he was glad to see me. At least at first. I was not sure how he was going to receive me today.

After I browbeat him yesterday into including me on his private detective agency payroll, we talked about a complicated case I had found. At least then it was a singular case, with a closet queen by the name of Frederick Crosby being the only stiff. Unless you counted up the bodies of some other queens, those being the "suicides" that Sly Harrington was exercised about during the pansy assault on the Sixth Precinct. Which it occurred to me was now reasonable to count. But then, who knew?

Harrington was now dead, his blood now stiffening the clothes I had to run over to the dry cleaner's sometime soon. And I had only just left the ghastly scene of the third murder in a now all-too-obvious series that was already developing the usual politics. Inspector Neglio was personally visiting crime sites, meaning that City Hall was aroused; meaning that now the press was starting to piece things together, which was causing palpitations in guys like Ben Peterson and the mayor. Soon, maybe the whole city would have the shakes. It happens this way in New York.

As for Davy Mogaill—who became a drunk, after all, for the perfectly good reason that he eventually cracked from being the head of homicide in a homicidal town—this could be a lot more than he bargained for when we threw in together. Maybe Davy would just as soon be at long last done with the bedbug work of serial murder; maybe he wanted to spend the rest of his days in the peaceable pursuit of weasels and hookers up and down hallways of places like the Harmony Arms; and maybe, unlike myself, he felt he had nothing to prove by doing otherwise.

"So, partner—how are you feeling this morning?" I said

to him with all the good cheer I could manage after what I had been through, first at the Ladies Auxiliary and then Devil's Heaven. And oddly, a little shaky in the knees at learning how lucky I was in being officially HIV-negative.

I had not addressed Mogaill's face but the open covers of the *New York Post*. Even so, there was no mistaking the man behind the paper. The cigar smoke pluming up from behind the pages was Mogaill's rank brand and nobody else's. I looked at his crossed legs and recognized the pale, hairless shins beneath the trouser cuffs.

I saw the big black streamer on page one of the *Post*— AT TRANSVESTITE DANCE CLUB, THE LADY'S CHOICE IS MUR-DER—and recognized Slattery's delicate journalism.

Mogaill lowered the paper. He stared at me through slitted eyes for a couple of seconds before answering.

"You ask me how I'm feeling, Hock?" he finally said. "With the help of God and four Irish cops, I've got maybe half a chance of surviving the onslaught of yourself."

I lifted my wallet out from my back pocket, cracked it open, and said, "Yeah, you're obviously into something way over your head, Davy. Here—why don't I give you back this generous three bucks' advance?"

"Keep your bloody wages."

"Deduct it out of my share of the retainer check I'll be collecting from our client, okay?"

"Get straight with me good and fast, Hock. And understand, it's not three little dollars nor any other amount of money that's on my mind."

"What then?"

"Tell me where you're taking us under risk to my PI license."

"I want to say there's going to be a regular orgy of gratitude when we close down this case. I want to say they're going to have us down to City Hall and the mayor's going to pin medals on our chests and the commissioner's going to personally reinstate us. And then we'll ride in a convertible down Broadway and people will throw ticker tape down on us two heroic harps."

"And why can't you tell me these lovely things?"

"Don't you see the answer already taking shape, Davy?"

"What I asked for was an explanation from your own two lips, friend. Not your shooting me back a sarcastic question."

"I was hoping you'd want to talk. So let's talk. Somebody out there has organized a game, okay? The object of which is killing people of a despised class. Which in the case at hand is gay men ..."

I paused to inform Mogaill that the body count had tripled since the *Post* went to bed with Slattery's late-edition splash, that I had in fact just walked across town from a place called Devil's Heaven, where King Kong Kowalski had preceded my arrival like he had the other morning in the Nineteenth at Crosby's place.

After telling him, briefly as I could, about this necro parlor in the shadow of Lincoln Center, we both took a longing look across the lobby to where Moses the bartender was wiping the crystal in front of his mirrored rows of colored bottles. Moses caught our desirous look, and smiled his knowing smile.

Also I confirmed Davy's suspicion that the unidentified off-duty detective in the newspaper accounts of Harrington's death at the Ladies Auxiliary was none other than me. And I told him about the cryptic epitaphs the killer had left on the bodies of Crosby, Harrington—and the latest victim, too.

"Now, the player is being selective," I continued. "He's picking off the most repulsive element of these despised people. This way, a lot of cops and a lot of civilians ask the same question, So what if these creeps are snuffed? That way, the game goes on for maybe as long as he wants it to."

"Aye, it reminds me of the bedbug who goes murdering himself a bevy of prostitutes," Mogaill said. "It ain't the pross he's singling out for hatred, it's all the female kingdom he fears and loathes. See my meaning?"

"Pathology."

"Sure, that's it. The bedbug would just as soon kill regular, respectable types—housewives and Girl Scouts and debutantes and candy stripers. But even a bedbug's got a survival instinct. He knows he can't get away with killing sugar and spice and everything nice. But pross—now there's the dark and secret type of women. It's sort of expected a whole bunch of them should get whacked now and again."

"Speaking of fear and loathing, let's consider another pathology here. We've got an armed and powerful organization in this city that hates gay men just like bedbugs hate pross. It's classic. And chief among these armed phobics is a certain overweight brute on the Sex Crimes detail with his own little torture chamber."

"Are you saying the killer here's our slob Kowalski?"

"That's doubtful, but I'm not ruling him out. I am wondering something, though. I've cracked a lot of serial murders, right?"

"Aye, you're the one for bedbugs, Hock."

"Now, this time out the victims happen to be repulsive little queers. And what does the department do? Me they put on furlough, leaving the way clear for King Kong Kowalski to muck around . . ."

Mogaill finished my thought. "Leaving the bedbug a nice prejudicial climate in which to keep on killing. You put your finger on the cynicism, Hock. Namely, there's little or no urgency for protecting this particular brand of doomed life and limb."

"This case, it's half about finding the demons inside the killer's head, and half about calculating the wiles of cop politics."

"We'd best keep two things in mind if we want to stay breathing, my friend."

"That would be nice."

"We're outsiders, Hock. And therefore the only ones fit to catch this killer. That's number one. Number two is, absolutely nobody's going to thank us for a job well done."

"That last part—that's the personal risk you're talking about?"

"Aye. When you want to renew your PI license, take a guess which armed and powerful group in this city reviews your application?"

"Are you saying you'd rather be in bed with the cops on this?"

"I'm only expressing my proprietary concerns open and honestlike. But so you shouldn't worry, know that I'm a great believer in an old Irish chestnut—one you could say's about being alert to the intentions of your bedfellows."

"What's that?"

"There's no sense in going to sleep early to save on candles if twins is the result."

18

DAVY AND I SHOOK HANDS, THUS SEALING OUR MUTUAL AND cautionary sentiments about the tricky business ahead of us. Then we divided up the day's tasks.

Mogaill would run a line on the ownership of the tenement house over on West Sixty-eighth. This he could do by telephone from the hotel, although it is by no means an easy matter to track down the personal identity of a New York slumlord. Most of them are well advised by their highly imaginative lawyers and accountants to be shy about having people know their actual names and home addresses.

Meanwhile, I would check out the place where the dead man in Devil's Heaven used to sleep, when it was still safe for him—before his corpse was violated by the necros. I would go to his apartment, pick off the cream of the clues for myself, and then maybe ring up Kowalski and make him a deal: my location for whatever tidbits he got from sweating Roberto the towel boy. This was an offer I figured that Kowalski's prurient little heart could not refuse.

I left Davy at the hotel desk, where he had commandeered a telephone and a pad of paper. "Still, I've got friends here and there in the department, and other bureaus of the city, too," he said, dialing. A porter was sweeping up ashes around Mogaill's chair as I passed by. I waved so long to Moses at the bar, and went out to the street.

The dead man I knew, of course. Where he lived exactly was another question. But the answer was well within walking distance.

Along the way, I looked in the shop windows and thought about some kind of gift I could buy for Ruby. I wished I could afford something spectacular. But maybe with even a small gesture Ruby could forget about my leaving her alone in bed last night. Maybe buying a little gift would take my mind off myself and I could forget about how much I wanted a big drink.

I stopped at a candy store and bought a bag of sweets. They came all wrapped up in black and orange ribbons for the holiday. Halloween was tomorrow night, after all.

I checked my wristwatch. First I would go get the address I needed, then I would call up Betty.

With the arrival of his second double bourbon, the first half of which he drank down like it was lemonade, Hiram Foster poured forth with his version of how Jay Schuyler and Frederick Crosby muscled him out of the agency. As promised, it was an uncomplicated tale of greed, hypocrisy, and amorality. But Foster's case history of corporate etiquette was heightened by the added element of association with a known criminal—a Russian criminal, neatly enough. Or so it went according to Hiram Foster's assumptions and allegations.

"Neither one of them alone had the balls to come after me man-to-man," Foster said. "And even between Jay and Freddy, they came up short. They needed a guy who knew all about long knives. They needed a silent partner, you could say."

"And just who would that partner be?" Ruby asked.

"You mentioned table eighty-nine. The Four Seasons. Anybody there strike you as, say ... a little out of place?"

"Maybe the guy at the poolside table with the nonstop cellular telephone and the hot-and-cold-running bimbos ..."

"So, you've seen him," Foster said. He pounded the table between them. "So—you know what I mean!"

"I suppose," Ruby said in a noncommittal way. It was the sort of lie that Hock had taught her, something to keep the conversation going along a one-way street. Hock had his tactical reasons for such lies, now Ruby had hers. Much of what Foster had told her made sense, some was bitter conjecture. The problem was to sort it through like Hock would, to think inside out. *What is this? Two detectives in the family now? And what was that "Nails" crack anyway?* Ruby took a stab at provoking something useful from Foster, though she was not entirely steady about it. "He looks like a thug who one day learned how to shave and put on a suit."

"A man can't hide his colors, can he?"

"No, most men can't. But besides that, Hiram, what makes you think this guy's a thug?"

"It adds up."

"Does it?" Ruby smiled to herself, satisfied that she had been steady enough.

"I'm telling you, your boss needed the type with unlimited cash. The kind you don't go to the bank to get. So just ask yourself, Where else would Bradford Jason Schuyler the Third, for God's sake, meet a living, breathing criminal?"

"Here's a flash, Hiram. The world that you and Jay Schuyler come from is lousy with criminals so far as we're concerned in the world where I come from. Your criminals are unfailingly well dressed and pleasantly well schooled—and, notwithstanding this one we're talking about, they are very gentlemanly in all the best rooms of the city. But tell me, are their hearts any different from subway muggers?"

"I can't say."

"No, of course you can't. Every night on the television news you see these guys in nice pinstripes being led off to jail in manacles. I'd bet a lot of money you've known a few of them."

"You'd win that bet. So what?"

"So do you think you've got anything in all this you've been telling me that might get the DA jazzed?"

"Nothing as concrete as that." Foster finished off his bourbon, and stared at the empty glass like he was considering another. "Not yet anyway."

"Even so, it might be useful."

"For your husband the cop?" Foster's slurry eyes danced. "I'm only trying to be helpful. You know—doing my civic duty by passing along something I honestly feel could be useful."

"I'll tell Hock, I promise."

"I'm an old advertising man who's been around schemers all my life. I've known my share of rotters, too. There's a difference." Foster stopped talking and waved over the waitress. He had decided on a third bourbon. "And I'm telling you, Ruby, this one at the poolside table—he's a bad number."

Hiram Foster had said everything he had to say, and now that he was prepared to get drunk Ruby worried that things could soon become repetitious. Hiram was a dearheart, but he did like to go on. And so Ruby, lying again, said, "All this reminds me, I'm supposed to call Hock right about now."

"Good. Be sure to tell him what I told you." Foster took a quarter from his pocket and handed it to Ruby. "Here you go, it's on me. I'll be right here, waiting to hear what he thinks."

"All right, Hiram." Ruby took the quarter and went up to the front of the bar where the telephone was, encased in one of the city's last honest wooden booths. She dialed the agency, reaching the eternally agitated Arlene. "I just wondered, has my husband called by any chance?"

"Oh, my . . . !"

"Arlene?" Ruby asked into the dead air. She shook the telephone receiver.

"I'm here, dear."

"Is something wrong?"

"Well, your husband . . . Actually, he's been here. And gone."

"He spoke to Jay?"

"No, he didn't want to see Mr. Schuyler. Oh, no."

"What did he want, Arlene?"

"An address, which I gave him. Oh, and he showed me his badge . . . !"

"Is Jay there right now, Arlene?"

"Mr. Schuyler is in his office. But . . . Well, I would certainly not say he is capable of conducting any business, not in his condition."

"He's drunk?"

"Oh, my."

"Arlene—?"

"That badge!" Arlene began sniffling. "I've never been so frightened in all my life. I suppose he carries a gun, too!"

"Actually, not these days."

"My—I've nearly forgot, dear." Arlene pawed through a mass of call slips on her reception desk.

"Take your time."

"Here it is, I found your husband's message. He wants you to meet him there."

"Where, Arlene?"

"Oh—sorry. I'm still a little upset. That address I gave him? That's where your husband went."

Ruby took down the address.

"Hiram, dear," she said when she returned to the booth, "something's come up. My husband wants me . . ."

"What's the matter?"

"I don't know. I just hope . . ."

Ruby turned in a daze, and left the Ebb Tide.

Given the last two scuzzy places I saw the guy, his apartment was a lot more than I expected. It was an eyeful for the super, too.

The super's name was Sammy. He was short and round with a two-day beard and a head shaped like a bullet. He wore a sleeveless undershirt, chinos, and a pair of those rubber flip-flops people wear at the beach. His mouth reeked of Fritos corn chips.

Sammy put me through the usual drill after I badged him and said I wanted him to let me into an apartment with his passkey. He used the exact same line they all do, like once he heard the phrase he decided it was a tattoo. Which is to say, he looked me up and down, and asked, "Got a warrant?"

I answered Sammy the way I answer them all, with a mild growl. "No, pal, but I can go get one in about ten minutes flat if it'll make you a happy little citizen."

"Okay, okay," he said, backing off, buying my incomplete story about a missing person like I was the world's finest used-car salesman. "I was only just asking, for crying out loud."

People like Sammy the super spend way too much time watching television cop shows written out in Hollywood by people who never read anything useful. This I say because it is obvious to me, as a cop who has seen enough of these TV fictions, that none of the scriptwriters has ever read the fourth article of the Bill of Rights to the Constitution of the United States. This is the one that puts the brakes on cops like me—and soldiers and IRS auditors, and anybody else employed by the government—when we want to search where somebody lives and maybe seize a little property for some evidentiary reason or another.

For me to get a New York judge's ink on a search warrant, for instance, it takes at least a whole morning waiting on some assistant DA to make up his mind if I have reasonable cause; then the assistant has to talk to the big man, which can take me until way past lunchtime; and then most of the time I have to round up at least a police lieutenant reasonably familiar with my needs, along with the same assistant DA all over again, so we can all have a chat in the judge's chambers about why I am feeling nosy.

So unless the reason I have to search somebody's place has to do with the fact that it is wartime and the Congress has just suspended various personal freedoms—which was not quite the case now, as I informally presented it to Sammy the super—getting a warrant is not like ordering a ham sandwich. Try telling that to the people who watch TV cop shows and believe anything the glowing glass tells them. But I should not complain, as this stupidity often makes it easier for me to do what I have to do.

So this is why I had to tell another big fat lie. This time to Sammy the super, about what a snap it is to get a search warrant. Besides which it turned out that Sammy had his own reasons for being curious about the apartment in question.

"Jeez, there ain't like nothing else I ever seen like this anywheres in the building," he said, whistling his approval as he followed me through the door. "The rest of the tenants, they don't got the kind of money it takes to doll up a room like this here. Also they're mostly a bunch of hogs anyways."

It was a very attractive place, probably decorated by a professional. Ruby would like it, I thought. It was a little dark, though, since there were only a pair of small windows on the east wall. I snapped on an overhead light in the foyer, then a floor lamp just into the parlor.

The parlor walls were peach colored, glazed in a soft brown wash. There was a short, chunky couch in a red and gold pattern with half a dozen pillows on it. And a nearby chair that was also red and gold but in a different pattern and furniture style. There were huge pots of flowers everywhere, heavy on the roses. And gauzy drapes over the windows that somehow made a fourth-floor view of sooty bricks and fire escapes dramatic. There were even more books around the place than flowers.

"You've never been to this apartment?" I asked the super. He was walking around in little circles, with his hands on his hips, whistling. "No emergencies, no repair calls?"

Sammy shook his bullet head, and said, "Nope, nothing like that. But man, you got no idea how many times I dreamt of being up here instead of the place where I usually am all the damn time."

"Where would that be?" I took a quick scan of the bookshelves and spotted three novels I had read myself and very much enjoyed—William Spackman's *An Armful of Warm Girl*, and *The Leopard* by Giuseppe Di Lampedusa, and Robert Heinlein's *Stranger in a Strange Land*.

"Oh, you know—laying in the rack with the old lady, watching some dumb old movie on the tube," Sammy said, watching me as I poked around the room. There was no television set in the place. "You married, Detective Hockaday?"

"It happened to me last April."

Ruby! Betty!

"Well then, you still practically got a honeymoon going on for you," Sammy said. "So what do you know from married?"

"I know one of my favorite things is lying in bed with my wife watching old movies."

"Yeah, wait'll you're twenty years down the line like myself. That'll wear off, believe me. Wait'll some night when you're thinking you might want to give the missus a little poke in the pants, and you look over to see the girl you married's got a face all globbed with cold cream and she's peeling off nail polish with some of that godawful stinking remover they use."

"Nights like that, you're saying you'd rather be up here?"

"Hey, why not?" Sammy snorted, the way we did when I was a choirboy and somebody told a dirty joke during the mass and we all passed it on. "Getcha little something you don't get at home. Know what I mean, brother?"

Believing as I do in allowing a man whatever fantasies might soften life's hard edges, I did not have the heart to set Sammy straight on the object of his fevered dreams. Who anyhow was dead. So I changed the subject.

"Let me just take a look down there," I told him, nodding my head toward the hallway.

I stepped around back of the chunky couch, running my hand over the nubby material. I could well imagine Ruby sitting on a fine couch like that, reading a book with her bug-eye spectacles and her legs tucked up under her. There was another floor lamp at one end of the couch, where most of the pillows were. Obviously this was where the guy did all his own reading. On the red lacquered chest that served as a coffee table were a couple of books that looked like they had been pored over lately, *Manners from Heaven* by Quentin Crisp and *Stories of the Great Operas* by John W. Freeman.

The hallway was lined with framed lithographs. Off to one side, through an open arch, was a dining room as smartly furnished and lavishly flowered as the parlor, and a sleek kitchen beyond that. Down at the end was a bedroom. I knew it was a bedroom because the door was standing open and I could see the bed and a nightstand. On the nightstand was another one of those boudoir telephones like I had seen at the Crosby murder scene.

On the end of the bed was something else that reminded me of murder, a blonde wig. I started moving toward the wig, but stopped where I was in the hallway when the intercom buzzed. Sammy turned and went to the foyer. Before answering the buzzer, he asked, "You want I should let anybody up here, Detective?"

This required a lot of thought in a short amount of time. It might be Kowalski already, if he had been lucky with Roberto—and maybe he had Neglio along for the ride. Or, it could be Ruby. Or else it could be some friend of the deceased, in which case I would naturally be interested in conducting an interrogation.

"Go ahead and answer, Sammy."

Ruby's voice on the intercom. Naturally, she was excited. "Ruby Flagg, calling for Detective Neil Hockaday."

Sammy looked over at me, a shoulder raised so that he looked like a question mark standing there with his finger on the intercom button. I gave him the go-ahead.

Then I said to Sammy, over my shoulder as I stepped into the bedroom, "I'm going to make a call in here while I'm waiting for the lady."

Quickly, I rang up my friend Betty at St. Vincent's.

"Like I said," Betty said, "chances are you're lucky."

"Sylvester Harrington's clean?"

"Clean as you get when you kick." Betty laughed darkly. "Sounds like some joke you cops would make, doesn't it?"

"Certain cops."

"Anyhow, Detective Hockaday . . ." Betty paused, maybe a little nervously. Maybe she thought I was the type of cop with no sense of humor. "It turns out Mr. Harrington was last tested for HIV just the day before yesterday. Negative. And then besides that, he's been tested half a dozen times over the last two years. All negative."

"That's such good news . . ."

"Well, so unless he got infected during the last two days—which is pretty unlikely, since he's been so diligent with the blood-testing program—you're home free. Just take care. Know what I mean?"

"I think so."

Hanging up the phone, I felt like a kid again, all carefree and slim-waisted. The silver lining in the age of the almighty shadow.

Then I heard noise out in the foyer, and Sammy the super opening up the front door, and saying, "Jeez—you's two must be sisters, or cousins at least."

"What . . . ?"

The question hanging in the air was Ruby's. I hurried out from the bedroom.

"I only mean, you're a couple of real good—"

I interrupted Sammy. "I'll explain all this, Ruby."

"Okay, but . . ." Ruby stepped in, a little out of breath from climbing four flights. She grabbed me. Her eyes were soft and foggy. "Oh, Hock, I'm sorry for this morning . . . I read the paper, and—"

"Never mind that now." I put my arms around my bride's shoulders and pulled her against me and kissed her hard.

"Hey, what's going on?" Sammy asked, annoyance and suspicion in his voice. He tapped Ruby's back with a finger that was sticky and orange from Fritos. "This ain't like no police work I ever seen."

Ruby turned into Nails. Nails does not take well to being touched by strangers. So Nails broke our embrace and glared at Sammy the super and his orange finger, and said, "My big boyfriend here, he's a cop, right? Take your scummy paws off me or I'll have my big cop boyfriend shoot you dog dead."

I played good cop to Ruby's bad guy. "Sammy," I said pleasantly, "let's just say we wouldn't want to keep you from your work."

He snorted and flip-flopped back out into the corridor. Before going back downstairs, he popped his head into the door and said, in a kind of nasty singsong, "Getcha a little something you don't get at home . . ."

"What kind of tune is that, rat face?"

"Never mind him either, Ruby. Come on over here by this nice couch." I steered her away from the entry and sat her down. Then I gave her the Halloween candies, and she smiled. She was not Nails anymore. "I wish it was a bag of rubies, Ruby."

She untied the black and orange ribbons, found a caramel and ate it. "Thanks," she said. "Whose apartment is this?"

"It's your secretary's place."

"Sandy? She lives here?" Ruby looked, twisting around on the couch, taking a quick survey of the furnishings, the books, and the flowers. Her face then filled with worry, and she asked, "Please, Hock, she's not—?"

"She's dead."

Ruby's hands flew to her open mouth, and all the candies and the orange and black ribbons spilled from her lap to the floor. "My God!"

"That's not all."

"She was murdered?"

"Make that, *he* was murdered."

Ruby held her head with her hands, like she suddenly had the world's most painful headache. "He—?"

"Sandy Malreaux wasn't a woman. We don't know exactly how she was killed, but we did find her body this morning. And it was a very bad scene."

"Well . . ." Ruby was trying to make sense of all I had told her. "How do you know she wasn't . . . I mean, how do you know Sandy was a man?"

"He was naked."

"When you called the agency, Arlene never said anything to me about your coming here."

"I asked her to keep quiet."

"She sure did. Give me a minute, Hock. This is all pretty overwhelming. First Crosby, then this murder last night . . . Now this." Ruby took a breath, then stood. Then she knelt down and scooped up the candy. "Sorry for dropping this."

"Forget it. Tell me about your Russian clients."

"The Likhanovs?" Ruby gave me a look like I had just slammed her jaw with an uppercut. "Funny thing, Hock. They seem to have disappeared."

"That figures."

"Oh . . . yes, maybe it does." Ruby seemed to be thinking out loud. Then she seemed to want me to help with her thinking. "How?" she asked. But she did not look up at me for an answer. She saw a certain book on the red coffee table instead, the one about opera. She picked it up.

"It figures because it's meant to figure," I told her. And I was likewise thinking out loud.

Ruby did not entirely hear me. For some reason she was suddenly very absorbed with the opera book and not paying me her fullest attention. I myself was only half clear about what I had just said, and why. All I knew at the time was that I had hold of one of those ideas I had to sleep on. And when would sleep come again to me? I wondered. Maybe we were both like this, with thoughts drowning out each other's words.

Ruby raised her eyes from the opera book, and asked, "Hock, she didn't die here in this apartment, did she? I mean *he*. Is Malreaux his real name?"

"I haven't made a close search of the place yet. But no, I don't think he was killed here. And yes, it's Malreaux. Maybe Sandy's short for Sanford. Anyway, he fooled a lot of people. Including the super, that's for sure."

"From what I hear, including all the men at the agency, too."

"Speaking of the agency, how's the boss doing today?"

"Not so good with the loss of the big project he hired me to run. This morning—I suppose right around the time you found Sandy's body, whenever that was—Jay had to give me a new job. He needs somebody he can trust, he says."

"You?"

"I'm trustworthy, aren't I? He seems to think you are, too, Hock. So while you're looking into Freddy Crosby's murder for him, I'm going to be playing detective myself. I'm officially looking into the disappearance of the clients Freddy brought us—namely Alexis and Dimitri Likhanov."

"How's their English?"

"The Likhanovs? Not so good."

"It figures." I cut Ruby off before she could ask me why this figured. "Schuyler didn't look so steady to me when we talked yesterday. You're saying he's not much better?"

"He was talking this morning about deep sea divers and how they have to train themselves to *see* disorienting *sounds* while they're down below in the ocean depths. In other words, he was drunk."

"Does he have a bad habit that way?"

"Not that I ever knew."

"Could it be he was talking sense?"

"Maybe. What about you, Hock? What's with the interest in my wandering Russians?"

"I think we're running around in the same circle on all this, Ruby."

"You don't know the half of it. Let me tell you what I heard at lunch."

19

THERE WAS A SHORT BUT CRITICAL TIME TO KILL, AND A GOOD appearance to make. And so it was helpful to have a companion.

In fact, this was his rule: He always made certain he had a companion at this stage—and to appear to be having a perfectly pleasant conversation, in the event anyone was watching. These days, who knew? He insisted, always, that his companion be an actual client, as was the case today. In his line of work, it was simply good insurance to have the client at some physical risk as well; this demonstrated sincerity.

He was as prone to boasting about his successes as any other professional man. And so in answer to his companion's question, he did not mind revealing that today was the twelfth time in three years he had completed this particular mission.

"It's that easy?"

"No, my friend, I'm that good."

"Good and expensive."

"You get what you pay for."

"It didn't take you long to learn the ropes, did it?"

"Ropes are so difficult to learn?"

"Well, I should think they are when the only thing you

ever knew your whole life turned out to be the wrong way of climbing them."

"So, maybe you like to talk about politics?"

"Not really, I never cared for politics. I think you have to be a lowbrow and a sadist to be political, ready and willing to see people sacrificed and slaughtered for the sake of an idea—whether the idea's good or bad."

"Ideas don't matter, money does."

"See what I mean about how quick you learn? All your life, from your schoolboy days and on through the party hierarchy, you were trained to be an idealist. Now here you are, as good a running dog capitalist as I've ever known— and I've known quite a few."

"I tell you a secret. Before in my country, there were plenty of us who knew the truth about socialism."

"And what is that?"

"Socialism is what happens between capitalism and capitalism."

"Very funny."

"Yes, I think so."

He turned from his English-speaking companion and smiled at two men in matching blue business suits sitting patiently on his other side. He spoke to them briefly in Russian. The two men laughed at what he said.

"What did you say?" the companion asked.

"I translated my funny joke about socialism."

"Your friends, they're rich new capitalists like you?"

"One day maybe, if they ever apply themselves and learn to speak American. There's so much opportunity in the United States for men of their abilities. It's such a shame to be sending them home."

"By your lights, maybe. But I'm making it well worth your while to throw them back, aren't I?"

"Yes, that's so true."

He opened an elegant leather briefcase and pulled out a stained paper bag and a bottle of catsup. He opened the bag for his companion. "Would you care for a bagel?"

"I don't think so."

The others likewise declined bagels.

He shrugged and picked out one for himself, which he

doused in catsup, then ate. When he was through, he asked his companion, "You brought the rest of my money?"

"Yes, of course."

"Good. It's time now."

And just as he said this, the boarding announcement was made for the daily Aeroflot run, direct from New York to Moscow with a one-hour layover at London's Heathrow Airport.

He rose from his seat, and his companion stood up with him. The other two men stood, and then all four proceeded to the gate.

"Goot bye-bye!" the two men in the blue suits said.

He hugged them both. His companion did the same. Should anyone be watching—and these days, who knew?—it appeared to be an ordinary farewell.

Thirty minutes later, when the plane for Moscow was aloft, he and his companion left the terminal building. They walked together to the parking ramp, where each had a car.

In the ramp, he accepted an envelope from his companion. Who in return accepted a satchel from him.

"Thank you," he said, with a short bow of the old-world fashion.

"And I thank you."

He placed the envelope in his breast coat pocket, and asked solemnly, "This is your written pledge to make me a genuine American businessman?"

"Yes."

"And to that end, you have accepted my money. And you are prepared to carry out the last remaining detail?"

"I am."

He touched his companion's satchel, and said, "If you like, my friend, I tell you the secret of America."

"Do tell."

"Justice is swift for those who can afford to corrupt it."

✐ 20 ✐

I FINISHED UP ON FOUR TELEPHONE CALLS JUST AS RUBY RE-
turned to the late Sandy Malreaux's parlor after washing her
face with soap and cold water in the late Sandy Malreaux's
bathroom. The first three of the calls I made partly in order
to take my mind off something bad for me and partly in
order to have something nice to look forward to when this
awful case was over. The fourth call I had to put in to
Kowalski, who was still across town at Devil's Heaven.

"Okay, he's on his way over," I said, hanging up the
phone receiver.

"Find anything helpful around here besides the wig?"

"Not really."

"What did you do with it?"

"The wig? I left it alone, except for pulling out a few
strands of the hair, so I have my own samples." I patted the
side pocket of my coat, where I had a few of the blonde
tresses sealed in an envelope.

"All right, let's get through this before I forget everything," Ruby said. She sat down on the couch and rubbed
her face. I settled into the adjacent chair. "By the way, who's
on his way over?"

"You'll have the pleasure of meeting Sergeant Joe
Kowalski."

"The one you told me about? King Kong Kowalski, the dickprints guy?"

"In the flesh. Which on him there's a lot."

"Maybe you've managed to keep your hands off his neck so far, Hock, since you didn't have to be personally offended by what Kowalski does. Now there's a reason you should be personally offended. Let me tell you about a friend of yours ..."

Ruby then told me about Angelo. About the sweet mystery of his life, and how he liked to think that in the many years of our friendship I had been able to see the truth all along. And had I seen? The answer was no. But so as not to disappoint my friend, I would tell him a lie when next I saw him.

"Quite some lunch you had," I said to Ruby when she finished her story.

"That was only the first course. Then came Hiram Foster."

"Schuyler's retired partner?"

"Muscled-out partner. So understand that what I'm about to tell you is all from Foster's skewed point of view."

"Shoot."

"Jay and Freddy—mostly Jay, I'm surprised to say— couldn't be content with what they had. Which was a nice, profitable medium-size New York ad agency doing about seventy-five million a year in billings. Along came the decade of greed, and the two of them bought into the whole sorry ethos."

"But not Foster?"

"Hiram's a fool like myself. I saved up all my money to buy the theater. And all Hiram was ever interested in doing was making a pile to support his little farm up there in Putnam County, and his sailboat."

"Definitely not an eighties kind of guy."

"Worse than that, he was in the way of some guys who were. Which is why Freddy and Jay tunneled under him, by persuading him that the agency should make a public stock offering. That way, the character of the shop could be preserved, and the partners would control a lopsided majority of the stock in perpetuity. But it was all a scam, and as soon as the shares were let, clients started disappearing."

"As I recall, a lot of companies sold themselves thin like that," I said. "Toward the end of the decade, when the bubble was beginning to burst but before anyone wanted to admit something was wrong."

"Sure, a lot of that happened. Capital went out that wasn't replaced with new revenue. People got scared, stock sold short. A lot of people who maybe should have known better were left holding empty bags."

"Which is what happened at your agency?"

Ruby shook her head. "Not exactly. According to Hiram, Jay and Freddy hit themselves with manufactured losses."

"How so?"

"They went out and solicited business they knew to be slow payouts, or surefire flops. That time you mentioned when the bubble was bursting—?"

"Middle to the end of the eighties."

"Right. You know what ad agencies did by way of ignoring reality?"

"No. Tell me."

"The common practice was to work on speculation. You'd invest the time and effort of your shop—your account services people, your creatives, your media budget—and you hoped to God your advertising campaign worked to increase sales for your cash-starved client, who never put up a dime of support."

"So you had a lot of what they call shakeout?"

"Like flies the agencies were dropping."

"And this kind of speculative business is what your boss actively sought?"

"Right. The question is—why?"

"Because that was the way to scare old Foster so bad he'd sell back his stock. That's not so complicated."

"Well, that's the small picture, which isn't complicated. And which in any case worked. Foster was afraid of his whole life's effort being dribbled away, so he gradually sold off his stock ..." Ruby paused, and picked up the opera book again. She asked, "Do you think I could take this with me?"

"I don't know why not."

"Anyway," Ruby said, continuing, "the stock that Hiram

let go wasn't sold to Jay and Freddy directly. Hiram *thought* he was selling to minor shareholders."

"Who in reality turned out to be?"

"That's the sixty-four-dollar question. Hiram claims to have this whole thing puzzled out, even though he could never prove it in a court of law." Ruby stopped for a second, to make sure she had Foster's train of thought firmly in her memory. She rubbed her face again, and also her temples. "Hiram says that Jay and Freddy were pulling in weak projects all that time with the help of a backer—sort of a fourth partner, a silent one. So silent even Jay and Freddy never knew exactly who he was. All they cared about was deep pockets, which they knew they had to have in order to get rid of Foster."

"Tell me again. Why get rid of Foster?"

"Because he wasn't hell-bent on bloating up the agency like Jay and Freddy were, and everybody else on Mad Avenue," Ruby said. "Because he thought that making a couple million or so to support his farm and his sailboat was plenty enough for one man."

"I see Foster's point. Also I can see where his bad attitude wouldn't fit Madison Avenue."

"It didn't. Hiram's an odd sock, which is why he's one of my dearhearts. Back when I was at the business full tilt, the two of us would take time out of the middle of the day and talk about things. Important things, not Mad Avenue things." Ruby shut her eyes. "What a glorious waste of company time. I can still sometimes hear him holding forth."

"What did he like to talk about?"

"Very often about mediocrity. Hiram saw the problem of this growing worse every year. Once he wrote a letter to the Harvard Graduate School of Business Administration suggesting that students should research corporate mediocrity."

"What did Harvard say?"

"Nobody wrote him back. Either that or his letter was lost in the mail. Anyway, Hiram had a theory: mediocrity is contagious. He also said a corporation's mediocrity level increased in direct proportion to the ratio of time spent by the big boys in dreaming up ways to get bigger purely for the sake of getting bigger."

"A very big ratio in the eighties."

"It still is," Ruby said. *Bigger than big.*

"So, tell me if I understand the play," I said. "Schuyler and Crosby conspired to drive down the stock value by taking on losses. Then they took money from a silent partner to buy up Foster's shares—on the cheap."

"Exactly. You've got the small picture, just like Jay and Freddy."

"Small picture?"

"There are all sorts of different-size pictures when you deal with the devil. Among the small ones was buying out Foster. For all their talk, Jay and Freddy never saw pictures any bigger."

"If they were alert, what would they have seen?"

"They might have tried seeing how their silent partner was buying up a lot of the loser agencies at the same time he was buying out Hiram Foster. How he put everything together under Jay and Freddy. How all his shares from a whole passel of losers added up to more than the shares owned by Jay and Freddy, who somehow thought they were big winners."

"Smart."

"And profitable, in the short run. Today the agency's billing better than three hundred million a year. So this is called an American success story. Never mind what the devil wants in payment for all the expansion."

"I'll bet that's not too complicated either. He wants a boatload of money laundered."

"Hock, my love, you're beginning to see larger pictures."

"Who's the devil behind the soiled money, Ruby?"

"Somebody who's been under Jay's nose all along. Hiram swears he's one of New York's biggest Russian gangsters. I've even seen the guy. I don't know his name, but he has lunch most days at the Four Seasons. They call him the Bullfrog."

We had only just begun to compare notes, in an attempt to figure out which of several twisting paths through the maze of clues and suspicions might eventually lead us to the failings of somebody's best-laid plans.

I had no sooner finished detailing for a numbed Ruby my

night at the Ladies Auxiliary that ran into my morning at Devil's Heaven—and the unfortunate run-in with Inspector Neglio—when I heard the unmistakable sounds of King Kong Kowalski clunking up the stairs, preceded by Sammy the super.

"Jeez, how was I s'posed to know?" Sammy was saying. "He shows me a gold shield and all, I never thought to ask if he was packing heat or not. Give me a break, will you, Sarge?"

"I'll give you a break. Right in your freaking spine." I heard Kowalski wheezing out in the corridor. Lucky for Sammy, some uniforms had come along with Neglio, and so I did not hear any bones actually snapping. "Okay, we're all the way up," Kowalski bellowed. "Which door, Sammy?"

"That would be King Kong?" Ruby asked.

"Ready or not."

The door fell open and Kowalski steamed in, along with a trail of uniforms. "So, Detective Pissbum—I trust you never touched nothing here. If you did, I will personally see about getting you retired out of the department so you can go fishing every afternoon with your buddy Mogaill. Or whatever retired pissbums do with time on their hands."

"I don't think you'll find anything disturbed, Kowalski. You know why?"

"I'll bite."

"Because you're the kind of cop who couldn't find a pubic hair in a whorehouse."

Kowalski's face went purple with blood and his massive head shook, and for one proud moment I thought I might have inspired a coronary. He looked at Ruby, then at me, and asked, "Who's the broad?"

"Watch your mouth, Sergeant," Ruby said. "I won't tell you nice again. Next time you talk garbage like that, I'm taking down names in this room and you and I wind up in front of the Civilian Review Board."

"Joe," I said to Kowalski, "may I present my wife? Ruby Flagg."

"Christ!" Kowalski picked a cigar from his pocket, bit off an end and spat it out on the floor. "All right, Hockaday, let's just get with it. Who's the dead faggot?"

"Sandy Malreaux. I don't know if that's a legit name, but

it's the one he goes by. Your men will comb the place, they'll find out if he goes by anything else."

"How is it you come to know this Malreaux?"

"He works for the ad agency—Fred Crosby's agency. As a woman."

"Ain't that lovely."

"You'll find a blonde wig back in the bedroom. Maybe it matches the one that Sly Harrington's killer was wearing."

"Not only that, maybe this here faggot was the one all duded up that night at Crosby's. The one that signed in as, whatever ..."

"Veronique Unique," I said, cutting him off. "I'm way ahead of you, Kowalski. Everybody is."

"I'm suddenly in such a good mood I'm going to ignore all your disparaging remarks from now on, Detective Pissbum. Just for you, I'm turning the other cheek. Say—I guess many a cheek's been turned in this here dump, hey?" Kowalski laughed his sickening laugh and apologized to Ruby by saying, "Please forgive the off-color humor, Mrs. Pissbum."

Ruby started rising up from the couch, but I caught her, which was lucky for Kowalski. "Later, Nails, and in a much sweeter way."

Kowalski sneered at us both, then said to his crew of uniforms, "Let's go, boys—it's yellow tape time."

Poor Sammy had heard everything. His dreamboat baby doll Sandy Malreaux was a man. Sammy the super looked ready to faint or throw up. He staggered backward out through the foyer to the corridor, where I heard him say, "She's a goddamn guy? I been gooey on account of a *guy?*"

"You ought to feel real proud of yourself right about now, Kowalski," I said.

"Damn straight."

"It ends here, doesn't it? This is enough for you and the department, right?"

"Bet your ass it is."

"King Kong Kowalski cracks the case."

"Don't be calling me that."

"King Kong Kowalski, he always gets his man. And wouldn't you know it, it's a guy that his whole crowd loves to hate."

"Say what you want, pissbum. You're on the outside looking in. Kind of cold out there, ain't it?"

"I'm warming to it."

"You better, since it ain't looking good for you returning no time soon. Not with this grief you're giving me by interfering with my case out of jealousy."

"You got me wrong, Sergeant. I think you're doing one bang-up job of old-school police work here. I can see that. Bust 'em, burn 'em, try 'em, and fry 'em."

"Give me that old-time religion." Kowalski spat on the floor again. He was out of patience with me now.

"You're not much of an ecologist, are you, Kowalski?"

"Up yours with ecology. Show's over, pissbum. Move it the hell out of here now. That's an order from an actual working cop."

"But we made a deal, Kowalski. Remember? You being a member of the Holy Name Society and all, you wouldn't want to be lying."

"Oh yeah, sure. What do you want to know?"

"I hate to spoil your old-time religious happiness with such a piddling little detail, but exactly what are you planning to write down as the cause of Malreaux's death? I still remember Earl's interesting lecture on the variable rates of muscular resistance, and how Malreaux was killed sometime before the necros raped him."

Ruby stood up, a little unsteadily, and announced she would be washing her face again.

"Earl and anybody else, they can be persuaded to go along with little alterations here and there. Main thing is, we got the killer of Crosby and this Harrington."

"Sure you do, Sergeant."

"I lay you ten to one that wig matches up with what forensic took out of the Ladies Auxiliary, and a look-see through Malreaux's closet here gets us a fiber match with the stuff we picked up at Crosby's."

"I'm sure you're a hundred percent correct."

"Little matter like this Malreaux got himself canceled out ... Well, that was only what he had coming to him anyhow. You think people are going to see any different?"

"No. It looks all very neat and tidy."

"For freaking once, yeah."

"Just one thing."

"What's that?"

"Your boys ever find the missing penis?"

"Oh, that." Kowalski made a sound like a suction plunger unclogging a drain, which for him constituted a laugh. "I guess one of the escaped clientele dropped the prize dick on his way out. Anyhow, we found it stuffed halfway inside of a rat's mouth. The rat, he choked to death trying to eat it."

21

Davy Mogaill telephoned at five o'clock and said he had something big to tell me. I yawned and he scolded me for this lack of enthusiasm. But only two hours earlier, I explained, I had enjoyed the great luxury of being at last home for a hot shower and a nap. And how the long overdue rest was just nicely beginning to settle into me when he called. This seemed to molly him some.

While I was soaping my head in the shower those two hours ago, Ruby made some quiet telephone calls of her own. Then she tucked me in and went off to the Four Seasons, she said, for a nose-about on the topic of a high-profile customer known as the Bullfrog.

Ruby and I agreed we should use Angelo as our answering service and the Ebb Tide as a relay point. When I suggested to Mogaill that under the circumstances it would be senseless for me to meet him anyplace else, he balked.

"I remember far too many of the good old bad days in that saloon," he said. "In all Hell's Kitchen, you've surely got some dryer and less reminiscent spot."

"The neighborhood's swimming in booze, Davy. What good is it going to do my recovery if I deny that fact of life?"

"Ebb Tide it is then. I'll be hurrying over."

"Please—don't insist on being my guardian angel. I'm not willing to accept the responsibility of that."

"Nae, I'm not—"

"And listen careful, Davy. Don't break your neck getting over here. I'm not tempted. I don't want a drop, hear?

This was the truth, the whole truth—and nothing but the truth, so help me God and all saints who might be listening.

"I hear, and my ears burn with joy at the sound. Nevertheless, I'll not waste time."

"See you soon, Davy."

The only thing on my mind having to do with the Ebb Tide and what was behind the bar was my pal Angelo Cifelli. What was I now going to say to this guy who had exposed his own private furnace room to Ruby? Who I had failed myself to properly understand during all the years of *his* understanding help, given freely to me? Had I ever myself done such a manful thing as had my friend Angelo in telling his truth to Ruby? Had I ever done like him, and truly said the devil be gone to a lonesome secret of my own? I, whose opinions and respect Angelo valued?

Or had I been a wussy? Spending so many years mewling and puking about my petty travails in love and marriage over jar after jar of whiskey?

At that moment I felt as if I should run out into the street with my hands stretched out, palms up, and ask the first nun I saw for ten whacks of a ruler. I felt like a fraud. And the last thing in the world a fraud needs is a belt of Johnnie Walker. Too much of that for too many years had blinded my eyes, bloated my brain, and thickened my heart. *And so help me God, and all saints listening—just for today, I'll not be such a man!*

Having prayed this while pulling on my chinos and sneakers and a ragg sweater and a raincoat, I then raised my hand in a fist and shook it in the direction of heaven, and offered an additional prayer of defiance. *If I have to be a cursed drunk, why in the name of God do I have to be a Catholic, too?*

It is not fair, after all. There are so many frozen moments in the life of a helpless Catholic such as myself. I am not a priest, and so I do not know why this is. I only know that I am often stunned, as now I am; thinking this impossible summary of myself, how I came to where I am and what in the world that means.

I look into a mirror. And I see myself: a cop with graying hair, in a well of tears. And I think of all that I meant to do in the pursuit of beauty and justice, and have not done. I think of my mother and father under the earth. And how I am crouched, big as I am, against the shrinking future. I greedily count up the few fond stories that might conceivably be told of me by mourners, and how these stories will quickly go to vapor. And how, if I had to select one innermost craving at the expense of all others, it would be this: lying in a field of green with Ruby, as on our Irish wedding day.

Before I left the apartment, maybe to lift my palms in the street, I made some quick telephone calls. Oh yes, for I knew exactly what I had to do.

I confirmed all arrangements, save one.

There was Angelo, as so many times I have seen him on walking through the Ebb Tide's swinging doors: stooped over hot, soapy water behind the bar, rinsing out glasses. Had I ever seen him dressed in any colors but black and white? As ever, he wore a crisp white shirt and black four-in-hand under a black silk vest. A white apron to his knees and black trousers completed the ensemble.

And high above him, up over the spray of flowers on the back bar along with all the pretty bottles, was a painting of himself. Angelo Cifelli, bent to the unending task of dirty glasses, and a woman in a hat with a green feather, sitting at the bar talking to him.

I walked to the end of the bar, and around to the back. And Angelo looked up in natural surprise. I took him by the shoulders and kissed his cheeks, one and then the other.

This occasioned a very good round of belly laughs amongst the unknowing boyos gathered at the bar. And I continued their good cheer by standing the house for a round.

Angelo pulled away from me and wanted to know if I needed a doctor's attentions.

"I'm only telling you in my own way, Angelo, that it was a hell of a good thing you did—telling Ruby about yourself." dropped my hands from Angelo's shoulders.

"You mean it about standing the house, Hock?"

"Sure I do."

Angelo told the assistant down at the other end of the bar to set up and pour.

I said, "Angelo, I've been waiting for years for you to tell me the same as you told Ruby, not wanting to intrude on your line. But telling my wife . . . Well, you know, that's as good as finally telling me."

Angelo mumbled, "I don't know what to say . . ."

"Well then, it's been said."

"Thanks, Hock." He took my hand and we shook hard. "Really—thank you, from the bottom of my heart."

"What you must never allow a friend to do," I said, words coming to me from I know not where, "is to suffer a terrible expense of the spirit in a great waste of shame."

"I'll never forget this moment," Angelo said.

"Me neither. And by the way, my friend, it's me who thanks you from the heart. I'll do it the way my mother used to, in the Irish. *Gora maith agát.*"

I thanked Angelo because I no longer felt the need of an avenging nun, or Ruby's loving scoldings. I felt, at least, as if I had learned what it is to be a man, with the added irony that this lesson had come at long last by way of the secret hardship of a different kind of man than me—the kind of man sneered at by ignorant choirboys, like me.

I felt, too, as if I were crouching a bit less in the face of my future. For I had made a proper deposit into the favor bank of heaven, and had earned the right to ask a return favor of Angelo.

I asked him the favor.

"Done," he said.

"Should I save us some time?" I asked Mogaill when he slid into the booth and sat down across from me. "Should I tell you what I think will be your great important news?"

"You could try guessing if you like. There are merely twenty-six letters to the alphabet. If you lived long enough and kept at least half the wits you now own in your sobriety, and if you talked incessantly every day—then you'd possibly conjure up the right information."

"But it would be saving us no time."

"Oh, do save us, Neil."

"The ownership of the tenement that houses Devil's Heaven—you've traced it down finally to one of those corporations with mysterious numbers for names?"

"That's no proper guess. Of course I done my job, like we agreed this morning."

"I'm not through guessing. I'm ready for naming names behind the numbers."

Mogaill reached into his breast coat pocket, to where he kept a casebook like mine. He opened it and turned to the page he had made that day. "Let's have it," he said. "See if you're smart as you think."

"Bradford Jason Schuyler the Third, no less, and the late Frederick Crosby."

"Jaysus! What do you know? That's right."

"It's no trick, it adds up when you consider the subtotals."

I then told Davy what Ruby had reported to me, on the basis of her luncheon right here at the Ebb Tide that day with Hiram Foster. The tale of how a Russian gangster with a colorful moniker had outslicked a pair of American hucksters and was busy taking over their ad agency for the purpose of converting it into his financial conduit for a variety of ill-gotten gains.

"Among the illest being slum properties," Mogaill said, imagining the range of possibilities in the nimble mind of a New York Russian gangster. "That, and the equally depraved enterprise of renting out human hide in a place like Devil's Heaven."

Then when I told Mogaill of the official solution to the iceberg's tip, and how King Kong Kowalski would surely be trumpeting the news for all afternoon deadlines and not failing to include mention of his own worthy escapades, our mood turned sullen.

"Of course, he'll have the all-important political upper hand," Mogaill said. He looked over toward the bar, and I recognized the look. It went away. "That pig, Kowalski, he'll be strutting like a plumed peacock in the stirring glow of the tabloids alone. And there's not much to be done in bringing justice to a New York landlord, not once they bring out the lawyers."

"These landlords being Crosby and Schuyler?"

"Aye. But with Crosby gone, please God, we're only really speaking of this Schuyler."

"He's not so well off, Ruby tells me."

"No?"

"He's in a free-falling panic for some reason, and making himself sick with booze."

Soon after I spoke Ruby's name, in she walked.

She was accompanied by a cop, or so some would say. And the sight of him startled me, jolting me into a small but critical realization.

I smiled then, and said to Mogaill, "Kowalski can have his day to crow. But there's a last laugh coming. My instincts tell me tomorrow night—Halloween."

"And it's not to be Kowalski laughing?"

"No way."

Ruby sat down next to me. Her companion, Inspector Neglio, slid into the booth alongside Davy Mogaill.

"You're a lucky man to be married to Ruby Flagg," Neglio said to me.

"Well, sure, she's got a fine big job in Madison Avenue. My own career seems to be faltering just now, as I'm duly warned by you, and so it's good somebody in the house is bringing home some bacon."

"If I were you—"

"Which of course you're not," I said, interrupting the inspector. "And so why bother crapping up the advice you want to fling on me with piety?"

Ruby said, "If you want back on the department early, Hock, you should now close your mouth and listen."

"I'm all ears."

Neglio said, "Ruby tells me you're working this little series of homosexual killings into one of your whole big megillahs."

"That's not the way I put it, Hock," she said.

I told her, "I know, babe. The inspector here doesn't understand a cop like me. That's too bad, since I consider myself only slighty past unremarkable. In other words, and contrary to the kind of cop the inspector here can understand, not only can I find a pubic hair in a whorehouse—sometimes I come across two or three."

"You're blowing this whole thing way the hell out of proportion, Hockaday." Neglio let loose with this cliché while he was poking at me with his finger, which as a matter of personal policy I do not enjoy anymore than Nails would appreciate somebody like Sammy the super touching her.

"Which way out of proportion?" I asked Neglio. I noticed he was wearing onyx links in his French cuffs. Some cop.

"Come on, Hock, stop busting my chops! Christ, I don't know ...". Neglio turned to Ruby, and said, "I thought you told me he'd be halfway reasonable."

"Naturally, I assumed you'd be at least the same," Ruby told him. "Why do you want to go saying things like *this little series of homosexual killings?* As if it's no big deal to anybody?"

Neglio appealed to Mogaill. "Help me out here, Davy. These two are ignoring the facts of life—including the fact that I never wrote them."

"Sorry to say, Tommy, but I'm seeing by a whole new light ever since the brass hats persuaded me to retire," Mogaill said. "The fact is, I'm with Hock and Ruby. And all the statistics down through the years crying out for justice and hearing only admonitions from the likes of you, such as if we don't let sleeping dogs lie dead—why we're only just *blowing things out of proportion.*"

"You're all three of you slightly crazy," Neglio said.

"Nae, we're sick and tired. There's a difference."

"To think I came here to help!"

"You still can," Ruby said. "Go ahead, Inspector, tell Hock and Davy what you've done. See if it redeems you, even ever so slightly."

"It looks as if a certain character by the name of Mikhail Rustavi is a good prospect for me to kick over to a friend of mine at the IRS," Neglio said.

"Rustavi is the Bullfrog's real name," Ruby said.

"He's dodging taxes?" I asked.

"Very likely. And big-time. This is preliminary, I have to tell you that. But between what Ruby tells me this Rustavi character spends on lunch at the Four Seasons, and according to what her ..." Neglio asked Ruby, "What'd you call Foster?"

"My dearheart."

"According to what her dearheart has dug up on the guy, Rustavi's my IRS guy's kind of meat."

"So we get this guy for taxes," Mogaill said, a little dispirited. "God only knows what all else he's doing. You know the stories as well as me, Inspector. The big ones like this Rustavi, they're bringing in the little ones from Moscow every day to do their dirty work—then popping them right back over the ocean when the deed's done. With nobody caring much to be the wiser."

"This is true," Neglio said. "I think a lot of these Russki wiseguys, they've got a basic soft spot. Which is, they grew up believing in all that commie propaganda about how any kind of crime always pays big over here in decadent America. So by the fate of history, here they find themselves in bad-guy heaven."

"Which in a way is partly true," Mogaill said. "But also I see your main point."

"Bad guys tend to get careless thinking it's only angels looking over their shoulders," Neglio said. "For instance, you heard of Capone, right, Davy?"

Mogaill nodded.

"A little matter of housecleaning," I said after the four of us were quiet for entirely too long. "Do we know if Rustavi has a hand somewhere in motion pictures?"

"That would fit the profile," Neglio said. He consulted Ruby, asking, "You told me he's always got this entourage of starlet types with him at the Four Seasons?"

"Correct," Ruby said, visibly shaken. "You could make him a suspect in the murder of Sandy Malreaux. Hock and I came across her last night, waiting on Eighth Avenue for some big shot to come pick her up for a private audition. Maybe some big shot named Rustavi."

"All right!" Neglio said. He seemed enthusiastic about the possibility of doing some police work. I took this as a good sign. "We'll pick him up on a twenty-four-hour tag for suspicion of homicide."

"Tell your friend at the IRS."

"I'll do that," Neglio said. "Tax fraud, that'll be our ace in the hole."

Ruby smiled at me, then at the inspector. Like she was a counselor up at some summer camp in the Adirondacks and

Neglio and I were a couple of kids from the city who had been in a scrap and were now under orders to shake hands.

Neglio said, "Hock, about that furlough—"

I knew what he was going to say. But I was not anxious to hear it just then. First, I did not want to insult Davy by hopping back into bed with the department at the first opportunity. Second, I did not really know, after what I had been through, if I wanted to be a part of something that included the likes of King Kong Kowalski.

"I'll be staying out for a little while longer if you don't mind," I told the inspector. "Keep my options open. Also, it's going to be a lot easier for me to pay attention to the case I'm planning against Sergeant Kowalski if I'm on the outside."

Before Neglio had a chance to say anything, Mogaill offered his support, and a suggestion. "I'm throwing in with my partner on the complaint against Kowalski. I think we'll do it whichever way makes the bigger stink—the regular IAD route, or Civilian Review Board. We've got a solid case against the swine. If I was you, Tommy, I'd join up with us here and now."

"Of course, if you don't," I added, twisting the knife, "that alone is grist for Slattery's mill in the *Post*. Which is the ultimate smelliest way for us to move forward on this."

"Don't be talking about Slattery and the *Post*," Neglio said. "Be reasonable."

"For once in your bloody life, be a righteous cop," Mogaill told him.

There was quiet at the table again. As there is from time to time at any war council, which is what we had become on this night of my prayers.

"All right," Neglio said. "I make you this deal. Keep my name out of your comings and goings on this, and you can call on me for backup."

"Deal," said Mogaill, as senior partner in the firm.

Somewhere in Manhattan on an office door, white calcimine letters on the glass, did I see MOGAILL & HOCKADAY, PRIVATE INVESTIGATIONS . . . ?

"A little housecleaning item of my own," Neglio said. "What about the clientele of that sacrilege up on Sixty-eighth Street . . . ?"

"Devil's Heaven," I said. "You've got a line on who shows up there?"

"Kowalski persuaded something out of a poor kid who works the place. Roberto's his name. He's either retarded or punch-drunk, I don't know which."

"Come out with it, Inspector."

"It's some kind of regular crowd from the opera."

"From just down at Lincoln Center."

"The Metropolitan, yes. This Roberto, he says they call themselves the Boys Club."

ME, A COP AND A SHAMROCK CATHOLIC BESIDES, IN THIS UN-
holy place.

Those songs! O Lord in heaven, if ever I needed a
drink!

No, I will not ... Just for today, I swear I will not!

God in Heaven, how could Irma be singing those songs
and telling those jokes? On Halloween—with the gaudy parade of potential victims, and the West Village crawling with
gay bashers like no other night?

And how had Irma fatally put it? *"The wounds of cruel
laughter are frequently salved by murder ... My poor, poor
children. They only want to turn the laughter around. That's
what it means to be gay, Detective Hockaday."*

Big Irma told another boozy joke, her rouged candy apple
red minstrel lips lurid beneath the blue light:

"Let me ask all my dears a question. What's old, brown,
and wrinkled—and smells of ginger?"

The crowd of her adorers pounded their tables, and
shouted, "What ... What ... What?"

Irma raked some piano keys, and shot them the punch
line, "Fred Astaire's face!"

Someone in the audience went one better, shouting,
"She wished!"

I winced, and waited for Ruby's return. These jokes were not my type . . .

I reflected back to only a few hours earlier, when at Angelo's Ebb Tide we had had a second session of our war council. Which included not only Inspector Neglio but his black cop-chauffeured armor-plated Chrysler, ready and idling out on Ninth Avenue.

The chauffeur in blues had rested the slow-moving red flasher atop the roof, no doubt thinking this would ward off any and all disrespectors of New York's finest. This was unwise, as the kids today in my neighborhood of Hell's Kitchen, although not so Irish as a generation back, are little different than we were in spirit. Meaning they are attracted to bright and shiny objects, especially when they belong to expensive cars with liveried drivers.

By way of warning the inspector about this local folkway, I related the story of the time back some years ago when George Bush was the president and one day pulled up in front of a juvenile homeless shelter with his two-block caravan of armored Secret Service limousines. Whereupon the president took twelve noble minutes from his busy schedule to inform a sweaty roomful of gainfully employed television reporters and a few carefully selected Times Square urchins that America was a glorious place for all who applied themselves to flipping hamburgers and such.

One of the urchins told the president of the United States of America, "Get real, man. I ain't working no whole hour for no four dollar twenty-five cent. You crazy? I make a hundred dollar for two hour on the Deuce dealing whack to vics look like you, man." This exchange was not felt to be suitable television viewing material, and was thus unseen by the nation. However, some of the media admitted the next day that a Secret Service presidential decoy limo had been taken for a little joyride around the West Side of Manhattan by a person or persons unknown.

Fortunately for the inspector, his own Chrysler remained where it was all through the war council. The little red siren, however, was stolen clean away. As if it had somehow evaporated.

Nonetheless, we did manage to lay down a Halloween

night strategy. Even as King Kong Kowalski was no doubt celebrating his press notices, which now included a photograph of himself that was ten years younger and better than a hundred pounds lighter than the current statistics.

"All right, tell me again why you're so sure there'll be a postscript tonight," Neglio said. I could imagine him altering these words slightly and asking the same basic question at scores of committee meetings down at One Police Plaza.

"It's because of something Hock said," Mogaill answered the inspector—with deference, as Neglio was now on our side in this highly unusual action. "Which was, 'Somebody out there has organized a game ... the object of which is killing people of a despised class ... The player is being selective, picking off the most repulsive element of these de-̶̶̶̶̶̶̶̶̶̶̶̶̶̶ ... That way, the game goes on.' Do I have that about right, Neil?"

I said he did.

"Now, there is objective—and there is purpose," Mogaill said. "These things are related, but they can be different. They can even be opposite things. Hock has stated the *objective* well, and that is clear enough. But, might there be a *purpose* not yet so clear? And could the purpose be unclear because we're still in the early stages of a potentially lengthy game?"

Ruby had brought with her the opera reference book she had taken from Sandy Malreaux's apartment. Three of the pages were dog-eared. She opened to one of the markings, and read a quotation aloud, " 'Such is an evildoer's end: death is the just reward for a misspent life.' " She stopped, looked at us all, and said, "That's from *Don Giovanni* by Wolfgang Amadeus Mozart."

"And the message left by Crosby's killer," I added.

The second deadly message—"There is no love here, we go from judgment to judgment," pinned with a knife to Sly Harrington's chest—was also from Mozart, *Le Nozze di Figaro*.

The third was Russian—"Why don't you have them killed, the way you did our Czarevitch?"—and had been inserted into Sandy Malreaux's rectum. This from Modest Mussorgsky's *Boris Godunov*.

"Do we have some common theme here?" Neglio asked.

"All day I've spent reading these operas," Ruby said. "And nothing leaps out and smacks me in the forehead and says, 'This now—here's your connecting element.' Except that I can say this, there is treachery in all these stories."

"But then, what would opera be without treachery?" Neglio said. He shook his head and asked another question that had an obvious answer. "Do we have absolutely any idea of what we might be looking for out there?"

"No," we said, one and all.

We made a quick decision on deployment. Mogaill would go up to West Sixty-eighth Street and, from Lottie Pinsk's apartment, keep watch on the comings and goings in the hallway route to Devil's Heaven. Ruby and I would take in the show downtown at the Ladies Auxiliary. Inspector Neglio would remain mobile in his Chrysler, on call via cellular telephone and the regular police radio channel for commander's vehicles.

And then as Ruby and I left the Ebb Tide and flagged a Ninth Avenue taxi to take us downtown, I remember thinking of something that Mogaill had just said . . . *There is objective, and there is purpose . . . These things are related, but they can be different . . . They can even be opposite things.*

There was Ruby coming at me, a bona fide female on her way back from the ladies' room. She sat down at our table, crossed her legs, and asked, "Miss me?"

"For the love of God, don't leave me here alone again."

"Don't flatter yourself. I don't see anybody hitting on you."

"That's not the point. This isn't just another downtown avant-garde club where everybody's wearing black and whispering bitter nothings in each other's ears. That I can live with. This is . . . different. I can't help it, it creeps me."

"I told you, Irish, you're not that good-looking."

Up onstage, beyond the haze of cigarette smog tinged with the slightest scent of Scotch, Big Irma had another joke.

"So, this well-meaning straight guy, he thinks he's doing the right and modern thing. He arranges a blind date for his two gay male friends. What he doesn't know is what we all know only too well, my dears: it's no damn use matching a femme with a femme, now is it . . . ?"

The crowd roared, "Hell no!"

"And so, the one femme turns up her little pug nose at the other femme. Then complains to her straight friend, 'Say, what do you think I am anyway—a lesbian?' "

There were waves of hard, forced laughter. Then gradually, Big Irma toned things down by crooning a couple of misty Judy Garland signature tunes. When she was through, she leaned toward the slender redhead sitting alone at ringside, the one in the black body stocking with a cropped jacket of black ciré, the one with the sad, baggy eyes welled up in tears. In her throaty, plaintive voice, Irma said to her, "Honey, you and me, we know how it is. I may be too old to cut the mustard, but I can still lick the jar."

Maybe Big Irma was trying to coax a quiet moment with this remark. I have seen chanteuses play one mood against another this way, the comic versus the pathetic. Maybe some other time, and in quite another collective frame of mind, this crowd might have reflected on the bittersweet joke, as intended. But not tonight. The mood tonight, as much as the desperate laughter, was competitive. And the contest was deadly simple: Who in this crowd might be lucky and survive Halloween?

Big Irma put the microphone close to her lurid red mouth, breathed hard, and said, "My dears, I'll be leaving you now 'til next set. Remember this—turn soft and lovely every chance you get because cruelty is just around the corner."

Sweet Jesus, I needed a drink. If only to make a toast to bravery.

I swear, not tonight!

In that trice of swearing, everything fell clear to me. *Opposite things.* Then burning in my mind was hawks swooping down from the sky into verdant Central Park, picking up food and material for their home in the city's high stone ledges. Like those hawks, I now picked from all the confusing squalor the key to cracking my case, and thereby ending a murder spree.

I stood up, grabbing Ruby by the arm, scratching her by accident. "Come on," I shouted over the nervous din of the place, "we haven't got any time."

She zigzagged behind me as I cut through the crowd of sad-faced Halloween revelers. I reached the public telephone. A butch was hogging the line. I pulled him away, badged him, and dropped a quarter into the slot.

Neglio answered in his car.

"Where are you from me?" I asked urgently.

"I'm just nearing Eighteenth Street, heading uptown on Sixth Avenue."

"Turn around. Pick us up."

I hear Neglio give his driver the order. Then he said to me, "Where are we going, Hock?"

"It's hit me, like the smack in the head Ruby was waiting for all day reading through the librettos to the operas ..."

"What?"

"We have to go where people are sleeping and see if they're safe."

"You been drinking, Hock?"

"I swear, no. Hurry."

"I'm so sorry, dear. It's late, and we're simply not receiving."

"But, please—I have to see you tonight. Right now! It's an emergency!"

It was no use. Ruby turned her face away from the intercom, and said as much to me. She had been trying for several minutes now.

I asked Inspector Neglio, "Will you back me, like you promised?"

"I'll make you that promise, Hock," he said. "It'll be a lot easier for me, since you're not actually on duty."

Ruby patted his back, and said, "We know you're sticking your neck out, Inspector. Thanks."

I lifted my foot and rammed the glass between the iron grillwork of the main door. It did not give. I tried again with no better result.

Ruby, meanwhile, pressed every intercom button on the board. People either refused to answer, or refused to believe her pleas of emergency. Undoubtedly, a Nineteenth Precinct prowl car was on its way to the scene, in response to numerous calls to 911 from the tenants of the building.

"Some penthouse your boss has," I complained to Ruby. "Doesn't even have a doorman after midnight I could just run over. Say—that gives me an idea."

I ran to Neglio's idling armor-plated Chrysler and rousted his driver from the wheel, throwing him out into the street, which was growing slick from a light rain. I gunned the big engine, aimed it at the front door of Jay Schuyler's apartment house, and dropped the pedal to the floor.

The door crashed into the lobby, and the Chrysler followed through, skidding to a stop against a marble stairway. I leaped out from the driver's seat and took the stairs by two, up a few levels to the elevator floor. Ruby and Neglio were close at my heels.

The elevator door closed just as a squad of uniforms from the precinct came barreling into the glass-strewn lobby, sliding all over the place as if they had ice skates strapped onto their shoes. The elevator bumped, slowly, up ten full flights before landing at the small penthouse floor.

There were two doors at opposite ends of the short reception hall, heavy with rosewood and mirrors and lilies in giant Chinese vases.

I looked at one door, then the other. I asked Ruby, "Here we are, babe. Door number one—or door number two. Your call."

"Two."

"God, I only hope you're right," Neglio said to Ruby. He saw me crouch down, my good right shoulder ready to smash into rosewood. He joined me, and together we ran at door number two like a couple of crazy men.

"What the—?"

Neglio and I flew headlong into a cocktail cart, spilling a pitcher of martinis all over a salmon-colored rug, breaking the pitcher and four crystal goblets in the process. We rolled to a stop, both of us on our backs, and looked up to see a startled man about fifty years of age standing at the door he had pulled open just as we had made our powerful lunge.

He wore a smoking jacket, a paisley pattern in mostly pearl gray with a black silk shawl, over pajamas and romeo slippers with red bows. His hair was black, his eyes dark brown. He held a long steel cigarette holder in a delicate hand.

"My, my," he said. "And welcome."

"Oh Christ, she got it wrong," Neglio complained. He lifted himself into a sitting position and extended a hand to the man in the smoking jacket who helped him to his feet. I stayed where I was.

"I'm awful damn sorry, sir," Neglio said. He pulled out his badge and displayed it, then a notebook. He asked for the man's name.

"Norman Applebaum."

"So you're Norman," Ruby said. She had been watching all that happened from the reception hall. Now she stepped through door number two. She looked at Neglio, and said, "I did get it right."

Neglio turned to me, needing confirmation.

"When she's right, she's right," I told him. I held out my hand. Neglio pulled me up.

"Let's see the bedrooms, Norman," I said. From out beyond the reception hall, I could hear the elevator rumbling upward. There would soon be uniforms all over the penthouse floor, I would soon be under arrest.

"I beg your pardon?" Applebaum said. "Would you people kindly leave? Or else I'll be forced to call the . . ." Applebaum stamped a romeo on the floor in frustration.

Ruby stepped closer to him, and saw beyond him to the woman standing behind a pair of potted date palms midway down a dark gallery corridor.

"Margot?" Ruby called to her.

I turned at the sound of running feet, and saw the hem of a dress disappear through a doorway off the gallery.

"Come on, you're the only one with a gun," I said to Neglio, grabbing him, and running.

As it turned out, though, the inspector was not the only one armed.

Ruby screamed.

I turned.

Norman Applebaum's face was obscured by the barrel of a large pistol, probably a .45 caliber, and he was knelt down in tripod position, aiming for us.

"Inspector Tomassino Neglio—and Detective Neil Hockaday!" Neglio shouted from behind me. "The color of the day is orange!"

Neglio shouted this because of what he saw, the first arrival of a small sea of blue uniforms. One of the uniforms drew his service revolver, and fired past Ruby, hitting

Applebaum's thigh and sending him sprawling harmlessly to the floor.

I jumped through the doorway, in further pursuit of Margot Schuyler. Neglio's feet pounded behind mine.

We heard her scream.

Then we heard a man's muffled screams.

Again, we crouched into a pair of battering rams. And this time we needed the force. A bedroom door cracked under our assault.

Margot Schuyler turned, her whole head and face a scream. She held a Turkish saber in her hand, and waved it over her head. Her face was splashed with blood that was not her own.

Behind her, strapped down onto a massive bed, lay Bradford Jason Schuyler III. He was nude, his shins and thighs a lacework of slashes, his private organs a bloody mutilation. But he was alive.

Neglio dove for Margot Schuyler's knees, crashing instead into her ankles. But he managed to knock her over, and cause her weapon to fly from her hands.

Six uniforms burst into the room then. They took over from Neglio. It took all of them to subdue her, and finally they had no choice but to club her into unconsciousness.

I pulled a wad of tight-wound cotton the size of a grapefruit from Schuyler's mouth. The way his jaw moved, I could tell it had broken. No doubt Applebaum had cracked Schuyler with his .45 while his dear wife did the honors plugging him up with the cotton ball.

A uniform put in the emergency call for a full portable medical unit and backup ambulances.

I fell to the floor, exhausted.

Later, as an unusually balmy and purpled morning of the year's first November day broke over the East River, all four of us sat out on the Schuyler terrace. The Nineteenth Precinct cops had not arrested me. In point of fact, they were serving me coffee and strawberries and croissants from the well-stocked Schuyler kitchen.

"Opposite," I said, absently. Ruby stood next to me, near the railing of the terrace. She took my hand.

"In this case, opposite meaning the starkest difference between the two parts of an unlovely game," Mogaill said. "The idea being to make the objective completely obscure the purpose."

"The purpose belonging to Margot Schuyler and Norman Applebaum, who both saw themselves as spurned lovers," I said. "Margot was angered by her husband's infidelities, Norman by those of his lover, Frederick Crosby."

Ruby turned from the railing. She picked up a leather manuscript cover. "It's no theory, gentlemen. The lady's a novelist, and a very imaginative one." She said to me, "The way it struck you how everything fell together, Hock—it's pretty much point-for-point the way her plot outline reads."

I had not yet bothered reading that outline, nor Margot Schuyler's self-damning evidence. Maybe I should have known it would be there like that, black on white. That would only figure, all the questions answered. But even so, with Ruby's help and Davy Mogaill's and even the unmet Hiram Foster, I knew this all could only be Margot's story.

Also I knew the central weakness of her piece: Writers make lousy killers. This is because they are forever trying to make murder something it is not, neat and tidy—and complex.

The fact is, murder is nearly always simple and usually pretty sloppy. And murder, carried out by anyone besides a writer, has unanswered questions. Not so in Margot's world of orderly pages.

Margot Schuyler the novelist had it all figured. Everything was accounted for, right there in her outline of crime—from the smallest picture to the biggest; each theme carefully constructed; every jot and tittle covered. Which is what bothered me about the whole thing as I finally saw it unfold in front of me—how all the players seemed to be puppets on somebody's string. All I had to do was look for the person most likely to be holding a wad of string.

The key to Margot's plot action—her basic tool—was Mikhail Rustavi, who Margot had observed for some considerable time at the Four Seasons. Clearly, she reasoned, the man had cash to burn; clearly, any such man had his uses; probably such a man was unfettered by ethics.

Unlike other regular diners at the restaurant, Margot was no mere amused observer of the Bullfrog. She had need of a useful man. And so, she made discreet inquiries. Classy ladies like Margot Schuyler can often accomplish such with nobody the wiser. Men will dependably underestimate shrewd and stylish women, from the First Lady on down.

Margot's shrewdness in this case turned on the early match of several fortuitous facts, which she was able to quickly match to her purposes.

Her pal at the Metropolitan Opera—Norman Applebaum, guardian of the so-called Boys Club—filled her in on the little matter of a sadistic homosexual club called Devil's Heaven, a highly profitable cash-only racket operated by a shady-looking Russian, so it was rumored by the tenants. Applebaum did not like it that his lover, Frederick Crosby, was an habitué of that sort of place. He liked it even less that Crosby's frequent guest was a romantic rival, a would-be faux starlet whom Crosby had even placed on the ad agency payroll, one Sandy Malreaux, aka Veronique Unique.

The address of the tenement building housing this basement club was familiar to Margot, the place being one of a number of casual real estate investments jointly owned by her husband and his partner. The operator of the basement club, rumored to be Russian, was a guess on Margot's part. Not much of a guess, but what had she to lose by throwing it up to Rustavi? Anyhow, she was right on the money.

Hiram Foster's instinct about Rustavi was likewise correct, although he was mistaken in assuming that Jay Schuyler was dealing with the Bullfrog directly. Schuyler had no clear idea what forces of money and murder were conspired against him, although he certainly did sense an ocean of danger.

Margot Schuyler was the one who approached Rustavi directly. She proposed a mutually beneficial pact. She would find a way for Rustavi to burrow tarnished money into a respectable enterprise, namely Schuyler, Foster and Crosby; Rustavi, in turn, would be pleased to arrange a camouflage of murders.

This was to be a killing spree of homosexual men who frequented the wrong places, a pattern into which her despicable husband's dead body would eventually fit, neatly and tidily. After all, Jay Schuyler was the business partner of Frederick Crosby, was he not? And with him co-owner, however unwittingly, of a building that sheltered the ghastly Devil's Heaven. Had Schuyler been murdered as well as all the others, this is how it was to play; this was to be a series of murders that the police and the public, in their darkest hearts, well might consider the acts of a gravely offended God.

In the big picture, then, Margot Schuyler would take safe revenge on her husband. For his bloody services, the widow Margot Schuyler would sell Rustavi her late husband's shares of the agency—and thus provide the Russian a means of consolidating his various gamy holdings into a respectable front, complete with respectable bank accounts.

The details of smaller pictures were Margot's to develop. And would that not make for a fine broth of a crime novel?

It was Margot, then, who hatched the notion of an ersatz Disney World in Russia. This was just the sort of hare-brained, sure-to-fail, bigger-than-big account that Jay and Freddy were willing to lavish money on—for their own devious purpose of cheapening SF&C stock and at long last snatching away the last of old Foster's shares. Rustavi supplied the stooges for this bluff, namely the brothers Likhanov—untouchables who could be later dumped back into the lawless streets of the new Moscow.

Margot was doubtless surprised, and not a little annoyed, when Jay saw in the phony Likhanov account a chance to bring back to the agency one of the objects of his peripatetic desire—Ruby Flagg. Nevertheless, Margot pushed on with the plot, unmindful that Ruby entering the story was her fatal flaw as well as Jay's. For among other things, Ruby begat my own entry into the murderous tale.

The *purpose*—always—was to murder two treacherous men, Frederick Crosby and Jay Schuyler. If need be, and with the considerable help of a man like King Kong Kowalski, Crosby could be tarred with the same brush as the murdered transvestite hookers of the Ladies Auxiliary, say. As extra insurance, it would be helpful to make certain it was not too terribly difficult to track down Schuyler's name along with Crosby's as owners of the Devil's Heaven site. Margot dutifully took care of these items.

Of course, the purpose was only half-successful. Crosby

was dead, but Jay Schuyler was alive in a hospital bed. Barely alive, but alive.

There was a message found in the ball of cotton that I pulled from his mouth. The very final line from Ruggiero Leoncavallo's *Pagliacci:* THE COMEDY IS ENDED.

I ran through this all as I sipped coffee.

Then I turned to Ruby, who was holding the manuscript in its cover, running her finger down pages as I asked, "And it's all pretty much there, black on white, you say?"

"Sure is," she confirmed. "The names are all different and facts are embroidered some, but the plot line pretty much follows what's been in the press. The initial murders down on West Street, done by the Likhanov brothers. The Crosby and Harrington murders, done by Sandy Malreaux—in three different drags."

"Three?"

"Number one, Veronique Unique."

"Which got her into Crosby's apartment house. From the looks of Crosby's closet, I'd say he received Veronique plenty of times, and maybe some other baby-doll visitors besides. The building staff probably had regular jokes about the traffic in and out of Crosby's place."

"Probably," Ruby agreed. She looked up from the manuscript for a moment, and said, "Then after she killed Crosby she had to have the perfect disguise for leaving. So she put on his hat and trenchcoat."

"Drag number two, which Otto the doorman fell for. Perfect. And of course, drag number three—"

"The Harrington murder at the Ladies Auxiliary," Ruby said, interrupting. "Sandy wore the yellow wig for that one."

"Attracting no particular attention in that crowd."

"No. Poor Sandy, she was dead meat for Devil's Heaven when she'd finished serving Rustavi's purpose." Ruby paused to collect her thoughts. She skimmed some more pages. "Personally, I think the operatic clues are a little over-the-top."

"Probably," I agreed. "Mystery novelists can be like that."

"And then, right before the denouement, there's Rustavi out at the airport . . ." Ruby paused to read a paragraph. "He's seeing off Vasily and Alexis, and meeting with a certain soon-to-be-murdered partner in SF&C who's going to at long last make him a respectable businessman."

"By selling him shares in the agency?" I asked.

"That's right."

"So, let me guess Margot's version of the story. All along, it's the Jay Schuyler character who's playing the Rustavi character for evil ends—for which Schuyler only winds up getting murdered himself. And this is where the facts she created for the story give way to the only fiction in the piece—the denouement. Which is, Rustavi is supposed to have murdered Schuyler."

"Right again. Margot certainly isn't going to cast herself in that role."

"But she did kill her husband. And she was the mastermind here, from the beginning to the end. From the Ladies Auxiliary to the airport scene with Rustavi. Then just for added insurance, and unbeknownst to Rustavi, she drafted the outline for the novel and had it come out that Rustavi murdered Schuyler."

"I'd say so." Ruby put down the manuscript.

"You should pardon the expression, but what balls," Neglio said. He shook his head. "Margot Schuyler wants to pull off a string of murders to cover up killing her old man, so what does she do? She writes down practically her whole damn plan as notes for some cockamamie book."

"Keep in mind, she wasn't a character."

"Still, it's unbelievable."

"But that in itself was part of the plan," Ruby said. She looked at me and saw that I was on her thought wave. "She even left this outline sitting around here so it would be found like it was."

"She wanted cops to read it?" Neglio said, utterly amazed. The inspector's naïveté was touching. He had been off the street for so long.

"Naturally." Ruby smiled before moving in for the kill, so to speak. "Most cops aren't bright enough to figure a killer to be a classy lady who writes murder mysteries."

Ruby was dead right. And there was nothing Neglio could say. I almost felt sorry for him. It had been embarrassing for the inspector to see a major crime wave solved by the likes of Ruby Flagg and a couple of pissbums.

"Margot figured she might be a suspect somewhere along the line," I explained to the chastened inspector. I stepped over to Ruby and touched the papers she held. "So, what better way for a novelist-suspect to switch the light off herself than to be doing her job? In other words, working up this blueprint of a book right in the middle of a crime wave that captures the public's fancy, what with disgusting characters in it like King Kong Kowalski. A blueprint that's conveniently discovered when Schuyler finally gets the business—and which just might convince the cops to go after Rustavi, the perfect fall guy."

Ruby finished for me. "Who better to draft the blueprint? Since she's married to him, Margot knows about Jay Schuyler's double-dealing on Mad Avenue. That's plenty of steamy tale in itself. The murders are the icing on the cake. And the information, complete with all the gory details, is in all the newspapers. Put this stuff all together as crime fiction, quote-unquote, and you've got any halfway attentive publisher frothing at the mouth. Follow?"

Neglio still had nothing to say. But Mogaill laughed.

"What's so damn funny?" Neglio demanded to know.

Mogaill stood up before answering. He moved to the railing, gripped it with his stout red hands, and looked down toward the East River. His eyes swept over hundreds of grimy apartment house rooftops, combing downward to streets below, which were beginning to swirl with morning traffic.

A hawk lazed in the sky, drawing my attention. I could almost hear its wings flapping.

Davy looked up at the bird, too. Then down again to the streets.

"This bloody, bloody city," he said. "She heaves and palpitates, she has a mayor and she's full of wild-haired writers. God help us all."

Epilogue

I DID ALMOST EVERYTHING I KNEW I HAD TO DO. THE LITTLE matter of King Kong Kowalski was the exception, but his day would come. I promised myself that.

Meanwhile, I had done a pretty good job of being a cop, even though I had to do it from the outside. In the process, I scored one for the pissbums. Also, I had surmounted a prejudice, which was more than my father had done with his life, and this had made me a better man than he.

Most importantly, I had done it all without a drink.

But there was one thing more.

It was the first Saturday of the month, a clear and chilly day, and Ruby and I walked from the apartment over the well-worn streets to Angelo's Ebb Tide. We planned a light dinner there, or as light as Angelo allows on his premises. Then maybe we would go to the movies.

We never got to the movies.

This was because of the people who were waiting for us at Angelo's.

At first, Ruby was put out when she saw the sign on the Ebb Tide's door: CLOSED FOR PRIVATE PARTY.

"Since when?" she complained.

"I think they'll include us in," I said, pushing open the door.

Somebody threw rice, Inspector Neglio I believe. He was early by about fifteen minutes. Which was the time it took for Father John Sheehan to properly—and, in accordance with the solemn laws of the State of New York—pronounce us really and truly man and wife.

Davy Mogaill gave away the bride, Angelo Cifelli was my best man.

No offense to Father Sheehan, but I am still considering our Irish gypsy wedding as our anniversary.

"I didn't have time to arrange for a wedding cake, Ruby." I was not truly sorry, though. "Maybe these will do."

I turned to Angelo, and said, "If you please."

Angelo snapped his fingers and a waiter bearing a covered silver tray came gliding out from the kitchen.

"Open it," I said to Ruby.

She did, and found three genuine Louisiana moon pies in cellophane beneath the cover—one vanilla, one chocolate, and one banana.

I then pulled a pair of Amtrak tickets from my breast coat pocket, and gave them to Ruby.

"Happily ever after to us, babe. We're taking off on the Crescent tomorrow night. We've got a first-class private compartment, and once we board we'll be down in the land of dreams twenty-six hours later."

There was a lot of champagne drunk that night at Angelo's. None of it by me. I did not feel I was missing anything, and this was a pleasant revelation. Father Sheehan took me aside for a quiet moment to talk about it, just between us.

"You know what you've done tonight, son?" he asked. He looked at me with pride in his bearded face.

I could think of nothing to say.

"I'm not your all-time favorite priest, that I know," Sheehan said. "But indulge me, will you?"

"Okay."

"I believe you've now seen the two paths before you. You can live your life, or you can act your life."

"An epiphany. Is that what you call it?"

"No, it's what I call the last station of the drunkard's cross."

"I see what you mean." And I did. "But I have to tell you, it doesn't look so much brighter on the sober side."

"That's true. There's so much evil in the world."

"Why is that, Father?"

The baker's chocolate eyes on Sheehan's wide face danced, and he said, "To thicken the plot, son."

"You're actually all right, Father."

"Go kiss your pretty wife."

I did just that. Then my bride and I left Angelo's, at shortly after midnight, and walked back slowly through the cold air to the apartment. Ruby talked about her family in New Orleans with great excitement, and "good food cooked by colored people."

Inspector Neglio walked with us. His newly assigned Chrysler was waiting at our corner, West Forty-third and Tenth Avenue, as in *Slaughter On.*

Before we said good night, Neglio took my arm, pulled me close to him.

He whispered, "You want back on the force right away after your honeymoon, Hock, I'll pull the right strings."

"I'll think it over," I said. "Good night, Tommy."

POCKET BOOKS HARDCOVER
PROUDLY PRESENTS

THROWN-AWAY CHILD

THOMAS ADCOCK

**Coming in Hardcover
from
Pocket Books
April 1996**

**The following is a preview of
Thrown-Away Child . . .**

"Afternoon, mama," said the loud one, stepping through the door and right past Violet Flagg, scanning the small front room, drawn revolver in his hand. He looked straight through Ruby, as he had Violet—as if they were windows instead of two black women. He was less cocky when he spotted me. In fact, he smiled and reholstered his .38, reassured by the presence of ... what? Someone from his own gene pool? He motioned the other one through the door, then addressed Violet with too much courtesy to have meant it, "I'm Detective Mueller, ma'am, and this here's Detective Eckles."

Violet folded her arms and stared at the two white cops, saying absolutely nothing. I had the idea she felt the same as I did about the courtesy. Also I had the idea that her silent treatment was a useful technique that had come to her with time and much experience. The cops were reliably dazed for a couple of seconds.

Detective Mueller fumbled with the cheap brown suit coat draped over the shoulder of his short-sleeved yellow shirt. His flabby sides were wet with perspiration, from the armpits clear down to his gunbelt. Detective Eckles looked at the pointy toes of his snakeskin boots, like he was a smart-alecky school kid waiting to be disciplined by the principal. Mueller shot a look over at me, deciding I was no ally after all. Maybe it was the way I looked back at him, like he was a sick person's former lunch.

"Ma'am . . . ?" Mueller's voice turned soft as funeral parlor talk. "You know why we're here?"

Violet was having none of Mueller's new tune. "What you mean by mangling my door, knocking it down with your damn gun, then calling me your *mama?* And how come you suddenly develop a case of the nices?"

"How's that?"

"You deaf, too? I know your eyes is poor. You haven't got the first idea what your ownself looks like."

"Ma'am, I—"

"Elsewise, you know I'm not nearly ugly enough to be your mama. What's your real mama name?"

"Florence . . ."

"Poor Flo. I bet you was her ugliest child."

Detective Eckles had a spasm of laughs. Mueller cracked a hammy elbow into his partner's ribs.

Eckles accidentally chomped his tongue, which took all the humor out of the situation for him.

"Look here, ma'am," Mueller said to Violet. He rested his hand on his gun. "We'd like to have a little talk with your boy."

"No boy staying here, sir. Only a grown man— name of Mr. Duclat."

"That's just who I'm talking about. Perry Duclat."

"You had a mind, you could to learn how to talk respectable about a black man."

"Ma'am, respectable's got nothin' to do with the bidness we got with Perry Duclat."

"What you think Perry done?"

"Where is he, ma'am?"

Mueller drew himself a step toward Mama Violet. So did Eckles. Which brought me off the sofa and to my feet. I moved in on Mueller, warning him, "You want to gear down some, Detective?"

"Who in goddamn hell are you?" Mueller drew out his gun again, which stopped me. He held it barrel-down to the floor.

"Put it away," I said.

But Mueller kept his gun where it was. Eckles now drew his piece, and dangled it the same as his partner.

"Don't sound like he's from 'round here," Eckles said, having difficulty with the letters *d* and *s*, on account of his injured tongue.

Mueller pressed me. "I as't you a question, Yankee-boy."

"I asked you to put the gun away."

"You best answer me first."

"I'm family," I said, smiling brightly.

"Oh, man—that's choice!" Mueller laughed hard, expecting me to join in the joke. When I did not, he took a second look at Ruby. This time he did not look straight through her. He turned back to me, eyes lowered like a couple of broken sunshades, and said, "Now, ain't this just special. The pretty one, she your missus?"

"That's right."

"Where y'all from, Yankee-boy?" Mueller asked.

"The gun, put it away."

"'Fraid I can't accommodate you. Not until I got me a name, at least."

"I've got identification." I pulled open my coat, slowly. Mueller could see the inside breast pocket. "There's all the ID you need in my pocket. Come and get it, Detective."

Mueller gave his gun a shake, directing Eckles, "G'wan over there, take it off'n him, Ricky Ray."

Eckles removed what he naturally thought was an ordinary wallet, opened it and whistled at the gold shield he found inside. He handed the wallet over to Mueller, whose lips moved as he read my name off the shield.

"Says here your name's Neil Hockaday," Mueller said.

"I know that."

"Says here you're a detective up there to Jew York City. Hoo-whee! a po-liceman, just like me."

"I doubt it."

Mueller handed back my wallet and shield, and ignored me for the time being. He put his gun away, though. So did his trained seal with the sore tongue.

"Say there, Mrs. Pretty..." Mueller said to Ruby, shifting his lopsided bulk. I said to myself, Now, that was a very unwise manner of addressing Ruby. As I had not warmed to Mueller and his anthropological sentiments, I decided he was on his own. "...You down from Jew York to visit some ol' Louisiana kin for a spell?"

"Listen up, you ignorant peckerwood. What I'd like to do is cram a rat in your mouth and sew your greasy lips shut. But I'm going to be polite instead, at least this once." Probably Mueller would have preferred being in a dentist's chair than having Ruby drill her eyes into him the way she was. She said, "State your fool *bid*ness. Then kindly move your big lard ass out of my mama's house."

Mama added, "Go, girl!"

Mueller and his red face exploded, "Missy, I just ain't accustomed—!"

"No, I'm sure you *ain't*," Ruby interrupted. "A cracker like you pisses in my face, I call it piss—not rain. Have we established an understanding, Detective Mueller?"

I stepped in at this point, and advised Mueller, "In the interest of being professionally helpful, I'd take things from the top if I were you." I nodded to Eckles, including him in this counsel. "Take a little beat, fellows. Then make like you're actual gentlemen."

The two of them sputtered for a couple of seconds. After their feathers were smoothed down, I asked Mueller, "Now then, Detective, what do you want with Mr. Duclat?"

"Got a few questions."

"About what?"

"None of your affair, Detective Hockaday. We ain't up North right now, we in New Orleans. But I don't mind tellin' Miz Flagg here." He turned to Violet and said, "Little matter about a friend of Perry's, ma'am—by the name of Cletus Tyler."

"Mr. Tyler, as I understand it, was a cellmate of Perry's up to Angola," Violet said to Mueller. She explained to me, "That's the penitentiary—Angola." She turned again to Mueller, and said, "Now you know my Perry's not going to be taking up with Cletus Tyler. That'd be a violation of parole, wouldn't it?"

"You happen to know Cletus, ma'am?"

"That's no affair of yours," Ruby said to the detective, "unless you plan to arrest my mama for whatever trouble you've got with this Mr. Tyler."

"Yes, ma'am, I guess you got me. Of course I ain't going to arrest your mama. All the same, I thought she'd like to know about poor Cletus." Mueller smiled at Violet, taking pleasure in telling her, "Fact is, Cletus got himself dead."

"La, no!"

"Oh, yes. I got to say, ma'am, when we found Cletus Tyler he was deader than a deep-fried palmetto. That's about as gruesome a corpse as I ever want to see. Got him shot up with a dum-dum, got his neck whacked so bad his head pretty near rolled off."

"Oh, La . . . Oh, La . . ."

Ruby jumped off the couch and stood by her mother, taking one of Mama's hands into her own. Violet looked up at me, hazel eyes beaded with grief.

"Must of been somebody familiar with the prison ways got to poor Cletus," Mueller continued, unmercifully. "Yes, ma'am, somebody whacked him—Angola-style."

I had to ask. "What style is that, Detective?"

"Them little rascals up to Angola, let me tell you. Always innovatin'." Mueller laughed wetly. "Latest thing, somebody gets him a nice stiff wood club for whacking. But before he does the job, he sinks razor blades into the club, along a couple of parallel lines—about a half-inch apart. That way, there ain't enough stitching surface between the wounds so a doc can sew the skin back together proper."

Detective Eckles added, "Leaves a big old snakey scar."

"Take a man down Angola-style, every time he looks in a mirror he's reminded about his whacking. Unless a' course it croaks him, like our boy Cletus." Another wet laugh from Mueller, and chimes from Eckles.

"Haw, Cletus got him whacked real good!" Eckles said. He was as jazzed as a kid fresh off a carnival ride. "Got him shot through the heart and creamed in the gut. That Cletus, boy—he's really, truly dog dead!"

Violet's head was bent low. I could not see her face, but I heard her crying softly. The air felt especially heavy just then, like a graveyard in the rain.

I felt I was in a room with a long history of mourning.

I had a decision to make, fast. Should I do what I had to do and get these two thugs out of the house? And what would it take to accomplish such a feat? I should sic Ruby on them? Or should I encourage the usual predilection of rabid thug cops to shoot off their mouths? But to what advantage? And why was I thinking like a cop so far south of my jurisdiction?

"How do you mean Cletus Tyler also took injury to his *gut*?" I asked Eckles.

Eckles tried to say something, but another one of Mueller's elbows cut him short of breath. "Ricky Ray, you ought not to be blabbing like some old gal with a dryer on her head," Mueller said. He had a warning for me, too.

"Obstruction of justice ain't a particularly pleasant thing, 'specially when I'm the obstructee," Mueller said. "Follow me? Don't be getting any strange notions about messing around in my case, Detective Hockaday."

"I imagine notions around here are strange enough as they are."

Mueller's pasty face was a study in wrinkled confusion, which did nothing to improve his appearance. "What exactly's your meaning?"

"Skip it, Detective. Say, didn't you come here looking for something in particular?"

Mueller turned to Violet, whose uptilted face had grown calm. She brushed her eyes with the backs of her brown hands. Violet's hands were large as a man's, but they moved in a delicate and purely feminine way. Mueller asked her, "All right now, where is he?"

"How'd I know where Perry at?"

"Ma'am, I as't you nice as pie."

"And I answered the same. Trouble is, you don't hear what you want to hear." She raised her eyes to the ceiling, and I wondered if it might be somebody up in heaven she was really trying to see, somebody mortal. "Trouble is, nobody ever want to know where Perry Duclat is bound to go."

"Ma'am, for the love of Christ—please!" Mueller was close to boiling over. Slow-witted people and overheated kettles are alike that way. "Do you suppose I might get one straight answer to one simple question before I leave?"

"I suppose you could leave easy enough," Violet said. "Being just a little old colored woman, I don't suppose too much otherwise."

"Goddammit to hell—!"

"Don't be talking ugly. I'm a church woman."

"Sorry, ma'am."

Violet laughed at him. Mueller was smart enough to know he had been made a fool fair and square, so he said nothing for the moment. But I had a fleeting thought as to how a rabid cop like Mueller might express himself later that night, after some drinks. Maybe there was a Mrs. Mueller he could punch around.

"All right," Violet said. "You want it straight and simple? Perry ain't here, and I ain't got a clue to where he at now. Okay? But I know where Perry been. That I do know. You want me to tell you where he been?"

"It'd be real nice." Mueller smiled, not out of friendliness. He reached into a sweaty shirt pocket and took out a Woolworth notebook and a ball-point pen. He clicked the pen.

"Been up to Angola a time or two," Violet said.

"Ma'am, we already know that kind of thing. Perry Duclat's a thief."

"Yeah, you right. That man he steal everything but a red-hot stove."

"That ain't nothing to write down," Mueller complained. "You said something about where Perry'd *been*?"

"My Perry been in a place much different than you ever going to know about. Remember when you was a little boy?"

"Ma'am, I—"

"Probably you had nothing more to worry about than Mickey Mantle's batting average. Probably you played in the street all night with your little white friends, and the sound you dreaded most was your mama calling you home to supper. That's not where my Perry been."

Violet took a deep breath. "Perry mama Rose left him, and his daddy Toby wouldn't have him. My late husband Willis took a shine to Perry and looked after him some when he was little. Then Willis took sick from a snakebite and couldn't even look after his ownself. I did what I could, but the street got hold of Perry. The street's like quicksand, you know. Anyhow, all the little street boys he run with? They either dead or up to Angola, same as dead. All his life, Perry lie awake at night thinking on all this. Thinking on what he is—nothing but a thrown-away child. You understand what I'm saying . . . ?"

I doubted if Detective Mueller understood anything of what he had just heard. He had the dazed, stupid-looking face of a fat man whose own snoring had roused him from a nap in front of a TV set. Mueller closed his notebook and stuffed it back into his shirt pocket. He said to Eckles, "Come on, Ricky Ray, there's nothing here for us but a damn waste of time."

Mueller handed Violet an embossed New Orleans Police Department business card with his direct-dial phone number on it, and said, "Now ma'am, we got us two ways of catching Perry Duclat—with you, or without you. You want to give up Perry to me, I'll see things go easy on him. But I don't extend no such guarantee otherwise." Mueller tossed a sneer in my direction, and added, "Ask your blue-eyed family if I ain't talking fair and reasonable like."

"Neil . . . ?" Mama Violet looked up at me.

"Oh, I'd say the detective's a fair and sporting man," I said. "Those qualities are most probably bred in his bones. I can imagine his daddy before him persuading a mob to give a man the fair and sporting chance of fifteen minutes' head start before they run him down for a lynching."

Violet ripped up Mueller's police department calling card, dropped the pieces to the floor.

Mueller grunted at me, and said to Violet, "Just you remember, ma'am, we going to get that boy, one way or another."

Violet glanced heavenward once again, then said to the back of Mueller's sweaty shirt as he walked out the door, "First thing y'all do, you come steal our bread. Then you want us to butter it for y'all."

Look for
Thrown-Away Child
**Wherever Hardcover Books
Are Sold
April 1996**